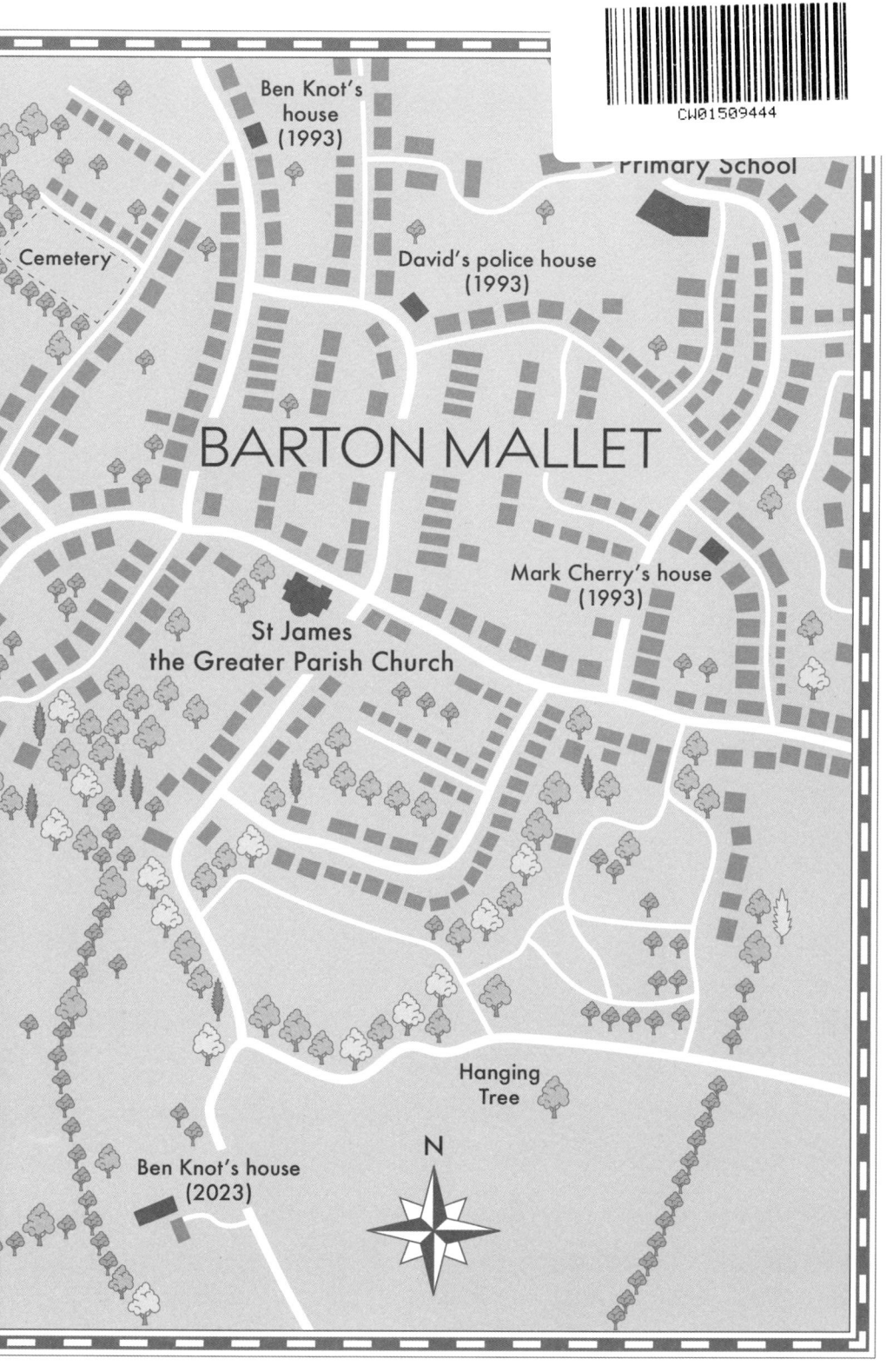

CW01509444

Ben Knot's house (1993)

Cemetery

David's police house (1993)

Primary School

BARTON MALLET

Mark Cherry's house (1993)

St James the Greater Parish Church

Hanging Tree

N

Ben Knot's house (2023)

THE CUT

THE CUT

RICHARD ARMITAGE

faber

First published as an original audio book by Audible

This edition published in the UK in 2025
by Faber & Faber Ltd
The Bindery, 51 Hatton Garden
London EC1N 8HN

Typeset by Typo•glyphix, Burton-on-Trent, DE14 3HE
Printed in the UK by CPI Group (UK) Ltd, Croydon, CR0 4YY

Map © Bill Donohoe, 2025

*This is a work of fiction. All of the characters, organisations and
events portrayed in this novel are either products of the author's
imagination or are used fictitiously*

A CIP record for this book
is available from the British Library

ISBN 978–0–571–39350–3

Printed and bound in the UK on FSC® certified paper in line with our continuing
commitment to ethical business practices, sustainability and the environment.
For further information see faber.co.uk/environmental-policy

Our authorised representative in the EU for product safety is
Easy Access System Europe, Mustamäe tee 50, 10621 Tallinn, Estonia
gpsr.requests@easproject.com

2 4 6 8 10 9 7 5 3 1

For my late father who taught me to fight my own battles.
'You are what you are.' John Turner Armitage

PROLOGUE

It had to happen at night. There had to be a forest, a full moon and a thunderstorm. A masked man chasing through the dark or a vampire hunting its sacrificial prey. Sometimes there had to be both.

The crack of thunder was closely followed by a sudden blinding flash of sheet lightning, tearing open the sky like an atomic bomb. From the top of the imposing tower of Blackstone Mill, the fourteen-year-old boy teetered precariously, trying to hold the video camera steady against the force of the gale. Blinking away the sudden glare of electricity, he pressed his eye back to the viewfinder. A stifled scream cut through the cacophony of noise. At first, he thought it was a fox, but the second time he heard it, there was no doubt: the sound was human and racked with fear.

The scream was drowned out by a car alarm, blasting a warning into the night.

The boy pressed himself into the smoke-blackened wall of the chimney, feet slipping on the narrow ledge. He found his balance and tried to focus the lens of the video camera on the ground, fifty feet below.

The night had been full of pranks. A flank of Stormtroopers in white spray-painted skateboard helmets had pursued him from the school gates, all the way down The Cut to Cheney End. Indiana Jones had chased Sarah Connor out into the thunderstorm, squealing with laughter, towards the flooded river. The reason the boy had sprinted out of the woods and mounted the makeshift ladder inside the chimney stack was to film the fireworks from the Crow's Nest. The view from up there was spectacular. Shrieks of joy echoed across the meadow as comets and willows exploded and fountains of golden rain burst into the sky. But the two figures who now appeared in the shot did not seem to be having fun at all.

One of them, dressed in pale chiffon, stumbled out into the mud, pursued by a terrifying demon, heavy black robes billowing in the gale. Sprinting across the footbridge, the apparition in white took the towpath towards the wheelhouse at the side of the mill. This definitely wasn't part of the festivities. There was a desperate urgency to the chase; it was a real fight.

In the distance, the deafening roar of a motorbike engine ricocheted off the stone walls of the mill. Emerging from the thicket of trees, the beam of its headlamp ignited the scene – and then the heavens opened. A drenched Chewbacca draped in a sheepskin rug stumbled out of the ruined mill, pulling an R2-D2 Henry vacuum cleaner behind him, followed by two Terminators and a bin-bag Darth Vader with dying sparklers. Everyone ran for the cover of the trees as the rain extinguished the last of the Roman candles. In the chaos, the two figures he'd been tracking in the frame of the camera had disappeared over the broken stone wall of the mill race. He'd lost them.

Droplets of rain splattered across the lens, obscuring his vision. The boy tried to shield the camera with the sleeve of his denim jacket. The red body warmer and high tops of his Marty McFly costume had seemed like a good idea earlier, but now he was soaked through, and the clothes were clinging to his skinny body. His trainers slid against the wet stone walls as he braced one foot either side of the narrow chimney and tried to climb higher. He slipped and chunks of crumbling mortar clattered down the chimney to the first level, fifty feet below. He grabbed the side of the turret and, regaining his footing, he put the viewfinder back to his eye. Panning the camera, he retraced the route of the two figures from the footbridge to the weir, following the swollen stream to the wheelhouse on the far side of Blackstone Mill.

There. He adjusted the focus and zoomed in closer. He had them in his sights. Two shapes moving frantically along the wall that led towards the dilapidated water wheel. He held his breath as they battled against the rain, staggering dangerously close to the edge of the deep water. The black-robed demon reached out towards his quarry, grasping at diaphanous chiffon billowing in the storm. The girl in white was cornered. She grabbed at the rotten wooden frame of the wheel and began to climb. The demon pounced on her, pinning her down. For the boy filming, it was too much to bear.

'HEY!' He broke cover, leaning out precariously from the top of the tower. 'LEAVE HER ALONE!'

A massive volume of water was now rushing into the mill race as the torrential rain flooded the already bloated river. The noise of the torrent muffled the boy's cry, but the black-cloaked demon turned for a second, scanning the area. Then he looked directly above him and stared right down the barrel of the lens. The boy with the camera froze. Oh shit, he'd been seen. He ducked out of sight, his feet slipping on the iron pitons hammered into the walls and his legs quivering with fear as he began to descend. He had to get out of there. The motorbike engine revved a warning below, and in a flurry of speed the accelerating bike mounted the wall and then disappeared from sight.

The boy's legs buckled as he reached the first level, landing on the scaffolding that was keeping the whole structure of the mill from collapsing. He found the ladder and began to climb down.

As he reached the middle rung, the ladder dislodged itself from the platform, swinging out over the void and hitting the wall on the other side. The camera slipped from his grip and clattered on to the ground below. He hung from his arms and dropped on to the flagstone floor, twisting his ankle as he landed. He cried out in pain but didn't stop; there wasn't a second to lose. He had to move. Now.

He grabbed the camera and sprinted to the exit, his ankle burning and already swelling inside his trainer. Outside, the gale was driving the torrential rain sideways. He braced himself, raising the viewfinder to his eye as he crept through the cavernous doors out into the darkness of the meadow.

BOOM! A demonic grey face punctured with rusty nails suddenly lurched into the shot. Holy shit! The boy jumped back in shock. The mask was torn, menacing eyes staring directly at him. The boy backed away in fear, stumbling in the mud, then turned and sprinted for his life. His heart punched at his ribcage as he pelted towards the cover of the trees. Bare sapling branches whipped his face as he dodged through the looming arms of the birch trees.

As he reached the ditch at the edge of the thicket, fenced in with chain link, he could see the lights of the motorway in the distance. He launched himself over, hitting the bank too short, and began to slide into the waterlogged brambles. Waist-deep in rising water, the boy tried to keep the camera dry. Sharp thorns caught in his hair and scratched his face as he fought to climb out. Then, out of the darkness, a hand reached over his face and grabbed his jacket, hauling him up the bank. His left fist cracked against the skull of his attacker as he broke free and scrambled over the fence, tumbling down the other side. The steep cutting of the motorway, covered in shale, broke his fall as he skittered down towards the glare of oncoming lights. His head hit the tarmac of the hard shoulder and he lay there, motionless.

The distant roar of traffic melded with a ringing noise in his ears and even the wind and the rain didn't seem to touch him anymore. Maybe this was it. The end. Suddenly he could feel someone breathing, very close to his face.

'Give it to me.' A hand grabbed at his throat, holding him down. 'What did you see? Huh? GIVE ME THE CAMERA.'

The boy tried to hold on to the evidence of what he had just witnessed, but a balled fist slammed hard into the bridge of his nose and his head whiplashed against the ground. He released his grip, and the camera was gone. All the tension began to drain out of his body, leaking across the hard wet tarmac of the motorway, and as the ground became soft and fluid, he melted into oblivion.

1

SEPTEMBER 2023

Benjamin Knot gripped the steering wheel and chewed on the small cut on the inside of his mouth. This trip had been as frustrating as the last one. Ben was CEO of the Ignis Fatuus Group, an award-winning architecture firm based in Stockholm. He had once made the list of *Fortune* magazine's '40 Under 40' and graced the cover of *GQ* as 'The New Architectural Innovator'. His star had risen, along with the jaw-dropping glass skyscrapers he was famous for, but those days were well and truly behind him.

He glanced up to look at his face in the rear-view mirror. He was still handsome . . . just about. Greying at the temples and in decent shape for his age, but his eyes were red from lack of sleep and deep indelible frown lines ran across his forehead. His phone rang and he tapped the touchscreen on the dash. Dani's face appeared on the video call.

'Oh, sorry, love. I didn't realise you were driving.'

Ben watched as she flitted around their Italian high-spec kitchen, stopping at the mirror on the way out to touch up her lip gloss. Dani was fifteen years younger than him, and her Scouse spirit was like an adrenaline shot. He was instantly dragged out of his stupor.

'Just landed. I'm en route from Stansted. The guidance is saying 5 p.m., but you know what Fridays are like.' He glanced at the road map as he glided past Peterborough.

'I'm heading out now to watch Lily at the football.' Dani was bending down, trying to pull on a pair of pristine white

Reeboks while holding the phone close to her face. 'Will you want to eat later?'

'What do you think?'

She hesitated, then smiled. 'I'll pick up something, or we can Deliveroo?'

'Again!'

A pair of glossy lips pouted into the frame as Dani multitasked her way out of the house, grabbing her bag and closing the door with her foot. 'Don't forget Nathan has Kidsmet tonight.' She slammed the front door and headed to the car. 'Can you pick him up from there on your way over, love?' Dani had taken charge of the kids' social calendars. She had taken charge of a lot of things.

Kidsmet was Nathan's beloved after-school drama group. Ben's older child, Lily, was turning into the star footballer that Ben had always aspired to be. She was a good player, spurred on by the success of the Lionesses, and he was enormously proud of her. Nathan, on the other hand, took after his mum; he was more of an introvert, more artistic. Ben's first wife, Ellie, had wanted their kids to follow their passions rather than be bogged down by academic career choices. But Ben knew that the luxury they lived in hadn't come from a pipe dream about scoring goals for Nottingham Forest, it had come from a laborious physics degree and a seven-year master's in architecture.

'How did it go in Stockholm? Are they going to restart your St Petersburg Project?'

Ben fixed a smile and turned to the camera. 'Not sure. There are still some financial hurdles to leap over. The toxicology ground report was a dud, but you know me, I'm like a dog with a bone. I just hope . . .'

Dani wasn't listening. She was 'yep yep yepping' in all the wrong places as she threw her bag into the back of her Jaguar

E-PACE and slid into the driver's seat. Big car, small woman. 'Fill me in later, love, I've got to get going, see you at the footie.' Dani smiled, touching her manicured nail extensions to her lips. And with that, she killed the call.

Ben floored the accelerator and raced up the A1 towards Grantham. He drove in silence for a while. Somewhere in a dark corner of his mind, an alarm was sounding, like the nagging blip of a distant heart-rate monitor. He flicked a button on the wheel and turned up the volume on the radio.

'Protests outside the Crown Court this afternoon descended into violence, as residents of Barton Mallet forcibly objected to the release of the notorious murderer known as "The Mill Killer". The ruling made by the parole board yesterday has been met with hostility—'

Ben's thumb hit the button, killing the bulletin. He turned off at Harlaxton. His foot pressed hard into the pedal as he tore down the country road, breaking the limit like a man with a death wish. He dropped the window an inch and breathed in cold air.

A lump had started to form in Ben's throat as he drew closer to home, a huge wave of emotion building, lapping at the edge of his composure. His old friend Stress could usually be tempered with a few large glasses of whisky, but this felt different. He'd always known this day was coming. That bastard was about to be released. For the last thirty years he had been safely locked away in HMP Gartree, but now he was going to be free and who knew what he was capable of? Ben's chest tightened as he gripped the steering wheel until his knuckles turned white. A pain grabbed at his chest, like fingers twisting his heart until he couldn't breathe.

He indicated and pulled into a lay-by, sat still for a second, then opened the door and stepped out into the evening air. The surrounding fields stretched out for miles, that patchwork quilt of English countryside gently rolling into the distance, carved up by hedgerows and barbed wire on wood. Decades had passed since he had gone 'bleggin', picking blackberries, in a place just like this. As kids, they'd hunted for conkers, built bivouacs in ditches, and got into all kinds of trouble.

On this winding road that led into the village of Barton Mallet, there was a large rock protruding from the verge, around which the road had been awkwardly redirected. A notoriously sharp bend that circumvented a 'death trap' on the site of an ancient Hanging Tree. Thirty years ago, the tree had been struck by lightning, and over time that burned-out husk had slowly disintegrated back into the earth, along with the terrible memories of that night. A gentle breeze blew around Ben and he took a deep breath. He watched as a single magpie landed on the jagged granite rock.

People don't forget when children are murdered. It is seared into the heart of a place, etched into the very foundation of the community. Ben stared at the lonely black and white bird, then glanced around, looking for its mate. The magpie balanced on the sharp tip of the granite rock, staring him down. Neither of them moved, frozen in time. Ben slowly brought his hand up to his temple and saluted the captain.

'One for sorrow.'

2

SEPTEMBER 1993

There is a bench on the corner by St James's church that sits on a little triangle of grass. On the wooden back slats is a small engraved brass plaque dedicated to Marian Knot, 1944–91. The bench is the morning meeting place reserved for the Year 11 girls of Barton Mallet Secondary School. The boys, on the other hand, have their own little hangout: a red-brick electricity substation with two huge metal doors of peeling grey paint. They climb up on the roof, like dumb chickens instinctively trying to find the highest perch. A row of sports bags sit like soldiers, lined up against the coping stone next to the little triangle of green grass, worn brown by football feet. The queue of bags allows the boys to mess around before the bus arrives, without having to stand in an actual queue.

Annabel Maddock is perched on the back of the bench, fingering the brass plaque, passing a half-smoked Benson and Hedges to her friend Amy Hartshorn. She never inhales; she just sucks in once and blows it out. It gives her a headache. She grabs a Polo from her bag and watches the boys. He's not here yet, he's always late, but the bag queue doesn't apply to him. He's Top Dog so it goes without saying that he'll be getting on the bus first. Mr Popular is a few inches taller than everyone else, he's got hair on his chest now and under his arms. His hair is golden – her sister Catherine calls it strawberry blond – and it shines in the sun like a crown. They're doing the Plantagenets in history: the Wars of the Roses. Mr Ashton says Ben takes after Edward IV, who was tall and blond apparently, but Annie thinks he looks more like the cute one from Take That.

Catherine Maddock nudges her older sister and giggles as they watch the boys play a ridiculous fainting game. It never works, but they live in hope of at least one of them hitting the deck.

'Hey, Annie, Mark's up next, look.' Cat grips her leg nervously.

Cat and Mark Cherry are best friends; they play music together. She's brilliant on the clarinet and Mark plays the cello so obsessively that they call him Mark Cello, or Marcello for short. In fact, right now his cello is propped up on the bench, with Cat silently guarding it.

The girls watch Mark puffing in and out to the countdown from the circle of lads, gathering pace.

'Four, three, two . . . blow!' The chant is led by Lynette Davis. She's not quite one of the lads but wants to be and is just one initiation away from being 'allowed in'. Mark has his fist to his mouth, his cheeks red and bloated as he blows into his thumb. For a second, everyone stands and watches in silence.

'Oh shit!' Cat is up on her feet as Mark sways unsteadily and then collapses to the ground, hitting his head on the kerb. 'Mark, are you all right?'

'Gaylord's down!' The boys are raucous, whooping and jumping off the substation, gathering round to look. Mark Cherry is out cold. Cat is gently tapping his cheek.

'Mark? Mark, are you OK?' His eyes flutter. Cat grabs her bag and pulls out a Kia-Ora juice drink. She pops the straw into the little hole and tries to put it into Mark's mouth as Annie cradles his head.

'He looks really pale . . . Mark?' Nurse Cat's voice is frantic as she tries to loosen his school tie. It's been cut short and is frayed at the bottom, the knot yanked tight into a 'peanut'; another of the boys' silly rituals. She leans in slowly, almost close enough for a kiss, but Mark suddenly revives with a huge grin on his face and quaffs a mouthful from the straw.

'Get off me.' Orange juice dribbles down his chin. Cat pulls back, a little startled, and then winces at the rebuttal. 'How long was I out?' He turns and clambers on to his knees, still woozy, eyes flicking to the circle of lads. 'I did it! Everyone look, I did it . . . I fainted!'

Cat props him up, keeping the juice straw in his mouth like she's administering fluids in ICU. 'Just sit still for a while.' She places a hand on his forehead and he shrinks back from her touch, slightly embarrassed, his eyes still searching for validation from the other boys. He did win the game, after all. If hyperventilating to unconsciousness was some kind of new Olympic sport, he just took gold. But the wall of black-blazered backs tells him nobody's bothered. Something far more important is happening. Top Dog has arrived.

Ben slings his red leather Nottingham Forest football bag to the front of the line and sweeps a hand through his mop of golden hair. Annie is up on her feet and moving towards him, her body gliding without consciousness like metal to a magnet. There's a huddle of chatter as his mates gather round the Gary Barlow lookalike. Cat and Mark watch on from the sidelines, not old enough or cool enough to be part of the gang.

'All right, listen up. I know we have GCSEs and all that, but this is the last year that we're all going to be together.' He glances at Annie. 'So, I have a plan. I want us to build an amazing den down at the mill.' Ben juts his chin towards the church, in the direction of The Cut that leads to Cheney End.

Blackstone Mill is legendary around these parts. A colossal, smoke-blackened stone structure built by the Victorians in the mid-1800s, it was originally a weaving shed powered by a water wheel. Over the years, it has been a printing house, a school, an air-raid shelter and even a garage where the local dads would get their cars MOT'd. But a fire put an end to that, and it's been wrapped in barbed wire and declared out of bounds ever since. To Ben, it's a forbidden fortress, a challenge waiting to be accepted.

'I want us to get to the top of the chimney stack and make a lookout post. We'll call it the Crow's Nest. We'll need all hands on deck. Everyone in?'

Mark and Cat watch as backs are slapped and fives are highed. Ben finally glances over at Annie and smiles as the sun breaks through the clouds.

A burgundy and cream coach pulls around the corner by the phone box, creating a sudden flurry of boisterous energy. A riot begins as bags are snatched from the kerb queue and the boys shove and jostle to be first on the bus, as the girls hang back, rolling their eyes and chewing gum.

'Oi, Marcello, get out the way, you big poof.'

Mark is elbowed and pushed as he tries to get in line, hugging his cello like it's a small child, protecting the bridge from being crushed. Annie is last to board. She looks up to the back seat as Ben watches her, drawing a heart on the steamed-up window with an arrow through it and patting the seat next to him. Annabel smiles, shakes her head and begins to parade slowly up the centre aisle of the coach. She looks over to Mark and her sister, who are deep in conversation, fixes her chestnut hair into a ponytail and turns over the waistband of her skirt to shorten it an extra inch above the knee. She slides in next to Ben and turns to him with serious eyes.

'No distractions this term, Ben. My mocks were a disaster and Dad says I need to knuckle down.'

Ben glances down to the inch of skin between her short skirt and thigh-high socks.

'No distractions.' He swallows and slides his arm over her shoulder, slumping deep into the seat.

As the coach pulls away, headed for the sports complex, across the aisle a pair of eyes spy on them through the reflection of the glass. Watching Annie's every move as she nestles her head into the crook of Ben's arm, scrutinising every detail.

Ben smiles at Annie. 'Your dad's right, better knuckle down and buckle up.'

3

SEPTEMBER 2023

Lily Knot tore down the right wing, boot studs flicking up mud and grass as she dodged defender after defender, the ball glued to her feet. She'd been wearing down the team from Heston Lacy since the very start of the game. A blocked penalty, following a handball in the second half, had their striker hitting the bar again. Barton Mallet were still pushing, but the excellent Kate White from Heston had capitalised on a gap in Barton's defence. Lily Knot was hot on her heels, deftly taking the ball from between her feet, thwarting their chances of a goal yet again.

'GO ON, LILY! DRIVE IT FORWARD!' Dani screamed from the sidelines, trying to keep her brand-new white trainers out of the mud. Her phone, held high overhead, filmed every second of the game, while the Heston Lacy dads watched from the other side of the field in a grumpy gaggle of folded arms.

Lily was a few feet away from the penalty box when Heston's Charlotte Roach was suddenly on the ground, rolling around in agony. A whistle sounded and everyone checked their watches in expectation of a fair whack of injury time.

Dani leant into her friend Margaret Carson, waiting for the referee to stand from his crouched position and deliver a verdict.

'Roach clearly dived. COME ON, REF . . .' She tapped her watch. 'GET THE BALL BACK IN PLAY!'

Margaret smiled politely and winced as Dani's talons dug into her arm. 'She does appear to have blood on her face. Let's hope there's no concussion.'

Ignoring the polite diplomacy, Dani focused on the verdict through the iPhone movie she'd be posting on TikTok in about twenty minutes, zooming into a tight frame on the injured girl. The referee's hand reached into his top pocket and his arm shot up, clasping a yellow card.

'IT WAS AN ACCIDENTAL KNEE!' Dani exploded.

Margaret intercepted her before she burst on to the field and accosted the referee. 'Doesn't really matter, does it? It's just a friendly, after all.'

'Friendly? It's about as friendly as cystitis. Of course it bloody matters.' Dani's head whipped back sharply as Charlotte miraculously staggered to her feet and the ball was back in play. A goal kick from Heston was intercepted by Lily once again.

'GO ON, KNOT!' Dani blasted like a foghorn. For such a small person, the lungs on her were impressive. Lily took an audacious shot from the halfway line that went high and wide, provoking a big groan from the Barton Mallet supporters. Then, on a second wind, Lily propelled the ball forward and drove it straight into the bottom corner of the net.

'GOAL!'

The Heston dads stood across the field, mouths open, hands on heads. Dani was about to get up in their faces when Margaret coaxed her off the field towards the safety of the sports centre car park.

'Come on, Dani, let's not gloat, not today, not with everything going on.'

Dani looked up into a pair of troubled eyes. 'What do you mean, "everything going on"?'

Margaret dug into her tote bag, pulling out a Tic Tac to freshen the foul taste that was forming in her mouth. 'We were at the Crown Court earlier.'

'Who were?' Dani shook her head at the offered sweet. 'Who's we?'

'Me and some of the ladies from the WI, a few from the lunch club and Barton Mallet PTA.'

'Why didn't you tell me? Why didn't you invite me along?' Dani stopped in her tracks as Margaret glanced back to the field and smiled sympathetically but didn't answer the question.

'There were . . . some arrests. It got violent.' They had reached Margaret's car and she was delving for her keys, avoiding eye contact. 'I don't blame them, to be honest. Susan Peterson, our so-called MP, is doing absolutely nothing to intervene . . .' She winced and swallowed back words as she clicked open the lock.

'What was the verdict?' Dani's mouth grew dry.

Margaret was about to confide in her when Gaynor Carson jogged over towards her mum and hopped into the back seat. Margaret's eyes flicked to her daughter, and she lowered her voice to a barely audible whisper.

'There will be certain conditions but he's definitely coming out.' There was a deep resignation in her tone and she squeezed Dani's hand. The two women were suspended in disbelief when a tap on the glass, telling them to hurry up, pulled them out of their silence. Dani smiled and waved at Gaynor as Margaret closed her car door and pulled away.

The blood rushed from Dani's head. What conditions? Her thoughts immediately turned to Ben. Did he know? She needed to call him. She wandered over to her car and climbed in, but before she could dial Ben's number, Lily was there, smushing her cheek against the glass, pulling a face.

Dani jumped. 'Oh. My. God. Come here, you.' She forced an animated smile and climbed out of the car, pulling Lily into a hug. 'You are an 'effing superstar.'

'Where's Dad? I thought he was coming?' Lily kicked off her boots and shimmied out of her muddy shorts as Dani held a modesty towel around her, like they were at the beach.

'Yeah, his flight got delayed . . . but he will be so proud of you when he hears. Tw-oo nil . . . two nil . . . two nil!' Dani chanted. It suddenly felt fake.

'Yeah OK, calm down.' The flicker of embarrassment on Lily's face was replaced by disappointment. This wasn't the first time her dad had been a no-show. She cracked a smile. 'I was pretty good, wasn't I? I mean, the game was good.'

'Good doesn't come close. You were a warrior.'

Dani was already scrolling through her phone, finding the best video clip to post as an Instagram story. She was all over social media, Threads, X, TikTok, Facebook. She was into everyone's lives and assumed everyone was into hers. Within seconds, the footage of her Barton Mallet star player was up online for all to see. The 'likes' started tumbling in and Dani put down her phone with a satisfied smile.

She glanced up to the rear-view mirror. Lily was sitting with her arms folded, staring out of the window.

'Indian? Chinese?'

'Can we get Thai?' Lily was looking out across the field, watching the losing team in their debrief with the coach, a sea of sad faces and soggy kits.

'Love, you can have whatever you want.'

Lily remained still, silently transfixed.

'What's wrong?' Dani tidied her hair in the mirror, eyeballing Lily.

'I dunno, just . . . I dunno.'

'Are we giving Katie a lift? Want to invite her for supper?' Dani smiled, trying some positive bravado.

'No, her mum wants her to go home. Everyone is going home tonight.'

As they pulled out of the car park, Lily stared out of the window at a man wearing a tweed flat cap lingering across the other side of the playing field with a majestic German shepherd next to him. He was standing still in the middle of the field, like a zombie, looking right at her as his dog ferreted through the brambles of the Barton Mallet landfill.

'Everyone was talking about him today.' Lily spoke quietly as Dani eyed her in the mirror.

'Talking? About who?'

'The Mill Killer.'

Dani shuddered but held it together. 'What were they saying?'

'I don't really know . . . they all clammed up when I walked into the changing room.'

Dani turned and looked over her shoulder. 'Hey, you. You just won us the match. You're a Lioness.' Her smile and sparkling eyes were full of genuine pride.

Lily looked at Dani. The word 'Mum' had almost slipped out so many times over the years, but staring at her now, face to face, this was definitely Dani. More like a big sister, full of fun and bubbles and too much make-up. Lily suddenly welled up and turned back to the window. Dani clocked it. Something was going on with her stepdaughter.

Something was going on with all the Barton Mallet daughters that evening. And all the parents of Barton Mallet's daughters. Parents who were new to the village and some who had grown up there. The foundations were trembling, an old rumble of collect-ive trauma was shuddering to the surface.

'Pad Thai and green curry it is then.'

Dani adjusted the rear-view mirror of the Jaguar, fired up the engine and slowly pulled away. Lily stared out of the back window as the car drew slowly up the hill, away from the sports complex and back towards the village. He was standing still in the middle of the road now, arms hanging limp by his sides, a husk of a person. The man in the flat cap with the German shepherd.

Dani had seen him too, but pretended she hadn't. She knew exactly who he was.

4

SEPTEMBER 2023

Exterior. Night. July 1994. 'Pearls Before Swine.' A siren sounds in the distance, a helicopter overhead. A manhunt was already underway.

Max opened his eyes and stared at the blank screen under the heading: final draft.

His fingers hovered over the keyboard as a long shadow lurched across the table, the candlelight flickering over the red brick of the low vaulted ceiling in the wine cellar.

She was late. The traffic on Santa Monica on a Friday evening was always hell on earth.

'Same again?' The cute waiter had been flirting with Max from the moment he'd arrived.

He closed his laptop and twinkled back at the wannabe actor's white teeth, gleaming for tips. 'Trying to get me drunk?'

His eyes looked to the wrought-iron gates framing the modest entrance to 'Pace'. His favourite Italian, midway up Laurel Canyon buried under the shabby Country Store, was like some illicit speakeasy. He returned to the waiter. 'Sure, why not. Make it a double.'

Moments later, two crystal highballs hit the table, ice clinking in the glass, as she slumped into their booth, out of breath.

'Sorry I'm late, the 405 was a nightmare.' She loosened her ponytail and tousled her white-blonde hair over her shoulders before taking a sip of her Tito's and tonic with a dash of lime.

'So . . . Did they bite?' Karine Mickelsen picked up the menu. 'I am starving.'

'Just pinning down the last few investors . . .' Max slid his laptop into his bag and caught the eye of the waiter. 'But we're in good shape.'

'Studio?'

'Probably one of the big streamers.' Max lowered his voice. 'Nordics are obviously chomping at the bit because of you.'

'Obviously.' Karine popped an olive into her mouth and glanced up to the waiter, who had reappeared to take their order. 'The rib eye please, rare.'

Max sat back and folded his arms. 'Karine . . .' He paused for a second. 'He's coming out, that's the only reason your financier finally came through. We have to ride this wave . . . it's now or never.'

'Just give me the green light and I'm on that plane.' Her eyes narrowed as she scrutinised his face. 'I'll need full access, and to be left alone.'

'Of course.' Max chewed his lip and inhaled, bracing himself. 'There is just one condition.' He shifted in his seat. 'I want you to shoot on Hi8.'

Karine blew out through her lips. 'You're joking, right?'

Max stared at her.

'Video.' She snorted. 'Why?'

Max sipped his drink. 'You know why.'

Karine paused, pursing her lips. 'What's the budget for post?'

'Don't you worry about that.' Max glanced up as the scampi piccanti appetiser floated down on to the table.

'It'll be difficult to find any Hi8 film stock.' Karine shook her head and dipped a shrimp into the sauce. 'But I guess I can trawl eBay for some cassette tapes. I think I have an old Panasonic I can dig out from my kit.'

'No.' Max was sharp, abrupt even. He checked himself, then lowered his voice. 'There's a very specific camera that I will need you to . . .' He paused, eyes drifting to the middle distance.

Karine raised her glass to her lips. 'To . . . what?'

'To source.'

Karine took a long slow draught of her drink, draining the glass. 'And where will I acquire this "very specific camera"?' Her soft Danish precision accentuated his choice of words.

Max stared into Karine's eyes, his face softening.

'You'll find it.' His mouth curled into a smile. 'I have every faith in you.' He raised his glass to hers. The crystal chinked in a toast and glittered in the candlelight.

'That's why I hired you.'

5

SEPTEMBER 1993

The old blue Ford Fiesta belongs to his dad. It hasn't been driven much the last few years because his dad can't leave the house. Ben hasn't passed his test yet, and with his L-plates he's supposed to drive under supervision. He sometimes puts an old shop dummy with his nan's fur coat and hat on in the front seat, to fox the police. But Barton Mallet is a small village, and no one really cares. PC Davis has pulled him over a few times to rap his knuckles and tell him to stick to the farm roads. But Ben is a special case, what with everything going on at home, and Davis has his back.

The car pulls up slowly to the Maddocks's farm. It's about two miles out of the village in the middle of nowhere, on the road to the pretty cottages, past the dog rescue, on the corner of Sienna Lane. On summer days, when they disappear into the woods on their mountain bikes, the sound of dogs barking melds with the smell of manure from the dairy farm. The headlights of Ben's car brush the dirt path and the hedgerows glow with an orange light as he slows down, crunching the gears and jump-stalling to a sudden stop. Now he's here, he needs to figure out exactly what to say. Not to Annie, but to her father, John Maddock. He switches off the head-lights and waits, steaming up the windscreen as he zips up his bomber jacket and tests his breath in the cup of his hand.

The Maddocks's is a perfectly symmetrical white-rendered Georgian farmhouse with dark green moss tumbling down the bowing slate roof. It's modest but rather beautiful in its own way. Lights are on in the ground-floor snug, where Ben can see two silhouettes through the faded net curtains. The voice of a clarinet sings through the silence, then, joining in harmony, the deep melancholy vibrato of a cello. For a moment, Ben's hand hovers over the car door handle. He is transfixed. Slowly, he winds down the window so he can hear the music. The hair on his forearm awakens as if roused by the sound. This melody is one of his dad's favourites, but he can never remember the composer's name. The harmonics rise to a mournful climax, hanging in the air for a second, before drifting up and out of the window, into the rustling leaves of the oak trees.

Can she see him waiting out here in the dark? The room upstairs is in shadow, but the shape of the girl is just visible, and as the curtains adjust, light from the landing spills across the wall behind her. Suddenly the music stops and a peal of laughter rings out, as Cat and Mark get up and move across the snug.

Ben turns to his lifeless passenger. 'All right, Nan, I'm going in. Wish me luck.' He opens the car door and crunches down the gravel path towards the house, his hands digging deep into his pockets.

John Maddock doesn't like him at all; he is well aware of that. He's also well aware that his dad is always late paying the Maddocks's milk bill and has stopped leaving the generous Christmas box that his mum used to give. Lots of things stop after the mums have gone. As soon as he taps on the heavy iron knocker of the front door, the dogs will go mad and there'll be no turning back. A little tap-tap on the window above him and Ben glances up to see Annie tugging on the old, over-painted sash window. The wood creaks and shudders as the tiniest crack opens, just enough to slide an arm through. Annie presses her face to the gap.

'Don't get stuck.' Ben stifles a giggle as Annie attempts to wriggle her shoulders through. 'Just whisper through the gap.'

'I can't come out, Ben. Dad won't let me.' Annie keeps her voice down.

Ben's shoulders sink. 'Not even for half an hour?'

'I have to study.'

'How come baby sister's allowed guests? I mean, I don't know what they're getting up to in there, but it doesn't sound very homeworky.'

'Orchestra practice. Mum's really cross with me. I only got Ds for my maths and biology mocks.'

'Just come down for ten minutes, then . . . we can listen to the radio in the car.'

'I can't believe you drove here, Ben. You know you're not allowed.'

Ben raises his eyebrows, his hands still buried deep into his pockets, trying to stop the little bulge from growing down there. 'Please?'

A stark light spills from her bedroom door and the room is suddenly illuminated. Annie turns sharply, putting her back to the window and sitting on the sill. Ben watches as she closes the curtain, the slightest shake of her head warning him off. And then the dogs go crazy. The hall light flicks on and the front door swings open, triggering the outside light. Mr Maddock stands in slippers, holding the dogs back with his legs, a half-eaten cheese sandwich in his hand. His rough Derbyshire accent bellows across the silence.

'Go on, buzz off. She's not coming out, and if you keep comin' back, she'll be grounded.'

'Sorry, sir. I just wanted to ask her about some biology homework.' There's a blend of defiance and sarcasm in Ben's tone that doesn't go unnoticed.

'Biology? I'll bet you did.' The remainder of the cheese sandwich is shoved in whole as the massive frame of Farmer John towers in the doorway, thick muscular arms folded tight over a bulging stomach. Catherine and Mark Cherry appear sheepishly in the hallway behind him.

'Fuck's sake,' Ben mutters under his breath as he turns away.

'Oi, clean your mouth out. And how many times do you need to be told about driving without a licence? You're irresponsible, Ben Knot.'

Ben slams the car door and hits the headlights on to full beam, before crunching the gears into reverse. He's actually a pretty good driver, truth be told. He's had to be. His dad needs help and there's no one else to do the shopping and fetch prescriptions.

At the gate at the end of the lane, instead of heading back on to the main road, Ben turns on to the farm track that runs around the edge of the field. Through the open window, he inhales the smell of damp leaves and manure from the field: the dank scent of autumn. The furrows of earth rutted deep by the heavy tractor treads scrape at the loose exhaust pipe of the old Ford Fiesta. Ben flinches. He can hear his dad berating him for not checking his oil or sorting out the clutch. The car bumps and grinds slowly around the back of the farmhouse, towards the vast cowshed.

As the car emerges from behind an enormous compost heap, he can see a figure clinging precariously to the drainpipe and dropping gently on to the flat roof of the outhouse. Annie slides over a wood pile and then crouches down on the ground next to the back door, as a clatter of chopped logs tumble on to the paving. Ben holds his breath. She is all rebel tonight in her leather bomber jacket. His heart pounds in his chest as he watches her daredevil escape from the house. In an instant, she's free and heading directly towards him across the paddock. Through the drawn curtains of the living room, Ben can hear the jaunty theme tune to *Only Fools and Horses*. That'll buy them half an hour.

The passenger door opens and a breathless Annie leans into the car. 'Oh! Who's your friend?' She giggles. The passenger seat appears to be occupied.

'Decoy! Hold on . . . I'll just pop Nan in the back.' Ben grabs the shop dummy, shoving her roughly into the back seat. Annie slides herself into the car, cool air passing from her mouth to his as he breathes her in. Talcum powder and strawberries.

'You're gonna get me into so much trouble.' She smiles, as Ben leans in for a kiss. She gently turns her cheek to him, blushing. Ben's apologetic smile turns into a grin as Annie produces a handful of kitchen roll, containing some of Mrs Maddock's homemade chocolate brownies.

'Where to then?' Ben asks as he bites into the crisp top of the chewy chocolate slice.

'Where do you think?' Annie glints at him as she pops a corner of brownie into her own mouth, savouring the sweetness.

Ben's eyes shine in the dark, fizzing with mischief. 'At this time of night . . . no way!'

'Why not?' Annie fixes him with a defiant glare.

'I can't drive this old rust bucket through, it's too deep. Remember what happened last time?' Ben chews his lip, considering her proposal.

'Let's get stranded together. You can carry me out.' Annie pulls down the visor and wipes rogue chocolate crumbs from her lip in the mirror, before turning back with a huge conspiratorial grin on her face. 'I dare you.'

Ben starts the engine and slowly reverses the car, backing into the circle of the pen-fold, and then heads off in the direction of Water Ford Gate, known to the locals as the Water Splash.

'You're a bad influence on me, Annabel Maddock.'

6

SEPTEMBER 2023

The Bashnya Evolyutsiya in Central Moscow was an extraordinary feat of engineering. The fifty-five floors of a twisted double helix, fashioned from glass and steel, won Ben Knot and the IF Group the 2015 NOPRIZ prize for architecture. The fountains, terraces and cafes bustling under a geodesic glass structure, inspired by the spiral geometry of human DNA, was simply breathtaking. But the eye-watering two-billion-dollar price tag, along with all the dirty corporate fingers in the pie, was the beginning of a snowball of broken promises and backroom deals that heralded the beginning of the end for the IF Group. The building remained empty and was a universally acknowledged commercial disaster. It had not only sent the firm into bankruptcy but had triggered an investigation for fraud.

Ben had gone to extreme measures to keep his name out of the picture. Shell companies and various entities had ensured that each new architectural development had no paper trail leading to him personally, but the IF Group was in deep water and sinking fast. Loans were being recalled with immediate effect and some of the lenders were unscrupulous to say the least. Russian money in sheltered tax havens, avoiding the scrutiny of Western governments, had found its way into the IF Group's accounts and now the investors wanted it back.

Ben stood in the hallway of his home, staring at the model of his 'Evolution Tower' in miniature. He'd always known it was far too ambitious, but he'd had something to prove back then, and hubris had fuelled his ascent to stardom. Ben's fingers traced the sharp edges of the glass box encasing all his creative dreams. It was everything he'd had to offer; every innovative idea he'd ever had had been ploughed into this venture, and it had failed. Ben was stubborn. He thought he could borrow his way out of this mess, but things were spiralling. The eye-watering numbers had stopped meaning anything to him, they were just jumbled figures on spreadsheets. The only thing left to do was to hold the banks off for as long as possible and try to bury the evidence. Eventually, they would come for the company, then for all his assets, and finally for him. They were out for blood.

Ben was convinced his phone had been hacked and his bank was flagging up fraud alerts every few days now. They'd been phishing. This is what they did: stress-testing the security of his personal accounts. He'd resorted to setting up a private server at home to try to ensure secrecy, but he knew they would get to him in the end. The question was when and how.

Nathan Knot kicked his school shoes off and skidded them across the polished concrete, aiming for the black marble base of Ben's pride and joy. EarPods in, vacant and unaware, he slung his school bag into the Macassar ebony veneered wall.

'Hey.' Ben glared at his son. 'HEY!'

Oblivious, Nate bopped his head to the music blasting into his ears and slouched into the kitchen. 'Dani?'

'Nate . . . give me a break, will you?' Ben tried to catch at least a glimmer of eye contact with his son, who was now charging up the cantilevered glass staircase to his room.

Nobody else was home when they got back, and the security system was enabled. Ben thumbed through the images of each room on his smartphone. He stopped at Nathan's bedroom and watched the door as his son entered and flopped down on to the bed. The room was a mess, clothing and trainers strewn every-where. Nathan's camera equipment – his tripod, cables and ring lights – was scattered around the room.

'NATE! TIDY YOUR ROOM BEFORE DANI GETS BACK. IT'S A TIP.'

Ben tapped his phone and pulled up the feed from the various cameras positioned around his house. He scrolled through the kitchen, den, master bedroom, basement, Lily's room and then back to Nate's. He stood at the door to his office, the one place where there was no camera, watching his son. Nathan stared up into the lens with a sarcastic smile, before climbing on to the bed and slinging a pair of dirty underpants over the camera. The screen turned black.

Dani had scoffed at Ben's obsession with security – 'It's like bloody Fort Knox in this house' – but he loved the power of technology. He could charge his car remotely and turn on the central heating and lights if no one was home. Sensors in the garden flickered on and off, triggered by every passing fox. The Google Nest cameras did what they said on the tin: his nest was secure.

The Lagavulin hit his throat and burned as he swallowed. The second quaff emptied the glass and was mellower, as the warmth of the whisky got to work. He began to soften as he poured another and sank into the Eames chair in the corner of his office, fingering the track pad to open his computer. He began to check his unread emails, opening the first of a long chain between Gazprombank and Kotak Mahindra. Subject: 'СРОЧНЫЙ/ URGENT'. His bowels moved.

A WhatsApp message dropped into the top corner of his phone.

On the way. Got Thai. LOL. 20 mins.

Dani. How on earth was he going to tell her that they were about to lose everything? He glanced at the pile of books stacked on the corner of his desk. There was a biography of one of his mentors, Bjarke Ingels. Sitting on top was an unread paperback, *Finding Meaning in the Second Half of Life* by James Hollis. It had been a joke present for his fortieth that Dani had found hilarious. The spine was unbroken, the pages untouched, but the title alone had planted seeds in Ben's mind. He poured another measure of whisky.

He would have to sell up and even then it wouldn't be enough to cover his legal bills. He was going to prison. If he could just buy himself a little more time. He closed his eyes for a second and drifted.

A shriek of laughter from the kitchen roused him. He ran his hands through his hair, scratching his scalp, trying to claw the anxiety from his mind. He took a deep breath, closed his computer and went to join the others.

'Hey, Dad! We won . . . two nil! I scored both goals. Wish you could have been there.' Lily's sing-song, dismissive tone punched a fist of guilt into Ben's stomach. She pecked him on the cheek and grabbed one of the plates Dani had just got out of the cupboard.

'Proud of you, Lils.' Ben eyed Dani, who was standing at the huge kitchen island, spooning rice noodles into a bowl. She inclined her head with a sad smile on her glowing face.

Lily threw a parting shot over her shoulder. 'Be there next time and I'll hat-trick the f—'

'Hey, language.'

'All right, keep ya hair on . . . what's left of it.' She giggled, stuffing a spring roll into her mouth, walked into the den and slumped in front of the TV. Dani remained silent and perched on a bar stool.

She smiled as Ben chewed on his lip and gazed at the food. His stomach turned; he had no appetite.

'She really wanted you at the footie, Ben.'

'I know . . . it was just bad timing.' He snapped open a pair of wooden chopsticks and fumbled them into the hot noodles, trying to slurp them up into his mouth. Dani smiled as she slid a fork across the counter towards him. She went to the fridge and pulled out a half-finished bottle of Riesling.

'Want one?' Her hand hovered over the two wine glasses.

'What do you think?' Ben persevered with the chopsticks.

'That bad?'

'Yep, the banks are calling in loans left, right and centre, and we just don't have the funds. I don't know what to do . . .' His tired eyes met hers, but they were glazed over. He knew she didn't want to hear it. She didn't want to hear about losing the house, tightening the purse strings, forgoing the luxuries that had become necessities. Dani's selective deafness sometimes appealed to him, but right now he needed her. 'Anyway. How was your day, angel?' His socked foot found hers on the bar stool.

'Yeah, great . . . Busy.' Dani's 'busy' was most people's bank holiday. She knew that and always had her 'how was your day' answer ready. 'Did Pilates, sorted out the MOT on the car, met Maggie at the football . . .' Her voice faded into the distance. Now it was Ben's turn to tune out. His shoulders seemed to droop, and his eyes drifted to the window. 'What you thinking about?' Dani twisted noodles on to her fork like spaghetti.

'Hmm?' Ben was elsewhere. Dani followed his gaze; he was staring out into the garden.

'I know, I know, I need to call the gardener as well. I'll do it tomorrow.' She finished her wine and topped up her glass.

'What did Margaret have to say for herself? I know you two like to put the world to rights.'

Dani paused and took a deep breath. 'She went to the Crown Court earlier – didn't tell me they were going. Did you hear . . . he got parole?' She took another deep swig of wine, steeling herself for what was about to come. Ben sat frozen for a second. A noodle slipped from his chopsticks, slithering back into the bowl. 'Ben . . . love?' She reached out a hand towards him, which he took. 'We are going to have to talk about this.'

Ben's eyes finally found hers. They were red rimmed and haunted. 'He murdered your girlfriend.'

Ben gently pulled his hand away, picked up his wine glass and smiled confidently at her. 'Skin looks good.'

'Yeah? Um . . . I did a microderm at Leslie's.' The words floated out without meaning as Dani stared at him. 'Ben, it's OK to talk to me about it. I think it's important that we do.'

Ben looked as if he was going to vomit on to the glittering black quartz worktop. He swayed down from the stool and moved to the window. Standing with his hands on his hips, he propped up his torso on shaking legs and faced the huge wall of glass. The evening light was fading in the garden and, without saying another word, he slid open the door and stepped out.

He made his way down to the bottom of the lawn towards the dense woods that extended far into the distance, towards Cheney End and the Water Ford Gate. The thick canopy of trees concealed the distant view, visible only from the very top floor of the house. That view was the reason Ben had purchased the parcel of land on which he had built his 'castle'.

He stood in silence, the water of the infinity pool reflecting another Ben. His eyes strained through the thicket of trees in the direction of Blackstone Mill.

7

SEPTEMBER 1993

(Vince:) *I'll slit the villain's nose that would have sent me to the jail!*

(Baps:) *But do you hear, sir, have you married my daughter without asking my goodwill?*

(Vince:) *Fear not, Baptista, we will content you. Go to! But I will go in to be revenged for this villainy.*

'Off you go then.' Mr Waller, the drama teacher, is on his feet, waving his arms like a mad conductor. 'Exit stage left . . . that means you, Davis. Go on . . . get off . . . please.'

Lynette Davis slouches down the rickety steps of the stage, making a 'wanker' sign behind Waller's back. She slumps into one of the orange plastic chairs lined up in a circle on the floor of the school hall as her twin brother, Chris, steps forward with a huge grin on his face.

Look not pale, Bianca. Thy father will not . . . er . . . er . . .

'Frown . . . FROWN,' Waller bellows from the stalls.

Chris Davis's face contorts into a comic grimace under his shaved head, gurning at the audience, who erupt into laughter.

'No . . . not literally, you idiot.' Mr Waller waves a bedraggled-looking *Complete Works* in the air. 'You've got the text in your hand, just read what it says.'

'FROOOOWWWNN!' Chris bellows, before performing a flourishing Elizabethan bow to rapturous applause. 'Sorry, Mr Waller, this ain't my part. Dave Patel's not here so I'm just winging it . . . innit!' The scruffy class clown and resident thug exits the same way his sister did, giving it jazz hands as he tiptoes down the steps. More laughter as the concentration of the class starts to disintegrate.

Next up, it's Annie Maddock. She touches the back of her neck with her hand and swallows nervously as she takes the stage.

Husband . . .

There are already a few titters around the hall as the Year 11s brace for what they know is coming.

. . . let's follow to see the end of this ado.

Ben takes his place to deliver his line. You can hear a pin drop. There is a collective thump of pulses around the room, racing in anticipation.

First kiss me –

'Pucker up, Knot!' someone pipes up from the back row.

Ben has another crack at the line.

(Petruchio:) *First kiss me, Kate, and we will.*

(Kate:) *In the midst of the street?*

(Petruchio:) *You ashamed of me?*

'It's "art thou" ashamed of me, Benjamin, please . . . this is the bard.' Waller is sweating in frustration.

(Kate:) *No, just ashamed to kiss.*

(Petruchio:) *All right, let's go home then. Oi, Grimmers!*

(Kate:) *Wait . . . I will give you a kiss.*

Here it comes. Ben Knot is holding his ground as Annie Maddock puts her script down, ready for the moment everyone has been waiting for. Nobody breathes until a wolf whistle from the back row breaks the tension.

Then, a slow, intimidating hand clap begins, goading them on. Annie Maddock frowns and huffs out an exasperated sigh. Then, walking slowly towards Ben, she pauses for a second, closes her eyes and quickly pecks him on the cheek. A loud farting raspberry issues from the back of the hall.

'Boooo . . . slip 'er a tongue, mate.'

'All right, settle down.' Mr Waller is now red in the face. 'Continue, please . . . I SAID SETTLE DOWN, YEAR 11!' There is a clattering of chairs and a scuffle, as someone storms the stage.

'Wait, I'll give you one.' Lynette Davis mounts the steps and shoves Annabel Maddock out of the way. She grabs Ben Knot's face and plants her lips on his. The entire hall erupts in a massive unrestrained cheer and feet pummel the wooden floor.

'GO GO GO GO GO!'

Lynette releases Ben, who appears stunned for a moment but then turns his head to the baying crowd and pumps the air with his fist, eliciting more shrieks and whoops from the crowd.

Lynette turns to Annie. 'That's how it's done, love!'

Annie reddens but smiles sarcastically. 'So. What? You think Kate should just give in to her "master"? Just give him what he wants?' The crowd in the hall hush as Mr Waller holds out his hand as if to stop time for a second.

Lynette screws her face up. 'What you on about, Maddock? You frigid or what? Yeah . . . I reckon she needs to give him what he wants . . . or he'll go somewhere else!' A rather subdued laugh bubbles out from the audience.

Annie turns to Mr Waller. 'I was being ironic, making him wait. I don't think Katherina should be controlled like that.' She looks back to Lynette with a smirk. 'She's just not that easy . . . love.'

This gets a bigger laugh and Lynette lurches forward to strike Annie. Ben reacts quickly and catches Lynette by the arm, dipping her into a dance move to cover the awkward moment.

(Kate:) *Now pray thee, love, stay.*

(Petruchio:) *Is not this well? Come, my sweet Kate. Better once than never, for never too late.*

The rowdy teenagers applaud as Ben spins Lynette around the stage in dizzying circles, defusing the tension.

At that moment, unseen by the rest of the class, Dave slides into the back of the hall and sits silently on one of the chairs in the corner. He's very late but relieved that he seems to have got away with it. He pulls out a video camera from his bag, inserts a tape and presses record. Holding the device gently in his lap, he stares into the viewfinder.

He follows Ben and Lynette as they spin around the stage. Then pans across to Chris Davis, hands clasped on the top of his head, chewing gum, his Doc Martens plonked on the back of the chair in front of him. He zooms in on Mr Waller, shirt buttons straining, sweat beaded on his waxy brow, his class totally out of control.

Finally, the camera falls on Annabel Maddock. She is standing to the side of the stage, in the shadow of a drab grey curtain, waiting in the wings. Patel adjusts the lens with his fingers, trying to find focus, but he can't seem to hold her form sharp. Then, almost sensing his gaze, her eyes find his. A knowing smile spreads across her face as she looks directly down the lens before backing away into the shadows.

Taking centre stage, Lynette Davis appears to have Ben in a 'Strictly Shakespearian' ballroom chokehold. Lynette keeps her eyes glued on Annie, who is studying them both from the darkness of the wings.

If looks could kill then one of them would be dead in an instant.

8

SEPTEMBER 2023

Nate glanced up at his pants dangling off the camera on the wall. He hated being watched like some prison inmate. He wanted to control who could see him. He smirked to himself at his temporary fix to thwart his father's surveillance and settled down to begin work.

In the background, Spanish guitar music picked and strummed as Nate opened a Grenade protein bar wrapper with his teeth and triggered the electronic blackout blinds. As the room went dark, he tapped his foot on the box lamp fader, setting the scene. Placing his phone into a cradle, he chewed on the peanut butter crunch as he lined up the shot.

He pulled out a dog-eared cardboard box from under the bed and took out hair gel and a comb, a small pot of adhesive, a stick of shaving soap and numerous palettes of tattoo paint. His open laptop was propped up on the small table, showing him the image that would be livestreamed. He opened his movie-maker app and set the timer for fifteen minutes, activating the AI editor to record with a thirty-second delay. A nondescript computerised voice counted down.

'Five, four, three, two . . . welcome to RetroFX. Your time starts: now.'

A green light flicked on in the corner of the screen. He was live. He dipped a large kabuki brush into a palette, then slowly and ceremoniously placed it on the centre of his forehead and struck down. A gash of vivid red severed his face, cleaving it in two between a river of painted blood. The brush hit the right side, then the left, the scarlet streaks of war paint lying on top of his skin as he leant forward into the lens. Just for a second, his eyes flicked to the screen below him, deep auburn hair scraped back, his eyes lowered like a hellish geisha. He watched as the instant messages dropped. Bursting hearts and emoji party poppers exploded over his screen as a festival of likes flooded his DMs. Now his energy changed, and he began to move faster. Fingers dipped into the paint as deep reds and blacks found the structure of his face, hollowed out his eye sockets and cheekbones, a broad swipe across the line of his jaw in the sharp angles of that iconic V shape. The transformation was remarkable.

'Is it Darth Maul?' A DM appeared at the bottom of the screen and travelled upwards as comment after comment, abused and ridiculed, celebrated and fawned over this performance.

Nate's hand suddenly covered the lens, plunging the frame into darkness. He only had thirty seconds, so he had to move fast. Stripping off his T-shirt and slipping into a black hoodie, he dug his hand into the cardboard box and found a small plastic container. He shook the liquid inside and carefully opened it. Without using a mirror, his fingertips found one of the contact lenses, which went quickly to the moist surface of his eyeball, and then the other. Nate blinked them in, allowing the blurred vision to settle before glancing at the timer. He pulled the hood over his head and replaced his palm over the lens. As he slowly withdrew his hand, an unearthly, angular red face stared out from inside the hood, through stone-cold black eyes.

The show was over.

There was silence in the room but a plethora of clapping emojis lit up his DMs. Fist bumps, fanfares and disco dancing gifs dropped in a muted ovation.

One by one, the followers logged off as Nate leant into the

screen and watched the number of attendees dwindle to just a few bots and hangers-on. He sat still in the darkness of his bedroom.

'Darth Maul? What a dick!' he muttered to himself as he checked the number of Amazon orders that had been placed. A few had searched for the contact lenses and someone had ordered the Uniqlo hoodie, but that was it. His numbers were lower than last time. He needed a new trick.

'You are very talented. You could be a professional.' A DM dropped into his feed. The Bitmoji graphic of a red-haired girl with glasses and freckles made him smile.

'Hi.' His own Bitmoji character, with its red-haired quiff and backwards baseball cap, gave a thumbs-up. He was met with a crying laughing face. Instant friends. Two lonely redheads in a world of mouse brown.

'Cute . . .' Nate typed.

'Thanks. U2.' Freckles replied. 'It's Red Skull from Captain America, isn't it?'

Nate beamed and hit the thumbs-up emoji. 'What's your name?'

'Freckles. I get teased a lot because of them.'

Nate's fingers tickled the keyboard. 'Me too . . .' He hesitated for a second then tapped the middle finger emoji. 'To the haters not you.'

Freckles beamed and hearts popped from her ears. 'You home alone?'

'Always.' Nate's emoji cried floods of dramatic tears.

'Lonely?' Freckles had two red embarrassed cheeks.

Nate typed 'No way' then deleted it. He was about to style it out when Freckles sent another message.

'Stand up and turn around . . .'

'What?' Nate's surprised face with a questioning hand to the chin.

'I want to check you out.' Three love hearts.

He noticed the camera was still running; he'd forgotten to turn it off. As he leant into the frame, his finger poised to stop the feed, he glanced at the followers online. Were they all still watching? Nate's emoji-head exploded.

'Uh . . . OK.' He stood and turned as instructed.

'Take your hoodie off.' A little monkey emoji covering their eyes, all shy.

Nate's stomach dropped, just for a second. He glanced at the viewer count, the numbers had started to grow again, something was happening. Followers were gathering for the 'torso show' and maybe something more? Nate's mouth grew dry. Who wanted to see his pale spotty skin and xylophone ribcage? Go on. Sell yourself, Nate. Dani's voice echoed in his head. The numbers were climbing at speed now as his fingers slowly reached for the zip of his hoodie.

'Off . . . off . . . off.' Just like the chants at school in the play-ground but in silent clap graphics.

'Nate?' Dani was knocking on the bedroom door. 'Lights out, love.'

Nate jumped in shock and smacked the camera to the side, knocking it off the cradle. He exhaled. What was he thinking? As he sat for a second, he could see the shadow of a pair of feet breaking the light under the door.

'Thanks, Dani, see you in the morning.' The feet moved away. Slowly, Nate packed up his gear with an empty feeling in his tummy. He kicked his dirty clothes under the bed, doused his armpits and crotch with a spray of Lynx and slid under the duvet. The groan in his gut made him wonder if he was hungry, but this hollow feeling and his thumping heart were something else. He lay on his side, facing the wall, choking back tears with his eyes wide open, thinking about the lonely little red-haired girl with glasses and freckles who was just like him.

9

OCTOBER 1993

The bridge of Mark Cherry's cello has been bumped and bruised as often as his nose. The tiny scars in the varnished walnut are frequently repaired in his dad's garage with epoxy resin and a brown felt-tip pen. The damage to his cello can easily be fixed but the other bruises always take a bit longer to heal. Mark's cello is on loan from the school, and although the sound it produces is decent, Mark longs for an instrument of his own.

The track, worn into the grass by runners and riders, is soft under Mark's feet as he walks across the recreation ground. Head down, buried inside a grey hoodie, the clouds of his October morning breath trail behind him like a steam train. As the cold weather draws in, Mark's grateful for an excuse to wear more layers, because that means more ways to hide his face. There's a weight on his shoulders but it's not the cello, it's something else. His silhouette is curved like an old man deep in thought. Shoulders back, lad. Stand up proud. It's what his dad would say. But he isn't proud, he lives under a shadow of shame.

Mark passes Lynette and Chris Davis's house. A detached red-brick box from the 1950s with a pale-blue Ford Cortina propped up on bricks on the front lawn alongside a rusty VW camper van. It's still dark as Mark turns into the alley, the streetlamps dying as a ribbon of frosty morning haze hovers over the fields. From the edge of the tree line at the top of the rise, something catches Mark's attention. Someone's coming. The heavy breath and pounding of feet make him turn suddenly.

Not again! How do they always find him? Out of the gloom, a faceless figure surges towards him. The assailant turns sharply on to the road, skidding on the damp grass and grabbing Mark around the waist in a rugby tackle. They both slam into a concrete lamppost.

'Oi, watch it, Marcello!' A furious and sweaty Lynette Davis pulls off a black running beanie. As usual, everything is always someone else's fault.

Slightly winded, Mark hunches over his cello, checking for damage. 'You scared the shit out of me.' He glares angrily at Lynette, scrutinising this walking ball of chaos. Mildly thuggish in appearance, she is considerably taller than everyone in her year, including her twin brother, Chris. Their father is the local bobby, which is why their house has been nicknamed the 'Pig Sty'. Lynette's a chip off the old block: untouchable, undisciplined and, like the rest of the Davis family, thinks she rules the village.

'You burying bodies again?' Lynette gasps for breath, smirking as she points at Mark's cello case. Mark rolls his eyes at the joke he's heard a million times before. His cello does resemble the curves of a corpse, mummified in faux leather. He often has thoughts of how easy it would be to murder someone and carry them around for weeks. They'd keep making their stupid jokes but eventually a trail of blood and the smell of rotting flesh would shut them all up, once and for all.

'Cat got your tongue? Who've you got stashed in there, Gaylord?' Lynette sneers with her signature charm.

Mark smiles sweetly. 'Saving that special place for you.' He runs a finger across his throat like a knife.

'Sod off, limp wrist.' She slings one of the bin bags stacked by her gate over the tall leylandii hedge into the garden next door and fishes her hand into the letter box to pull out a front door key attached to a piece of frayed grey string. Mark brushes the dirt from his trousers and heads off towards Forest Hill.

Dr Sandeep Patel's surgery is a makeshift conversion in his double garage, separated from the main house by a small porch, which serves as a waiting room. The old vicarage, a sturdy Georgian mansion, is no longer affiliated with St James the Greater, and is set behind a dense hedge of privet with an arch cut into it, leading to a wrought-iron gate. Mark follows the path around to the small blue door and takes a seat in the tiny waiting room, listening to muffled voices from Dr Patel's first appointment of the day. He glances at the ornate polished mahogany grandfather clock, standing erect against the wall in the porch. Its heavy pendulum marks time and the ominous tick-tock fills the air with a sense of interminable boredom. The clock says 8.55 a.m. but the distant chime of the church bells of St James tells him it is already nine.

On the dot, the door opens and Ben emerges, his complexion pale. He glances at Mark with a scowl, then takes the furthest seat in the corner and pretends to read a dog-eared copy of *Auto Trader*. Mark stares at his scuffed Clarks shoes.

On the first day of school, when Mark's mum, Jean, had dropped him off at Barton Mallet Primary, Ben had been there. The reassuring pictures of trains painted on the wall, the orange carpet and the smell of glue had distracted the nervous five-year-olds from the true horror of waving goodbye. But the tall blond boy from Year 2, sent to help Reception settle into their new school, had made everything seem OK. That day, Mark had peed his 'Monday' pants and Mrs Fisher had sent Ben to get fresh shorts from the lost-property box. The older boy told him it had happened to him on his first day too, and from that moment, Mark Cherry had idolised Benjamin Knot.

An awkward silence hangs in the air before Ben breaks the ice. 'What's up with you then?' He doesn't look up from the magazine.

Mark clears his throat. 'Tonsillitis again.'

Ben's chin juts upwards in acknowledgement and the conversation dies a death.

'How's he doing?' Mark gives him a sympathetic smile.

Ben sighs and chews his lip, swallowing down a ball of emotion. 'Not good.'

He's still thumbing through the magazine but his hands tremble. There isn't anything more to say. Cancer has come for his dad and he knows that the time they have left is fleeting. Mark squeezes out a tight smile of sympathy and glances up to the ticking clock. As they both stare at it, it begins to chime and a pristinely groomed Dr Patel, in a grey pinstripe suit and blue tie, pops his head around the door. 'He's ready.'

As Ben stands, his eyes shoot to Mark, wishing him away, wishing he wasn't here to witness this. A few moments later, he reappears in the doorway of the doctor's consulting room with his father. Anthony Knot is slumped awkwardly in a wheelchair. There is a blanket covering his legs and he appears to be dressed in a blue pyjama top, with a robe over his shoulders. The stale smell of sweat and urine suddenly fills the room. Mr Knot's eyes are glazed and unfocused and his once sturdy frame appears shrunken inside his clothes. His mouth is half open with a trickle of saliva dangling from his bottom lip, dripping on to his chest.

Sandeep smiles, his Edinburgh accent enhancing his gentle bedside manner. 'You can wait inside, young man.' He holds the door for Mark, who hurries in and takes a seat in front of the desk, but he can still hear everything being discussed in the waiting room.

'I've given him a shot of morphine and we'll arrange for a district nurse to visit over the next few days.' Dr Patel hands Ben a prescription. 'Is there anything else you need from me?'

Ben stands with his hands on the back of the wheelchair, his shoulders hunched. 'Um . . . is he going to be OK?'

'Let's just wait for the test results to come back from the oncologist, shall we?' Sandeep places a hand on Ben's shoulder. 'Do you need any help at home?'

'No, I'm fine, I can deal with it.' Ben's eyes catch Mark's through the half-open door. There's an expression of loathing on Ben's face, disgust that his private business is within earshot of the weedy little geek, Marcello.

Dr Patel returns to the consulting room and closes the door behind him.

'That boy deserves better than this.' He gathers his notes from his desk and places them in a manila file. 'First his mother, now his father. Life is very unfair, dear boy . . . very unfair.' He breathes in deeply and then smiles at Mark. 'Right then, let's have a wee look at this throat of yours.'

The Patels are influential. Sandeep's wife, Akshata, is an investment banker, and they have high hopes for their only son, David. The Patels try to keep a low profile, hiding their wealth with a respectful modesty, but Barton Mallet is such a tight-knit community that everyone knows everyone else's business. Mark wonders about all the private information the doctor must have to hold on to and how difficult it must be for him to keep everyone's secrets.

There is a secret happening in the Knot household, something that a kid of sixteen shouldn't have to deal with alone. Mark aches to reach out and help Ben, but he knows he would never accept the help, especially not from him. Then a strange feeling begins to flood into Mark's chest, a feeling that he tries to suppress, guilty that his mind is capable of such manipulation. He has peeked into Ben's world and in that single moment, he is filled with an overwhelming sense of power.

Mark has seen how vulnerable Ben is. Top Dog isn't quite as invincible as everyone believes. Ben has something to hide. Just like him.

10

OCTOBER 2023

Condensation had formed in the vacuum between the triple layers of the argon window that spanned the rear wall of the ground floor. Ben stood gazing out towards the woodland at the bottom of the garden. The sun was cresting over the canopy of russet autumnal leaves, its golden rays diffusing through the glass. A sudden wave of anger coursed through him as the memory of his father's painful struggle in the last few months of his life passed through his mind. Ben had made promises that he was unable to keep; there'd been no room for his father at the hospice and his final hours had been spent in a hospital corridor, waiting for a bed. He'd failed him.

Ben squinted as a beam of sunlight breaking through the drifting clouds blinded him momentarily. For a second, the reflection in the glass was someone he didn't recognise. He was sixteen again and Mark Cherry was staring back at him through the surgery door; but as his eyes adjusted, the face looking back was his. He appeared haggard and world weary. A deafening crash behind him sent an electric shock through his spine.

'You didn't eat your eggs!' Dani was clattering around in the kitchen, loading breakfast crockery into the dishwasher.

'We need to get that window fixed, the seal's broken.' He forced a smile.

'I'll call them on Monday. Not everyone works on Saturdays, love.' Dani dropped the used coffee filter into the recycling. 'Any plans for today?'

Ben's head turned back to the garden. He approached the glass again; this time, his fingertips touched the surface.

'HEY!' Without warning, he hammered hard on the glass. There was someone out there. He darted to the side door, yanked on the handle and stumbled out into the side return, socked feet pricking over sharp stones like hot coals. 'HEY!'

His ankle caught in the jumbled mess of the garden hose, nearly tripping him. He shook off the coiled snake and darted around the corner. Hovering for a second, Ben saw a figure crouching at the bottom of the garden, hiding in the undergrowth. Someone was watching his house.

He strode purposefully down the lawn, not noticing his sodden feet on the wet grass. 'What do you want?' As he got closer, he saw the person more clearly and hesitated. It was a boy, small and rake thin. It couldn't be . . .

'Mark?' The name formed on his lips and the sound rumbled in his chest as if he was feeling the word, not speaking it.

As he drew nearer to the boy bent over in the shrubbery, he heard Dani shouting from the house. 'BEN! What are you doing?'

At the sound of Dani's raised voice, the boy shot up and turned to look at Ben, who was now looming over him. Fear crossed the boy's face as he looked down at the spade in Ben's hand.

'What are you doing here?' Ben's voice was brittle.

'I . . . I'm sorry, Mr Knot. I was just . . . looking . . .' The kid was utterly terrified, his fingers clenched into nervous fists at the ends of his skinny arms.

'Mark . . .' The name floated out again.

'No . . . it's Joseph . . .' The boy took a small step back, stumbling on the stone edge of the lawn, never taking his eyes off the spade in Ben's hand. 'Can I have my ball back, please?'

'Joseph?' Ben's brow furrowed in confusion.

'Sam kicked it, not me . . . Sorry.' Tears filled the corners of the boy's eyes.

'All right, Joe, love . . . did it come over again?' Dani marched up to them, out of breath. She took his hand and started rooting through the shrubs. 'There it is.' Her foot slid under a hawthorn bush, fishing out a small white soccer ball with a Welsh dragon printed on the leather. 'Here you go, trouble.'

'Thanks, Mrs Knot.' Joseph scuttled away down to the bottom of the garden and climbed over the fence that led on to a patch of scrubland by the edge of the stream. The kids still played over there, after everything that had happened on that piece of land. Ben's brow furrowed.

'What's up with you?' Dani frowned as she held out a pair of lime-green crocs. 'And what's with the spade? You frit the life out of him.'

Ben looked down to his hand. He was shaking. 'I swear they kick it over on purpose.' Ben slid his feet into the shoes and stabbed the spade into the flower bed.

'Why? So they can spy on your deluxe eight-burner barbecue? I don't think so, big shot.' Dani placed a hand on his arm. 'I put more coffee on. Shall we take the kids to the cinema this afternoon? Be good for us all to get out . . .' Her voice drifted off into the distance as Ben stood squinting into the dense woodland, shaking his head.

From the upstairs window, Nathan watched his dad standing in the garden. He looked lost, disorientated, like a zombie from *The Walking Dead*. He couldn't remember the last time his father had made eye contact with him. Maybe he *was* a zombie and too afraid of being outed and exterminated. The ping of a message dropped into Nathan's inbox with a jingling flourish. Freckles had sent a burst of firework emojis that filled his screen. A rush of serotonin shot through him as he returned to the RetroFX site and logged on. Three dots moved in rotation; his new-found friend was typing.

'Are you a scaredy cat?' Two cute cat-face emojis.

Nate typed, 'What's a scaredy cat?' Three laughing emojis.

'A pussy,' Freckles wrote. 'A wimp.'

'No way.' Sunglasses cool emoji. 'Why?'

'Check this out.' Three more symbols slowly popped into Nate's DM. A ghost, a camera and finally a scream emoji.

Nate typed a question mark. Freckles responded, 'Click the link . . . this is right up your street.' Wink emoji.

Nate moved the cursor and opened the link she'd sent. The screen flickered and a high-definition close-up of a shiny 50mm vintage lens from a film camera filled the frame. It turned slowly and an out-of-focus image grew closer and sharper in the reflection of the highly polished lens.

An orange streetlamp brushed the silhouette of a faun standing in the shadow with an umbrella tucked under his arm.

'Come with me, Son of Adam.'

A graphic faded up briefly on the screen, then died. Nathan had played Mr Tumnus in the Christmas play the year before and ever since then he'd been tapping on the backs of wardrobes, obsessed with *The Chronicles of Narnia*. He felt stupid, like a little kid, but he'd re-read *The Lion, the Witch and the Wardrobe* every year since he was ten.

The faun with the umbrella leant in close to the screen and knocked on the glass; his eyes twinkled with a digital flare. A graphic appeared on the screen.

Are you coming or Knot?

Nathan blinked as the graphic faded. Knot was spelt with a K, like his surname. Was this some kind of a joke?

Mr Crow wants you . . . click the link.

Nathan racked his brains; there were no crows in Narnia. Friendly beavers and all kinds of other strange creatures, but no crows. Click the link. His fingers scrolled and the cursor tapped on the little box, shaped like a wardrobe. Knock knock and the doors opened.

I'm hunting for young storytellers to come on a brand-new adventure. A feature film made especially with you in mind.

As the graphic faded, a tiny bead of light appeared in the distance. The lamppost from the opening sequence.

This is a spine-tingling story: unlike anything you have ever seen before.

The darkness grew brighter as the lamppost came into the foreground, illuminating a tree-lined alley, leading to the silhouette of an industrial building with a tall tower.

Submissions before the end of October. Requirements below.

The curious faun glanced over his shoulder, waiting in expectation.

Well?

As Nathan read through the description in the article, his throat became dry and his fingertips tingled with excitement. The brief outline of the film made the hair on Nathan's arms stand on end. It was spooky – frightening, even – but Nate loved ghost stories. He wasn't a show-off or a natural performer but when it came to drama class, something special happened to him. It always felt deeply personal and he could never talk about it afterwards, like trying to hold smoke in his hands. He had the same feeling when Mr Tumnus tapped on the glass: it was just for him and no one else. It made him feel special. It spirited him away from all the loneliness.

Nathan's finger hovered over the track pad. The cursor moved slowly across the screen and he clicked again.

The figure standing by the lamppost winked, swung his umbrella over his shoulder and began to saunter down the lane into the distance. In a final flourish, more words appeared on the screen.

You're in. Prepare to be spooked!

11

OCTOBER 1993

The ritual of hiding in the blackberry bushes to avoid the first cross-country run of the year is always a thorny affair. Mr Branchflower, the strapping sports teacher just out of Loughborough College, watches from the second-floor window of the chemistry lab, eager for the sprinters to turn the corner by the Nag's Head so he can sneak off to the back of the French huts for a crafty cigarette. Coast clear, Mark Cherry and Catherine Maddock emerge, scratched and giggling, from the brambles and pool their 50p emergency phone money for their afternoon skive. The straggle of Year 8 runners has long gone by the time they're heading down Miller's Lane and past Hayes Hospital in the direction of the legendary local chippy, Codswallop.

The vinegar tang of the fat chips dipped in curry sauce leaves a tingle on their lips. A sudden gust of chilly wind whips their bare legs pink as they huddle together on the broken bench inside the bus stop. Greasy fingers pinch the salty scraps at the bottom of the newspaper before Mark screws up the soggy remains and lobs it at the bin, missing it by a mile.

'Shot!' Catherine wipes her fingers on her gym shorts and hugs her legs into her chest to keep warm.

'We should get back, although I'm not sure I can run on a full tummy.' Mark lunges into a gangly leg stretch.

'I thought you had a sick note?' Catherine stands, nudging her head into him and knocking him off balance.

'I did, but Branchflower recognised my handwriting. He hates me.' A grin spreads across Mark's face as he spots the exhausted group staggering around the corner of Chapel Street. 'Come on, let's tag on the end, he'll never know.'

'You still up for orchestra practice later?' Catherine jogs ahead, calling over her shoulder as they approach the school gates.

'Always.' Mark feigns his limp as the silhouette of Mr Branchflower miraculously appears in the science lab window, just in time.

The last days of the late balmy summer have given way to the grey gloom of October downpours. But the occasional bright autumn morning with crystal-blue skies and plunging temperatures promises the coming of Halloween, Bonfire Night and then Christmas. The darkest months of the year are illuminated with many beacons of light. The playing field would be cleared of leaves for the village bonfire and kids would stuff clothes with newspaper and wheel 'Guy Fawkes' around the village in a shopping trolley, begging a penny before chucking him on top of the blaze.

Remember, remember the fifth of November,

Gunpowder, treason and plot.

They'd burn their lips on baked potatoes in foil and drink hot flasks of oxtail soup to ward off the chill. When that was over, all that remained was the final sprint towards Mark's favourite holiday of all: Christmas.

The hood of Mark's petrol-blue parka is now hooked over his head, trailing behind, billowing in the wind as he and Catherine head home along the motorway path towards Blackstone Mill.

'Too lazy to change out of your gym gear again?' A freshly showered Cat is polo-necked under her school blazer, long woolly socks slowly drifting down to her ankles.

'Yeah.' Mark buries his head into the fake fur of his snorkel hood. He doesn't ever admit the boys' changing room is a 'no-go' for him. The taunts and the jeers, the 'don't bend down when Cherry's around' little sing-along that always happens at the end of PE, are becoming too much to bear. His radar for danger has grown acute; he can sense it.

Boys in blazers leaning against a fence? Turn around and walk the other way.

The footsteps in the alley behind him? Just run.

Check over the door before you walk into a room. Check your pencil case. Check your bag. Check everything for dog shit, chewing gum and all the other hilarious 'booby traps' that were always being set for him.

Oh, how they laughed.

A deep cavern of resentment was building inside of Mark and he vowed that one day they'd be laughing on the other side of their faces. All of them.

'I just didn't want to be late for practice.' Mark clutches the cello slung over his back and smiles at Catherine.

There is a sadness in her eyes as she smiles back. 'Well, you stink. You can shower at mine, if you want.' She knows the truth.

The lights from the motorway cast a sickly yellow hue over the line of leafless skeleton trees at the end of the footpath that turns into Cheney End. As they round the corner into the lane, Mark's feet halt before his eyes can even focus.

A group of eerie figures silhouetted against the tree line: Dave Patel, Chris and Lynette Davis, Benjamin Knot and Annabel Maddock. The Gang of Five, the usual suspects. Standing in a line, they block the exit and seem to grow taller in the streetlights. It's too late to turn and run.

'All right, you two lovebirds? Gonna play us something?' Ben leers at them both.

'Oh, leave them alone, Ben!' Annie Maddock is leaning in, his arm clasped around her waist. 'Hey, Cat, you walking home?' She makes a move towards her sister, but Ben pulls her sharply back and holds her tight.

He presses his lips to her cheek. 'Oh, leave them alone, Annie,' he parrots, tickling her ribs.

'Yeah, come on, Marcello, giz a tune.' Chris shoulder-barges Mark as the two younger kids attempt to sidle past. Mark stumbles against the larch lap fence, refusing to respond. Keeping their heads down, Mark and Cat continue towards the end of the lane and down an incline to the car park, unfortunately named Doggers Dive.

'Where do you think you're going, mardy?' Lynette's jarring voice taunts them. 'Oi, queer! Are you deaf or what?'

Mark suddenly stops in his tracks. A furnace of rage rises within him. Just one more time. Just one more. He closes his eyes and exhales, trying to calm himself. They want him to break, they want a reason to hurt him, but he won't give it to them. Not tonight.

Mark turns and smiles at Lynette's angry red face. It's not a pretty sight. Chris, chewing and bouncing nervously on his heels in an attempt to seem taller, spit forming on his lip, is even uglier. Dave hangs back, passive as ever, behind Ben and Annie. Very slowly and deliberately, Mark unhooks the strap of his cello and begins to unzip the case, glancing at Catherine. She looks stunned for a second.

'What are you doing?' she whispers to him, but as she realises his game, a smile spreads across her face.

Mark's fingers find the neck of the instrument and he gently pulls it from the leather sheath. Resting the waist on his shoulder, he withdraws the sharp metal spike from the base, aiming it at them all like a bayonet.

'Woooaaahh.' Chris jeers awkwardly, like this is some kind of striptease. Lynette folds her arms and taps her foot.

Annie turns to Ben and puts her hand on his shoulder. 'Ben, don't do this,' she whispers in his ear.

'No . . . I want to hear them play.' Ben gently raises his hand but there is a cruel smirk on his face.

Mark perches on the fence of the kissing gate and begins to tighten the nut of his bow, staring at Catherine, who is assembling the mouthpiece of her clarinet. Mark strokes rosin on to the taut horsehair, eyeballing Ben without blinking.

Out of the silence, very gently, Mark begins to bounce the wooden bow into the bass string in a slow, slouchy spiccato. He slaps his fingers seductively against the neck of the instrument. It's like the feathery shiver of a jazz drum, introducing the voice of Catherine's clarinet. The first few notes slide upwards into the silent darkness, in an achingly sexy melody. The Gang of Five were clearly expecting awkward, scratchy scales or some tight-arsed Bach, but this? This is something else. Everyone is speechless.

Annie leans her head into Ben and he brushes her hair with his hand. Lynette's hips relax, swaying to the rhythm as the sultry music infuses the night air with the sound of longing. They all feel it. Lynette turns her head towards Dave, who is looking sideways at Annie with an intensity on his face. His eyes cast down to Ben's fingers as he grips his girlfriend around the waist. A final rallentando eases the duet into an imperfect jazz cadence. Then there is silence again.

Nobody speaks until Chris cocks his leg like a dog and forces a fart. Ben smacks him around the back of his head. 'Twat.'

Ben turns back to the musicians. 'Marcello . . .' His voice is soft and unthreatening. He holds out the leather case, visibly moved by the music. Mark gingerly puts his instrument away with trembling fingers as a hand touches his shoulder. 'Well, well, well . . . you are a dark horse.'

Mark's shoulder retracts slightly from Ben's touch as he braces himself. He daren't breathe. Here it comes . . . the punch. But for once, it doesn't come. Maybe he finally did something right. It feels like an eternity before Mark can exhale.

Long after the gang have left, even at home later that night, Mark can still feel the heat of those fingers squeezing his shoulder. Ben's touch has burrowed deep into his flesh and a tremble of electricity courses through him. As sleep finally comes, he stares at the light dancing on his bedroom ceiling, remembering the sounds and atmosphere of the afternoon.

Must I go on like this? Shall I just be a lonely stranger on the shore?

Ben was right. He was indeed a dark horse.

12

OCTOBER 2023

'Name?'

'Nathan Knot.'

'Age?'

'Um . . . I'll be fourteen in May.'

'Height?'

'Umm . . . dunno . . . probably not tall enough.'

'OK, Nathan, now tell me something about yourself that no one else knows.'

The camera was moving very slowly upwards from chin and clenched lips to an anxious pair of eyes that darted between the lens and someone sitting slightly to the left. His body language said everything. Pale hands, clenched prayer-like, slid down between his knees and his shoulders hunched into a shrug. His cheeks flushed into the deep crimson of embarrassment.

'Um . . . well. I don't know what to say.'

'Tell me a secret.'

Timid eyes flicked in the direction of the person beside the camera again.

'I . . . I can't.' One of his shoulders lifted higher than the other, as his chin buried itself into the other shoulder. He was coy and self-conscious. 'Can I do this on my own, please? I'm embarrassed with you here.'

Nathan reached out to pause the video. 'Sorry, I just can't . . . not with you watching me.'

Dani was sitting with the piece of paper she'd printed off earlier scrunched in her hand. 'Well, if you really want to be an actor, you better get used to everyone looking at you, pet . . . even me.' Nate chewed his lip nervously and shrugged. 'There will be other kids auditioning too, you know.' She saw the colour drain from his face. 'But they're not like you, Nate. You're talented.'

Nate frowned. 'I don't know. This is just the first round. I think we have to get selected, then meet the director. What if he doesn't like me?'

Dani smiled. 'Just be yourself.'

Getting permission to audition for the film should have been straightforward, but like most things Nate wanted to do, his dad was reluctant to agree. His bedroom was its own mini film studio, and he had all the bells and whistles for making great-quality video content; how hard could it be? There was a list of questions he needed to answer on camera, about height and weight and experience. Did he have an agent? Of course, Nate didn't have one, but over the dinner table earlier, Dani had come up with a plan: she would act as his manager.

'OMG! Dani struts around the field like she's Jürgen Klopp at Anfield. You sure you want to let her loose on your acting career?' Lily stuffed a meatball in her mouth with one hand as she scrolled TikTok videos with the other.

'Oi, you. Watch it! Barton Mallet Girls are on the map now thanks to me.' Dani sipped a glass of wine. 'I'm great at organising, aren't I, hon?' She nudged Ben with her knee under the table.

'Hmm . . . What's it about?' Ben sat back and folded his arms, one eye on the BBC six o'clock news playing on the TV in the den.

'What's what about?' Nathan glanced at his sister.

'This silly film, genius.' Lily inclined her head sarcastically. Nathan was silent.

Ben gently picked up the remote control and muted the TV. He sighed and turned to Nathan with a tight smile. 'Tell me all about this film then, son.'

'Um . . . I don't know really. It's kind of improvised. Found footage. Have you heard of *The Hoax*? Same director, apparently.' Nathan pushed spaghetti around the plate and squirmed uncomfortably in his chair. His eyes shot over to Dani for help.

'You're joking? I was just watching that on Netflix. They're not going to cast you. Not in a million years.' Lily didn't glance up from her phone.

Ben's attention was pulled back to the TV, images of HMP Gartree and a man's mugshot on screen.

'Will you be galloping around the school playing field wearing a cardboard box horse again?' Lily sniggered into her can of Fanta.

'Shut it! It's got nothing to do with school.' Nathan reddened and chewed his lip, toes curling inside his socks under the table. He looked to Dani again. Help me out here.

'"Found footage" is, apparently, how they made, er . . . *Paranormal Activity*, was it? . . . and . . . *The Blair Witch Project*. Remember that one, Ben? Bloody terrifying that was.' Dani had clearly been on Google and IMDb.

Nathan was done. 'Can I get down, please?'

Dani pushed her plate aside and reached for the half-empty bottle of Pinot to replenish her glass. 'Your dad and I are excited for you. Aren't we?' She kicked Ben under the table. 'A chance to earn himself a bit of pocket money.'

Ben's head turned back to Nathan. 'Wait . . . what? It's a paid job?' The wheels in his mind creaking into action.

Dani ruffled Nate's hair. 'I expect so.'

'How much?' Now Nate really had his dad's full attention.

Dani put her wine glass down and stood up. 'Oooh, I should say . . . a couple of million at least.' She rolled her eyes as both Lily's and Ben's heads snapped round to her. 'I'm joking! No idea how much. It's not about the money, though, is it, love?'

Nate jumped down from his stool and headed to the door.

'Er, Nate . . . dishwasher . . . I'm not your personal slave.' Dani rubbed imaginary cash between her fingers. 'Not yet anyway.'

Nathan trudged back and obediently dumped the dirty plate into the dishwasher. Just as he was leaving, Dani pulled him in for a hug. 'It's very exciting, pet. Just don't get your hopes up. There'll be lots of boys auditioning, OK?'

'Only boys?' Lily glared angrily at her brother.

Dani kissed Nate on the cheek, which made him squirm. 'Give me a shout if you need coaching. I'm more than happy to help. You know I once played Sally—' She hadn't finished the sentence before Lily jumped in.

'*Understudied* in the local am-dram production of *Cabaret*. Yawn!' Lily's hand clapped over her open mouth, taunting her.

Dani flicked her hair and pouted at Lily. 'I'll have you know I was pretty good. I got on for two matinee performances as Sally Bowles.'

'Sally Bowels, more like – crapping herself, I heard!' Lily was up from the table in a shot, laughing as Dani launched herself into a tickle tackle.

'I got a standing ovation.' Dani laughed as Lily struggled to get away.

'Only because they were leaving.' Both of them were now in fits of giggles.

Later that night, after dinner was cleared and the house had settled down for the evening, Ben, having suddenly cultivated an intense interest in Nate's trajectory to stardom, had encouraged

Dani to go up to his room and help him win the role. They were both pleased he'd found something he wanted to get involved in. It was better than him being stuck upstairs alone in that bedroom all the time. Dani also believed in her own talent as a manager, or 'momager'. Yes, she could totally see herself picking up Instagram collabs and walking down red carpets.

Now she was standing at the side of Nathan's camera, with the list of questions in her hand. 'All right, love, you do your thing. I'll be downstairs if you need me.'

'Thanks.' Nathan waited for the door to close. The footsteps on the stairs faded away and he was alone. Just him and the camera.

In life, this boy's face wouldn't be one you'd notice; he was just a regular, awkward kid. But on screen in high definition, this face was a landscape of hope and promise. Deep-set lids and intense dramatic brows, his irises were a kaleidoscope of soft brown hues, with flashes of gold. Long neck, pale skin, freckled and sensitive, wild wavy auburn hair. In close-up, the camera did something to Nathan Knot. He'd need to change that name, of course, but he was a star in the making.

Nathan exhaled and looked down to his hands before he began to speak.

It was as if the floodgates of his memory had been swung open. Now that he was alone, the story flowed out of him.

This was no ordinary audition. This was no stage school kid. Nathan Knot had something special and the most compelling thing of all was that he didn't know it.

None of them knew.

13

NOVEMBER 1993

'Five may keep a secret if four of them are dead.'

Ben's ghostly face, drained of blood, leans forward into the flickering candlelight. The gathered fellowship sits inside a 'pentagram of power', chalked on to the stone floor in charcoal.

'Is that how it goes? I thought—' Ben raises a finger to silence Annie. She bites her lip.

'Sshh.'

On the upturned beer crate in the centre of the cavernous ruin is a broken saucer containing tea lights, and plastic cups into which Dave Patel carefully pours full measures of Diamond White. As he hands one to Annie, his fingers accidentally brush hers and he smiles with embarrassment before picking up his camera. She gags on the sweet, fizzy cider as Ben's voice echoes off the damp stone walls of Blackstone Mill.

'Listen! (Listen!) (Listen!)'

Ancient rusty hinges creak and the candles gutter as a gust of cold air rushes in through the crack between the two huge, rotting oak doors braced with iron struts. Dave's video camera slowly finds each frightened face, brushed with slivers of candlelight in the blackness: Chris, Ben and then Annie. Dave tilts the lens down to capture frantic hands finding each other in the dark.

Ben's voice trembles with excitement. 'By the power vested in me, I decree that Blackstone Mill belongs to us.'

The camera scans the vast hall, searching for something that might be hiding back there in the gloom. Shadows on the wall, cast from the candlelight, point towards a dank pool in the flag-stone floor that seems to be sucking in the light, pulling everything into an abyss. Outside, the rusty barbed-wire fence and the 'keep out' sign that has been ripped off its nails shiver and creak as the shadow of two long bony fingers reaches around the door, pene-trating the crack.

'Who's there?' Ben blows out the candles and the circle closes. The shadow slowly stretches across the floor, like a hand clawing for its prey. A metallic rasp shatters the silence.

'*No. STOP. Please don't!*' Patel's camera whips up to find Annie on her feet, back against the wall, hands over her eyes.

Ben stands and squeezes her hand, laughing. 'It's OK, it's only Lynette with the gear, look.'

'It's me, you nutters. Give me a bloody hand, this thing weighs a ton.' The top of a ladder pokes through the door, and is swiftly followed by Lynette Davis, overloaded with bags and equipment. 'Tell you what, why don't you lot just sit there on your fat arses and I'll break my back over here?' She slings a huge rucksack down on to the stone floor.

'All right, Fatima Whitbread, chill out.' Her brother, not lifting a finger, ducks into a corner, unzipping his fly and taking a leak.

'Outside, you filthy animal!' Ben boots Chris in the backside, and Chris turns and sprays over Dave.

'Oi, watch it, that's bloody disgusting!' Patel dives out of the way as a drunk Chris stumbles past Lynette.

Annie leans into Ben, whispering through the darkness, 'Are you sure this is a good idea?'

'Trust me, this is going to be the icing on the cake. We're finally going up there.' Ben picks up Lynette's rucksack and opens it. 'Or, at least, one of us is.'

The camera darts from Ben to Annie, then to Chris's backside mid-pee. He turns and splutters, 'Wait, what? Who? Who exactly is going up?'

Finally, the camera lands on a flustered Lynette. 'Don't look at me, I can't do it.' The contents of her rucksack spill out on to the floor. 'It's my dad's climbing gear. Not that he's used it in about a decade, fat git.'

'Who are you calling a faggot?' Chris is back, wiping his hands on his jeans.

'Everyone, just shut up and listen. We get to the first floor and figure it out from there. OK?' Ben drags the ladder over to the rotting rafters, where a small section of new wood and sheets of chipboard have been nailed down to create a platform. With the ladder secured against the sturdiest-looking beam, Ben starts to climb.

As he reaches the top, he stands heroically, Maglite held aloft like a lightsaber. 'My fellow Jedi! Who is next?' He shines the beam down at the four nervous faces below. Selecting them one by one, Lynette, then Annie, then Chris climb the ladder. Leaving just Dave behind at the bottom.

'Come on up, I'll hold the ladder for you.' Chris is now at the top with his hand out, gesturing for Dave to go next. Dave stares up in horror then steps tentatively on to the first rung.

'I . . . I need to get going . . . my dad said I needed to be back before nine.' Dave glances to the door, stomach churning with anxiety.

'If you don't get your bony arse up here *right now*, Patel, you are out of this gang.' Ben's voice is serious.

Annie rolls her eyes. 'Come on, Ben, you know he doesn't like heights.' The ladder shifts and creaks as Annie glances back to see Dave already braving the climb.

'See, my Jedi Initiate just needed a little persuasion.' Ben flicks a glance to the others and winks.

75

As Dave nears the top rung, he glances back over his shoulder to survey the twenty-foot drop beneath him, and the ladder suddenly detaches from the beam and swings out into mid-air.

'Oh, God, help me, HELP!'

'HEY! What are you doing? STOP!' Ben dives forward to grab the ladder as the cackling twins swing it further out into the dark void. Dave, screaming and barely clinging on, tries to find the wooden rungs with his flailing feet.

'He's sweating curry! I can smell it!' Chris Davis pinches his nose as Lynette falls about laughing. 'Eugh . . . gross.'

Annie shoulder-barges Lynette out of the way and yanks the ladder back hard against the rafter.

Dave scrambles to the top. 'Bloody idiots,' he mutters under his breath, shaking his head as he lands on the wooden platform, visibly trembling.

'Yeah, you idiot.' Chris kicks Lynette as she stifles a laugh.

Dave checks to see if his camera is broken. He scoots back across the platform to the brick chimney stack and points it at Chris and Lynette. Lynette sulks, flipping the bird at him, and Chris moons into the camera, performing like an idiot.

'You really are a pair of absolute morons, aren't you? Your dad must be so proud of his little piglets.' Dave keeps the camera rolling.

'Turn it off.' Lynette is on her feet now, angry.

'Make me.' Dave zooms in closer.

Chris's shaved head looms into the lens. 'Go on back to your corner shop.'

In a flurry of rage, Patel boots him in the shin.

'Ow . . . shit, that hurt.'

'Oi! That's enough, all of you, PACK IT IN!' Ben's voice ricochets around the cavernous stone walls.

Annie looks at them both in disgust. 'Don't say things like that! You're awful people, just awful.'

'Oh, come on, lighten up, it was only a joke.' Chris Davis rolls up his jeans to inspect the cut and bruise forming on his shin.

'It's always "only a joke" with you lot, isn't it? Until it isn't. Come on, Dave, let's go home. This isn't fun anymore.' Annie is kneeling in the corner, checking on Dave. She glares at Ben, who eyeballs both of them. 'Ben? You coming?'

'No way. I'm going to do what we came here for.'

Without waiting for her to answer, Ben moves swiftly to a broken section of the stone wall leading to the blackened firebox of the chimney stack. An upward draught seems to be sucking in the air, urging him to climb. 'Lynette, help me with the light.'

The chimney is massive, at least fifty feet high. The moonlit sky is just visible in the distance, as droplets of water run down the smoke-stained walls of the flue. Ben hammers at the bricks with an ice pick, banging iron pitons from Davis's climbing kit into the mortar to create steps. He threads rope and secures finger grips, building a makeshift spiral ladder around the narrow square sides of the chimney. Slowly but surely, Ben hauls himself up on to the lintel of a smoke shelf and stares up through the brick shaft to the sky above. Broken pieces of masonry crumble down into the void below. The distant sounds of hammering and heaving echo down the brick stack and out into the vast cavern as Ben finally summits, pushing himself up on to the chimney crown.

'Hey, come on up, to the Crow's Nest. I can see everything from here!' His voice seems miles away.

Annie's head cranes in through the broken gap. 'Ben (Ben) . . . Ben? (Ben?)' Her voice echoes off the walls. 'I'm going home. It's too dark. We'll come back in the daylight, OK? (OK?)' There's no answer. Annie withdraws and starts to head back down the ladder.

'Chicken shit,' Lynette mutters, just as Annie is out of earshot and before her hand grabs the rope. 'Room for one more up there? I'm going all the way, Ben.'

Annie waits at the bottom of the ladder as Dave jumps down the last few rungs, trying to style out some last-ditch bravado. 'Glad to be back on terra firma . . . that was a close call.' He checks the camera slung over his shoulder, wiping the lens with his sleeve.

'I'm sorry about what they said. I hate it.' She places her hand on his arm.

'It's OK, we're used to it. All the names, all the games.' He winks at her.

In the half light, Annie suddenly notices his deep-green eyes, perfect skin and jaw line, his beautiful black wavy hair. For a second, she can't breathe. Dave moves his arm away from hers and flushes.

She inclines her head towards him. 'Why do you film everything?'

'I dunno . . .' In the darkness, his eyes sparkle at hers. 'It's a documentary . . . of life, I guess.'

'Hmm. Endless hours of nonsense, probably?'

'Not always. Sometimes you catch something really special. Like now.' Dave stands smiling at her.

A shaft of moonlight between moving clouds momentarily drapes Annabel Maddock in a gossamer cloak of ethereal white light. She smiles at him. 'You missed it.'

'Nah . . . it's up here.' He gently taps a finger to his head. As Annie turns, he secretly switches off the camera, held at his waist like a gunslinger. It's all there on Dave Patel's video tape, shot with a very specific camera. In truth, he never fails to capture what he needs.

14

NOVEMBER 2023

Standing at the pinnacle, on the top floor of a tower he had designed, had become some kind of ritual for Ben. The year the IF Group collaborated with the Danish design team under Bjarke Ingels on the Serpentine Gallery, they'd hit the headlines. It had been a hard climb to the top, from those first rough rungs crudely hammered into the brick of a disused chimney.

That night, all those years ago, Ben had stood at the very highest point of Blackstone Mill in his Crow's Nest. He'd surveyed the surrounding villages and farmland in the moonlight and felt a profound sense of disappointment. His heart had sunk as he scanned the flat, uninteresting landscape of the rural Midlands, wondering how the hell he would escape from the drudgery of this life. A life that was slowly dragging his father into a painful grave and most of Ben's hopes and dreams with him. But that night, he had followed the source of the River Soar, glistening in the darkness as far as his eye could see. Later, at home, he had found an old Ordnance Survey map in the sideboard and had traced its course, following it out to the sea and far beyond. He vowed that one day he would carve a path for himself just like that river.

Over the years, he'd become famous for the extraordinary storytelling hidden within his architectural designs, but deep down Ben knew he wasn't really an innovator. The evolution tower in Moscow was just a twisted facsimile of Norman Foster's Hearst Tower in New York. The series of thrusting shards that assaulted the sky out in the United Arab Emirates desert had been audacious vanity projects, empty cathedrals of architecture for architecture's sake.

The flurry of emails he had received just before take-off was weighing on his mind. The second the plane landed from Stockholm he'd turned his phone back on, to a tsunami of texts from Lars Sorensen.

'Call me ASAP.'

The IF loans were leveraged with overinflated valuations. At the time of the transaction, no one batted an eyelid, but now that IF was sinking, they'd suddenly been paying a lot more attention.

Ben took his foot off the accelerator and let the autopilot take over. Something had to be done, there had to be a way out. A black shape shifted aggressively into his rear-view mirror. Ben checked his speed and moved over from the outside lane. A motorbike sped past, nearly clipping his wing mirror. Ben clamped his jaw tight and gripped the wheel. He was tired and irritable from his trip, and he wanted to get home.

The call from the IF business manager came through. Ben hesitated then tapped accept. 'Hey, Ben, it's Lars, I've been trying to get hold of you.' His face was pixelated on to the touchscreen display.

'Yep. Just landed. Driving home, then . . . family time, Lars, you know how it goes. Why are you calling me on a Friday night?'

'You didn't sign off on the Petersburg bridging loan. Mukash Das is livid. He wanted this done and dusted before the weekend.' Lars's tone had lowered into a passive-aggressive threat.

'I told you, the lender hadn't received the toxicology report, they're withholding funds until Monday, they want the data.' Ben's hands gesticulated sharply off the wheel; he was exasperated.

'I had an intern do some work on the forms; I sent them over.' Lars was now leaning in close, his red face on the touchscreen like he was peering into a shop window.

'I'm not an idiot, Lars. This is my neck on the line.' Ben's head was about to explode.

'If the report doesn't hit their inbox by the end of play, we don't get a sign-off on the loan.' Ben heard Lars light up a cigarette and take a drag. 'And you know what that means.' He exhaled angrily.

'So, dig again and doctor the sample, put this on someone else's fucking shoulders.'

Ben slammed his hand on to the wheel. They didn't know about the loan recalls. Only he did. There was no way back and he had to keep going.

'Just switch the sample. If you won't, I will.' Ben's voice was threatening now.

Lars was silent for a second. He glanced around the office and leant in tight to the screen. 'This conversation never happened.'

Ben killed the call and tried to steady his breath. He looked up to the rear-view mirror, his guilty eyes reflecting back at him. He'd bent the rules so many times in his life. He'd been flexible with the truth, he'd evaded and avoided for most of his career in order to get ahead. This wasn't the first time Ben had doctored samples. A hollow feeling churned in his stomach.

The light over the fields had shifted from a golden sunset to fast-moving heavy clouds, threatening rain as his car slowed to turn on to the road for Barton Mallet. In the rear-view mirror, Ben noticed the bike that had overtaken him earlier tearing down the road behind him, burning the throttle. It sped up close, weaving in and out of his blind spot. The headlamp caught the mirror and blinded Ben for a split second. The growl of the engine brought a wave of nausea up into his throat. He passed the turn-off for Blackstone Mill. A word had been graffitied over the sign in red paint, dripping like blood. Ben's palms became clammy, he thought he was going to be sick. 'Mill Killer'.

He was coming out. The locals would never tolerate Dave Patel returning to Barton Mallet, would they? Ben couldn't tolerate it. Would he really come back here after he was released? Ben swallowed down a ball of regret. He should have got out when he had the chance. University and then his internship in Stockholm had offered him the perfect exit, but something had pulled him back. His family home had lain empty for a few years after his dad passed away, and those trips back to pack up all the boxes and bin bags full of his parents' precious possessions gradually became less frequent. The place was full of stuff. Tools and knick-knacks that had meant so much to his parents, but after they were gone seemed like nothing, just junk. Eventually, the house had been sold and a clearance company had taken care of all the furniture. But Ben simply couldn't stay away. He would take what he called his 'nostalgia tour' on the anniversary of his dad's death. Flowers were laid up at the cemetery, but then he would sit in his car across the street from his old house, trying to figure out what the new owners had done to the place.

When a plot of land went up for sale on the scrub opposite Cheney End, Ben made an offer. Land that had once been his playground: cornfields for summer hide-and-seek, tree houses with rope ladders and snow igloos built into the rocks skirting the perimeter of Fosse Meadow. He would build a home. All his perfect design ideas, the space he had longed for, the organisation, the aesthetics he craved, but most important of all, that view over the fields and across the river towards the mill. It was almost as if he was keeping guard, watching and waiting for some kind of return. It was one of the reasons his wife had left when she did:

she didn't want anything to do with Barton Mallet, she had cited 'irreconcilable differences'. The difference being that she wanted to move on, and Ben couldn't.

Ben slowed then stopped at a traffic light. His eyes darted to the mirror and the rider in the helmet, straddling the bike, waiting to speed off again. He sat back in his seat. The weight pressing down on his shoulders moved to his chest. Ben placed his hand flat on his sternum and moved it in a circle. Heart burn or heart break? Nothing that couldn't be tempered with a shot of Pepto-Bismol washed down with a whisky chaser. He closed his eyes for a moment, trying to calm his anxiety. He thought of her. But it wasn't Dani who came into his mind, it was another face. A face that seemed to be tattooed on to the inside of his eyelids.

A blaring horn sounded behind him. Ben stared at the green light, paralysed. He inhaled sharply, glancing up into the rear-view mirror. The motorbike was revving its engine, waiting for him to move. What the hell were they doing? The rider was clad head to toe in black leather with a matt-black helmet, like an apocalyptic assassin from *Blade Runner*. Ben pulled away, heading for the steep incline into the village as the bike engine growled again and shifted back into his blind spot. The bike was tailing him. 'Tourists' from Moscow trying to run him off the road. The Russian financiers were not people who negotiated. Had they been listening in on the call?

The emergency auto brake suddenly slammed down hard and the bike shot out in front, cutting across the road and hanging a sharp turn towards Mallet Hill. Ben was wrenched violently forward, the seat belt cutting into his neck. He grasped the wheel and fought to gain control of the car as it swerved violently across the road and mounted the verge. The wheels hit the kerb with an almighty metallic bang. A huge, jagged slab of granite rock slammed into the door, the stone ripping into the carbon-fibre side panel. The airbag exploded in Ben's face as the car shuddered to a halt.

The crooked tip of the Hanging Rock had splintered the side window, shattering the glass. Ben lay motionless, the side door airbag pressing him into the bucket seat. The car horn screamed a constant warning as Ben lay still, not breathing. But then his eyes opened, chest heaving painfully as he tried to breathe. Wiggling his feet, he attempted to move himself out from behind the steering column. His head was bleeding and he could feel blood trickling into his eye, but his adrenaline had gone to work. Ben scooted over to the passenger side, straddling the front seats, tumbling out and collapsing on to the pavement. He sat for a second on the tarmac, resting himself against the wheel.

He stared at the door panel. It had been ripped open like a tin of sardines, the window was shot: a couple of grands' worth of damage to add to his list of worries. He sat in silence, staring at the wreck of his car. Maybe he was in shock, but he felt numb. He could sense something else being torn open, something ripping at the fabric of his life.

15

NOVEMBER 2023

'My earliest memory is sitting in the neighbours' garden, strapped in a pushchair. I must have been three years old. Mum was busy chatting in the kitchen and I had somehow shuffled the buggy forward. I wanted to look at the goldfish swimming in the pond.' Nate swallowed, his complexion white as a sheet.

His face was projected through the darkness on to the cinema screen that covered the entire wall. A pair of unusually clear, light-brown eyes shone like windows into a young, uncertain soul.

A hand reached for the track pad built on the laptop; two fingers expanded the image. Zooming in closer. So close that the blood vessels in the teenage boy's pale cheeks were clearly visible. He was blushing. The text at the bottom of the frame read, 'Knot, Nathan. 14.' The frozen image was released from its digital inertia and the boy continued to tell his story.

'The wheels caught on the edge of the paving stones and the buggy tipped over.' He closed his eyes tight. 'I was suspended underwater, trapped. I couldn't breathe.' Tears streamed down his face now. 'I nearly drowned. Mum wheeled me home, dripping in green algae.' He wiped his face and smiled. 'It became something they all laughed about . . . the green slime bit anyway, especially Lily.'

The boy on the film inhaled deeply as his eyes lit up. 'I still have dreams about her – my mum, that is. We see her at Christmas . . . well, not last year but the year before. She gave me a scarf of hers that I keep in a drawer, it has her perfume on it . . . that's my secret. It's a bit silly but no one knows about it.' He wasn't acting; this was all real and deeply personal. His voice lowered into a conspiratorial whisper. 'I think Mum felt guilty that I nearly drowned and Dad blamed her for not looking after me properly. But it wasn't her fault. Lily said they got divorced because of me.'

Nate paused for a second, gathering himself as he tried to swallow the sadness.

'Ever since then, I've been terrified of water. Can't swim, even now.'

The film was paused once again on the face full of pain, and this time something else lingered behind the boy's eyes. Fear and guilt. The hands controlling the film reached for a laptop on a side table. The overwhelming urge to reach out to this boy, to heal and nurture him, took hold. But that would be overstepping the line.

Nimble fingers tickled the keyboard and a web page flashed up on to the screen. The RetroFX blog site. Logging on, the cursor found the last thread of the conversation they'd been having. Nate's light was amber, which meant he wasn't online. In the empty box at the bottom of the thread, a new message was typed.

How did the audition go? Did you nail it?

A fingers-crossed emoji.

As he pressed send, the freckled face of the girl with glasses and bouncing pigtails waved on to the screen, carrying her message to Nathan Knot's computer.

Then Freckles, the lonely little girl, the emoji with the red hair who was just like Nate, stood up from her lonely chair, moved across her lonely office and stepped out of the darkness. She crossed to a drinks' cabinet, threw a handful of ice into a highball and poured herself a gin. The man in his forties behind the friendly emoji passed a hand over a well-groomed beard.

In the darkened room, a heaviness hung in the air. The digital footage was uploaded on to the hard drive and a retro filter was processed over the iPhone video of the audition. It still wasn't good enough to use in any large format, but all he needed to know was if this boy could convey the truth. That's what he was hunting for: truth. Not some stage school kid who had been coached, but someone real and touching. There was something about Nathan Knot, something you just couldn't take your eyes off. Maybe there was an imprint there, an endowment of an essence he wanted to see, a memory of the past. Max Crow had found his muse.

He squeezed his eyes closed, trying to shut out the cacophony of thoughts cluttering his mind. He needed a break, needed to think. He leant back in his chair and stretched his arms as the door behind him was nudged open. A dog padded across the room, hopped up on to the leather couch and nuzzled under an outstretched arm.

'Good boy, is that dinner or garden?' The tail wagged as the good boy cleaned the hand with his warm tongue. 'All right, all right.'

Max stood and stretched. That was enough for today. He opened the shutters, letting the bright sunlight stream into the room, before pulling open the door to the terrace where warm evening air perfumed the stifling atmosphere with bougainvillea. As he turned back to the paused screen, the face in the darkness stared back at him. Max tried to imagine him in the role. Was he up to it? Could this kid take what was about to happen to him, physically and emotionally?

The Cut was deep. It wasn't his intention to make it bleed. After all this time, old wounds were supposed to have healed. But if he would insist on picking at the scab, forcing the skin to tear, enjoying that moment of stinging pain and the relief of blood flow, then what did he expect?

Max hesitated for a second. Was he really going to do this? He slowly pulled his phone from his back pocket and opened his contacts. He scrolled down to her number then dialled. It went straight to voicemail.

'Hey, it's me, it's a green light. Offer him the role.' He hung up.

There were many pieces to this puzzle that would need to be found, but the first, most crucial piece was Nathan Knot.

He was the muse. He was also the target.

16

NOVEMBER 1993

How should we like it were stars to burn
With a passion for us we could not return?
If equal affection cannot be,
Let the more loving one be me.

W. H. Auden

She's his muse. Her hair is gathered up into a knot on the top of her head, revealing smooth skin on her neck. The cervical vertebrae are visible through the fine layer of pink fabric stretched tight over perfectly aligned shoulders. Her head inclines forward then backward in hypnotic motion, keeping time to the glissando of the piano. The muscle that runs from the back of the skull behind the ear guides the eye down into the soft skin of the shoulder and along the arm, now extending into a beautiful arc overhead. Then, light as air, her arms float down and scoop as if the atmosphere in the room is like sand running through fingers. She is bathing in a ring of light as the rays of the morning sun flare through the glass and blow out the camera frame for a second. Zooming in even closer through the reinforced windows of the classroom, his eye passes through the buried wire in the glass that imprisons these caged swans.

Annie Maddock is an inch or so taller than the other girls holding on to the barre. Her neck seems longer than the rest, her arms more expressive, as if she is suspended on a soft cloud. She is mesmerising, in every possible way.

Dave holds the camera in his right hand over his shoulder, and for a second his eye leaves the viewfinder and he watches her with naked eyes through the window. Her ruddy cheeks betray the concealed effort in her body and the small beads of perspiration on her forehead and neck are dabbed with a towel from her bag, before the dancers move into the centre of the room. Dave ducks down slightly, bringing his camera to the floor outside the window to change the tape. Once reloaded, he peeks back up. His eye glues itself to the viewfinder. The frame in and out of focus judders to find its subject then bang! The crack of metal on glass. An angry, heavily made-up face, filling the lens, is glaring at him, ringed knuckles rapping on the window. Patel sharply backs off from the viewfinder as Mrs Clarke, the ballet teacher, orders the piano to stop. She mouths something and shoos him away dismissively with her hand.

'Go home, Peeping Tom.'

Dave cuts his camera and slinks away as the girls grab a break, to sip water and towel down. Annie stands in the centre of the room, watching him leave. She stares at him, smiling, then lifts her leg, pulling it high behind her ear like a gymnast, inclining her head towards him as she mouths 'Bye-bye'.

The roar of the throttle and the spluttering backfire of Dave's motorbike tears up Forest Hill. He skids to a halt outside the vicarage and cuts the engine, removing his helmet and shouldering the gate. He wheels his bike quietly around the side passage of his dad's surgery to the back of the house. He opens the kitchen door and starts upstairs to his room.

'I thought you were going to help me on reception today, young man?' Sandeep's stern tone makes Dave stop midway up the stairs.

'Sorry, Dad, I got stuck at school.' Dave unzips his bag and pulls out the camera. 'I'm making a montage for my GCSE art course work.'

'On a Saturday? Hmm . . . well, so long as you're not just wasting time.' Sandeep eyeballs him over the rim of his glasses.

'Don't worry, this will be worth it, you'll see.' Dave turns to head up the stairs.

'They'll try to sabotage you, you know.' Sandeep's voice catches him as he reaches the top.

Dave stares back to his dad. 'You always do this, kill all the fun. It's always homework and coaching and hard graft.'

'I just don't want you held back by shirkers.' The electronic sound of the door opening signals Sandeep's next patient.

'So, what am I supposed to do? Hide myself away and have no friends?' Dave reddens as the anger reaches his face.

'Now, you listen to me.' Sandeep pulls the door and lowers his voice. 'Just be careful who you allow into your life. Do you know how many patients left this practice when they found out the new doctor had an Indian surname?' Sandeep's mouth clenches. 'It's not always what they say . . . it's what they don't say.'

'I really like her!' As soon as the words tumble out of Dave's mouth, he wishes they hadn't.

Sandeep's face falls.

'She'll turn you down.' His voice softens. 'Oh, my dear boy. I'm only trying to protect you.'

'I don't need your protection, I have friends . . . good friends.' Dave begins to pull the camera cables from his bag, ready to set up to the TV.

'But they're not true friends.' Sandeep stares back at his son. 'They never will be.'

They regard each other for a second, a deep wedge of resentment fracturing the bond between them.

'Why did you bring us here? Why did we have to leave Edinburgh?' Dave shakes his head as he turns and slams his bedroom door behind him.

He closes his eyes, leaning his back against the door, and gathers himself. Then a rush of heat rises into his chest as he remembers the film he has just shot. He kneels on the floor and begins his familiar ritual of marking the tape case with a black felt-tip pen: time and the date. He pulls out a brown leather box from under his bed. With a small key, he opens the padlock and lifts the lid. Inside, he runs his fingers along a line of other tapes, about thirty in total. His finger hovers over one (31/10/92 Spirit in the Woods. A. Maddock) and then another (10/11/93 The Crow's Nest. A. Maddock). Each tape that Dave has collected since his father bought him the camera has been dedicated to her. Dave plugs the camera into his portable black-and-white TV and presses play. He slots a CD into his Walkman, and slides headphones over his ears.

The sound of Radiohead blasts into his ears as he bathes in the image of the ballet dancer fading up on the screen. His breath stolen by the gravity-defying Annabel Maddock balancing in front of him. Floating like a feather, in that beautiful world.

The image is slightly blurred, but she takes her hand from the barre and extends a lifted leg slowly into a perfect arabesque. She really is just like an angel.

'You are so friggin' special,' Dave whispers to himself. There is something about her that he can't describe. Capturing her on film like this feels like the most natural thing in the world. He wanted her to notice. He wanted control. In his juvenile brain, he somehow understands that these years are transient, none of us can remain like this forever.

In time, every millisecond of this footage will be pored over. The grainy image slowed down, made clearer, analysed and dissected. Not for its beauty but for its meaning.

The reflection of the boy holding the camera in the glass window of the dance studio would be the final exhibit that would seal his fate.

17

NOVEMBER 2023

Karine Mickelsen emerged from the footpath that led through a dense thicket of trees at the base of Mallet Hill. Half of the ancient burial mound to the north had been eaten away by an open cast granite quarry, but the south side of the hill, the sacred side, was still intact. The frosty gorse bushes shivered in the breeze and the crispy remains of fallen leaves crunched underfoot as she approached the kissing gate that led to the river's edge. She stared out towards the stone walls of the austere structure nestled in woodland, inhaled sharply and let the icy vapour escape from her mouth as she crossed the bridge over the river. Hands thrust deep into her jeans pockets, Mickelsen pulled out her phone and took a photograph of Blackstone Mill.

At the beginning of every venture, at the moment when the theoretical research was over and principal photography began, there was a feeling of anticipation for what was about to happen. The entire narrative needed to be clear in her head because when the starting gun fired, there was no turning back.

Karine already knew *The Cut* would be a different kind of film from her previous work. This one would test her in a way that would be hard to predict. 'Genre' was a euphemistic term the film industry preferred to use instead of 'horror', to elevate itself above the tropes of the eighties' slasher flick. For Karine Mickelsen, it was a step down, but the pay cheque would sweeten the blow, especially if the film was a smash at the box office.

Sometime later, she was standing in the driveway of the Knot house, taking shots on her phone. The pale buff sandstone facade was warm and welcoming, but the house stood aloof on the border of the village and at odds with the faded grey council estate of Barton Mallet, which seemed trapped in the pessimism of the 1970s. A shiver of depressing recognition coursed through her. In a way, it was perfect, like the drained palette of *Misery* or *The Silence of the Lambs*. Karine's moment of reflection was broken by the honk of a horn and she turned to see a rust bucket Ford Transit scraping its hubcaps along the kerb. She gathered her ice-white hair into a ponytail and indicated for the van to pull up on to the drive. She watched it park and went back inside the house.

'Excuse me . . . what are you doing? This is private property!' Behind the Transit, a flatbed pickup loaded with the wreckage of a pearl-grey Polestar had crawled around the corner of the grove. Ben Knot was leaning out of the window, shouting at the van parked up on his drive. He swung the cab door open, jumped down on to the pavement and stormed towards a bemused-looking stoner in work boots, jeans and a T-shirt, chugging on a vape and pulling a trolley loaded with monitors and cables across the grass.

'Didn't you hear me?' Ben tapped at his ear. 'Move the van off my drive.'

A cloud of vape smoke that smelled of pear drops billowed into Ben's face as a tattooed hand pulled out an ear bud. 'You what? Sorry?'

'Your wheels are chewing up my lawn, mate.' Ben wafted his hand through the cloud of vape as Dani appeared at the front door.

'Ben? . . . Ben, he got it . . . he got the part!' Dani appeared to be in full stage make-up and had shimmied into a festive sequined tank top at 4 p.m. on a Friday afternoon.

Ben frowned at her, confused. 'Wait . . . What are you on about?'

'Didn't you get my text?' She was sipping a glass of blush Prosecco. 'The film Nate auditioned for! He's doing it.' Some kind of celebration was afoot. 'The director's here, come in and meet her.'

He flinched. 'Her?' Then checked himself. 'Hold on a second, this is all a bit sudden, isn't it?' Ben stared at the equipment strewn all over the driveway and front lawn.

'You've got something on your face, love.' Dani scrunched her cuff and leant in to wipe Ben's cheek but he pulled away. 'Come in. Karine will explain.' Dani turned to Fruity Vape. 'I opened the garage door for you, love. You can put all your gear in there.' Her heels click-clacked their way into the atrium. She was in full party mode.

'Where do you want it, mate? I got another call out.' The driver of the flatbed, clipboard in hand, was scribbling on the paperwork and checking his watch. Ben's shoulders sank as he signed the form and watched as the wreck of his car was dumped on to the road.

Minutes later, Ben was standing in the kitchen, awkwardly holding a glass of the pink fizz as Dani and Karine, who appeared to have bonded instantly, machine-gunned their way through all the facts and details of the film in which his son had apparently managed to bag the lead role.

'When did all this happen?' Ben slung his coat over the back of a high stool by the kitchen island. 'I've only been away a week.'

'Well . . . they liked his audition tape.' Dani smiled over at Nate.

'We loved the tape.' Karine touched her arm.

'They got him in for call-backs along with some of the rest of his year.' Dani was flushed with excitement. 'And he smashed it!'

Nate was slumped on the sofa in the den, playing on Lily's Xbox, one eye on the TV, one ear listening to his fate. 'I am the lead, though . . . tell him.'

'That's right. Nate's the leading man.' Dani beamed at Ben. 'Timothy Charmly eat your heart out, right?'

'Timothée Chalamet . . . That's how you say it.' Nate cringed.

'Whatever,' Dani muttered under her breath, topping up her glass. She leant against the quartz worktop and fluttered her fake lashes at her new-found friend. 'Is there a part in it for me?' There was a pause as Karine Mickelsen diplomatically sipped her wine. 'Only kidding. Can't act to save my life. Well, apart from that one time—'

'Dani . . .' Ben stepped in, just in time to stop her straddling a chair and belting out the opening bars of 'Life is a Cabaret'.

Karine flashed a professional smile and then turned her head to Ben. 'I can assure you, you won't even know that we're here, Mr Knot. I'm originally from a documentary background.'

'She's got an Oscar.' Dani nudged Ben, her eyes full of boastful pride.

'Actually, a César . . . it's kind of a French Oscar.'

'Ooo la la.' Dani filled her glass and clinked with Karine.

Ben glanced over at Nate. 'So . . . what's the film about?'

'It's a horror film. Max Crow.' Dani shivered with excitement.

'Well, we like to think of it as elevated genre.' Karine smiled reassuringly.

Nate piped up from the den. 'She says it's going be like *The Hoax* . . . and that was massive.'

Karine smiled. 'Yes. Unexpected blockbuster. Horror and superheroes are the only things keeping Hollywood in the black these days.'

Ben frowned. 'Well, before he gets involved, don't we need to see a contract? Is he going to be paid? What's the deal?'

'Jumping straight into the legals there, typical. He's getting paid, aren't you, pet?' Dani gave Nate a thumbs-up. He smiled back and returned his attention to the video game. 'Don't bother your head about all that, Ben. I've sorted it.' Her elbow slipped on the counter, her Prosecco sloshing on to her sequins. Intoxicated in more ways than one, as money, fame and film premieres flashed before her eyes.

'Er . . . OK. Look . . .' Ben shook his head in disbelief.

Karine jumped in. 'I'll have all the paperwork prepared for you. Trust me, we need insurance as much as you do.'

Ben nodded, allowing himself to be drawn into Karine's calm gaze. He studied her extraordinary face. She looked almost like an apparition: pale skin and white hair with eyes so light it was hard to identify the colour. She smiled at him.

'You cool with all this?' Ben addressed Nate in the den.

'Yeah, Dad, I'm sweet . . . Do I get time off school?' He rose from the sofa.

'NO!' Ben and Dani chimed in unison.

Karine placed her glass down and stepped forward towards Ben, smiling. 'Please don't worry, Mr Knot, the whole film will be seamless. We will be completely invisible. Most of the content is remote capture or found footage. We usually ask for access to phone cameras but that's totally up to you.'

Ben raised an eyebrow and opened his mouth to protest, but before he could say a word, Dani chipped in.

'Nate loves all that, don't you, pet? You're OK if we use the camera on your phone, aren't you, love?' Dani turned back to Karine. 'They live their lives on camera, don't they? Film everything.' She beamed with excitement.

The tattooed crew member with the fruity vape stomped past them towards the utility room. 'All right if I use the bog?' Ben's eyes followed him, uncomfortable with all these people in the house.

'Is there a script we can see?' Ben placed his glass down. 'I'd just like to know what he's going to be involved in.'

'Script? . . . All right, Scorsese! Honestly, I can't even get him to read a WhatsApp message.' Dani was refilling that glass again, sidling up to Karine.

Karine smiled, but her lips remained clamped over her teeth. 'It's largely improvised. We'll guide Nathan towards a narrative by setting some goals. Does the phrase "fly on the wall" ring a bell?' Her crystal silver-blue eyes sparkled at Ben. 'Think of me as a giant bluebottle with all-seeing eyes.'

The toilet in the utility room flushed as Fruity Vape emerged, a slightly more pungent smell following in his wake. 'Mate. You got high-speed fibre I assume, judging by the place. Can I grab access to your router and Wi-Fi code?' He scratched his balls. Ben squeezed his eyes tight, trying to block everything out. 'I'll just run a cable to the equipment loaded in the garage.'

'It's in the basement, I'll show you.' Dani placed her glass down and wobbled on her heels towards the hallway.

'We usually set up something called a "video village". It's like the hub of the film, where all the equipment lives.' Karine leant against the counter and stared calmly at Ben. 'But you won't even know we're here.' She toasted her glass to Ben with a reassuring flourish. 'I'm fastidious. I hate leaving a mess!'

Dani was drunkenly tugging at the door that led down to the basement.

'It's locked, hon . . . you have the key?'

Ben sighed. 'I . . . um . . . I need the paperwork before we dive in headfirst. I'm sorry, it's just . . . it's all a bit of a whirlwind, isn't it?'

'Welcome to show business. Once a film is green lit, everyone is on borrowed time.'

Ben stood clenching his jaw. 'Look, I had a prang in my car, shattered the windscreen. I just need to deal with that right now.'

'You what?' Dani stood open-mouthed.

Karine glanced at the small cut above Ben's eye. 'But of course, I understand. I'll email you the contract and you can sign digitally . . . if it gets your approval.' Then she looked at her watch and zipped up her jacket.

Ben moved over to the sink in the kitchen to wash his hands. Grabbing a sheet of kitchen paper, he dabbed his eye.

'Great meeting you, Dani. We'll be in touch sooner rather than later.'

'Where are you staying, by the way? We've got a whole granny annex downst—' Dani's eyes flicked to Ben. 'Sorry . . . studio flat.'

Karine made eye contact with Ben. 'We checked into the Red Lion. Seems nice. Creaky and quaint. Enough room for the rest of my crew.' She gently ushered Fruity Vape towards the front door.

'Beer, ciggie-stained walls and cheese and onion crisps . . . right up my street.' He took another drag as Karine clicked the door closed, and they were gone.

'I can't believe you crashed the car.' Dani was unfocused and not quite present. 'That'll bugger up your no claims.' She slouched back towards the fridge for a refill with a face like thunder.

'I'm fine, thanks for asking.' Ben felt a pair of arms slide around his waist.

'Oh, don't be like that. Of course I'm glad you're OK. I just wish you could be a bit more excited about the film.'

Ben sighed and leant into her embrace. 'I'm excited for Nate . . . Happy now?'

'You're letting him do it then?' He felt her lips kissing into his neck, he turned and pulled her closer.

'Anything that makes you smile like that gets my vote.' There was a relief in Ben's voice as he exhaled. Dani's sparkle always made everything better.

'Oh my God, Nate! You're gonna be a film star . . . we're going to Hollywood.' Dani planted a kiss on Ben's lips and closed her eyes.

Hollywood. He winced at the thought. What on earth were they letting themselves in for?

18

NOVEMBER 1993

'One. And. Two. And. Three.' The speed of the bully sticks thwacking against each other sends the striker into a panic as the ball is fumbled down the centre line by Annie Maddock, pursued by a rabid Lynette Davis virtually foaming at the mouth. The wooden shaft of Lynette's weapon slams into Annie's shin with a sickening crack, nearly tripping her. But Annie is no novice to Davis's dirty tricks. Four years of ballet training kicks in as her legs fly backwards, her hockey stick held high in the air with two hands. She appears to float above the slicing blow, legs behind her in a double 'pas de chat'. It's like something out of a martial arts movie. The excitement sends a raucous explosion of cheers around the field of spectators. Dave Patel, filming everything as usual, punches the air as Ben Knot calls out from the sidelines.

'GO, ANNIE!'

Lynette glances over her shoulder, eyes thinning. Chris Davis juts out his chin, egging on his sister. 'COME ON, DAVIS!'

Annie's feet pound deep into the field, wet clods of earth splattering into the path of a diving Lynette, Jackson-Pollocking her furious red face and pristine white jersey with a spray of wet mud. Maddock sprints away towards the goal as Lynette wipes her eyes and drives forward in a second attempt at an underhand foul.

Annie moves like a bolt of lightning down the centre. It's almost impossible to catch her. The rest of the team form a defensive phalanx as she approaches the goal, four of them feathering out down the wing. Ten metres from the shooting circle, dribbling forward, Annie hits the ball gently a few feet ahead, then raises her stick to strike the winning shot. At that moment, Lynette appears to catch her, the gap between them closing fast. Annie swings from her shoulder in a perfect arc and in the very same second, Lynette swipes low, the hook of her crook wrapping neatly around Annie's ankle, yanking her face down into the mud.

'Foul!' the crowd jeers at Lynette.

'HEY! Stick obstruction. GET UP, ANNIE!' Catherine is jumping up and down on the sidelines.

The ball spins high in the air, heading directly for the goal. Lynette Davis attempts to chase it down but the velocity of that strike bypasses the goalkeeper and slams into the back of the cage. The crowd explodes and the final whistle blows.

A mud-soaked Annie watches as Lynette smacks her stick into the goalpost in anger, splintering it in two. She spits into the grass, turns to face the crowd and walks back down the field. As she passes Annie, still on her hands and knees, Lynette stamps into the mud, spraying filth into her face. Annie snaps, hooking her foot around Davis's ankle, bringing her crashing down. The crowd erupts again as Mr Branchflower blows his whistle. The red card goes up.

'Bad sport, Maddock. Intentional foul.' Mr Branchflower turns to Davis. 'All OK? Nothing broken there, I hope?' His Welsh accent somehow softens his angry tone.

Davis is on her back clutching her ankle, squirming in pain.

'I'll be OK, but that was definitely a foul, sir.' She glances over to Annie, who is standing over her now with her hands on her hips. Her middle finger spread out over her hip bone, secretly flipping the bird to the girl on the ground.

Branchflower isn't an idiot, not when it comes to sport anyway. He looks at Annie, who is pulling the double shin pads out of her blood-soaked sock.

'It's a draw, Davis, but I'll need to see both of you in my office after you've cleaned up.'

'Sir? The rules state extra time when—' Davis attempts to negotiate.

'Save it for my office.' Branchflower turns to walk away and Ben charges in towards Annie.

'You OK?' He kisses her on the cheek, mud transferring from hers to his. 'Wouldn't like to meet you down a dark alley, you bruiser . . . you're lethal.'

Annie nudges him away. 'Sod off,' she sighs. 'Better go and face the music. See you in class.'

'Double maths . . . boo!' Ben wipes the mud from his face and gently kisses her cheek again. Laughing, he jogs back to the others.

Lynette scowls, watching Ben leave, then turns to Annie with hatred in her eyes.

Branchflower's 'office' is really just a glorified equipment cupboard with no windows that he's requisitioned to make himself feel like he actually has some status at Barton Mallet Secondary School. The stacks of orange plastic chairs form a barrier around him as he sits behind a makeshift desk, shaking a plastic beaker full of bright-blue energy drink. He cricks his neck and sighs with exhaustion, then takes a swig. The place stinks of body odour and vinegar; the warm, windowless room emanates the perfect marinade of sweaty cricket pads and trainers. The two freshly washed girls sit opposite him: Annie all crossed legs and folded arms, Lynette Davis chewing gum.

'You're team captain, Davis, I don't want to see that kind of rubbish out on—'

'No idea what you're talking about.' The chewing becomes even more slovenly.

'I'm talking now. I don't want that shit out on my field.' Branchflower's overworked guns bulge through his T-shirt as he scribbles in a ledger.

'Then you should have benched the shitty player.' Lynette's head flicks to Annie, refusing to make eye contact.

Branchflower leans in close. 'I'm not quite sure who you think you are, Davis.'

'Daddy's girl!' Annie pitches in under her breath, tightening her arms. Lynette kisses her teeth. Everyone knows exactly why she's the captain of the team. Her dad is the local bobby and Branchflower's collection of unpaid parking tickets has miraculously disappeared since Davis became team captain.

'Thank you, Maddock, you are on a two-match suspension.'

'What? Why?'

'Because we don't go around tripping our teammates into the mud. We're not animals.'

'Well . . . she acts like a pig in shit.' Annie immediately knows she's overstepped the mark by the sudden clatter of Lynette's chair and the arm that lashes out.

'ENOUGH, YOU TWO!' Branchflower is up on his feet and between them like a shot, his cheap aftershave almost doing the job of knocking them out. 'SIT DOWN . . . both of you. Davis, you will remain head of the team but I'm selecting Maddock as your striker once she's back from suspension.'

'No, sir. No way.' Davis kicks out sideways towards Maddock, that instinct to smash bone, just itching to make contact.

'WAY! You two will work together. Do you hear me?' In the silence, you can almost hear the grind of molars as both girls bite down on their rage.

'Do . . . you . . . hear . . . me?'

'Yes, sir.'

'Yes . . . SSSIR,' Lynette hisses in the poor man's face.

'Good, now shake hands and get out of my sight.'

Annie stands and turns to face Davis, a mocking smile spreading across her face. As their hands join, Davis's middle finger bends inwards and a sharp pain stabs Annie in the palm; the stiletto of a killer fingernail digging deep.

To make an enemy of someone like Lynette Davis is a grave error. Annie has crossed a line. There would be no warning, there never was with people like her. They wait, biding their time.

The cruel sting will strike when she least expects it.

19

NOVEMBER 2023

The goal that exploded from Lily Knot's boot was sublime. No one was surprised; her speed and agility, along with a sense of something to prove, were like fuel in her engine. A lot of unapologetic rage was expended on that football field, and Lily was the leader.

Old Mr Branchflower blew the whistle, and the ball was back in play.

'DRIVE IT HOME, LILS!' Nathan Knot was standing on the sidelines, shouting out what he thought was football jargon. He sipped on hot soup, holding the cup with one hand and filming her on his iPhone with the other. He and his sister lived for embarrassing each other with TikToks. A montage of hilarious football fails would go down well.

Another camera panned across the backs of the bodies standing on the sidelines.

Karine Mickelsen hadn't wasted a second setting up. Initially, she had held back, standing some way off under the cover of a line of cypresses, but slowly she began to creep forward until she was closer to the action.

She wore a baseball cap and headphones and had a handheld Sony Venice Rialto'd into a split body, the lens on her shoulder, battery in her backpack.

A guy in a fedora, with a mullet and sunglasses, was sitting in a lawn chair a little further off, with a portable sound-mixing desk on his knees. A younger, scrawny kid wearing a puffer jacket and combats, who didn't look much older than Nate, loaded the shot with the clapper board and then concentrated on working the focus.

Lily Knot glanced up from the field to the chemistry lab window, where she could see a line of bare buttocks mooning her. If that's what the boys thought of girls' football, she would show them.

A flurry of trouser hitching was met with the red-faced Mr Tacey, struggling to drop the blind. Lily shook her head and looked over to Nate, who shrugged, trying not to snigger at the boys of Year 11.

Nate clocked Karine out of the corner of his eye and sidled up to her. 'That's a lot of kit.' Karine removed her cans and slipped them down to her neck.

'Lily's a good player.' Karine smiled at him. 'She looks great on camera too, athletic.'

Nate smiled. 'Have we started making the film already?' He blew on the surface of his soup to cool it.

'Not quite . . . I'm shooting plates and establishers to get a feel for the geography.' Karine's eyes scanned the field.

'Will you tell me what the story is about?'

'It's about love.' Karine's gaze moved from his face, passing over his shoulder across the field.

'And pain.' She lifted the camera and continued recording. 'It's a simple story, really. Like football, we all know the rules but we won't know what will happen in the game until it's played. That's what makes it exciting.'

The score was one all, and with five minutes left they would most likely be going into extra time. Lily knew this wasn't good. If it ended in penalties, they would lose; she was the only decent striker on their team. The final minutes seemed like a blur. Backing up into the halfway line, the ball was thrown in and Lily was off like a shot. Whitney Briggs, the other team's attacker, had been salivating for months at the opportunity to bring the team captain down a peg or two.

Karine continued. 'Barton Mallet's a quiet village . . . I like it. I live in the city but it's nice out here in the peace and quiet of the countryside.' She breathed in the cool breeze and surveyed her new location.

'Yeah, not much happens here though . . . it's pretty boring.' Nate shrugged and chewed his lip.

'Well . . . Not anymore.' She winked. 'Not now I'm here.' She jolted to attention as a loud boo surged through the crowd. 'Ouch! That must have hurt.' Karine's eager eye returned to the viewfinder and Nate's head whipped back to the pitch. The brutal foul from Whitney Briggs, akin to a rugby tackle, had swept Lily's legs from underneath her. Winded, she lay on the ground, tasting iron in her mouth.

'Briggs, what are you playing at? WRONG SPORT.' Branchflower was striding across the field from the sidelines.

Whitney Bully Briggs was up on her feet. 'She fouled me, innit . . . I was clinging on.'

'With both hands wrapped tight around her knees, Briggs? I wasn't born yesterday.' Branchflower was fiddling in his top pocket for the inevitable yellow card.

'Wha'ever.' Briggs shrugged, turned to her gaggle of friends filming everything on their phones and smirked.

Nate was standing shaking his head. 'SHOULD BE A RED CARD!' He turned to Karine. 'That girl never plays by the rules . . . she's a bad sport.'

Karine eyed him beadily. 'And what about you? You ever break the rules . . . just to win?' She raised her eyebrows. 'No matter the cost?'

Nate finished the soup and drop-kicked the cup over the chain-link fence. His head snapped back to her as if caught out.

Karine laughed, throwing her head back. 'Is that all you got?' She stopped for a second. 'What? No necking on the swings, no smoking weed, no joy rides?'

Nate shrugged. 'I guess not.' He didn't have a lot to say. His eyes focused back to the sports field, where his sister was still lying on her back. As she sat up on the grass, a trickle of blood rolled down her cheek. A stone had caught her temple and opened a small cut close to her eye. Whitney Briggs glanced over in the direction of Karine Mickelsen's camera. Then, unseen by the referee, Briggs booted Lily hard in the ribs. Lily flinched with pain, holding on to her side. Nate noticed Karine's energy lift. He thought she was about to wade in and break it up, but instead she moved in closer and continued filming.

Hordes of kids began to pour out of the school doors and something in Lily snapped. The attack took her opponent by surprise. Briggs was down on the ground in a second and Lily Knot was on top of her, pummelling her face and pulling on her braids.

'KNOT, KNOT, KNOT, KNOT.'

Karine moved like a bullet from a gun, striding across the field with Nate in tow, homing in on the action. 'Go on, Nate, get in there . . . do your brotherly thing.' Karine guided him to his sister's aid, filming his every move.

'Get off me!' Briggs fought back as the crowd began to gather round. Karine's camera captured every moment and the circle of spectators were too preoccupied filming the action on their phones to do anything. A girl-on-girl fight was the perfect click bait. It would most likely go viral, especially if hair got pulled or clothes got torn and body parts spilled out. It took Nate barging through the tight circle and pulling Lily off the massive physical form of Whitney Briggs to bring the vicious fight to an end. Nate held Lily's arms and tried to calm her down as she continued to lash out.

Mr Branchflower helped Briggs up from the floor and ushered her inside as the clique of girls, checking their phones to ensure they'd captured all the drama, finally rallied to their friend's aid. As Whitney passed Karine, they made eye contact, a moment of recognition. Karine smiled at her and she nodded back. She'd set the whole thing up.

Nate clocked it, but busied himself with his sister, talking quietly into her ear, stroking her head, and using the corner of his shirt to wipe some of the blood from her face.

Karine had witnessed the fight in close-up. She had captured everything, just as she had promised. From a safe distance, the focus puller, Freddie, had sharpened the frame as Karine pushed in close on the rage boiling across Lily Knot's face and witnessed it melt under her brother's touch. The effect was dramatic; a score was already playing in her mind, something poignant, strings or a solo sparse piano. She needed to cut to a wide shot to close the scene, so she changed lenses and dropped back to the very edge of the sports field. School was out, the game was over and the girls were cleaning up in the changing room. Karine saved the data to her hard drive. She had decided to defy Max and shoot on digital where possible; the vintage camera would come later.

She sent Freddie and Fedora back to the Red Lion for a well-earned pint and waited for Nate to leave the main school building. She watched him cross the tennis courts, then headed him off at the shortcut between the houses.

Karine was leaning against the fence waiting for him, her eyes focused on the end of School Lane, where glittering Santas, robins and bells already hung from each lamppost in the distance, lining the path. 'Mind if I walk with you for a bit?'

Nate paused for a second. 'Is this about filming?'

'Yeah . . . Nate, listen . . . Those rules we were discussing. I am going to need you to break some of them.' Karine walked alongside him, hunched over against the icy wind that was now picking up. 'Just for me . . . for a bit of extra drama, you know?'

'Like you just did?' Nate looked down to his feet.

'How do you mean?' Karine kept her eyes fixed on his face.

'Whitney Briggs . . . the fight with Lily.' Nate turned to Karine and stared her down. 'You set that up . . . the foul.'

Karine stopped for a second and smiled. 'I'm just testing the water.'

'She could have got hurt.' Nate's brow furrowed.

Karine inclined her head. 'Lily's tough . . . she can take it . . . but how about you?'

Nate was reddening, he swallowed and nodded.

'You have to go through the mill to get the best results. Did watching your sister make you feel something?' Karine was studying him, like a specimen.

'It made me feel sick.'

'Right? So, use it, Nate. These feelings are real.'

Karine pulled something from the bag on her shoulder, a bundle wrapped in a leather zip pouch.

'I'm going to set you a task. Do you know what improvisation is?' Karine was holding a small leather camera case.

'Oh course. We do it at Kidsmet . . . never invent . . . never deny.' Nate seemed energised now, his ruddy face beaming as they picked up their pace towards the amber lights of the small parade of shops in the village.

'Good mantra . . . we might need a little bit of invention, though.' Karine paused at the end of the lane. 'Will you take this and shoot some footage for me?' She held out the zip bag and opened it. 'It's a vintage camera.'

Nate frowned. 'Looks complicated. Can't I just use my iPhone?'

'This one will capture some interesting stuff.' Karine flicked open the cassette window and ejected a tape. 'It uses real film.' She blew into the reels, clearing it of dust.

'What do I have to do?' Nate's eyes glinted with intrigue.

'OK . . . how about this. I send you a text each day, with a time and a place to meet. I tell you what to wear and what to be pre- pared for, maybe a few lines of script but not exactly what is about to happen. I want you to be surprised and I want you to surprise me.' She crossed her arms and smiled at him down the lens. 'Does that sound like a good plan?'

Nate took the clunky-looking camera and turned it over in his hands. 'You'll have to show me how to use it.'

'Of course. Happy to! They don't make the tapes anymore, but I'll try and get hold of some for you. Maybe there are some old home videos stashed away in the attic you could use?'

'Yeah, maybe.' Nate smiled, tucked the camera safely into his bag and turned to head home.

'This will be exciting; we'll have some fun. I'll text you the first task tomorrow. How are you with stunts?'

Nate shrugged. 'Oh . . . I'm not sure.' He looked nervous. 'Why?'

'There's going to be a fight.' Karine's eyes moved to the path behind him. 'It might get a little tricky.' She seemed lost in her thoughts for a second. 'But don't worry, we'll choreograph it to look convincing.' Karine turned towards the old part of the village. 'So, my little action hero, I'll see you tomorrow. Yes?' Nate nodded and headed off home. Karine watched him trudging off into the distance.

His gangly awkward body, trousers too short, already outgrowing his school uniform, made her flinch with anticipation for what was about to happen. Max was right, he was absolutely perfect for this role.

Nate was grinning from ear to ear as he opened the front door to his house and headed up to his room. This would be exciting. He loved a new project, and experimenting with an old film camera was right up his street.

He felt like a spy on a mission.

It had already begun; blood had already been spilt, just a spot. A second audition had happened by accident and Lily had nailed it.

Karine had no intention of disturbing the water, but throwing in a catalyst now and then to get what she wanted would be essential.

The cast of characters was beginning to emerge in her mind. The lover, the rival, the outsider, the witness, there was always a bent copper and someone always had to die.

The Hoax had been a commercial success. *The Cut* would change everything.

20

NOVEMBER 2023

The blue-black glass surface of the ocean was dead calm. It turned orange at the epicentre of the jaw-dropping sunset far out to the west. Point Dume, the famous cove where Charlton Heston had stumbled towards a submerged Statue of Liberty in the final scenes of the 1968 movie *Planet of the Apes*, was a favourite hot spot along the Pacific Coast Highway. Hikers would descend to the beach and cars would pull over, pop the trunk, grab a beer from a cool box and perch on the hood for a 'sundowner'. There were no seasons here, not really; that was something he missed, especially fall, or rather autumn, but Max Crow missed very little else.

Malibu usually conjured up images of paradise: heavenly white sand, sun-kissed bikini bodies and movie stars. In reality, the massive eight-lane motorway trimmed with the windswept palm trees of the Pacific Palisades hid the fact that nature's majesty was often enjoyed from the stillness of gridlocked traffic. LA had a vehicular cholesterol problem. Highway 1 was one of the clogged arteries that brought commuters down from Santa Barbara, Ventura and Ojai into Tinseltown. Someone once said most of LA was perched on what was effectively compacted kitty litter: one big quake and the whole place would skitter down into the ocean. But traffic and doom-mongering aside, it was still quite breathtaking.

I've just sent you an email. FoxcatcherXX

The text dropped around 4 p.m. It was pretty late there; she was burning the midnight oil.

Max was detouring back from Thousand Oaks, after a very frustrating day. It was all over a badly received note he'd given on an edit. He had driven two hours to meet the director, only to find a bull-pen of bewildered casting assistants thumbing through a diary with no evidence of a meeting. LA was like that sometimes; piss people off and they would screw you over in a thousand tiny ways. But the thought of his time with Charlie had cast a ray of sunshine over the dark clouds furrowing his brow as he drove.

Every other Friday afternoon, Charlie was all his for the weekend. His ex, Brandon, lived in a remote part of Topanga Canyon. The plaid shirts and rough hands of the woodsman had appealed to him once, but their lives had become complicated. Off-grid living with oil lamps and shitting in an outhouse wasn't really conducive to the high-tech demands of film production. So, a detour had occurred. He often felt like he was on an eternal detour. But the route from Thousand Oaks via Topanga and back towards Hollywood was one of those tedious drives made a million times better with his son riding shotgun. They could stop at Patrick's Roadhouse by Ginger Rogers Beach for a surf burger; Charlie's favourite with mushrooms and Jack cheese, to go. He would drop the roof while Charlie ran in for a pee, before getting a head start on the traffic, cutting through Brentwood and up on to West Sunset towards Laurel Canyon. It was longer and windier but with the radio on and Charlie's shoulders shimmying along to the Beach Boys, everything was OK with the world.

It was dark by the time they wound their way up the steep canyon, turning past Charlie's school, Wonderland Elementary. Parenting through a divorce had been painful but Wonderland had lived up to its name, and it was walking distance from their home on Lookout Mountain Avenue. It was pitch dark when they pulled into the concrete underground carport and Charlie was asleep with a blanket over him. Max bundled him up and mounted the stairs to tuck him into his bed.

'I need to brush.' A sleepy-eyed face peeked out of the deep pillow as Max laid Charlie down. Cocoa stirred in his bed, then sleepily hopped up on to Charlie's and snuggled in, wrapping his front paws over Charlie's feet, like he always did. A lifelong friend.

'I'll bring it in.' By the time Max had returned with a toothbrush and a glass of water, Charlie was out for the count. The window was cracked ajar and the mosquito net adjusted. The cicadas clicked and brushed their metronome pulse as Charlie blew out a tired bubble from red flushed cheeks.

Max removed his sneakers and moved on silent socked feet out of the bedroom and down into the basement of this mid-century cantilevered box set into the canyon cliffs. The soundproof suite wouldn't disturb his sleeping baby boy. The door closed with a vacuum suction and the electric blackouts sealed in the darkness from the light pollution outside.

The note from Foxcatcher read:

Pre-lap. Opening establishing shot. We meet the main characters.

'Roll A001 Scene 6 Take 1a. Mark it!'

The figure on screen moved slowly through a gate, hesitated, then turned into the narrow pathway lined with high metal fences. The shaky video was handheld; someone was following close behind. It was real and intimate. The first few dailies were always nerve-racking to watch; it was the earliest impression of how the film would look and feel. Max liked what he saw. Karine Mickelsen wasn't a multi-award-winning director for nothing. The shot was dripping with atmosphere.

The frame panned up slowly into the face of a boy wearing a dark-green hoodie. There was just a glimpse of his profile as he glanced furtively over his shoulder; he was carrying something heavy slung over his back. A body in a bag, perhaps? The shot suddenly cut to a close-up of his face as he recorded himself. Clever: she must have gained access to his iPhone already. His pace quickened, eyes darting nervously around as the shadow of The Cut swallowed him. He was up to something.

A different angle now, from a distance, higher quality and well framed. The long lens with a narrow field of vision felt like surveillance. This was her master shot. The camera was framed up on a gap between two red-brick houses, a larch lap fence and the footpath that skirted the perimeter of the vast gardens. The frame pushed in close on three figures leaning against the fence at the end of the lane. They were waiting for him. As the shot pulled back wider, the three figures slowly stood up and the boy carrying the body bag halted. The timing was exact, almost robotic, as the three of them moved in perfect synchronicity, barricading his path. It was a stand-off. As he turned away, another form entered the frame from behind. This was an ambush: he had nowhere to turn, he was trapped. The boy dropped what he was carrying and braced himself.

Max already knew what was coming. He paused the film and made a note.

At 5.36 remove 10 frames, consider delaying the reveal for more impact.

The close-up selfie on Nathan's iPhone suddenly whipped around as the three boys charged at him out of the shadows in a sudden flurry of movement. From afar, it was like a pack of wolves devouring their prey: fists flew and clothing was ripped apart.

The handwriting on the notepad became scrawled and shaky.

Use a 90-degree lens effect here, if possible, for maximum dynamic.

Max breathed deeply, trying to steady himself. The fight was brutal.

A harrowing scream ripped through the silence. The kid was getting beaten black and blue. Max was used to all kinds of blood and gore; it was the currency of the horror genre, but this was savage. Kids against kids. It sent a wave of nausea through him. The shot pulled back to the master and faded out to the sound of boots thudding against flesh, accompanied by the screams of pain. The screen dissolved to black.

'Dada?' He was hearing things. He rubbed his eyes, inhaled deeply and tried to focus.

The second assembly began in the same way: 'Roll A004 Scene 6 Take 2. Mark it!'

The time code ran down and the screen faded up to the same path and the silhouette of Nathan in the distance. It was the same scene but from a different point of view and this time the boys waiting in the dark had weapons. Fingers closed on the handle of a baseball bat as the camera travelled at speed towards Nate, chasing behind the three thugs as they pounced. Jump cuts now into close-up shots of boots kicking into ribs and knuckles on a crowbar as it swung high in the air, about to descend with force and smash into his skull.

'Dada? NO!'

Max hit pause and the screen froze on that terrified screaming face. The image was bleached out by the stark light bleeding from the open door.

'Charlie, what are you doing up?'

'What's happening to him?' Charlie was trembling, as if awoken from a nightmare. Max stood up and gathered his son into his arms. 'It's OK, Chol. It's just a film. Something Dada's working on.'

'Don't let them hurt him.' Charlie's tiny balled fists screwed into sleepy eyes.

Max carried his son up to his room and tucked him in, popping Sonic the Hedgehog under his arm. He stood by the bed for a moment, watching over him. Kids were like sponges at this age, vulnerable and open, listening to everything and absorbing the smallest of details. Max flinched as a jolt of nausea surged from his stomach to his throat. The thought of his little boy suffering at the hands of a school bully was frightening. Max knew he had the capacity to kill anyone who dared to lay a finger on his kid. The overwhelming love and protective instincts were strong within him, as fierce as a furnace. Over the years, most of Max's story-telling instincts had been allegories of David and Goliath type battles between good and evil. It was his signature, and this one would be no different.

The scene he had just witnessed was hard to watch. She had thrust the viewer directly into the place of the victim. It was visceral and almost too much to bear.

But this was just the tip of the iceberg.

21

DECEMBER 1993

The School Lane runs left out of the gates at the rear of the building, off the concrete driveway where the buses pull in to Barton Mallet Secondary School. The entire site is contained by a chain-link fence. In the spring, it's covered in bugle vine, Rutland beauty or, by its more common name, 'granny pop out of bed'. When the buds of the white trumpet-shaped flowers are gently squeezed, they leap off the vine and parachute to the ground. By the end of summer, thousands of them are mulched into the tarmac path. As the lane narrows, the chain-link fence turns into high wooden panels of larch lap, which border the gardens closest to the school. The Cut is a dark footpath that slips between the detached residential houses with their posh conservatories and water features.

Midway down is a sharp bend that makes it impossible to see one end from the other. A huge horse chestnut tree marks the halfway point; its roots have pushed through the tarmac and broken the fence. Later in the year, around late September, some of the seeds from the tree fall on to the pathway, but the rest tumble into a vast overgrown garden. For the best conkers, the local kids have to knock on the door and receive rations from an orange bucket, meted out from the gnarled hands of the Conker Lady. They would be baked, vinegared, varnished and drilled, then strung on to shoelaces to become champion Six-ers that would annihilate One-rs into broken 'stampsies', crushed on the ground. But now the early frost of December has killed everything, ready for renewal when the spring comes.

Mark Cherry lets his hand xylophone along the chain link, making sure to stay tight to the left-hand side just in case they're there. They usually are. There is another way home, but it's heads or tails as to which one he risks. A broken nose on the toss of a coin. There is a smell of musty damp wood from mildew at the bottom of the fence. An ombré of moss green to silver-grey as it reaches the top is illuminated by the amber glow of a golden Christmas bell strung up to the streetlamp by the entrance. Another lamp at the sharp-angled turn has been smashed, plunging the passage into darkness. Mark's heartbeat quickens and his eyes take a few seconds to adjust. His footsteps slow as the shadows and shapes come into focus. His fingertips ripple across layers of splintered wood and he hoists the leather strap of his cello over his back, pulling it in tight. His eyes find the small, concealed gap in the fence as he approaches the turn, his potential escape route. As he reaches the corner, he pauses momentarily, peeping round. The coast is clear. He holds his breath, then hastens towards the light. Then he hears the footsteps behind him. Heads it is.

Every time Mark used The Cut, they would find him. The beatings were all too frequent and yet Mark still took a gamble on which would be the safest way home. Maybe he was willing them to finally finish him off. In his restless dreams they left him for dead, and he'd look down from heaven at his own funeral to see if the bullies were sorry for what they had done, straining to find a glimmer of remorse on their faces.

Mark turns his head to glance back, but the bend of The Cut obscures his vision. A shadow appears, stretching out of the darkness as the person behind him quickens his stride. Mark's head whips back to the sharp point of light and he runs for his life.

As he tries to make his escape, two black silhouettes calmly step out of the shadows and bar the way. They're holding baseball bats, the manifestation of his worst nightmare. Mark can't breathe, his feet skid to a stop on the damp tarmac. So near yet so far. He slinks deep into the shadow of the fence, wishing it would wrap around him, concealing him from sight. The figures stand still and wait. Mark's hands reach up to try and climb the fence, but the slimy wood is too slippery, his fingers catch on splinters and his feet can't find purchase. He crouches down and gathers himself for a second, head spinning. It will be another beating for sure, and in the dark they don't know how hard they kick and punch. They don't care. He slowly begins to walk towards his fate, legs quivering with fear and his head so light he might pass out. A sudden rush from behind and his cello is snatched from his back. It's Chris Davis; he can smell the body odour.

His bag is yanked, the strap cutting into his neck as it's torn free and flung over the fence into the Conker Lady's garden. Like predators about to pounce, there is a breathless pause, a gathering. The first kick slams into Mark's ribs as he scuttles sideways, pressing himself into the fence, instinctively protecting his face. Other feet and fists are winding up to strike and Mark braces himself.

A sudden burst of white light explodes out of the darkness: the headlamps of a car. A miracle. The attackers scatter like rats. Chris Davis launches himself over the fence, the other two barge past and run back towards the school. He can't see their faces in the dark, but the sister, Lynette, and Dave would be the usual suspects. Mark covers his eyes from the glare. Maybe it's his dad but, in a way, that might be worse. The high beam dims and the engine cuts out. A door slams, then a voice.

'Come on, Marcello, hop in.'

A figure stands, like a Messiah, back-lit in a halo of light, mist rising off the silhouette like smoke from fire. Epic.

Mark looks over to the garden; his books are strewn across the muddy lawn. 'I need to . . .'

'I'll get it.' Ben's hands reach for the top of the fence, and he is over like a cat. A few seconds later, Mark's bag flies back through the air, hitting him on the head, spilling the contents over the pathway. By the time he's scrambled to pick up his books, a pair of brogued feet are standing next to him. Mark looks up into Ben's smiling face, holding his cello out towards him. 'Wanna lift?'

'Why are you being nice to me? I thought . . .' Mark swallows down the rest of the sentence as Ben jogs to the passenger side and opens the door for Mark, gesturing like a footman.

'Get in, I want to talk to you.'

Mark settles into the passenger seat, gripping his instrument between his legs. He can hear loose wood rattling inside the case. Broken again.

Mark glances over to Ben. 'You're not supposed to be driving.'

'Shut it, Marcello.'

The engine fires up and Ben swings a U-turn. He floors the accelerator but still the car crawls up Forest Hill at a snail's pace.

'So . . .' Ben's nervous, he crunches the gears.

'So?' Mark can smell his aftershave, his heart thumps hard in his chest. What does Ben Knot want with him?

'I need a favour.' Ben glances to the rear-view.

Mark tries not to stare at him through the dark glass of the windscreen. He focuses on Ben's knuckles holding the steering wheel.

'You're good friends with Catherine Maddock, right?'

'Er . . . I guess.'

'Well, I've got a problem.' Ben's fingers grip the wheel tighter. 'I need you to . . . big me up.'

'How d'ya mean?' Mark chews on his lips and turns his head.

Ben runs a hand through his hair, frustrated. 'Put in a good word for me, with Old Farmer John.'

'Oh, I see.' Mark's stomach begins to sink.

'I want to go out with Annie properly, but Annie's dad hates me.' Forest Hill has turned into Albert Rise and Ben crunches the gear as Mark's street draws close.

'Is your dad doing OK?' The question comes out of the blue.

Ben slows to a stop just at the corner of Mark's road, the car bucks and the engine stalls. He switches off the ignition and turns to him. 'Not doing so good, mate.' The streetlamp casts over the lower half of Ben's face as he exhales, his moist eyes hidden in shadow.

'I'm sorry.' There is so much to say but Mark doesn't know how. 'If there is anything I can do . . .' He can't look at him and reaches for the door handle. 'Thanks for the lift.'

A hand reaches over and touches his shoulder. Fingers slide across Mark's back, pulling him in for a buddy hug. Static electricity snaps across his neck with a jolt.

'Easy there, jumpy.' Ben removes his arm. 'Just put in a good word for me with Mr Maddock, that's what you can do.'

Mark waits for a few more seconds, paralysed by Ben's touch. A combination of terror and desire. There is a shriek from a fox in a neighbouring garden.

'And in return, I'll call them off. The gang. They'll leave you alone if I tell them.' Ben's arm retracts and a cold breeze from the open door hits them both.

Was it as simple as that? 'Really?' Mark's eyes meet Ben's.

'Only if you do what I'm asking. Otherwise . . .' He shrugs. 'Not much I can do about them.'

There is some kind of pact between them now, a bond. Mark has seen into Ben's world; he has witnessed his vulnerability, and now Ben is about to lean on Mark for something he wants. In a reversal of fortune, Ben suddenly needs him.

Mark had fantasised about this. An impossible utopia, in which he and Ben are friends; or closer than friends, perhaps. Mark's imagination was a place he could disappear in, a place he often vanished to. His books, his artwork and music helped him to exorcise some of his demons, but there was a deeper level of contemplation where he found solace. Sometimes his dreams were so real it was hard for him to distinguish fantasy from reality.

But in that electrifying touch, in that squeeze of friendship to his shoulder, there had been something real. The glimmer of possibility.

22

DECEMBER 2023

Ben stood in the shower, letting the hot water cascade down over his thinning crown. He turned the heat to maximum, blasting the jet into the base of his aching spine.

'DAD . . . Come on! LET'S GO!' Lily was clattering around in the kitchen. The relentless jingle of Mariah Carey's 'All I Want for Christmas Is You' floated up the stairs to torment him.

Ben turned off the water and threw on a towelling robe, too lazy to dry himself; whacked some deodorant under his wet pits and took a mouthful of Listerine. He stood for a second on the threshold of the en-suite, stared at the unmade bed and searched his brain for where he was supposed to be going with Lily. For the life of him, he couldn't remember. Sleep had eluded him in recent months. He'd been jolting awake in drenched sheets to the sound of shattering glass as Russian gangsters in motorcycle helmets swarmed his house in the middle of the night. Dave crawling up the stairs from the basement door like a monstrous chimera emerging from the mouth of hell. He couldn't take the tossing and turning anymore and had finally resorted to Zopiclone, which left him with a metallic taste in his mouth and a blurred reality, like a video with out of sync dialogue.

'ON MY WAY!' Come on, Ben, snap out of it. He drifted into the bedroom and rubbed his face vigorously with his fingers to wake himself up, dropped his robe and stood in the middle of the room, naked and bewildered.

Downstairs, Dani wandered into the kitchen, mules clattering on the polished concrete floor. Nate was slumped on the floor in the den under a makeshift tent consisting of a cashmere throw from the sofa and a clothes airer. The curtains were drawn and the room was in darkness. Lily was sitting cross-legged on a bean bag, with a tablet open on her lap, the light from the screen illuminating her face in an eerie glow as she read.

'Say it again slowly.' Nate poked his head out from the makeshift tent.

'"Sod off!" The heel of a foot donkey-kicks him in the ribs. "Keep your hands to yourself, faggot."'

'LILY . . . language!' Dani was pouring coffee from a cafetière.

'What?' She huffed in annoyance. 'It's what it says in the script. I'm testing Austin Butler here on his lines.' She yawned and picked at the scab on her shin.

'Shut up . . . just read it.' Nate was sitting up now. He threw a bag of Haribo at his sister.

'Bribery will get you everywhere.' Lily stuffed a sour snake into her mouth and continued. 'E.X.T. Campsite. Night . . . What does E.X.T. mean?' She screwed up her face.

'Exterior, as in outside . . . idiot.' Nate tried to get into character, lying flat on his side listening to the imaginary howling wind, half of his face buried into the carpet. 'It's a camping trip to the Brecon Beacons. There's a wild animal in the forest . . . or at least that's what they think it is, but I think it's a werewolf. Karine says it's like that scene in A Quiet Place . . . if they hear you, they hunt you. Come on, I need to know these lines.' Nate pleaded.

'It just says "heavy breathing" and "he screams". It's not exactly Shakespeare.' Lily picked the remains of a Gummy Bear from her teeth.

'Give it me.' Nate tried to swipe the tablet, but Lily kept it at arm's length. She rolled off the bean bag and crouched on the floor, commando style, face-to-face with Nate. She continued, her voice intoning a suspenseful whisper.

'The patter on the tight canopy overhead is like fingertips on a drum skin. Outside, sheet lightning illuminates the boughs of a tree.' Lily glanced up for a second, a terrified expression on her face. 'Jagged shadows of branchy limbs reaching out across the sky, their nails scratching at the door.'

'ROOAARRAAGGHH!' Dani pounced on Nate from behind with an almighty growl, decimating the makeshift rehearsal tent.

'NOOO!' Nate nearly jumped out of his skin, squealing in shock. 'GET OFF ME! HELP! DAD!'

Upstairs, Ben heard the commotion coming from the den. His heart leapt into his mouth. Someone had broken in, someone was attacking his family. He threw himself down the stairs and turned the corner. He skidded into the kitchen, scrambling towards the worktop. Grabbing a carving knife from the block, he bolted into the darkened den.

'GET OFF HIM! LEAVE THEM ALONE!'

The chaos of the violent struggle suddenly broke apart.

Lily and Dani were rolling around on the floor in stitches as Nate tried to cover the fact that he had nearly peed himself laughing. Lily spluttered, 'Yeah, Dad . . . that's exactly what he says in the script. You know the lines better than Nate.'

Ben panted heavily, catching his breath. His face was white and his hands trembled. 'What the hell are you doing?'

Dani's eyes fell on the knife in Ben's hand. 'We're only playing around, love.'

'Christ . . . I thought there was an intruder.' Ben was hyperventilating. 'You scared the life out of me.'

His family stared at him, the smiles disappearing from their faces. Nate gathered himself up and draped the throw over the sofa, while Dani packed away the rest.

'Chill out, Dad.' Lily breezed by him to get her coat. 'It's just a rehearsal for the film. Exterior. Night. Some scary camping trip that Nate's shooting tomorrow . . . Can we go now, please?'

Ben stood staring at Nate in silence. He didn't move, he didn't breathe. An overwhelming need to cocoon his children washed over him.

'You look like you've seen a ghost.' Dani fussed past Ben. 'Come on, snap out of it, love. We've got guests,' she muttered under her breath. 'Don't want Karine to think you're a nutcase.'

'Well, this is all very exciting.' Ben turned to see Karine standing in the hallway. Had she been here this whole time?

'Can you show me down to . . . wherever your Wi-Fi and service board is?' She glanced down to Ben's hand. He tucked the knife behind his leg and hesitated, before moving tentatively towards the kitchen. He carefully replaced the long blade into the block and headed into the hallway. His hands were still shaking as he tried to fit the key into the lock of the basement door.

'Er . . . how long are you going to be? I have a work call in twenty minutes.'

'Wait. Dad . . . I thought we were going to Palmers to get a Christmas tree?' Lily interjected.

'Yeah . . . well, after my work call. It's important.' Ben shifted uncomfortably.

'It's Saturday . . .' Lily slumped back angrily on to one of the kitchen bar stools.

'Not now, Lily!' Ben snapped.

Dani and Lily exchanged a look as Karine defused the tension. 'I won't be long, I just need to run a few extra cables to video village, then I'll be out of your hair.'

Ben paused for a second at the top of the stairs to the basement. 'Fine, just give me a minute to tidy up a few things.' The door banged behind him.

Karine's eyes narrowed before turning back to the sulking teenager at the kitchen island. 'Hey, you're a really convincing actor, Lily . . . Do you want to be in the film? We need some female energy.'

Lily's face flushed and she pulled her hood over her head. 'Nah, that's Nate's thing.'

'Well, let me know if you change your mind.' Karine smiled at Dani, who had been frantically nudging Lily to say yes.

'Nate's been so secretive about the whole thing. I'm dying to know what you've been up to the last few weeks.' Dani leant in conspiratorially.

'He's doing great. He's a natural performer.' Karine winked at Dani. 'But we will need one or two night shoots, if that's OK with you and Ben?'

Something in Lily switched at the sound of Karine's praise and the idea of some exhilarating nightlife, anything to alleviate her teenage boredom and get out of the house. 'All right then . . . I'll give it a go.' The sibling rivalry overrode her reticence.

'Amazing! Just out of interest . . . are you a good swimmer?'

'She'd give Tom Daley a run for his money.' Dani was nodding encouragingly at Lily.

'He's a diver, love.' Ben was holding open the basement door for Karine with a face like thunder.

'Diving works for me.' Karine's eyes met Ben's as she descended the stairs into the darkness. He watched her go, then turned to

Dani, who was silently fist-bumping Lily by the door. Her new career as 'momager' appeared to be in full swing.

Ben stood at the top of the stairs, monitoring Karine's every move. He really didn't want anyone down there rooting through his private things, not right now with everything going on at work. And the timing of this film was making him feel uneasy. As Karine plunged into the darkness, Ben took one step down and gently closed the door behind him. He watched as she fumbled with her iPhone, trying to find the torch.

His hand hovered over the light switch but he decided to leave her in darkness. He watched as she shone the torch into the corners of the gloomy space. The light passed over the steel shelves bolted to the stone walls, loaded with crates of fine wine. Ben's collection, an investment of sorts. Several worthless oil paintings and framed prints were filed vertically against a mountain of plastic stacking crates full of junk. There was a pile of old suit-cases and the blue-painted wooden highchair that the little Knots had once sat in, passed down through generations. The silhouette of an old dressmaker's mannequin, propped against the wall in the corner, was draped with an old flea-ridden fur coat.

When they had sold the old house, Ben hadn't thrown a single thing away. It had all just been shoved down here and forgotten about.

Karine's torch light picked up the narrow corridor of Ben's wine cellar and followed the line of shelves into the storage area.

'The router is right behind you, in the service cupboard.'

The basement spluttered into light as Ben finally flicked the switch. Karine jumped and shielded her eyes from the glare of the strip bulbs.

She exhaled sharply. 'Thanks.'

'What exactly is it you need?' Ben took another step down.

Karine opened the metal locker bolted to the wall and held out her phone. 'Just a photo of your set-up for my crew. Ed will sort you out.' Her hand reached out to a large black box, flickering with green light.

'Don't touch that.' Ben's tone caught her by surprise. He softened. 'It's . . . for my work. The house Wi-Fi runs from a different system.'

She pocketed her phone. 'OK, I'll let the boys know.'

Ben noticed her eyes scan the basement again. He didn't trust her and needed to keep a tight grip on this. He was standing on thinning ice, the ominous creak of his fate about to shatter everything; unable to do anything about it, except fall. Ben stood his ground as Karine got closer.

'Before you do any more filming, I'm going to need to see this . . . deal.' He made air quotes with his fingers. 'You know what I'm talking about.' His phone vibrated in his back pocket. He looked at the screen. 'I have to take this.'

She smiled awkwardly at him. 'Then I'll get out of your hair.'

'I need the contract or I'm pulling the plug . . . You understand me?'

Karine nodded as Ben stepped out of the way, opened the door and permitted her to leave.

'Dad, come on, let's go.'

Ben left the basement, closing the door firmly behind him, and answered his phone.

'Lars?'

'What the fuck, Ben? The FSA are here at the office, they're confiscating everyone's computers.' His voice was a hissed whisper. He was clearly rattled.

'Listen . . .' Ben headed outside after Lily, halting on the threshold of the house. 'I'm gonna need to call you back, Lars.'

'Ben, don't hang up . . .' Ben killed the call and froze. A motor-bike was speeding off around the corner on to Barton Rise; the rider was wearing a matt-black crash helmet. It was the same one he had seen in the rear-view mirror, the one that had been follow-ing him and run him off the road.

His phone buzzed: a text from Lars.

What the hell have you done?

23

DECEMBER 2023

There was nothing unusual about the wall of photographs stuck to the whiteboard in lines with tiny magnets. On each photo, a black Sharpie had scribbled a date and time code. In tiny writing was a description, a 'headline', of what was happening and why. To the everyday person, it might have seemed obsessive. It was like the quintessential scene in a police procedural with the map and the red string, linking all the suspects together with photographs and Post-it notes. Editing a film like this was painstaking. At this point, the narrative was very much in flux. Of course, he knew how it ended, they both did.

The iPhone shots were jumpy and had a feeling of urgency, but the interviews along the found footage would balance the film with a much more grounded tone. The assembly so far was fragmented. It was like placing the corners and then slowly finding the edges of a thousand-piece jigsaw puzzle. There was just a vague outline to begin with, the skeleton of a narrative in which to thrust the cast of characters, waiting to find their place in the big picture. It would all climax into some CGI bloodbath but that would come later.

Max took a beat, then pulled up a shot from his Dropbox that Mickelsen had sent over.

The clapper board loaded. 'Roll A005 Scene 240 Take 7. Mark it.'

On screen, the surface of a dark river, splattering in the driving rain, reflected the quivering chimney stack of Blackstone Mill, casting a long shadow across the cascading water to the riverbank. Max clenched his jaw. He exhaled, gathering himself, then paused the roll, zooming in closer. He wrote a note on the side bar.

We'll need a stunt rider and incorporate a POV drone shot. Wide and high.

The door to the basement cutting room cracked open, spilling light into the den, and the padding of Cocoa's feet on the concrete pulled Max out of his work. Charlie chased close behind.

'Dada, can Cocoa and me go in the sprinklers?' Charlie had anticipated a 'yes' by changing into a pair of yellow swim shorts with pineapples and bananas printed all over them. He was wearing snorkel goggles with the air pipe dangling from the side of his ear as he stuffed a whole Reese's Peanut Butter Cup into his mouth.

Max laughed out loud. 'All right, Jacques Cousteau, how deep do you think you're going?'

Charlie was staring at the screen.

'What's that?'

'It's a weir.' Max held his arm out to Charlie, offering a cuddle.

'What's weird about it?' Charlie looked confused and Cocoa trotted over to lick his hand.

Max chuckled. 'Well . . . it's all covered with slippy green slime and it's really deep.' He bent down to tickle Charlie, picking him up and holding him tight as his skinny body squirmed and wriggled in his arms. Charlie leant into Max's neck.

'Can we pleeeaaase go in the pool?' The puppy-dog eyes from both his son and an actual puppy dog were impossible to say no to.

'You'll have to be quick. Papa'll be here soon.'

Charlie slipped out of Max's arms and sprinted up the stairs, Cocoa haring after him. Max grabbed a towel from the hall cupboard on the way up, before hearing the splash into the deep end. His stomach lurched. Somewhere in the back of his mind, an old fear resurfaced. Deep water, dark and murky. His knees softened slightly and his feet tingled on the polished porcelain floor. He paused for a second, waiting to hear laughter, but there was only silence, then Cocoa started barking uncharacteristically.

'Charlie?' Max raced up the stairs, almost slipping face down on the stone steps. Cocoa was racing round and round the pool in an absolute frenzy, barking at the surface, back and forth.

Charlie was face down in the middle of the pool. Max ran over as Cocoa dived into the water and swam towards the body now sinking to the bottom.

'Charlie!'

As Max reached the water's edge, Charlie suddenly exploded up out of the water between a giant inflatable flamingo and a slice of watermelon.

'I found buried treasure.' He spat out a mouthful of water and lifted his goggles, holding something aloft. The pair of yellow swim shorts he had been wearing, helicoptered over his head, spraying Max with water. Charlie was laughing his head off. Max closed his eyes and exhaled, allowing himself to get drenched in the spray and smiling in relief.

They were abruptly interrupted by the honk of Brandon's car horn. 'Quick, come on. Papa's here. Go on in and dry off.' Charlie scuttled out of the water naked, trying to get one foot into his shorts, hopping around on the other. 'Charlie, please stop messing around, you'll get me into trouble!'

'Having fun?'

Max turned, water dripping from his face and staining his white linen shirt and shorts with huge transparent blotches. Brandon, with a face like thunder and a tone to match, was checking his watch. He dumped a huge box of See's Candies down on to the table.

Max smiled. 'California brittle . . . you remembered.' He stared at the box.

'Happy Christmas. Don't eat them all at once.' For all the heartache between them, there was always room for a thoughtful gesture.

'Don't stress. We're all packed, he just wanted to cool off.' Cocoa came running up to nuzzle Brandon, then returned to Max's side, where he proceeded to shake himself dry in a double drench. Brandon's face cracked a smile, he just couldn't help it. Max was surrounded by the kind of chaos that made him want to throw his arms around his ex-husband and chuck him into the pool. They both started laughing.

A dripping wet Charlie, wrapped in a fluffy white towel, tiptoed inside. 'I'm ready. I'm ready . . . promise . . . please don't be mad.' He disappeared up to his bedroom.

'He'll be at least half an hour drying his hair.' Max glanced up to Charlie's bedroom.

'Like father, like son.' Brandon smirked. He was all open-necked plaid shirt and cowboy boots.

'Wanna beer?' Max headed inside.

'Driving.' Brandon wet his mouth at the prospect and glanced down at Max's butt in damp shorts as he passed.

'One won't hurt.' Max was at the fridge, two bottles of Stella Artois in his hand.

'Still drinking that European crap?' Brandon took the offering and cracked the top open on the door latch.

'Tell me again where you're taking Charlie on holiday?' Max swigged his beer.

'Italy.' Brandon put the bottle to his mouth.

'So . . . you gonna eat Jack in the Box and drink Bud Light all trip then?' Max ran his tongue over his teeth, grinning.

Brandon, for all his masculine bravado, was a shy country boy at heart. He fingered the St Christopher on the silver chain around his neck. 'You could still come, you know. There's "room at the inn"?' He reddened – that was really hard to admit. 'All that fresh powder and Bombardino on tap . . .'

Max was silent for a second. There was just the shiver of a moment between them when Brandon thought he was going to say yes, like a tear in silk.

'Skiing? With my knees? . . . Nah, too much work on.' Max glanced over to the stairs where Charlie was dragging a Spider-Man wheelie bag, clattering down the steps.

'What have you got in there? The kitchen sink?' Max ruffled Charlie's hair and kissed his head.

'Huh? No, just my boots, my helmet . . . and my Xbox, and my presents and . . .'

Brandon nearly spat out his beer. Both of them burst out laughing.

'Good luck with that excess baggage.' Max slapped Brandon on the shoulder and they headed out to the driveway for the farewells.

Charlie was all strapped in; the Xbox had been secretly extracted and left in the trunk of the '75 Mustang. Max and Cocoa came around to the driver's side to see them both off.

'Will Santa Claus be able to find me up the mountain?' Charlie's red teeth were stuck together with a Twizzler.

'Hell yeah! We sent him the address already.' Brandon fired up the engine and hid his eyes under a pair of sleek Ray-Bans. 'Hey . . . Don't get so busy with the past that you miss the present.' Brandon's parting shot was like a punch in the gut.

'What do you mean?' Max smiled at him, a smile that kept a brave face to the world.

'I've been paying attention, babe.' Brandon hadn't called him that in a long time. 'I just wish you'd pay a little more attention over here.' Max glanced at Charlie, who was fiddling with the stereo. Brandon leant out of the window and lowered his shades. 'Still havin' nightmares?'

'I produce horror movies . . . babe.' It was sharper and more sarcastic than he'd meant it to be, and he instantly regretted it. 'I'm dealing with it.'

'Sure you are.' Brandon pulled his baseball cap down over his eyes.

Max followed Brandon's car down the drive, bending into the window, smiling at Charlie. 'Stay on the piste . . . no daredevil stuff.'

Max stood at the end of the path, watching the blue Mustang disappear around the corner, Charlie waving frantically out of the rear windshield. And they were gone.

Max stared at the empty road and shook his head.

'I am dealing with it.'

24

CHRISTMAS 2023

Midnight mass had always been a bit of a chore to Ben Knot. As a kid, he resented being dragged out into the frosty night at 11.45 p.m. when all he wanted was to lie in bed, guarding the empty pillowcase that was hanging from the knob of his chest of drawers and waiting to be filled by Father Christmas. But Marian was raised a Christian and out of love for her, Anthony Knot would get them all bundled up in duffel coats, hats and scarves and insist they all head to St James's. In those days, the church congregation was a healthy smattering of devout locals and some who came from the surrounding villages. The handsome young priest, Father Allen, was a big draw. He was a fun and optimistic minister, who decorated the ancient whitewashed chapel with colourful tinsel and a huge tree by the altar. There was always a mince pie and a cup of mulled wine after the service, but it was his Christmas message of peace and goodwill, with a couple of jokes thrown in, that left a lasting impression.

Even though he hated it as a child, there was something in Ben that had made him carry on this tradition, even after he'd moved away. It's what families did at Christmas. So, that Christmas Eve, they walked in the pitch dark from Fosse Grove along Barton Road, feet crunching through the frosted grass of the verge, the twinkling lights from the trees guiding the way. Most families didn't bother with church anymore, but one or two hunched silhouettes gravitated towards the warm glow emanating from the stained-glass windows and the single bell chiming out the call to mass.

Ben sidled into the pew next to Dani, who was all wrapped up in faux fur. Nate was hunched grumpily over a hymn book, turning down the corners of the pages, while Lily filmed selfies to prove she was actually there, 'at frikkin midnight, y'all'.

There were very few people in the church, but old Father Allen, in his dotage bearing a vague resemblance to Gandalf, kicked off the proceedings. The chapel was unchanged, stark and simple. There was no heating and it felt colder in here than outside in the subzero night. Ben's eyes were blurred with wine and dazzled by the candlelight. He exhaled deeply. Two withered figures, well into their late eighties, were sitting in their place alone at the front. As usual, they were respectfully left in peace, aside from a whispered conversation and a friendly squeeze on the arm from Father A. This would be a difficult Christmas for them both. Their daughter's killer was about to be released from prison. Ben could see his cold breath trembling in the air as they sang, but something inside him became that child again. He gripped Dani's arm and pulled her in tight.

The candlelit service was as charming as it had ever been, the darkened church austere yet magical at the same time. As the organ piped up the introduction to 'Silent Night', the door at the back of the nave creaked open and a gust of cold air licked across the flagstones. Ben turned mid-verse.

Round yon Virgin, Mother and Child

All alone, a man had slid into one of the pews at the back, trying not to be seen. He kept his head down and, with hunched shoulders, removed the flat cap he was wearing. His eyes were cast to the floor, but he picked up the hymn book and began to sing along with the congregation. As the carol came to an end, and Father Allen once again took his place at the lectern, Ben glanced back a second time and his eyes met those of Dr Sandeep

Patel. They stared at each other for a second and Ben's stomach hollowed out. Sandeep looked like the shell of a man, thin and gaunt, his few wisps of white hair combed across his bald head.

Ben nodded his head in acknowledgement, as Father Allen began the 'in memoriam' of those who had died.

After the communion was taken and the collection bag passed around, Christmas morning was welcomed in with 'Oh Come, All Ye Faithful', and the service was over. Ben looked for Sandeep, but he had gone. Dani was in a deep conversation with Margaret Carson, leaning on the font under the portico, a cup of mulled wine in her hand. Ben agreed Lily and Nate could walk home ahead of them, while he waited for Dani. He grabbed a mince pie and stared vacantly at the congregation bulletin board.

'Bold of you . . . showing your face here.' A brittle-throated voice behind him. 'Bit brazen, isn't it?' The Derbyshire accent was still strong.

Ben turned. 'John?'

'Mr Maddock to you, son.' John Maddock gripped his wife's arm.

'Mrs Maddock . . .' Ben smiled at her.

'She won't remember you.' John kissed his wife's head. 'Barely knows who I am anymore.'

The lights on the Christmas tree were extinguished and the nave was plunged into shadows. The room was suddenly so cold they could see their breath.

'Happy Christmas.' Ben held out his hand to shake but the old farmer stared at it and kept his deep in his pocket.

'I don't think it's right . . . this film being made . . . it's not right.' John pushed past him.

'The film? Nate's film?' Ben was rooted to the spot.

'The whole village knows what it's about . . . it's not right.' John dabbed his wet eyes.

'What are you talking about?'

John took his wife's arm and muttered under his breath as he left.

On the walk home, over the glass of sherry before bed and even into his dreams that night, Ben tried to understand what John Maddock had been referring to, struggling to shake off that haunted look etched on to the old man's face. Why would John Maddock be upset about the film Nate was making? What the hell was going on?

A sharp pain wrenched at his chest. Ben gripped his sternum and tried to breathe.

That one was real.

25

CHRISTMAS 1993

On Christmas morning, Mark Cherry wakes and wiggles his toes, searching for the stocking propped at the foot of his bed. It sags, completely empty, and his heart sinks. The Cherrys aren't poor, there is always food on the table, but every penny of housekeeping is accounted for. Green Shield Stamps were saved year-round for the Christmas bills and all year, Mark would flick through the Argos catalogue, turning down the corners, dropping hints to his mum.

Mark is downstairs at the crack of dawn. Standing in the lounge doorway, he looks over to the Christmas tree. A suspiciously shaped present is leaning in the corner, half obscured by tinsel and baubles. He stares at it, his heart close to bursting. He sits patiently waiting until his parents finally come downstairs. He sits through breakfast, through *Tops of the Pops* and *Carols from King's*, eyes flicking between the screen and the plastic Christmas tree. When lunch is over, everyone sits round as Mark gently removes the wrapping paper, revealing the varnished auburn woodgrain, the elegant Baroque curve of the neck and the pale carved wooden bridge of the German Stentor cello. He can hardly breathe.

'Don't you like it, son?' His dad glances up from the *Radio Times*, under his glasses. Mark can't answer, he's choking back the tears that are threatening to come. His mum bustles off into the kitchen to fetch tea and mince pies. As the bags are dunked into the hot water, she feels two arms slide around her waist and a head snuggle into her back. She pats his hand, embarrassed to show him the tears rolling down her face. She knows so much about Mark that can never be spoken. Mrs Cherry was so worried about her son, but the only balm she knew was love. She'd sat with him on the stool in the kitchen and held cotton wool to his bleeding nose, she'd stroked his head in the early hours when he'd cried out with another night terror.

She knows him better than he knows himself, but they can never talk about it, they both have to pretend everything is OK, that everything is normal. That he is 'normal'. So, when she touches Mark's heart, like she has this Christmas morning, it is almost too much to bear.

After it happened, Mark Cherry had spent some time in Hayes Hospital. 'Rehabilitation', they had called it. Then he was packed off to boarding school. He had always attributed his complicated, almost reclusive nature to that time when he had left home at the age of fourteen, never to return.

But that child had been the father of the man.

Max Crow stood alone in his vast open-plan living room. The twelve-foot Christmas tree, tastefully decorated with plain lights and tartan ribbons, left him feeling empty. It was Brandon's year to have Charlie to himself. Last year, Max had taken him to the Hollywood Methodist on Franklin for the family evening concert, and they'd spent Christmas Eve cuddled up under a blanket watching *Home Alone* and munching on Celebrations decanted into an old tin from his childhood home. He wished he'd taken up Brandon's offer, jumped into the back of the Mustang and stowed away with them both to Italy, but their lives had become far too complicated for that.

The Sinatra Christmas Spotify playlist had looped its way back to 'The First Noel'. Max tapped his iPhone to turn it off and stood in the silence, feeling the emptiness in his stomach. Cocoa, asleep on his bed, didn't stir. The multiple WhatsApp pictures of Charlie and Brandon having a ball pelting down the Mottolino Valley at Teola faded up and out on the digital picture frame propped up against the grand piano. Max poured himself another drink, a Hendrick's and tonic, and slid open the huge glass door. The night air was cool and the fairy lights slung across the garden fence reflected in the still water of the swimming pool. Every now and then waves of loneliness would swarm out of the dark, like tentacles reaching from the past to grab hold of his heart and twist hard. He loved solitude but hated being alone.

Max breathed in deep, holding back a wave of sadness. He knew the remedy; his solace was hidden in the darkest recess of the room. A velvet blackout drape was obscuring the thing he was seeking. He walked over to the piano and drew back the curtain to reveal the instrument that was propped in the corner, facing the wall. He gently clasped the neck of the old German Stentor cello and spun it gently on its pin. He caressed his thumb across the four strings. It was out of tune. He sat on the piano stool and lifted the lid to the keyboard and softly played the A, then the D, the G and finally the C notes, tuning his beloved instrument. He lifted the bow, remembering how to spread his fingers and place his thumb. He paused for a second, awash with the memory of tearing away the wrapping paper to reveal the varnished walnut. He rested the horsehair on the string and, as if his best friend Catherine Maddock was right there by his side, he began to play.

Out in the garden, the sultry sound of Mark Cherry's cello drifted up and out into the LA night.

26

FEBRUARY 1994

'Mum, I'm only going for four days.' Annie glances up to the rear window of the coach, where a seat is waiting for her. The coach is already packed with sleepy students for their 5 a.m. departure for Wales.

John Maddock has his eye fixed on Ben, whose face is pressed to the window of the back seat. Ben was hoping that Annie's dad would have warmed to him by now, but it hasn't happened; he's as cold as ever. Marcello was supposed to have put in a good word. The little shit has let him down. Mr Maddock still sees him as nothing more than a bad influence on his little girl; he'll never be good enough for her.

'Please be careful, sweetheart.' Annie's mum cups her face. 'You know what I'm talking about.' She looks to Catherine, who stares at her shoes, reddening.

'Mum . . .' Annie's eyes flick to her dad, who looks away, embarrassed. Then he presses a ten-pound note into her hand. 'Dad, it's too much . . . you can't—'

'It's for both of you, for emergencies. Don't spend it.' Mr Maddock hauls their backpacks into the luggage area under the coach and glances up to the boy sitting on the back seat. There's no one here to see Ben away safely this morning.

The kids pile on the coach with the usual scramble, 'bagsying' their seats with their besties. Mark Cherry is last to get on as usual. He makes his way down the aisle, looking for a place as far away from the trouble-makers as possible. He sees Ben at the back of the bus and acknowledges him with a secret wave, but is met with daggers. He takes his seat alone and rolls his sweater into a pillow, leaning against the window. The coach finally pulls out of the school gates at 5.30 a.m. in the dark, leaving early to avoid the traffic on the A46 as they hit Tewkesbury. It's a slow road over the Welsh border, cutting through the Wye Valley and deep into the wilderness of the Bannau Brycheiniog National Park. The Black Mountains to the west and the famous Pen y Fan to the east will provide the dramatic setting for the challenging four days of camping on the banks of the River Taff.

'If it's good enough for the SAS, it's good enough for Barton Mallet Secondary School.' Ben leans forward across the aisle, passing a bottle of Coke to Annie, who is sitting next to Cat. Girls have to sit next to girls, and boys next to boys. No smoking, no radios and no fumbling under blankets. Those are the rules, although Mr Ashton has been assigned to marshal the trip and he's a pushover. He nodded off just after Solihull, so those silly rules are crying out to be broken.

Lynette Davis has taken off her Doc Martens and has her feet up on her twin brother's headrest, kicking him in the skull. Her Sony Walkman emits a tinny beat of Duran Duran. She's bleached her hair to look like Nick Rhodes and her crispy perm is pulsing in time like a demented chicken. Annie passes the bottle of Coke to Cat, who takes a sip and then passes it down the line until it reaches Lynette, who swigs a mouthful. Chris passes her a packet of sweets over the back of the seat. She opens the Mentos Mints and pops one in her mouth before taking another swig and secretly spitting it into the Coke bottle and holding her hand over the top. She rises from her seat, shaking the bottle vigorously before the whole thing explodes across the coach.

'Take that, ya muvvers!'

'Eeeww!' The screams of protest across the back row wake the whole coach and the driver suddenly brakes. Students tumble off seats and dive for cover as a shower of sticky projectile foam spurts down the aisle, while others hide under blankets, squealing in a riot of jeers and laughter.

'DAVIS!' Mr Ashton is up on his feet and storming towards the back, as the coach slows to a crawl and pulls into a lay-by.

'Sorry, sir, the bottle exploded.' Lynette slumps back into her seat, chewing and smirking to herself.

Mr Ashton glares at her and pulls out a huge roll of paper towel. 'Clean it up.'

'No way, sir.' Lynette tries to disappear into her seat. 'I wouldn't touch their shit with someone else's barge pole, let alone—'

'I SAID clean it up.' Ashton isn't a tyrant, he finds it quite hard to keep a straight face, but he knows exactly who the culprits are as his eyes shift to Chris, who is red-faced and giggling, eyes nearly popping out of his head. 'Both of you.'

'Sir, my seat is soaked.' Annie Maddock is on her feet, wiping her jeans with paper towel.

'She can sit next to me, sir . . . This one's dry.' Ben pats the seat on the back row next to him.

Dave, sitting across from him on the other side of the rear seat, watches intently as Mr Ashton agrees and Annie moves to the one next to Ben. Beaming, Ben wraps his arm around her as she snuggles into his shoulder.

'Cheers, Lynette,' Ben calls through the gap in the seat. He pulls the pillow from behind his neck and props it under Annie's head. Now that the disapproving parents are out of the way, he has her all to himself. The camping trip is off to a cracking start; they are in for the best weekend ever.

Lynette stares open-mouthed and slumps back, pulling on her headphones, as Aerosmith's 'Love in an Elevator' nearly blows her head off.

Unbeknown to any of them, Dave has his camera hidden under his coat and trained on the unfolding events. Peeping between the seats at the conspiratorial antics of the Davis twins, zooming down the aisle to Mark Cherry passing a bag of Black Jacks and Fruit Salads across the aisle to Catherine, and most importantly keeping watch on the lovers in the back seat.

Patel now turns his lens to the window and the pink breaking dawn over the Malvern Hills. 'Shepherd's warning,' he mutters to himself, then notices something in the reflection of the glass. The camera catches Ben and Annie snuggling under the blanket as the sun rises. Dave's stomach lurches, he feels sick, and his face burns hot with jealousy. He zooms in, watching closely. Ben's arm gently slides down Annie's shoulder to her waist, then to her thigh, crossing her leg, reaching for somewhere forbidden. He kisses her sleeping head lovingly, but Annie's body suddenly tenses, she sits upright and pushes Ben's hands off her. She stares at Ben in disgust. Then she shrinks away and slides out from under the blanket. Patel keeps filming through the reflection in the glass, pretending to be asleep.

'Annie . . . wait.' The hissed whisper has no effect. She doesn't want to make a scene, so she quietly moves forward to the centre of the coach and takes the empty seat next to Mark. Her head disappears behind the headrest and Ben pulls the pillow tight into his chest.

Dave's eyelids close as the rocking of the coach lulls him to sleep with a smile on his lips, and they head out into the unknown wilderness of Pen y Fan.

27

JANUARY 2024

'Roll B001 Scene 1 Take 1. Mark it.'

The clapper board snapped closed and lowered out of the frame.

'Where d'ya want me then?' A woman's arm appeared in the shot; she shuffled forward, her back to the camera, one hand clasping a walking stick for balance. Splinters of light through venetian blinds cast a sepia hue over the room and highlighted the face of a drug addict. The hollowed-out cheeks and greasy dyed-red hair with grey roots, tied back into a scraggy ponytail, missing teeth and retracted gums reflected a lifestyle lacking any sense of self-care. Her faded green velour tracksuit and sneakers had seen better days, as had the shady interrogation room in which she was sitting. A scene like this felt like a cliché but it would serve a purpose. The cast of characters was shaping up nicely. It wasn't an audition; she already had the role.

'I want me money first, before I say anything.' Her eyes were unfocused, casting up to the light and then scanning the room. She thrust her hands into the pockets of her stained track pants and hunched her shoulders. She was clearly in pain.

The interviewer took the same tone as before, calm and kind. 'Tell me what you remember about Annabel Maddock.'

There was a pause as Lynette Davis chewed and gurned, her knees jittering with addiction.

'Not much . . . she weren't all that.' Her dry mouth sucked in the air.

'Did you like her?'

'Not really. She were all lardy dah.' The knees calmed to stillness. 'Thought she were it . . . just because of Ben.' Lynette wrinkled her nose as if catching a bad smell.

'They were dating.' It was a statement, not a question.

'Stringing them all along, she was.' Lynette looked straight at the camera. 'She weren't a virgin neither.'

'Really? What makes you think that?' The voice remained calm, while Lynette's legs started fidgeting again.

'She were on the pill. Din't tell her parents.' Her tongue ran around the inside of her drug-blackened teeth. 'He was too good for her.' Her eyes cast down to her dirty sneakers. 'Way out of her league. She were playing 'em both.'

'Both?'

'Patel were sniffin' around her too . . . like flies round shit. Made for each other.' Lynette's tone deepened into resentment.

'And your brother?'

Lynette screwed her face up in confusion. 'Chris? He wouldn't have gone anyway near Little Miss Prissy.'

'But he was a suspect too.' The words were carefully chosen. 'He had to give a DNA sample.'

'Yeah, well, all our class did, the whole school did, the whole village; everyone between thirteen and thirty . . . and not just the boys neither.' She cleared her throat of mucus, muttering under her breath, 'Even Mark Cherry, like that poofter ould have had a go.'

Lynette's laugh was buried under the gravel in her voice.

'I were there. I saw everything. Heard the motorbike, when we was watching the fireworks. He were the only one who had a scrambler . . . rich kid . . .' Her eyes shot to the camera and she cut herself off, tightening the dry lips of her foul mouth. 'Anyway, it's all water under the bridge now.' She snorted at her own private joke, hawking up phlegm, and pulled down her cap, trying to shield her face.

'I've had enough now, just give me the money so I can go.' Lynette was scratching at her arm.

'Just one more question.'

'Fuck's sake.'

'Why did you hate Annabel Maddock so much?'

'Because she were a prick-tease. Thought she were better than me. Thought she were so special. Like she were above everyone else.' Lynette shifted in her seat. 'I don't know what he saw in her. She stank of manure . . . Farm girl.'

It was a ghastly face, racked with the ravages of time and a resentment that had burdened her for thirty years.

Lynette began to cough violently. 'She were asking for it.' Her face reddening, as if the vile words stuck in her throat.

'She were the monster.'

28

FEBRUARY 1994

'Master betrayed us . . . We ought to wring his filthy little neck. Kill him! Kill them both.'

Swaddled deep in a tight claustrophobia of darkness, Mark Cherry's eyes suddenly open with a sharp intake of breath. He claps a hand to his mouth. For a second, he can't remember where he is. He reaches out to touch the wall by the side of his bed, but his fingers find wet canvas.

'Sod off, Cherry.' The heel of Chris Davis's foot donkey-kicks him in the ribs. 'Keep your hands to yourself . . . faggot.' The hissed whisper from the pungent bundle next to him is a stark reminder of exactly where he is.

The door of the tent is half open. Lying still, not daring to move for fear of another kick to the ribs, he listens; cold breath filling the damp air with vapour. A globule of rain runs down the half-stuck zip, pooling in a little indent by the opening, as tiny rivulets of water creep towards his bed. The patter on the tight canopy overhead is like fingertips on a drum skin. Outside, sheet lightning illuminates the boughs of a tree, jagged shadows of branchy limbs reaching out across the sky, their nails scratching at the door.

The campsite is nestled in a small clearing between the Pentwyn Reservoir and the thick woods of Dol-y-Gaer. They'd pitched their tents earlier that day, after the exhausting coach ride, clearing what remained of the snow and hammering tent stakes into frozen earth. Finally, exhausted, they had built a fire and eaten half-cooked sausages and beans heated in a jerry can, cowboy style. Chris Davis had passed around a bottle of dandelion and burdock laced with Bacardi, which had made Mark feel really rough. He'd tried to take away the taste with a mouthful of Colgate, then immediately thrown up.

A low mist had crept from the surface of the lake into their small encampment as the boys and girls had finally retreated to their tents. Pen y Fan was invisible, shrouded in cloud, but its looming presence could be felt. Mark had immediately thought of the Dead Marshes, lying at the foothills of Mount Doom; he'd fallen asleep dreaming of Frodo and Sam and of a creature tied to a tree, wailing at the injustice of his wrongful incarceration.

Under the covers, the illuminated hands of his watch tell him it's 2 a.m., the witching hour. His head is thumping with tiredness and a hangover from the drink. He can hear the snores of the other boys, slowly becoming synchronised, all of them breathing as one. The trickle of water from the door seeps under his sleeping bag, soaking freezing water into his feet. He closes his eyes and tries not to shiver, as the hard, damp ground seems to fold around his shoulders, sucking him down into another troubled sleep.

'BAGGINS!'

The shriek that wakes him the second time sounds exactly like a winged creature of Sauron. Mark sits bolt upright again and listens. Was that screech in his dream or did that come from outside? The rain has stopped now and a gentle wind plays through the trees like notes on a flute, luring him outside into the darkness. Mark eases himself towards the tent door and slowly pulls on the tag of the zip. The cold hand of night presses against his face as he peers through the split canvas opening. His eyes slowly adjust to the reflection of the moon glittering on the surface of the undulating lake. A brief second of clear vision before clouds, moving across the sky, cloak the world into a starless night. There is nothing out there, just the sound of ice lapping against the bank and the scent of grass and manure. Mark inhales deeply. He is about to retreat into the safety of the tent when he spots movement in the woods. Something darting between the trees.

'There's something lurking out there.' Mark glances back. His trembling whisper to the line of snoring bodies gets no response. They are all dead to the world. He worms his way to the edge of the tent. He can't do this alone.

'Ben?' He reaches across to shake the shoulder two doors down, but the bundle of bags and coats stuffing the sack crumples under his touch. Another shriek, similar to the one that woke him the first time, pierces the silence, higher and further away now. Mark freezes, his throat constricted, terrified to his core.

'It's just a fox,' Mark whispers to himself, trying to shore up his courage, 'nothing to worry about.'

His mind is racing as he clambers to his knees, pulling on his damp parka and Wellington boots from the foot of his bed, but as he slowly peels back the tent flaps and eases himself out into the damp air, his heart begins to pound. There is something wrong. He can feel it. There is something in the forest.

A flicker of light in the distance burns bright for a second and then vanishes. There is now just an impenetrable wall of black at the edge of the woods, but as Mark emerges the cloud cloaking the sky eases away like a curtain to reveal two figures perched on the picnic bench by the shore of the lake. Moonlight brushes arms and shoulders wrapped in an embrace. Mark creeps on to his haunches and moves out slowly on his hands and knees. He can hear the sound of someone crying.

'I'm not afraid of him.' The girl being held in an embrace is clearly upset. 'But I feel so sorry for him.'

'I know.' The other speaks in a low whisper, barely voiced. Something indistinguishable follows and then he hears, 'but you're safe with me'. Mark can just about make out what they are saying.

'I'm just not ready.' Annie Maddock's face is suddenly clearly visible in moonlight.

'I understand.' Dave holds out a hand and she takes it. 'You can always talk to me.'

'I know.' Annie leans into Dave's shoulder. 'Thanks for listening.'

Mark presses his ear to the damp grass, breathing slowly, trying to still his heart. A strange feeling rolls in his stomach at the prospect of watching something so private. He shouldn't be looking but he can't help himself. Then again, they shouldn't be doing this. Annie is Ben's girlfriend. His eyes follow the line of the lake, back towards the tent, and he sees the silhouette of a person shrunk back behind a tree trunk. There's someone else watching from the shadows.

That animal shrieks again, deep in the dense thicket of trees. Then, the faintest chitter of laughter and the rustle of branches. Annie pulls away and stands up from the bench, wrapping her coat tightly around her. 'What was that?'

A flicker of light from a torch passes between the boughs. A thin streak of light lashing out across the scrub before disappearing into the darkness again.

'Over there,' Dave whispers, and he stands up from the bench. 'I saw it.' He looks deeper into the woods towards the fading light. That mocking cackle again, further away this time. 'Someone's spying on us.' He creeps forward. 'Annie. Stay here . . . don't move.'

Dave steps stealthily, pace by pace, then stops, waiting. Listening. No one moves a muscle.

In an explosion of light, Patel's face is suddenly illuminated in a stark flare. He shields his eyes.

'Who's there?' His voice trembles as he staggers deeper into the forest, blinded by the light.

Desperate to follow, Mark begins to crawl commando-style through the muddy grass into the undergrowth. A branch breaks with an echoing snap beneath him and he curses in the darkness.

Annie freezes and whips around towards him. 'Dave? Wait! I'm scared . . . come back.'

But Dave has disappeared into the trees, following the dancing faerie light, enticing him deeper and deeper into the densely laced fingers of tree branches.

Annie is on her feet now. 'I'm going back . . . Dave?' Her panic-stricken voice quivers through the silence. There is no answer except for her words echoing into the void. Nobody moves. Nothing stirs, not even the wind, as if nature is holding its breath.

In an explosion of breaking branches, the torch beam is smashed on, full flare, directly into Annie's face. A high-pitched shriek bellows from the mouth of something charging at speed out of the darkness.

Annie cries out in fear, turns and sprints back towards her tent. She stumbles and falls, almost tripping on Mark, who is still prostrate on the ground. He freezes, flicking his head towards her as she gets to her feet. 'Annie?'

'Leave me alone!' Her cry is frantic now as she staggers in the dark, back towards the safety of the girls' tent.

It's too much for Mark, who begins to scramble to his own tent as the wild animal bursts through the trees. A basilisk, or one of the Ring-wraiths hunting them all down. Brambles and branches give way to the charge. He hears Dave call out from deep in the pitch-dark forest.

'Ben, I know it's you . . . Leave us alone.' His voice is distant but drawing closer as he gives chase.

In her frantic escape, Annie darts across the dark campsite and as she turns a corner she slams into a body standing dead still.

'Oh my God!' Annie shrieks as two arms clamp around hers, pinning her hands to her sides and drawing her in tight.

'Easy, tiger . . . What's the hurry?'

The Bacardi on his breath is undeniable. 'Ben?' Annie tries to break free, but he holds her fast. Her head shoots around, back to the forest. 'I thought you were . . .'

'Thought I was what?' Ben presses himself into her body, turned on. Annie squirms, trying to extricate herself, but his arms just pull her in tighter. 'Ssshh.'

'Back there in the forest.' Annie's eyes search the darkness. Dark figures scuttle back into tents, the sound of zip flaps and hushed whispers. 'It's all right, we're alone now, everyone's gone to bed.' She is breathing hard, her chest heaving against his.

'Don't be scared, I've got you.' Ben stares down into her face. That cackle chitters again, closer now. Annie's head spins to see Lynette Davis, in a hoodie, crunching through the grass, heading back towards the girls' tent.

'Don't let me disturb you two lovebirds.' As she passes them and ducks down to unzip the tent flap, Lynette mutters to herself, 'Farm girl's having a crack at everyone tonight. Little slut.'

Mark's heart races, and in a frenzy of panic he crouches close to the ground, watching Ben and Annie, but then very slowly he crawls back towards the boys' tent. As he tries to get inside his wet sleeping bag, his Wellington boots catch on the fabric and his parka rides up over his head. His head thumping, almost suffocating, he hears the sound of feet outside, stalking in a circle.

Is she OK? Does she need help? Mark reassures himself that Ben is out there with her. Her boyfriend is there to protect her. He hears hushed whispers and a flurry of movement followed by someone entering the tent.

Mark lies as still as a corpse, not breathing as a body clambers over him, suddenly pressing his weight deep into his chest, breath close to his face.

'Saw you watching.' Ben's skin brushes Mark's cheek. He's paralysed with fear. 'Did it get you all excited, you little Peeping Tom?'

Then very slowly Ben rolls off and collapses into a deep slumber.

Mark lies awake, eyes wide, glued to the shadows on the canvas, as if he will never sleep again.

29

FEBRUARY 2024

'Roll A008 Scene 23 Take 1. Mark it.'

'I'm not afraid of him.' The girl being held in an embrace was clearly upset. Her tears seemed real. At distance, the camera crept painfully slowly towards them, as if stalking from behind, their faces obscured.

'I know.' The boy spoke in a low whisper, barely voiced. 'But you know you're safe with me.' He pulled her in closer.

'I've told him I'm not ready.' The girl's face was suddenly revealed as clouds passed across the moon. She appeared almost in monochrome; her eyes shone as the camera finally moved into a close-up.

'Good timing,' Max muttered to himself.

'I understand.' The boy stood and gestured towards the tents. 'You know it's just us here.' His hand reached out and she held it tentatively. 'You can always talk to me.'

He's a bit wooden, but she's good. Max made a note.

It was normal to introduce a jump scare early in the story. The boy and girl were about to 'split up', which always signalled that one of them was about to die. In the edit, they would lose him and focus entirely on her face. It was all about her reaction anyway – after all, it was her story.

An animal shrieks deep in the dense thicket of trees.

'That wasn't a fox.' The girl pulled away and stood up from the bench, wrapping her coat tightly around her as she backed off into the shadow of the trees. 'What was it? What's out there?'

Her improvisation was good, she was completely present, racked with fear. A flicker of light from a torch passed between the trees.

The boy stood from the bench and moved slowly forward, deeper into the thicket towards the fading light. The body language was stiff, he didn't know what to do with his hands. The camera followed, and then a peal of mocking laughter rang out across the campsite.

'Someone's spying on us.' His voice was like gravel. 'Stay here . . . don't move.'

The boy walked forward. The lack of wind and the unnatural stillness made Max lean in closer. The tension wound tighter and was about to break. No one moved a muscle. Then the camera moved rapidly in a startling push, up close, from a low angle, right into the boy's face. His breath trembled and tears formed in his eyes. Maybe he wasn't so bad after all.

'Wait for it,' Max muttered.

In an explosion of light, the camera turned on a hideous face, dramatically illuminated from below in a stark flare.

'Who's there?' The boy shielded his eyes and lurched forward, deeper into the forest.

The camera chased after him, 'cowboying' low to the ground, swooping across the surface of the muddy grass. Faster and faster, chasing a single beam of light dancing in the woods like a firefly. A branch broke with a snap. The girl froze and whipped around, truly terrified, her heart racing.

In an explosion of movement, something suddenly burst forward, charging at speed from out of the gloom. A high-pitched shriek erupted from the creature hunting her; her lover changed from man to beast, in a transformation of flesh to fur. The rabid werewolf hungry for blood, hunting its prey. She cried out in fear, turned and sprinted back to her tent. She stumbled, almost tripping on someone who was lying on the ground.

'Aaagh.' Lily stumbled to her knees, shielding her eyes with her hands.

'Ow!'

'Nate, what are you doing down there? That's not what we rehearsed. Get up.' Lily cried out in pain as her ankle buckled beneath her, twisting on the uneven, muddy ground.

Max leant in to study the screen. There was a sudden jerking reframe as the camera found focus. In the darkness, the terrifying silhouette of a body rose like a demon from the depths of the earth, leaving the devoured corpse of the boy dead in the grass. An all-powerful manifestation of evil loomed up from the ground. The figure grew taller than any man, then, spreading muscular arms wide, let out an animal howl of agonising pain.

'Kill it,' Max mumbled unconsciously from behind his fingers. 'You need to kill it, or it will never leave you alone.'

Out of nowhere, a huge chunk of a fallen branch swung violently into the stomach of the beast. Its hind legs buckled as it was cut down. The club was raised again, suspended in the air before swiping down hard like an axe. It was the final blow.

Max had always shied away from using children in stories like this. He felt responsible, like he was somehow cultivating an immunity to extreme violence. Or worse: putting ideas into their heads. But he also understood what children were capable of – Jon Venables and Robert Thompson, Danny and Ricky Preddie, Scarlett Jenkinson and Eddie Ratcliffe: children who had committed appalling acts of violence. How on earth had he allowed himself to stray into this territory for the sake of entertainment? It was the stuff of nightmares.

Deep down, he knew the answer. He had felt it himself in the cruelty dished out to him, the crack of knuckle on bone. He'd been terrified into silence. About everything. He'd bottled it up, kept it all secret, even from his parents, because he knew that the monster was always hiding in the shadows, waiting for him.

But now it was finally time to lure it out of the dark and into the spotlight.

30

FEBRUARY 2024

The club of the tree branch was gnarly with thorns. He raised it in the air above her head. As the jagged branch swung down to shatter the skull, the face of his own daughter suddenly stared back at him. He tried to scream but no sound came. Then the heavy branch slammed down hard, lacerating her perfect skin, cutting deep into the flesh. He gasped in horror, struggling to fill his lungs with air. He was suffocating in a deep, black pool, water rushing around him as he began to sink, something beneath him pulling him down. He was tethered. He reached down, fingers desperately searching for the weeds that were entwined around his foot. It was clamped around his ankle; something alive, like a snake. He tried to loosen it but the more he pulled, the tighter it bound itself.

His chest was exploding as his head tilted back, eyes stinging in the foul water as he tried to break for the surface. Shadows appeared out of the darkness: hands extending, fingers pointing. He reached back, freed his ankle and began to float upwards. The concrete base of the weir was close now, inches away, the vibration of rain pounding the choppy surface. He had no breath left in his burning lungs. Then the rope tightened again and yanked him down. He screamed out for help, but the black water rushed into his mouth, filling his lungs with a thick liquid. He was drowning.

Ben tried to wrench himself out of sleep. His eyes were open but his whole body was paralysed. He could hear a distant cry, someone far away screaming out in agony. With every ounce of strength he could muster, he wrenched himself out of his paralysis. Shaking and sweating, he caught his breath.

A hand flopped over on to his chest.

'All right, love? Night terrors again?' Dani wasn't awake; her voice was distant and her words slurred. She rolled over, cocooning the duvet around herself, while Ben lay still. The perspiration on his body began to cool into a clinging dampness.

Ben sat on the edge of the bed and pulled off his damp T-shirt. His head was thumping, blood pulsating in his ears. He stood up and went to the bathroom for a glass of water and a painkiller. He was just approaching the door to the en-suite when he heard the front door close downstairs and anxious whispered voices coming from the hallway.

He stepped out on to the landing, shirtless, wearing only his boxer shorts. His irises gleamed bright like a cat's as he held the door frame.

'Lily?' he hissed down the staircase.

Nate had his sister propped up under his shoulder. She was limping, hopping on one foot.

'It's OK, Dad, I'm fine. Go back to bed.' Lily winced in pain as she hobbled into the kitchen with Nate.

Ben moved silently down the stairs and followed them into the kitchen, sliding the door closed behind him.

'What time do you call this?' His eyes shot to the digital clock on the cooker. 'It's past two. Where the hell have you been?'

'Night shoot.' Nate was pulling a first-aid kit from the medicine cupboard. 'Didn't Karine tell you?' He found a can of freeze spray as Lily pulled off her sock. 'Out in Burbage Woods. It was meant to be the Brecon Beacons, but—'

Ben stopped for a second. 'The Brecon Beacons?'

'Yeah, we pitched tents and everything . . . Don't fuss, Dad.' Lily winced as the ice-cold spray hit her foot. 'I just went over on my ankle in the dark. Happens all the time at football . . . not that you'd know, you're never there.'

Ben didn't respond and instead flicked on the undercounter lights and scrutinised his son's face.

'You're bleeding.' A number of small lacerations were speckled across Nate's cheek.

'We were running through branches in the dark.' Nate pulled an ankle support on to Lily's fast-swelling sprain. 'It was brilliant, just like *American Werewolf.*'

Ben pulled cotton wool from the kit and soaked it in Dettol. 'Now, listen to me, both of you.' He pulled Nate in sharply by the shoulder and started to dab at his cuts. 'I'm not having you galli-vanting around at night in the dark.'

'Ow . . . you're hurting me.' Nate flinched and took hold of the swab, pulling it away.

Lily slid down from the stool. 'Karine said—'

'I DON'T CARE WHAT KARINE SAID!'

'Bloody hell, Dad!' Lily's wide eyes found her brother, who looked just as shocked.

Ben lowered his voice. 'I don't give a flying f . . . fig what Karine said . . . This stops now. I'm going to have words with that woman.' His eyes darted to Lily. 'You are both going to school in the morning as usual but you're getting that ankle looked at first thing, young lady.'

Nate sloped off to bed while Ben helped Lily up to her room.

A few minutes later, Ben returned to the top of the stairs and stood looking into the bedrooms of his two children before tip-toeing back into his own. The bundle wrapped up in the duvet rolled over to face the door. Ben walked over to the en-suite and flicked on the bathroom light.

'She's hurting them.' Ben's silhouette lingered in the bathroom door.

'What, love?' Dani leant up on her elbow then picked up her watch from the bedside table. 'It's 2.15. Come back to bed.'

'This film, I . . .' Ben's voice was barely a whisper. 'I don't know what's happening . . . Why did we let them get involved in this? This was your idea.'

'He just wants to make you proud. They both do.' Dani rolled over and fell back into a deep slumber.

Ben was frozen on the threshold. Something was stirring deep down, rising up inside him. An old animal instinct he had long forgotten. Fight or flight.

He needed to protect his family at all costs.

31

FEBRUARY 2024

'Roll B002 Scene 2 Take 1. Mark it.'

The man in the frame jumped as the board clapped; his eyes darted around the room, unfocused and nervous. After a few beats, he settled, and the interview began.

'Tell me about your son's friendships at school.'

'I warned him not to let them in. I grounded him, but he disobeyed me.'

The doctor's hair was thinning now. It had turned white and gave him a certain distinguished authority. The rest of his features told a different story. His face was lined with a road map of worry and stress, and there was a weariness that pressed down on his spine. He glanced over to the window, where the twilight outside made a mirror of the glass. He stared at his own reflection.

'Once they're invited inside, they have more potential to hurt you. Like vampires.' Sandeep closed his eyes slowly.

'David was an outsider . . . he was marginalised by his friends.'

'Devesh . . . not David. He anglicised himself to fit in.' The doctor sniffed. 'It means "chief of the gods".'

'It's a beautiful name.'

'Hmm . . . he didn't exactly live up to that mantle though, did he?' A flicker of pain and disappointment flashed across the old man's face.

The zoom tilted in a little closer, detailing every flinch of the broken man.

'Devesh was being dragged down by peer pressure.' He shuffled papers around on his desk as if this was a consultation with a patient and he was looking for answers.

'What kind of peer pressure?' She knew the answer, but her voice and the questions would be removed in the edit.

'Yes, that is rather a euphemism, isn't it . . . hmm . . .' The little hum was like a nervous tick that filled an awkward silence. 'Coercing him into drinking and smoking, running riot all over the village like he was a tearaway, all kinds of nonsense. He should have listened to me, then none of this would have happened.'

'Why did he cave in?'

'The dog shit wrapped in newspaper, set on fire and posted through the letter box was definitely a catalyst . . . that's another form of peer pressure, I suppose.'

'Did that happen a lot?'

'Mmm . . . Devesh just wanted to be popular, he wanted to be one of the gang, so he tagged along, did what he was told by the ring leader . . . His mother hated it, of course . . . especially that damned bike.'

The doctor looked up to the camera and fixed a smile on his lips, but his eyes were dead. 'Children can be cruel, beyond anything an adult could dream up. Their imaginations are so . . .' He sighed. '. . . stark. They despised everything about him, they othered him, so he buried himself in separate pursuits, solitary interests.'

'Yes . . . he liked making home videos.'

Dr Patel clenched his mouth into a tight smile and checked his watch.

'You've answered all these questions before, haven't you?'

'Oh, many times. Couldn't keep the newspapers and so-called TV journalists away back then. Had to close the surgery.' Sandeep swallowed and inhaled, bracing himself. 'My son wasn't the only one that was punished. But you're right to bring up the video tapes. It was one of the things that really swayed the jury. Pity they didn't find all of them.'

'You think there were more?'

'Well, let's just say some houses were never searched . . . not like ours. Like I said . . . shouldn't have let them in.'

Then the camera started to track in to an extreme close-up.

'When Devesh is released, do you think he'll return home . . . to you?'

Sandeep glared at the camera. 'I don't think the village would deem that appropriate, do you?' It was as if a veil descended over Dr Sandeep Patel's eyes. He was weary. Tired of carrying his son's sentence on his back for thirty years.

'There is a monster in all of us. We all have the propensity to kill, but we suppress the animal.' His face turned towards the black glass, his reflection again. 'This village used to be so full of life, full of young people and hope. But it's dying now, slowly fading until there will be no one left to remember . . . that's why we invited you to come.'

The camera was cut.

32

MARCH 2024

'Protesters outside Grantham town hall became disruptive and violent again this afternoon. Chief Constable Chris Davis, who was a classmate of Patel and his victim, Annabel Maddock, at Barton Mallet Secondary School, made this statement: "Dave Patel has served his full sentence and is deemed fit by the parole board for release back into the community." He refused to answer any further questions.

'And in London today, Just Stop Oil protestors were arrested for gluing themselves to the deputy prime minister's e-scooter . . .'

The newsreader's voice drifted off into 'other news'. Dani was sitting with her feet up on the couch with an empty glass in her hand and a hollow feeling in her stomach. She felt a presence behind her and turned on a sharp intake of breath. 'You made me jump.'

Ben was standing on the threshold with the half-empty wine bottle he'd pulled from the fridge, staring vacantly at the TV. Dani instinctively went to turn it off.

'Leave it on if you want.' There was a weary resignation in his voice. 'Top-up?'

She muted the TV. 'Did Lily get seen?'

'Yeah. We had to wait in A&E for nine hours, but it's just a sprain, nothing broken.'

'Did they say if they had fun though?' Dani smiled at him.

'I can't deal with all this right now.' He reached to top up her wine.

Dani held out her glass. 'Lily will be OK, you know, they both will. You worry too much.'

Ben set the bottle down on the table and faced Dani. He looked at her with a penetrating stare. Was he about to kill all her dreams?

Dani blinked and inclined her head. 'What?'

'I know I worry, but—'

'What, love? You're freaking me out.'

'A couple of years before I met you, just after Ellie left, Patel was released on parole.' Ben drifted to somewhere else, another place in his mind.

'I know . . . you told me.' Dani's foot made contact across the couch, tucking itself under his thigh.

'Yeah, but . . . what I didn't tell you is that . . . he broke it . . . his parole. There were strict rules, and he broke them.' Ben chewed his lip. He was holding something back.

'Go on.' Dani wiggled her toe, pressing him.

'It was ten years ago. Nate was only three and Lily was five . . . this house wasn't . . . I was too busy with work, trying to build this place, to make a home for us all.' His eyes were filling with tears.

'Oh, love, that's who you are, a homemaker. Look at what you've created. If Ellie didn't have the stamina to stay around . . .' She placed her hand on his cheek, but Ben gently pulled away.

'He came here. He was looking for—' Ben's voice caught in his throat.

'Looking for what?' Dani's whole body seemed to slowly contract.

'I don't know. Looking for trouble? Looking for me? I think he blamed me.' Ben's head tilted back, looking to heaven, or was he remembering something else?

'He was convicted on overwhelming evidence; the jury was unanimous. It was her blood on his clothes, his DNA on her.' Dani was emphatic and had done her research. Or at least Wikipedia had.

Ben's eyes were full to the brim as two huge tears dropped on to his shirt, but his face remained expressionless. 'She was my girlfriend, she had her whole life ahead of her.' His voice was wrenched with pain. 'What would she have become?' His chin was lifted again, head shaking. 'I'm sorry, love.'

'Ben. She was your first love, please don't apologise. What happened to her happened to you as well. You've had to live with that trauma for thirty years.' Dani wiped a tear from her own cheek.

'He'd only just been released from prison, and he came here. He was institutionalised, I didn't recognise him. He was like a wounded animal. He was incoherent, trying to rake up the past. I told him to let sleeping dogs lie. He'd served his time for what he'd done.' Ben was suddenly incredibly lucid. 'He freaked out. He became aggressive. It was clear he hadn't been rehabilitated, he was as violent and as volatile as the night Annie died.' Ben swallowed hard and ran his hand over his forehead.

It was all starting to make sense to Dani. The sleepless nights, the stress weighing upon Ben's shoulders. Trying to keep a positive face, while inside he was terrified that Patel would come back and kill again.

'I'm worried he'll never go away.'

'What about his father? He's always around . . . Can't you speak to him?' Dani folded her arms, hugging herself for comfort.

'I dunno. Sandeep is like a ghost these days.' Ben closed his eyes and took a breath.

'He's always hanging around at the girls' football.' Dani's militant mind was suddenly razor sharp. 'I don't want to use the word "grooming" but . . .' Dani pursed her lips and drained the dregs of her wine. 'Like father, like son,' she muttered, reaching for the bottle.

Ben sighed. 'He's a broken man, love.' They were all broken.

'Well . . . I always say there's no smoke without fire.' Dani was about to go on a rant, but Ben cut her off.

'He took care of my father at the end of his life. Sandeep is a good man.' Somewhere at the back of Ben's mind, he knew that the unconscious racial bias in their community had fuelled the police investigation back then. But the community was different now, the world was different. Wasn't it? Ben wanted this conversation to be over. He'd turned to Dani for comfort and, as usual, she'd turned it into something else. His voice was calm and quiet. 'I'll talk to Sandeep.' Ben stood up.

'What . . . now?' Dani stared up at Ben in shock and wrapped her cardigan tight around her shoulders, as if Patel was hiding somewhere in the house and she didn't want to be alone.

'I'll just go for a stroll around the village. He's usually walking that dog of his at night – best time to avoid people.' Ben turned to leave.

'I'm sorry about this film thing. Bad timing.' Dani bit her lip. She'd pushed for the kids to take part and now realised Ben had enough on his plate.

He picked up his keys from the kitchen counter. 'Put the chain on the door.' Ben stood on the threshold looking back at Dani. He was struck by how small she seemed.

Dani puffed out through her lips and flicked her hand, shooing the fear away. 'Pick up a bag of chips from Codswallop. I can't be bothered to cook.'

After Ben had left, Dani glanced up to the small camera high in the corner of the hallway, trained on the front door. If nothing else, this house was a fortress. She was beginning to understand why. She slouched towards the kitchen in her bare feet, empty glass in hand, and then stopped. Turning back, she tiptoed to the door, double-locked it and slid the security chain in place.

Ben had no intention of finding Sandeep. His focus was now on Karine Mickelsen.

He stood across the street by the petrol station, in the old part of the village, staring at the lights in the windows of the old thatched pub, the Red Lion. He could hear the chatter of regulars, huddled around the pool table and crowding the bar.

It was just one harmless drink and maybe a casual game of darts. He hesitated, but then what? What exactly did he intend to do?

He crossed the deserted road and headed inside.

33

MARCH 1994

Lynette Davis watches as Annie Maddock steps down from the school bus. Hands are pressed to the window, fingers drawing romantic love hearts and ejaculating penises in the breath on the glass. Annie has been avoiding Ben since the camping trip, but as he stands waiting for her, Lynette lets out a taunting 'whoop', effecting a ripple of applause around the jostling kids pushing their way off the bus. All eyes have been on Annie since they got back from the Wales trip. Giggling and whispering behind hands, furtive glances and notes being passed in class. A rumour is going around about Annabel Maddock, or at least Lynette is determined to start one. She's on the pill. She gave one of the boys a hand job on the bus. She lost her virginity in the woods. Rumours that were nasty and untrue, but once they started, they were like feathers in the wind.

'Hey, are you avoiding me?' Ben hops down from the back of the bench by the church. 'Just ignore them.' The whistles and jeers begin to disperse along with the crowd of kids heading home.

Annie stops. 'You weren't at school today. Everything OK?' Despite being upset with Ben, she notices a black eye and some small cuts to his face and neck. Dave had been off school too, grounded by his dad, who was apparently livid when he heard about what they had got up to on the trip. Annie pauses for a second. She can't seem to make eye contact with Ben; it's hard for her to look at him.

Ben's fingers tingle and his face grows hot. He hesitates. 'I called Mrs Bee, she wrote me a sick note. Dad took a turn, he needs more medication, but the doctor won't prescribe anything stronger.' He broke off. 'It's as if Dr Patel doesn't trust me.' His eyes betraying the fear growing inside.

'If you need help, my mum said—'

'I'm good.' Ben shuts her out, closing that door with a slam. He wants her love, not her pity.

Annie smiles sadly and slings her bag over her shoulder, heading for Forest Hill and home.

'Mind if I walk with you?' Ben's brow furrows. Something odd is happening between them, but neither of them have the understanding or maturity to deal with it. Deep in his gut, Ben knows that he crossed a line. The question is whether to pretend it didn't happen and carry on as before or address the issue and risk everything.

'Sorry about what happened on the bus to Wales.' Ben stares straight ahead with his hands in his pockets.

Annie chews her lip. 'Not just on the bus . . . in the woods as well. I was terrified, Ben.' She hesitates as she stares out at the trees.

'It was just a bit of fun. What were you talking to Dave about anyway? You two looked like you were getting cosy.'

Annie stops in her tracks and gives him a look.

'Sorry.' He sighs.

In Ben's house, brushing problems under the carpet is the way of life. When his mum got sick, the smiles and voices became faker and brighter. Cheerful outings and walks in parks they'd never been to before became the norm. But making plans and looking forward to things like Christmas became a stumbling block. He'd once come home from school bursting with pride that he had been selected to play for the local football team next season. As the news tumbled out of his mouth, he realised his mum wouldn't be around to see any of the matches. She'd smiled all the same and held her hand to his cheek, telling him how proud she was. It was his dad's turn now. Ben's carpet had a mountain of unresolved pain brushed underneath.

They walk in silence for a while.

'We still friends?' Ben shoulders Annie, who keeps walking but finally makes eye contact with him.

'Yeah.'

Her shy smile pierces his heart. He really likes her. His whole body swells with a warm tingling feeling. 'I'm sorry if I . . .'

'Lay off the drink, Ben, it doesn't suit you.' Annie stops for a second at the crossroads between the primary school and the housing estate that will take her home up Forest Hill towards the Maddock Farm. The flatbed trucks of the travelling fairground are parked up by the gates of the community centre. Bunting is being strung up between the lampposts, festooning the recreation ground with blue and red flags. The fox head emblem of the county rugby team, official sponsors of the Easter Wakes, ripples in the breeze. The end of term is coming; everything is about to change. Ben's spirits lift a little.

'We'll have the whole of the Easter holidays to hang out if you want.'

In the distance, the yapping of anxious dogs from the rescue shelter cuts through the awkward silence between them.

'I'm good from here.' Annie waits for Ben to leave.

'See you around then.' He turns, head dipped, hands in pockets as he backs away.

Annie watches him walk off with a heavy heart. Sadness shrouds Ben like a dark cloak. His mother gone, his father on his deathbed; if Annie isn't by his side, then nobody is.

34

MARCH 2024

'Roll B003 Scene 3 Take 1. End board.'

The old Red Lion pub dated back to the late 1600s. It claimed to be one of the oldest inns along the Fosse Way, built long before the rest of the village had settled, and an infamous haunt of high-waymen. The Lion was named after Richard the Lionheart, who once travelled incognito along the war route on his crusade from Wales to Jerusalem, a myth the locals liked to cling to for tourists. At the back of the pub, in the beer garden, the fulcrum of a ducking stool, which had once reached out into the river, was remarkably well preserved. They hadn't been so barbaric as to burn witches in Barton Mallet, they had just dunked them in the water and waited to see whether or not they would float. In 1665 the Malleus Maleficarum, the 'Hammer of Witches', fell on the unfortunate Mary Barton and so the village got its name.

The Barton Malleteers were acutely aware of strangers. No one ever visited the village by accident and they were a suspicious folk. It was hardly surprising, bearing in mind the tragedies that had befallen the place on more than one occasion.

The footage was deliberately grainy. The shot moved like a black-and-white silent film in flickering fast motion, crossing the road and plunging into the darkness of the inn. Max leant forward as the light adjusted to the dim saloon.

The Red Lion was all yellowing whitewashed lime plaster and black-painted beams. Ceilings so low you had to duck under to get to the roaring fire of the stone inglenook that spewed smoke into the room. Everyone had their regular table and the hum of chatter and thwack of the balls on the pool table gave a cosiness to the whole place. In a small, partitioned annexe, two figures sat across a table in deep conversation. The discreetly positioned camera was propped up on the stone window ledge behind her, hidden in a collection of woven baskets of dried herbs. The shot was dirty, clipping her shoulder and the white-blonde hair cascading over it. Her head was facing the protagonist of this particular scene: The Bent Copper.

'Throughout his incarceration, Patel has always maintained his innocence.' Her voice was low and conspiratorial.

'Not quite . . . he finally admitted his guilt in . . . When was it? 2010? He was tried as a minor, so initially he was only in a Young Offender unit. They were too soft on him . . . got his parole far too easily for my liking. They said he'd been rehabilitated, bloody ECHR lefty lawyers . . . good behaviour, my arse.'

'What happened? Why was he re-arrested?'

'He was tagged, broke a restraining order.' PC Davis screwed up his lip. 'I'd just come up the ranks, Dad was retired.' A smile spread across his face. 'He broke into private property and threatened the owner of the house.'

'Benjamin Knot?'

'Yes. We arrested Patel again and banged him up in maximum security. He finally got the sentence he deserved.'

'Do you know why he targeted Mr Knot?'

Davis paused. 'Well, obviously the two of them have history. But it was an unprovoked attack. If there was ever any doubt what kind of person Patel is, it vanished that day. Dave Patel is a psycho.'

'Why do you personally think there was doubt over Patel's guilt?'

'There wasn't . . . there isn't. His confession is now public record, signed and sealed. Condition of his final release.' Davis sniffed and turned to glance across the crowded bar to the pool table.

'But not all the evidence was heard at the trial, the DNA samples were not conclusive, the jury was divided.'

Davis's lips tightened as he chewed down on his teeth.

'If it had been an accident, Dave would have done the right thing and come forward immediately. Instead, he went home and cleaned himself up, tried to wash away the evidence, but they found traces of her blood on his trainers. My dad did his job thoroughly. The jury was not divided, just the media.' Davis thumped his empty glass on to the table.

'The murder weapon was never found?'

'Rarely is. In any case we didn't need it, the rest of the evidence was enough. Case closed.' He clapped his hands together, then wiped them down his trousers as if he was cleaning the memory of Patel from his fingers in disgust. 'Right. Want another half?' He stood up out of his seat and stepped out into the saloon. The camera tried to adjust its focus. 'My round, then I'm done.' He had moved out of shot.

'Just one more question.' The sound dropped out momentarily as the hubbub of the rowdy bar began to rise. 'Off the record.'

'IPA, was it?' The black frame burst into light again, revealing an empty stool, horse brasses pinned along the beam of the fire-place behind it.

'Patel always claimed he was filming that night . . . he said that footage was kept out of the trial.'

There was a pause. The digital auto zoom buzzed in and out of focus on the flames in the fire, trying to find a face to recognise.

'I wouldn't know about that . . . but like I said, my dad didn't leave a single stone unturned. His OBE says so.'

The sound of laughter burst from the back room, and a man, just a tiny figure in the corner of the shot, moved towards the jukebox. Max's hand shot out like a dart and froze the frame. He breathed in deeply and advanced the shot frame by frame as the figure slowly turned and stared over towards the nook and directly into the camera lens.

'There you are . . .' Max muttered to himself. 'Long time no see.'

A shiver of electricity rippled down his spine as he set eyes on Ben Knot for the first time in thirty years. He zoomed in closer. God, he looked so different.

His phone buzzed as a message dropped into his inbox from Foxcatcher.

Did you review the Davis footage?

Max was still staring at the frozen image on the huge cinema screen. Maybe she hadn't noticed him at the back of the bar in the midst of all the hustle and bustle. She'd been too focused on the copper. Max replied:

I think he's on to you. Be careful.

He let the tape run. The jukebox kicked in and the opening bars of Doris Day's 'Secret Love' drifted out as Ben Knot backed away into a throng of bodies at the bar and the shot dissolved to black.

35

APRIL 2024

The Warren House was an old junk yard near Thurcaston Lacey. The overgrown winding country lane led to an industrial building on the site of a disused airfield about three miles outside Barton Mallet. Karine tugged at the rusting chain and padlock wrapped around the wrought-iron gates and texted the farmer who was supposed to meet her there. She was out on a recce of the location for tonight's shoot. Her phone buzzed in her pocket; it was Dani calling.

'Hey, how's it going? I'm at the location, setting up now . . . just muting you for a second . . . hold on.'

Karine set a foot into the chain of the gate, hauled herself up to the top, threw a leg over and dropped down on to the other side. It wasn't the first time she'd had to gain access without permission. She stepped into a courtyard littered with junk, old refrigerators and scrapped cars. She unmuted the call. 'You still there?'

'Yeah, I'm here. Listen . . . there might be a problem.' Dani sounded nervous.

Karine approached the vast corrugated steel barn and dragged open the rusty door. 'Problem?' The smell of dank earth mixed with heady petrol fumes hit her nostrils. She flicked the switch on the wall by the door and the buzz of electricity illuminated a succession of sickly orange strip lights.

'Yeah, it's Ben. He wants to pull the plug on the whole thing. Lily did get injured quite badly and I . . .' Dani ran out of steam, her voice petered out.

Karine draped a cable of string lights over an old sign propped up against the wall. 'Lily seemed fine when she left.' A pile of dismembered shop mannequins made Karine freeze for a second. 'Do you think something happened on the way home?'

Dani's voice lowered to a whisper. 'I'm not sure . . . Can we have a quick chat when we get there?'

'Of course . . . Are you OK?'

'Ben doesn't know we're coming tonight.' Dani's voice was hushed and trembling. 'I said I was taking them to see *Stranger in the Woods.*'

'OK . . . look, I'm sorry about all this. Let me speak to Ben. But I'm at the location now and it's going to be great. There'll be a couple of others from Nate's year, just in the background, but how about you stay with us until we're done? You can be their chaperone.' Karine moved into an older part of the barn. The cowshed still stank of urine; she covered her nose with her hand.

'Just text me when you're ten minutes away. I'll have everything ready . . . and don't worry. You're going to love this, it'll be fun.' Karine ended the call. She glanced to the door where the light was fading and a low mist from the surrounding waterlogged fields was forming.

The location had captured her imagination in the day, but at night it was something else. She jogged back towards the perimeter fence. The farmer who owned the land had unlocked the gate and was glaring at the intruder on his property.

'Thought we said 8 p.m.?'

Karine smiled sweetly in the face of his scowl. 'You wouldn't be able to give me a hand with some heavy lifting, would you?' She pulled two twenty-pound notes from her jeans pocket.

The farmer snatched them away and grunted. 'What do you need?'

Karine busied herself in the van while the farmer removed canvas covers from three old dodgem cars and pushed them into the centre of the space. The handheld rig with a 4K lightweight camera on a gimbal would be perfect for tonight. She walked the route from the door, positioning small LED lamps here and there to create ambience. Under the faded 'Circus' sign with the blistering paint and the face of a sad, cackling clown – because there always had to be a clown – was another old hoarding of a fairground ride, 'The Mouth of Hell'. A gaping scream with peeling painted fangs formed an archway, which she dragged into position over the door to the cowshed.

'Hey, give me a hand with this.' Karine beckoned the farmer over as she began to haul naked mannequins from the burn pile. The midden stalls in the cowshed would work well if she positioned the dummies in strategic places. She killed the main overhead lights and set about placing lamps into the shadows, caressing the terrifying limbs of the lifelike figures with light.

Finally, Karine rolled out two heavy metal gas canisters and a coil of rubber tubing from the back of the van and began to run a line into the Mouth of Hell. The festoon string lighting flickered as the fuse strained to hold the voltage, but the scene was set.

She went back to her car and braced herself, waiting in silence for it to get dark, going through the motions in her head of what was about to happen. She jumped as her phone buzzed on the dashboard.

The text from Dani landed.

10 mins away.

She reached across and retrieved a torch from the glove compartment and quietly opened the van door. The night was still and silent; a fresh dampness from the surrounding fields filled her senses. She moved back to the main building, killed the lights and called Dani.

'Karine?'

'How are you getting on?'

'I'm just turning into Thurcaston Lacey Lane now. It's pitch dark. I can't see a thing.' Dani crawled along the single-track road and stopped the car. She glanced into the rear-view mirror. Nate was half asleep, his head lolled back on the headrest, and Lily was into her phone, her face illuminated in the darkness.

'Listen to me carefully, we only get one shot at this. I only want one take. I'm set for close-ups, but I want it to be real.' Karine was all business.

'What do you need me to do?' Dani's voice was shaking on the other end of the line. There was a sense of subversion about this whole thing. Outside, the fields were absolutely pitch black, no moon and not a breath of wind.

'When I hang up the call, I want you to kill your headlights and wait for my instruction.'

'OK.' Dani's heart was racing.

Karine could hear her breathing hard. 'On my signal, send Nate and Lily towards the cluster of torches in the distance.'

Dani felt like she was on some kind of sting, an accomplice to a crime. She felt like Jamie Lee Curtis in *Halloween*.

'They will be home and tucked up in their beds before you can say "Candyman". Whatever you do, whatever noises you hear, do NOT get out of the car. I'm shooting towards you, and it will break the take.'

'Right.' Dani braced herself. 'Don't move, don't react.'

'Exactly. Ready?'

Dani's palms were sweating and her heart racing. 'Ready.'

The line went dead. Dani turned into the back seat. 'Karine says we have to wait here and when we get the signal, you have to walk towards the lights . . . She'll tell you what to do next.'

Dani had fully immersed herself into the role she was now creating in her head, her voice was quivering at an unusual pitch.

Lily yawned and Nate rubbed his eyes. 'All right, Dani, chill out.'

Lily's phone buzzed. She opened her Instagram: 'Euugh! Whitney Briggs is here . . .'

'Give her hell, Lils. Don't let her take you down again,' Nate teased, laughing at his dig.

'Sod off.' Lily huffed into the glass and drew daggers on the window.

They waited in the car for what felt like an eternity. None of them spoke. In the distance, about two hundred metres down the pitch-dark lane, three small beads of light flickered on and started to move towards them. Torches. Dani closed her eyes for a second and listened to the wind and a distant car on the main road. She was about to nod off when her Muppets ringtone buzzed.

'Oh my shitting shit!' Dani leapt out of her skin and fumbled for her phone. A text dropped.

Send them now.

'OK.' She took a deep quivering breath. 'I'll see you both on the other side.' Dani turned to the back seat, Meryl Streep'ing the crap out of this moment. 'I love you.'

'Wait . . . Dani, are you crying?' Lily screwed up her face, and Nate stifled a giggle.

'Come on, Lils, let's get this over with.'

The rear doors opened and a distant flickering beam from the end of the road signalled the way. Dani watched as Nate and Lily headed towards their fate, brother helping his limping sister as the two silhouettes disappeared slowly into the darkness.

The scene was set, Karine's Wonderland of Terror was waiting for them. As the distant shrieks from the darkness began, Dani gripped the wheel and squeezed her eyes shut. She'd wound herself up into a state of dramatic tension.

'Don't break the take . . . you mustn't break the take.'

A single tear fell from Dani's eye. She glanced at herself in the mirror, the perfect image of a loving stepmother. If only there had been someone to witness this performance.

But there was a witness. A figure stood in the dark on the unmarked track. He had followed her there, followed the car, parked up at the main road and continued on foot. He saw her crying in the car, and then moved off across the field towards the glow of light and the screams of terror coming from the junk yard.

Ben watched as his children played on rusty old dodgem cars and chased through the maze of mannequins into the Mouth of Hell.

The face of John Maddock at the carol concert flashed into his mind. 'The whole village knows what this film's about . . . it's not right.'

Lily and Nate at 2 a.m. in the kitchen, nursing their wounds from a scene set in the Brecon Beacons.

The clandestine hushed conversation he'd witnessed between Karine Mickelsen and Chris Davis at the Red Lion.

And now this.

It was all starting to make sense but as answers formed, more questions arose. Was this just his paranoid brain joining irrational dots? No, there were simply too many coincidences.

As realisation hit, the blood drained from Ben's face and an odd feeling of calm descended over him.

How the hell did this stranger know all their secrets? His secrets. There was only one way to find out.

36

APRIL 1994

'In our darkest hour, before my final rhyme, she will come back home to Wonderland and turn back the hands of time.'

Sparks of electricity crackle from the metal posts as Annie Maddock and Ben Knot circle the perimeter of the Mad Hatter's Dodgem Ride. Mark Cherry hops in beside his best friend, already eagerly at the wheel of an orange-painted car.

'The Cheshire Cat, I see what you did there.' Mark nudges Cat, who grins at him and floors the pedal, but nothing happens. He glances over his shoulder to see Chris Davis racing towards them in a black-and-white-striped Tweedle Dum dodgem. He slams into the back of their car, jolting them both forward; but their pole connects with the grid above, sparking the electrical connection, and they shoot off. Attempting to swerve away from the edge, Cat crashes into Lynette Davis, driving the Queen of Hearts, and Dave Patel, trying to shunt his Dormouse out of the traffic jam.

Rounding the bend through a mouth-shaped tunnel, Ben and Annie in their Tweedle Dee dodgem take the corner at speed. Chris pulls up alongside, forcing them into a row of pink plastic flamingos, and they both grind to a halt with a crunch. Ben laughs, frantically reversing into a back spin, punching into the side of Patel.

Patel winks at Annie, who is flushed with the thrill of the ride, as Ben manages to free their car. As they speed away towards the gates of Wonderland Castle, Annie whispers something in Ben's ear then turns her head, tossing her chestnut hair over her shoulder, laughing at Patel. He floors it, slamming the pedal down, but his car is dead. He makes a daredevil leap from his dodgem Dormouse, trampling over the face of Tweedle Dum and landing on the Queen of Hearts. Lynette shifts over, letting Patel take the wheel, and they career towards the castle.

It's Knot vs. Patel: Tweedle Dee in one direction, the Queen of Hearts in the other. As they reach opposing sides, Patel spins the wheel to the left at the same moment that Knot turns his to the right. It's a stand-off. Patel stares at Annie and slams his foot to the floor. The sparks from the electrified connection pole explode on to the graphite platform. But Knot's reflexes are fast and the two cars lurch into a head-on collision. At that very same moment, the Cheshire Cat crawls languidly into the crosshairs. The little orange car is slammed from both sides. The wheels buck violently off the metal platform and slam back down with a crash. Cat and Mark are jolted sideways as the car tips, throwing them both to the ground.

The siren sounds and the electricity is cut. All the cars suddenly power down to a surge of boos and groans.

'EVERYONE OFF!' The operator, sporting a rather fetching top hat and red wig, strides across, more bothered about his damaged car than the kids on the ground.

Lynette smirks at Mark. 'Off with his head?'

Ben, Chris and Dave explode into a cackle of whoops and jeers as Mark lies there, dizzy from the fall.

Catherine stands up. 'You OK? You bumped your head, you're bleeding.'

Mark snaps. 'You're a dick, Ben Knot!' His frantic eyes flick from Dave to Ben, unsure exactly who is to blame. 'I hope your dad DIES.'

It's as if all the sound is sucked out of the air in a vacuum. Everyone stares at Mark, open-mouthed, speechless. Mark stands up from the platform, trembling. A trickle of blood runs down the side of his face as Ben slowly rises from his seat. He's beyond livid.

'What? What did you say?'

Mark, panting in rage, hesitates for a second. A siren for the next ride of dodgems suddenly pierces the silence and a crowd of kids race across the floor towards the cars. Mark bolts, weaving through bodies, pushing them out of the way, but Ben is off like a rocket, leaping over the bonnets of the cars, tearing after him.

'BEN! Leave it!' Annie calls to Ben as the gang gives chase.

Mark pegs it across the fairground towards the Fun House, barging to the front of the queue and pushing through the candy-striped double doors. His feet slip and slide over the polished boards of the shaking platform. The punchy beat of a rock song blasts through loudspeakers as Mark clatters down steps and dives headfirst into a ball crawl, pulling himself across to the other side. Turning back to make sure he hasn't been followed, he mounts a flight of jerking scissor stairs and darts through a pair of saloon doors into a maze of mirrors. He stops to catch his breath, panting heavily. The clatter of the doors behind him sends a shock wave through his body. In a panic, he turns to run down a passageway towards the exit, but his whole body ricochets off a pane of black glass as he slams into a wall and collapses on to the floor. Dazed and disorientated, he crouches down in the corner and tries to stay quiet. Shit, that really hurt.

'I know you're in here.' A voice melding with the lyrics to the guitar riff thrashing out through the speakers. 'You can run but you can never hide, Cherry.'

Mark's hands feel along the wooden floor until his fingers find the base of the mirrored wall. There is a gap underneath, just enough room to wiggle through.

He's no stranger to small spaces; hiding in cupboards and creeping under the school huts is second nature to him. He lies face down on the ground and squeezes through the gap into another corridor of mirrors, but this time Mark keeps his hands out in front of him and moves slowly. As he turns a corner, a figure appears ahead of him with his back turned. It's him. The thumping music sounds more distant. Shadows creeping up beside him.

From the shadow that's creeping up beside you.

Mark ducks down out of sight and watches the reflection of Ben as he moves off in the wrong direction. Slinking down and squeezing under another gap, Mark finds himself around the back of the ride now, in an area that is clearly out of bounds. He traces the wall with his hand, frantically searching for an escape. A red light appears in the distance, spilling through a crack in a half-open door. Mark makes a beeline for it, but it's yet another hoax: a fake exit into another room. A macabre light fills the space, like a darkroom. As Mark's eyes adjust to the sickly red gloom, he can see a figure standing in the doorway, barring his escape. Shit. He shrinks back into the darkness.

'Turn around, Mark, I'm two steps behind.'

'Gotcha.' Two hands grab his shoulders.

'Oh shit . . . please.' Mark flinches in terror and freezes. 'I'm sorry.'

'Hey, chill out, it's only me.'

'Dave?'

'Come on.' Dave places a friendly hand on his shoulder. 'Relax. I'll show you the way out.'

'Oh, thank goodness.' Mark exhales as Dave leads him into the room but then grabs his arm, pulling him to a stop. An overhead light flicks on, revealing the room in a stark glare. There are mirrors on all four sides and a vast chess board on the floor. Across the other side, Ben Knot stands leaning against the door frame, arms folded.

'Checkmate.' He stands smirking, and cracks his knuckles, ready for a fight.

Two kings on either side and Mark just a pawn in the middle. He turns to Dave. 'Why?'

'King's rook.' Dave shoves him forward and Mark stumbles on to the board.

But then something miraculous happens. As Mark takes a step across the board, his body is at least eight feet tall and seems to tower over a tiny child-sized Ben Knot. It feels so good to be this big: a Goliath in the face of this David. Brimming with false confidence, Mark begins to stride forward but with every step he seems to shrink, smaller and smaller, as the chequerboard floor slopes upward and the deceitful mirror reveals its trick until, finally, they are face to face.

'Let me out.' Mark tries to move past. 'I want to go home.' Ben grips his elbow.

'Don't cross me, Cherry, you'll regret it.' He slams him up against the wall. 'Thanks, mate.' Ben relaxes his grip and turns back to Patel. 'I owe you one.'

Dave acknowledges him with a nod, swallowing his guilt.

Mark's eyes dart between the two of them. 'You're working together?' His voice trembles. 'You pretend to be a friend, but you are just as bad as he is.'

Suddenly, out of nowhere, a fist smashes into Mark's face and he goes down. There's a searing pain in his head and tiny white lights begin spinning. Ben hauls Mark back to his feet and shoves him hard into the wall, one hand on his throat, the other clenched, threatening a second punch. 'Now, what did you say to me?' His fingers tighten, choking Mark. 'Say it again . . . to my face.'

'Hey, mate, take it easy.' Dave moves in to stop him, but Ben shrugs him off and slugs his fist into Mark's stomach. He doubles over, but Ben still has him by the throat. 'SAY IT.' He's about to go in for a third strike when Annie, Cat and Lynette burst in through the door.

'BEN! Come on, leave him alone,' Annie cries out to him, but Ben is now wound tighter than a spring.

'You're defending him?' Ben stares at Annie in bewilderment. 'But you heard what he said.'

Mark's face is red, he's choking and spluttering, but suddenly his lips become pale and his body starts to go limp as he loses strength and stops struggling.

'You're hurting him.' Annie shakes her head in frustration. 'Please just let him go, Ben. It's not worth it.'

'Well . . . you've certainly made your loyalties crystal clear.' Ben stares at his so-called girlfriend.

'You're just a bully, Ben.' It's now Cat's turn to wade in. 'Stop it, he's had enough. Can't you see that?'

'Oh! She's so brave . . . Little Miss Perfect.' Lynette Davis shoulder-barges Cat into the wall, willing the whole thing to kick off into a full-on scrap.

'HEY!' Annie grabs Lynette by the collar and yanks her back. 'Get off her.'

'Come on then, Farm Girl, give it your best shot.' Lynette turns, fists raised, squaring up to her like a boxer.

Annie shakes her head at Ben. 'See what you've done?' But then she turns on Mark as well. 'You provoked him.'

Ben turns to Dave. 'What do you think?'

Dave scans the faces in the darkness. He knows what he ought to do, the right thing to do. But his own neck is on the line.

'He's a little creep, isn't he?' Dave leans on the wall next to Ben. 'Little weirdo.'

It's three against three.

Annie stares at Dave with a withering look. 'Of all the people, I thought you would know better.' He reddens and his eyes drop to the floor.

She turns to Ben. 'Cat's right, you're all bullies and cowards. When are you going to grow up? This was supposed to be a celebration. This is our last term together and you have to go and ruin it. Come on, I'm going to walk you home, Mark. Let's go. Now.'

Annie steps in between them and frowns at Ben with such contempt in her eyes that he releases Mark.

'Cat, I'll see you at home.' Annie gives her sister a knowing nod. It's time for a heart-to-heart. As she turns away, her eyes remain focused on Ben. There is something scathing in her stare. She has a power over him. In moments of mutual connection that power is glorious, but this humiliation in front of the gang is a new experience for Ben. An uncomfortable feeling courses through him that is hard to comprehend. How dare she?

Outside, the air is cooler now. A light smattering of rain has started to fall and the handmade bunting for the Easter parade, which had fluttered with so much joy earlier in the day, hangs flaccid and damp.

Annie and Mark walk in silence until they round the bend of Forest Hill. Mark's nose has stopped bleeding, but the blood has crusted all over his face. Annie takes out a handkerchief and hands it to him.

'I'm sorry he hurt you. But you said something very cruel, Mark. Why did you say it?'

Mark dabs at his nose. 'I dunno, it just came out.' His voice is hoarse.

'But you know about his dad, right?'

'Of course. I was just angry at him. They all pick on me all the time and I've had enough.' There is anguish in his voice. As they reach the corner of his street, he stops. 'I know I shouldn't have said it.' His eyes dart to the light flicking on through the glass of the front door to his house. 'This is me.' Mark turns back to Annie. She smiles at him. His eyes are red rimmed. He looks so lost and alone.

'Cat really likes you, Mark, but . . .' She takes his hand, feeling him tense slightly. His eyes drop to his shoes. 'I . . . I think you like boys, don't you?'

Mark swallows, his face screwed up in pain, as his head turns to the silhouette twitching the nets in the window of the Cherry house. His mum is waiting up for him. Without looking at Annie, almost imperceptibly, he nods. There, it's done, it's finally out.

Annie holds out her other hand to him, her fist clenched. 'Here, I got this from the bran tub, 10p a go.' She opens her hand.

Mark takes the silver chain from her palm and looks at the small medallion attached.

'It's a St Christopher, patron saint of travellers.' Annie pulls Mark into a hug; his body stays limp, drained from adrenaline. 'Someone will carry you. I promise.' Mark has no words. He didn't want this. He didn't want to be seen or carried. 'It's going to be OK.' She smiles.

She really believed it would all be OK. But she was wrong.

37

APRIL 2024

Dani stood at the sink, filling a saucepan with water. She was watching Ben in his usual spot, pacing at the bottom of the garden on the phone, staring out across the river.

She'd lied to him last night when they got back, pretending she'd taken Lily and Nate to the cinema. She didn't feel good about it. What had started out as an exciting secret mission had ended in her not being able to meet Ben's eyes and regurgitating the Wikipedia page of a film she hadn't seen. She picked at the chipped lacquer on her nail extensions and slid the pan on to the ceramic hob, dropping eggs into the water. Her eyes had been glued to the morning news. The Mill Killer's imminent release wasn't just regional anymore; all the major channels had picked up the story and spun it into a national outrage. Everyone salivating over the past, trampling over the details of a case they had no real knowledge of. But he was definitely coming out, and soon.

The front door slammed, making her jump. Dani turned to see Karine standing in the doorway. She was coming and going these days like she owned the place. In a way, she did; they were all living on her film set and Dani was like a runner at her beck and call.

'Oh, it's you.' Dani's tone was flat. She muted the sound on the TV, the scowl on her face morphing into a pleasant smile that concealed the tension tightening in her gut.

Karine stepped one pace into the room. 'Lily and Nate were great last night . . . It was a tough scene – they surprised me.'

'Of course they were great.' Dani's instinct was to counter with something akin to 'they're my kids', but she checked herself.

Karine stared at Dani. 'It's boiling over.'

'Sorry?' Something passed between them before a hissing sound like pressure from a piston broke the spell. Dani grabbed the pan and shifted it to the side of the worktop as water spat and crackled on the hot ceramic.

'Nate will have a few bruises . . . Sorry about that.' Karine ran her hand through her hair and laughed uncomfortably. 'Don't sue me.'

'Seriously?' Dani turned to face her. 'Actually, Karine, I think we need to have a little chat.' Her voice was quivering with the anticipation of confrontation.

'Really, about what?' Karine's voice lightened.

'Umm . . . Lily's sprained ankle and cuts on Nate's face.' Dani's hands went to her hips. 'OK, look, I don't know how this filming lark is supposed to be but . . .' She was struggling. '. . . frankly, I'm concerned.' Their eyes met. Dani didn't blink. 'They're just children.'

Karine smiled and tossed her white hair back over her shoulder. 'Oh, Dani . . . I totally understand.' There was an arrogance in her tone. She took a breath. 'Yes, I admit there is a certain level of danger when we attempt a stunt, and sometimes things happen in the heat of the moment, but I can assure you, I am watching them like a hawk.' Her eyes flicked to the TV news bulletin. 'Lily must get a few knocks and bumps in football, no?' Karine smiled at Dani. 'She's a tough cookie.'

Dani swallowed. She didn't want Nate's dreams – her dreams – to be shattered.

Karine continued. 'Like I said before, I don't want anything fake . . . this film needs to feel real. I need to believe everything, I need to feel everything. It has to be visceral. You'll thank me at the Oscars.' Karine nudged Dani.

Dani smiled but her voice had an edge to it. 'All right, well . . . as long as you're getting what you need.'

'Oh, I am.' Karine glanced at the TV. 'We are.' Her eyes returned to Dani. The muted presenters had segued into a piece about paedophiles and AI.

'What was it you wanted?' Dani fished out the boiled eggs from the pan.

'I need to get everything over to the editor this afternoon. Can you please sign the release agreement?' She pulled an envelope from her coat pocket and slid it along the quartz worktop.

Dani inclined her head and smiled, feeling a sudden sense of empowerment. 'What exactly is being released? Do I need to read the small print?'

'It's a standard waiver for Nate and Lily's participation. We can't release the film without it.' Karine flashed Dani a confident smile. 'Aren't you curious, to find out what happens in the end?'

'No. But I am.'

Karine turned. Ben was standing on the threshold of the back door.

'I'm fascinated to find out.' His face was flushed and he gripped his jaw. 'You seem to be having a wild time with my family, Karine.'

Dani had never seen Ben like this. He had a look on his face like he was about to kill someone.

'Can I have a word?' He beckoned Karine out into the garden with a nod. 'In private.'

Ben was waiting by the edge of the river, as far away from the house as he could possibly get, hidden from sight behind the stack of fallen branches in the burn pile. Come autumn, this would all be ablaze. He heard her feet on the gravel path behind him, but he didn't turn.

'Where were you last night?' Ben thrust his hands deep into his pockets.

Karine stepped close to his side, her shoulder almost touching. 'Why?' She nudged him slightly. 'I didn't know you cared.' Ben flicked his head back to the house and pulled away from her.

'I don't.' His tone was flat. 'But we need to talk.'

She smiled but he cut her dead with his eyes.

'Oh, OK . . . well . . . I went to the cinema with Dani.' Karine smiled implacably.

'I dropped into the Red Lion. I'm becoming quite the regular over there these days.' He squinted at her, enjoying the power he had in this moment. 'Your tech guy was in the bar . . . Ed, isn't it? Yeah, I played a round or two of darts with him and your focus puller, Freddie. Ed and Fred certainly enjoy chewing the fat . . . so . . .'

'So?'

'So . . . They told me where you were.'

'Then why did you ask?' Karine's voice hit a register he hadn't heard before. It was intimate, seductive even.

'Why did you lie?' Ben held her gaze, matching her tone.

Karine moved her hair away from her neck, exposing her tantalising white skin, and laughed.

'Because I . . . I didn't want you to know.' She smiled to herself and turned her face towards the river and the mill.

'I warned you about overstepping the line with my kids.' Ben's voice tightened to a whisper. 'I'm going to pull them from your damned film.'

Karine breathed in the cool morning air. 'And I will sue you . . . It's all there in the contract you so diligently pressed for, Ben. Plus, of course, you would need to repay all their fees, plus bond and damages for shutting down a studio feature. Do you have any idea—'

'Why are you doing this?' Ben cut her off.

'Oh, come on, Ben, you're getting all caught up in the drama.' Karine turned her body towards the house. 'Which is maybe not such a bad thing.' She moved past him and began to walk back.

'Wait, I haven't finished. I was there, I saw what you did. The dodgems . . . the fairground set-up.'

Karine stopped and turned back.

'I followed you.' He hadn't intended to tell her that. Now he was the one who was being subversive. Neither of them spoke for a second.

'Hmm . . . so you're curious?'

'I know what you're doing. You're not the first person who has come sniffing around these parts, trying to rake up the past. Books have been written, documentaries . . . you have no shame, do you? Anything for a quick buck. People just want to be left alone.'

Karine shook her head. 'It's always like this, Ben. Everyone always thinks the story is about them . . .' She winced sympathetically. 'But that's what I do, I get under the skin.'

It was as if he were reliving the moment; it was as if she had been there, in every recurring nightmare that had haunted him over the years. A sharp pain jolted in Ben's chest, tighter than ever. He flinched.

Karine turned and smiled at him. She could see the effect she was having on him.

'Filmmakers are the truth tellers . . . you'll see.'

38

MAY 1994

Annie stands outside the Knots' house under the newly planted oak tree on the grass verge. The bare patches of earth where they'd dug small holes to play marbles in the spring are starting to grow new green shoots. She's perched on the faded road sign, bolted to two low concrete posts, that indicates the way to the council estate of Barton Rise. This is where they'd had their first kiss. She'd never done open mouths before; it had felt like two goldfish gasping for air. Their lives will never be like this again. After the summer holidays, they'll all be going their separate ways. Sixth-form college, or work experience stacking shelves in a shop somewhere. Ben will most likely sign up for an apprenticeship; there is a local mechanic that will take him on. Annie wants to spend the summer in London; she's been accepted on a summer course at Central Saint Martins school of fashion and design, the beginning of a dream. The dream of getting out of her small town and making something of herself is very much alive. But what about the two of them? Where do they go from here? She inhales deeply, strides across the green and rings the doorbell. There's no answer at the front door so she crouches down and calls through the letter box.

'Ben . . . it's me. It's Annie.' The kitchen door is closed but she can see movement through the fluted glass door. He's definitely in there. 'I'm sorry we haven't spoken since the Wakes. Can I come in?'

Annie drops the letter box and sits on the doorstep with her head on her knees. She should probably go home, it's getting late and she has revision to do. Exams start next week.

'Annie?' She turns to see Ben in the open door, bare feet and tracksuit bottoms. His shirt is filthy and his hair is a mess. 'You better come in.'

The house stinks, like someone died in here. They don't have any pets, but the aroma of urine is pungent. Newspapers are piled up on the hall carpet and letters are spilling over the telephone table. Annie closes the front door behind her as Ben heads into the kitchen at the back. As she passes the living room, she notices the stale stench has been masked with the smell of pine disinfectant. An empty hospital bed is parked in the centre of the room, with yellow sheets and plastic buckets of God knows what underneath. A commode and a small table loaded with pill bottles and a jug of stagnant water stand next to the bed. The couch in the corner has a rumpled-up sleeping bag and a pillow in a case that clearly needs a wash.

'You want a tea?' Ben calls from the kitchen, his voice flat with exhaustion. Annie places her bag in the corner of the hall and braces herself, trying to muster some courage.

'Come on, he won't bite, he's out for the count anyway.' The kettle in the kitchen begins to whistle as Annie tentatively steps into the room. The kitchen hasn't been updated since the fifties; lurid yellow and green flower-patterned wallpaper and aqua-blue cabinets, a Belfast sink in the corner and a stove that has seen better days. An electric fire is plugged in with a few bars on, despite the fact May has been pretty warm this year, but it's more for visual comfort than any withering heat it might emit. A wing chair with an old brown stretch cover has its back to the door. As she moves into the room, Annie can see a pale-blue, bony hand on the arm of the chair. Ben dunks two tea bags into hot water.

'It's OK, he's asleep, I gave him the morphine.'

As Annie rounds the chair, she can see what remains of Ben's father. It's hard not to show a reaction when faced with such a shocking transformation. Anthony Knot is hanging on to life by a thread. His sunken cheeks and hollowed-out eyes, open mouth and head tipped back give the impression of a man in a scream of ecstasy. His breathing is terrifyingly shallow; yellow fingernails hold on tight to the wooden arm of the chair with the only strength he has left. For a second, a rheumy eye splits open and he expels the faintest croak of breath that smells like yeast from the black interior of his mouth.

'It's Annie, Dad. She's come to see you.' Ben pops the tea on the table, along with a plate of biscuits.

She can hardly speak. What can she possibly say? Without thinking, she kisses Mr Knot's head. His fingers grasp hers lightly for a second, like a baby finding its first grip.

She picks up her tea and takes a sip, staring into Ben's eyes. 'Are you getting any help?'

'District nurse comes in in the morning after I go to school, but that's just to make sure I'm not stealing his drugs.' Ben stuffs a biscuit into his mouth.

Annie lowers her voice. 'He needs to go to the hospice, Ben. You can't do all this alone.'

'No beds.' Ben's eyes drift to the window, avoiding hers. 'I sleep in the living room. He wets the bed two or three times in the night . . . needs changing. No one else is going to do it.' Ben is on his feet now, at the sink, washing out the mugs.

'Oh Ben, I wish you'd told me. My mum would've—'

'I don't want to burden anyone.' He cuts her off, watching her closely through the reflection in the glass.

Annie pauses for a second, then suddenly stands. Ben turns, thinking that he's blown it. But instead, she steps towards him, gently moves him out of the way and starts to run the tap. She waits for it to get warm then puts in the plug. Under the sink there is a box of washing powder. She pours in a measure and then, without saying a word, heads into the living room, strips the bed and returns with the sheets. She is on a mission.

By the time they've finished, it is getting dark outside. The sheets are hanging out to dry and Anthony Knot is tucked up in fresh linen, washed and changed for the night. The floors have been vacuumed, surfaces scrubbed, and the place is as spick and span as it could possibly be in the few hours they've worked together.

'We make a good team.' Annie smiles at him with admiration.

'We do, don't we?' Ben slumps into his dad's chair and starts to pull on his socks and trainers.

'What are you doing?' Annie stands, sweating with exhaustion.

'Driving you home.' He grabs a set of keys from the table.

'I can call my dad.' Annie puts her hand on his to stop him. 'He'll pick me up.'

'It's no bother.' Ben is already pulling his coat on.

'You're not supposed to be . . .' Annie stops herself. There are a lot of things that a kid of Ben's age isn't supposed to be doing. Nursing his dying father, for one. Illegally driving a clapped-out Ford Fiesta is nobody's business. Annie smiles at him. 'OK, you can take me home – on one condition.'

Ben steps close to her. 'What condition?'

'Please stop bullying Mark Cherry . . . for me. Do it for me.' Their faces are close. 'Deal?'

Maybe he is fully conscious of the effect the bullying has on his victim. Then again, maybe the Ben here in this room is different from the swaggering Top Dog in the school playground who needs to secure his position. This Ben is soft and caring, but the boy out in the world wears a whole other mask.

He nods his head gently, but his voice is strangely detached. 'Deal.'

Annie moves in close to Ben and plants her lips softly on his cheek. Ben turns his face, so they are mouth to mouth, and pulls her in tightly for a deeper kiss. It lingers and Ben presses their bodies together. Annie breaks first but Ben clings to her as if starved of love. He wants to go further.

She presses him gently away with her hand against his shoulder. 'Ben . . .' She glances towards his father. 'Not here.'

'Want to come upstairs?' Ben holds on to her hand, pulling her in.

'I need to get home.' Annie turns and searches for her school bag. Slinging it over her shoulder, she heads out into the hall.

Ben follows. 'You always do this . . .'

'Do what?' Annie places her hand on the door latch.

Ben's hand reaches out and his palm presses against the door. 'Get me all excited and then run away.'

'I'm sorry, it's just . . . your dad.'

Ben's voice lowers, trembling with rage. 'You're always sorry . . . Maybe Lynette's right, you're just a tease.'

Annie pulls on the door, but Ben holds it fast.

'Ben. Let go . . . please. I'm going home.'

She pulls harder and Ben taunts her with the door. 'You play this game with Patel or is it just me you like to get all hot and bothered?'

He finally lets the door swing open and Annie stumbles backwards, falling on to the floor. Ben snorts to himself, leans back against the wall and just watches her pull her skirt down and clamber to her feet.

She moves quickly out on to the driveway, turning back, her face flushed with embarrassment. 'I guess I'll . . . see you at the leavers' party?'

The door hits the wood with such force that the glass almost shatters in the frame. Ben's shadow turns and heads back to his father.

As Annie moves away, she can hear shouts from the kitchen. He's taking it out on him, breaking crockery and flipping furniture. All their hard work undone.

It was her fault. At least, that's what she told herself. She knew the effect she had on him. Passion was a wonderful quality in a boy, but inside Ben was a heat that could burn too hot.

39

MAY 2024

A burning fire emoji.

'Hey . . . you there?' Freckles burst on to the screen.

Nate sat up from the bed as the message dropped.

'Hey, how's it going?'

'Check this out.' Nate turned his camera on, lifted his T-shirt and turned to the side. A rainbow of livid bruises peppered the side of his ribcage.

'Whoa, is that real?'

'What do you think?' A little artist with a beret and a paint-brush, then a wink emoji. Nate was a master with a make-up palette but the bruises looked awful against his pale skin.

Freckles' three dots rotated. As Nate waited, he noticed another follower had logged on. He frowned and turned off the camera.

'Did you shoot any of the vintage film yet?'

Nate had completely forgotten about the Panasonic that Karine had given to him. He typed back.

'I haven't got enough tape.'

'You're gonna be the next Spielberg.' Camera emoji.

Nate stood up from the bed, moved across the room and pulled out the camera from his desk drawer. He returned to the screen. Freckles was fast.

'eBay?' Detective emoji.

Nate sat back on the bed and opened the little door on the camera. There must be some old tapes somewhere. There was all that junk in the basement, the Atari game console with the geriatric tennis game that was like watching paint dry. Old VCRs, a Betamax and a beat-up ZX Spectrum, boxes of crap that should have been dumped at the charity shop. Maybe there were some video tapes buried in there.

'I have a plan.' He sent Freckles a fingers-crossed emoji and signed off.

Ben sat in his office staring at the screen in disbelief. Nate's RetroFX site was open on one side, Lily's Instagram on the other. He'd always allowed both of his kids their privacy online, he had never intervened or checked up on what they did . . . until now. He'd just witnessed Nate's live feed. He'd seen the bruises, but he couldn't see who he was talking to.

He cupped his face with his hands and exhaled sharply.

He didn't know how to stop this; it was way out of control. Ben gritted his teeth and hit the keys so hard his fingertips stung.

Karine Mickelsen.

The Wikipedia entry flashed up an old head shot of her from a few years ago. She was Danish, but a profile link listed her training at Stockholms Filmskola, and there was a short entry about her private life, including a divorce.

A link to a video of huddled crowds at a black-tie event. A line-up of winners, Cate Blanchett, Léa Seydoux, and Karine Mickelsen draped in red silk, her white-blonde hair pinned up in a chignon, surrounded by a gaggle of studio executives smiling and waving on the steps of la Croisette at Cannes 2018. That was the year she had received the Palme d'Or and a César for best adapted screenplay for *The Hoax*.

'The search for the truth is everything to a filmmaker like me.' Karine was standing at the microphone, making her acceptance speech. 'It's all about pushing boundaries. I see myself as an archaeologist digging into the earth, to reveal the secrets hidden in the past. Thank you to my agent and my backers at Sony and Ray of Light, and especially to Shiv Banerjee, who financed the movie – we couldn't have done this without you. Thank you.'

Ben paused the video and sat for a moment. Banerjee . . . that name rang a bell. He continued to scroll through more articles about Mickelsen as a rising star, coming from a journalistic background, through a successful career as a documentary filmmaker and in 2018 breaking out as a feature director. A *Hello!* magazine article of a UK premiere press launch. The after-party at Claridge's in London, and a sea of well-known faces whose names slipped the mind. Ben stopped and clicked on one particular picture. Karine was at the centre of a shot, with five or six others. Below, their names were listed.

'Karine Mickelsen entertains Shiv Banerjee and her husband, Mukash Das, at Claridge's for the after-party of *The Hoax.*'

Ben froze. Mukash Das was an Indian billionaire and one of the major backers of the IF Group.

'I knew it.' Ben's hands swept sweat from his brow as his heart raced.

Das was one of the financiers currently threatening IF with a major lawsuit. He zoomed in closer on the face. They'd never met but the name was etched into his brain. In the background of the shot was a bar; and sitting on a stool, facing away from the camera in profile, was a face Ben thought he recognised. He zoomed in closer still until the frame pixelated.

'It can't be,' Ben muttered to himself. 'What the hell?'

He couldn't be certain, but the profile was familiar. Ben strained to read the copy at the bottom of the picture. Akshata Patel and her husband, Sandeep. Ben's stomach dropped. Mukash Das, the Patels and Karine Mickelsen were all at the same party.

'Knock knock?' Karine was standing at the open door to his office.

Ben's hand whipped out like a shot and slammed the laptop closed.

'Sorry, I didn't mean to make you jump.' In her hands she held two heavy crystal glasses. 'Whisky rocks, peace offering . . . Looks like you could use a drink.'

'What are you doing here?' He looked absolutely terrible.

'I thought you and I needed to have a little chat . . . to break the ice.' The cubes chinked in the glass as she held one out to him.

He pressed his fingers into his tired eye sockets and pushed back in his chair. 'I have some business I need to deal with . . . in private. Work stuff.'

Karine glanced at his laptop and smiled. 'Come on. It's five o'clock somewhere.' Ben took the glass obediently.

'Dårligt er aldrig godt, før værre sker.' She smiled at Ben.

'Sorry?' Ben's glass hovered by his mouth.

'It's a Danish proverb . . . bad is never good until worse happens.'

Ben inclined his head. He inhaled through his nose.

'Are you having work problems?' Karine leant in closer.

Ben eyeballed her. What the hell did she know?

'This is cosy.' Dani's voice cut through the tension. She was standing at the top of the stairs with her arms folded. 'Cocktail hour?' Her eyes drifted to Ben and she pursed her lips.

'It's my fault. I'm corrupting him, Dani.' Karine laughed, brushing it off, and placed her glass down on the desk. 'But I do have an ulterior motive.'

'I'm sure you do.' Dani cut her dead. 'Ben, can I have a word?' She whipped around as best she could on four-inch heels and moved off into the kitchen. He set down the glass and wearily hauled himself out of his chair, following behind her. Karine shrugged apologetically but didn't move. Her eyes returned to Ben's laptop.

She downed her drink in one, then picked up Ben's glass and knocked that back too. She needed some Dutch courage. Karine slid an expensive-looking business card from a marble holder on the desk and studied it. He'd really made something of himself. A CEO no less; it was impressive how high he had risen. Just like her, he was at the top of his game. She pondered for a second; it was such a shame to have to do this. But Ben was the last piece of the puzzle; he was the most important element of all. She studied the phone number on the card. It was all just a game, a bit of artistic fun; a text from the director with a set of instructions – what could be simpler than that? Karine sensed that Ben would need a little more encouragement, a little more prising open than she had anticipated.

She had them all in her sights; the cat was among the pigeons, exactly as she had planned.

40

JUNE 1994

The endless weeks of revision and the stress of their GCSEs have taken their toll. Hours cooped up in sweltering classrooms, desks lined up facing the wall, inky fingers and aching necks from the head-down, frantic splurge of knowledge: from brain to paper. And now it's the calm before the storm, the no man's land before the exam results come in. Ben knows his grades will be shit, one more reason for Farmer John to keep him away from his daughter. Dave's dad has ridiculous expectations for his son. Annie has it for nothing; she's got a photographic memory, so her exams are always a breeze, except when she's distracted. The Davis twins would most likely suffer the most, having done zero work, fancying their chances to just wing it on the day. It hadn't gone well.

From the top of the chimney, high up in the Crow's Nest, Mark Cherry has Catherine Maddock in his sights. She's as tiny as an ant, by the edge of the brook in the distance below. Wrapping her legs tightly around the tyre swing dangling from the old willow, she braces herself for take-off. Annie stands behind, holding on to her sister's waist as she pulls back the rope swing and pushes her out over the water. Cat is suddenly flying out high into the sky, arms windmilling and skinny legs bicycling in mid-air. Her squeal of delight makes Mark smile as he watches his best friend splash down into the deep water of the mill pond at the top of the weir before rising up like a champion diver. She clambers on to the top ledge of the concrete slope and skids down towards the shallower brook below, splatting, bottom first, on to the surface.

Mark is just about to descend from the top of the chimney stack when he notices Dave Patel and Chris Davis on the wall of the reservoir by the water wheel. The sluice running from the brook is little more than damp mud. The wheel is still intact after all this time, half of it preserved in silt, half of it bolted together with a makeshift scaffold. A shopping trolley, old cans of paint, car tyres and pieces of timber have blocked up the tail race and the whole stinking soup is an absolute death trap. Chris has a rope around the branches of a tree that has sprouted in the walls of the old covered tunnel and Dave has a crowbar and tent mallet. He's hacking at the bricks around the roots while Chris hauls on the rope, gradually dislodging the tree as the crumbling ancient masonry loosens and a section of wall gives way. The smallest trickle of water begins to fill the sluice as Patel sets to work with his mallet.

Cat and Annie have set up a picnic blanket by the edge of the water and are lying on their bellies, picking daisies, making tiny holes in their stems with their fingernails and linking them together.

Annie is adjusting her crown of flowers when she spots Mark at the entrance to the mill. 'Where have you been?'

'Up there.' Mark turns back and regards the tower, from which he's just descended, with pride. He starts to jog over.

'Mark, wait! There's a load of cow sh—' Too late. Mark lifts his foot from the grass, flip-flop dangling ankle-deep in stinking green-brown gunk.

'Whoopsie.'

Cat puts her hand to her mouth, stifling a laugh. 'You can say that again.'

'Very funny.' He hops towards the edge of the water to wash his foot.

'Want some squash?' Annie calls out, holding a blue plastic flask from her open lunch box. 'We brought sarnies too, corned beef and Branston, and some Bakewell tarts if you're hungry. Mum made them.'

Mark flops down, all cleaned up. He flips the lid of the flask and takes a sip. 'Oh my gosh, it's scorching . . . I'm so hot.' He lies back on the blanket and lifts his foot, thrusting it into Cat's face.

'Eeuugh . . . it stinks. Get off.' She rolls off the blanket and charges towards the water to cool off.

Annie takes a piece of tart from the lunch box and offers it to Mark. They both chew on the almond sweet pastry, the midday sun beating heavily down on their heads.

'He promised to leave you alone, Mark.' Annie fills the small plastic cup with lemon barley water.

'What?' Mark's mouth is full of jam and pastry. 'Who?'

'Ben. I asked him to.' Annie sips her drink and swats a fly buzzing around the food.

'Oh no . . . what did you say to him?' Mark stops chewing and looks grave for a second, as a long shadow creeps up his legs and body.

'What did she say to who?' Ben is standing behind Mark and, in the glare of the sun, he cuts a heroic silhouette in nothing but football shorts.

Annie glares at Ben. 'Nothing. Talking about you, not to you.'

'Bad-mouthing me to your little friend?' He casts his eyes towards the mill: Dave and Chris are hobbling over, head to toe in mud, red-faced and sweaty. 'HEY . . . DID YOU DO IT?'

Chris drops the branch he's carrying and jogs over. 'Yep, next torrential rainstorm and the wheel should move . . . Patel nearly committed Mata Hari.'

'Hara-kiri, numb nuts.' Ben laughs and heads over to join them.

Patel calls over to Mark, 'Come on, Cherry, don't think we haven't noticed that you haven't been in the drink all day.' Goading him.

'Yeah, leave your gay little teddy bears' picnic and get on that swing.' Chris grabs Mark by the arm and hauls him to his feet.

Annie makes eye contact with Ben, a warning not to break their pact, not to renege on their deal. Ben, sulking, heads off towards the water's edge.

'OFF, OFF, OFF, OFF!' Dave claps, as Chris pulls on Mark's T-shirt. Lynette, arms freshly covered in lick'n'stick tattoos, jogs up, joining in the chant.

'All right, I'll go.' Mark pushes Chris as he tries to pull down his shorts. 'GET OFF ME! I can do it.'

'OH MY GOD! He-Man? Haaaah!' Lynette bursts out laughing at Mark's *Masters of the Universe* swimming trunks, having been stripteased out of his trousers. 'Come on then, He-Man, let's see what you got!'

Annie and Cat sit quietly, saying nothing.

Mark approaches the willow as the chanting and clapping continues, and grips on to the rope for dear life, terrified as the gang pull back on the tyre. The bough of the willow creaks and cracks ominously.

'One, two, three.' The push that comes is too violent and far too high. Mark swings out above the water and his hands release from the rope. For a second, he is suspended in mid-air, a look of utter shock on his face. Then he plummets, falling heavy as a stone, face-first into the pond, belly flopping on to the surface of the water. It smacks him in the face with a force like landing on concrete. Everything goes dark.

The sound of water and the sudden shift from hot to cold create a strange sensation that Mark hadn't prepared himself for. He could just lie here, still and silently floating, suspended, calm and happy. The feeling of sinking is oddly comforting. Sinking into the dark, he curls himself into a foetal position and takes a deep breath in.

The sound of voices around him, muffled and distant, gurgle into focus. A hard, painful pressure pounds on his chest, and something warm is clamped over his mouth, suffocating him. He's gagging, about to vomit. The ground shifts and he's tilted sideways. Daylight seeps in through his eyelids and he's sick, water exploding from his mouth and ears, out on to the warm grass.

'Oh, thank God. Mark? Mark? You're OK. You're OK.' The drifting voices swim in and out of his waterlogged ears, as he lies on the ground coughing. He opens his eyes and, gently falling into his eye line, Ben's face hovers over him.

'Quite a good kisser,' Ben laughs, looking down at the boy he just saved, white as a sheet and panting with exhaustion. 'You OK?'

Mark buries his face into the grass and vomits water again. 'I'll be fine, leave me alone.' He can barely speak.

'All right. Keep your knickers on.' Ben tuts and gets up off the grass.

'Yeah, keep your He-Man poofter pants on!' Chris chips in.

Mark flushes with rage. Everyone is gathered round in a circle, staring at him. Smirking. Mocking smiles, whispering behind their hands. For once in his life, it becomes too much to bear.

'Just fuck off, Ben Knot! Fuck off, all of you!' Mark staggers to his feet trembling with white-hot anger, his fists clenched, spit forming on his lips.

'Come on then, have a go.'

Mark squares up to the tall blond real-life He-Man who is towering over him. Nobody breathes. But then, almost out of nowhere, Mark's arm swings wide, cracking Ben across the side of the face. Ben reels back in shock, holding his hand to his cheek as Mark waits for the inevitable retaliation. Trembling from head to toe, adrenaline pumping and tears rolling down his cheeks.

'I just saved you from drowning, you little prick!' The look on Ben's face shifts from shock to menace. He steps forward. 'Was that your first kiss with a man? Well, it definitely won't be the last, will it?' He is close up in his face, but then turns to the crowd. 'We know all about you. He really is a bender!'

Mark swallows hard, his vision blurs and his head spins. His whole world is collapsing around him. How did Ben know? He looks at Annie Maddock. It must be her. She's betrayed him and now they all know. He pushes his way through a circle of shocked faces. Annie follows behind, catching his arm.

'Mark, are you OK? Come here.' She's holding out a blanket to cover him.

'Leave me alone!' The fury in him rises to his throat. 'Traitor.'

He couldn't forgive and would never forget.

She was dead to him.

41

JUNE 2024

The last few girls walked through the school gates as Ben sat waiting for his daughter to emerge from football practice. When she didn't appear, he opened his phone and tapped on the Meta app, scrolling to Lily's feed. She always posted after the game.

Lily Knot has blocked you.

'Shit.' Ben hated spying on his kids, but he was losing control. A tap on the window made him jump. The face of Mr Branchflower, the sports teacher, loomed into the glass. He dropped the window.

'Hello, Ben. How's tricks? Everything OK?' Branchflower must have been in his sixties by now. When Ben was his star pupil thirty years ago, he was like some heroic pin-up, tanned and strapping. Now his hair was grey, and his pecs had descended into 'moobs'.

'Just picking Lily up. She's probably messing around in the changing room.' Ben leant back wearily against the headrest.

'Lily didn't turn up tonight.' Branchflower pulled his car keys from his sports bag.

'What? That's not like her.' Ben glanced at his phone for missed calls.

'This so-called film they're both involved in . . .' Branchflower paused, chewing his lip. 'I just hope it's worth keeping them out of school for. If you want my advice, they both need to be getting their heads down.'

Ben frowned at him. 'What are you talking about?'

'I haven't seen Nate on the football field for a few weeks now, but maybe it's just me he's allergic to.' He pulled his bag over his shoulder and headed towards his car. 'Just give them a heads-up to prioritise their studies, Ben.'

Ben watched as Branchflower got into his car. It was starting to get dark as Ben pulled away from the sports centre and began to head home. Where the hell were they? He drove down Forest Hill and turned right at the small parade of shops. A group of kids were squatting on the wall outside Codswallop, sharing chips from a polystyrene box. Ben crawled slowly along the kerb, leaning over to the passenger side to scrutinise every face, hunting for his children. One of the girls in a pleated mini skirt flipped a finger at him, whispered to her friends and took a photo on her phone.

Ben headed down the winding lane past the Red Lion and over the small humpback bridge on to Barton Road, which wrapped around what was left of Mallet Hill. He pulled off the road on to Mill View and took the unmarked track towards the car park. Instinctively, he turned off his headlights. Doggers Dive was empty except for one other car, parked in the corner. Ben pulled up by the grass verge and turned off the engine. In the twilight, he sat staring at the mill tower. The sun was setting behind it and the long shadow reached out over the water, creeping closer to him, taunting him.

A tap on the glass of his window startled him.

'Can you step out of the car, sir?' Ben's stomach lurched.

'Oh right . . .' He wasn't here for that. He had just needed some quiet.

'Car trouble? Or are you walking the dog?' The implication that he was soliciting was buried in the sarcasm.

Ben recognised PC Davis's voice. 'Chris . . . It's me.'

'Aye aye . . . back to your old tricks, Casanova?' Chris stepped back as the door opened.

'Far too old for all that.' Ben got out and closed the door. 'Actually, I'm looking for my two . . . Sounds odd, but Lily wasn't at football tonight and Nate isn't answering his phone.'

Chris had been an unlikely late bloomer, turning his life around. Military fit and sharp as a razor blade.

'Well, you're not going to find them here, are you?' Chris coughed uncomfortably.

'Thought they might be playing at the weir . . . like we used to.' Ben glanced back to the mill and lowered his head with a sigh. He was about to get back into his car when Chris stopped him.

'You heard Patel confessed to everything? Only reason he's allowed out. We're bracing ourselves; the whole village is.'

Ben fixed his eyes on his old friend but didn't speak.

'We got him in the end though . . . served his full sentence.' Chris lowered his voice. 'You're welcome . . .'

Ben furrowed his brow. 'What do you mean?'

'Don't tell me you're suffering from dementia as well?' Chris folded his arms. 'Could have been you.'

A crackle of nerve endings rippled over Ben's scalp. 'Could have been any of us . . .'

Davis pursed his lips and glanced over the water to the tower. Ben didn't blink.

'Oh, cheer up, Knot . . . It's all over now. Patel's served his time.' Chris turned off the torch and wandered back to his car. 'He was stalking her, grooming her . . . we all knew it, smelt it a mile away.' Chris reached the car and opened the door.

Ben stopped him. 'I saw you talking to Karine Mickelsen in the Red Lion.'

Davis paused. 'I talk to a lot of people in my line of work . . . kind of my job.'

'What did she want?'

'Same thing that all of them have wanted over the years: gory details. They're all just rubbernecking ambulance chasers who get a thrill from raking up the past.' Chris climbed into the driver's seat and put the key into the ignition. 'Seemed to know her stuff though. Oh, don't look so shocked.' He tapped a finger to his nose. 'I didn't give her anything that hasn't already been said.' He turned the ignition and the blue lights spun against the trees.

'Unless she flashes the cash again . . . very tempting.' Davis winked then put the car in reverse and pulled away up the lane.

Ben stood in the muddy car park of Doggers Dive. Trees creaking and whispering as they bent in the wind.

He'd been lying to himself, and he'd been listening to the lie to the point that it had become his whole foundation. He needed to take a bold new step, to utter the words out loud. He couldn't hold on to it any longer, he had to tell someone, but it was what he feared most.

The rider in black straddling the motorbike, deep in the woods, watched as the police car left, and the camera focused in on Ben. He was sitting in the driver's seat, facing the water with his head in his hands. The shot moved in tighter, so close she could see his chest heaving.

It was happening. Fear was leaking out of him, like blood from a wound, unravelling and completely out of his control.

42

JUNE 2024

Max drove along Vista Del Mar to Manhattan Beach on autopilot, racing the surfers riding waves into the Santa Monica Bay. Access to the ILM studio was through a friend at Disney and Lucasfilm who owed him a favour. The sound stage, initially built for *Obi-Wan* and *The Mandalorian*, was no longer in use, but Max had the skills to work The Volume alone. The coast road from Marina del Rey took him to the very edge of the sea and the end of the runway of LAX. A crowd of surfers and beachcombers had gathered to film an incoming A380 that skimmed the tide, its engines blasting so close you could see the passengers' faces in the windows. Max checked the side pocket of his carry-on for his passport. After he finished up at the end of the day, he would head to departures.

'Hey, Letitia.'

The glamorous receptionist on the desk of Industrial Light & Magic wore sliders and cut-off denim shorts. She gave Max a huge grin and the grills on her teeth sparkled. 'Hey, Mr Crow, long time no see.' She sucked on a straw from an enormous plastic cup. 'I got it all set up in there for ya.'

Max dumped his bag behind the desk. 'Thanks for coming in on a Saturday.'

'Of course, Larry said it was for you so . . .' Letitia flicked her braided dreads over her shoulder. 'Just so ya know, I don't have anyone on Brain Bar to help run the program though.'

'All good, I'm not shooting today, just reviewing.' Max pulled his laptop from his bag. 'You're a star.'

'Well, ya'll need anything, just holla.' She clamped her glossy lips to the straw and her eyes returned to the screen of her phone.

The Volume was all set; the footage he had sent over digitally was loaded on to the multiple screens that formed the state-of-the-art immersive sound stage. They were nearly there in the rough cut, but there were still crucial pieces missing.

Max set up his laptop and ran the program that would hold his footage in the system. The surrounding light bleed outside The Volume faded to black as the first image of *The Cut* formed in three dimensions around him. He stepped out into the space about the size of a tennis court as the opening scenes of the film began. The silhouette of the mill was almost exactly as it was back then. Max breathed in deeply, holding his nerve. It was as if he was stepping back there. He made a mental note to extend the tower just a little bit higher than it really was, make the river just a little wider; everything needed to be exaggerated.

The assembly was seamless. Max stood at the very centre of the action, as if it was playing in real time around him. On the football field he ran with the players, he flinched as punches flew, ducking and diving through fight after fight. The blood and the aftermath all around him in a virtual backdrop. Then he lay on his belly in the terrifying darkness of Pen y Fan and the camping trip with the unseen monster in the woods. His heart raced as he chased through the fairground into the Mouth of Hell and felt the heat of the fire.

Max grounded his feet into the concrete floor as the image on the huge LED screen began to rock like a seesaw. Nate was on the rope swing tied to the branch of a tree overhanging the brook at Cheney End. A ripple of laughter and the sound of splashing kids enjoying the sunshine blended with the choral high notes of the choir on the soundtrack.

'OFF, OFF, OFF!' Nate's exhilarated face, flushed with energy, turned to the camera. 'MASTERS OF THE UNIVERSE!'

The camera moved slowly up the rope to the knot attached to the creaking branch, bending under the strain of the boy's weight. Max knew what was coming next and he braced himself.

Nate's face grew larger in the frame as he swung towards the camera. The director had dropped into monochrome, close on a mouth wide open in a silent scream, a moment of pure expressionism that would hold up to Murnau's *Nosferatu*. The image slowed to fifty frames per second . . . and the branch broke.

Max watched in horror as the rope twanged from the splitting wood. He couldn't believe what he was seeing: did they actually do this, or was it a stunt? Nate couldn't swim, he'd confessed as much in his audition tape; surely Karine knew that? He plunged headfirst into the river. Max's whole body juddered as Nate hit the water, and he gasped for air as if he himself was going under. As the camera panned across the surface, Max followed the river from one screen to the next. It was all around him, a continuous turbulent flood. He moved with the current along the bank, as if he was right there, waiting for Nate to resurface, but he was gone. The shot cut to a black screen, then a countdown to the next take.

Max crouched down and caught his breath. His heart thumping in his chest, he knew what was coming next. The story needed Annie's journey from the minute she left home that night, all the way to the school. He wanted to track everything that had happened after that, moment by moment. Every single detail of that missing half an hour when Annabel Maddock had disappeared had to be revealed for the story to be complete.

Out of the darkness, a thin silhouette stepped into a half-light, and black became grey, bleeding into the soft orange hue of the evening. She was moving fast but the camera was steadier this time, tracking from feet to legs, to spine, closing in on the back of her neck. Max followed her slowly, pacing across the space that led him deep into that dark alley. His heart raced; the emotional recall was almost too much to bear. He stopped as her hand reached out to caress the fence. Max reached out along with her, fingers gently brushing the climbing ivy, covered with cream-coloured flowers. Max closed his eyes. He could feel the metal fence on his fingertips turn to wood. He opened his eyes as Lily Knot, the girl playing Annabel, drifted through the shot in white chiffon, floating like an angel. She was heading up The Cut towards the school, full of excitement for their prom. Max followed her.

'Turn around. Let me see you.' He stepped in closer to the LED wall.

The image distorted and he backed off a little. Karine was good. This was exactly what she had intended; she wanted the audience to crane their heads to see the face of the protagonist. But she was denying them the satisfaction. Max exhaled as a sudden wave of guilt rose into his throat.

He closed his eyes and stood in the darkness, steadying himself. This had been a long time coming. He wasn't prepared for the surge of emotion that was flooding his body; it was a completely physical reaction to the immersion of The Volume. He wanted to crumple into the concrete floor; his stomach felt hollow and his heart ached for her. The girl on the screen.

The cuts of the penultimate act before the finale had been partially recreated, just as they had planned.

Nate's Marty McFly costume was convincing but the angle from the top of the tower looking down into the car park was shot against a green screen. Max tapped the keys of the computer and The Volume shifted sideways across the vast LED wall to a clearing on the other side of the river. It was a plate shot from the actual location at Blackstone Mill. That's where the car would need to be parked.

An eruption of sound and an impressive burst of fireworks from stock footage filled all four walls of The Volume. Max looked down at his hands and arms as his whole body was covered in the reflections of the glittering fire. A car alarm sounded, screaming over the explosion of a thunderclap. Max's hands flew to cover his ears as all four screens slammed to black. Max stood in the darkness waiting, his heart racing erratically in his chest. Every cell in his body was back there, remembering every impulse of that fateful night.

Slowly, the screen began to fade up, into an extreme close-up of a pair of eyes. As the camera pulled back, the pixelated face became clearer.

Although she was older now, there was still something so familiar about her features, the sad smile that he had known so well. Her hair was cut into a bob and streaked with silver, framing her delicate features, but the kind sad eyes that stared back at him sent a shudder of recognition through Max. Deep in the pit of his stomach there lingered a profound sense of guilt.

Her married name was Carter, but back then he had known her as Catherine Maddock.

43

JUNE 2024

'Lily? Nate?' Ben opened the front door to the dark house and called out. He began to head upstairs, desperate to see a light under Lily's door and the sound of Nate's Castlevania game spilling from his room. He was halfway up when he noticed someone sitting in his dad's old wing chair in the den, not moving. A wave of anxiety coursed through him before he realised it was Dani. She'd heard him come in but was just silently sitting there in the dark, like a corpse. What did she know? He descended the stairs and headed towards the kitchen. He decided to strike first.

'So, apparently Lily and Nate have been absent from school for this sodding film. I've just sat outside the school waiting for her . . . and I've been driving around all the villages looking for them both.' Ben was trembling.

'Course you were.' Dani huffed out a laugh. 'I'm not an idiot, Ben.'

'What's going on, Dani? Where are Lily and Nate?' His questions were met with silence. 'Dani . . . where are my children?' *My* children, he checked himself as their eyes met. 'What? . . . What have I done?' The sing-song tone was Ben's way of trivialising her. He did it all the time, turning her into the proverbial hen who enjoyed picking and pecking.

He moved towards her, rounding the armchair. On the glass coffee table was his computer, open on an email account, a thread of words and a collection of low-res attachments, too small for him to make out any detail.

'Is that my laptop?' She had gone through his emails. She had found out how deep underwater he was, that they were about to lose everything. She knew the house was going to have to go on the market and that a court case for fraud wouldn't be far behind. He should have told her while he still had the chance. He took a step closer to her.

'Is there something you want to tell me, Ben?' Dani's voice was soft and calm.

'Sorry?' Ben rooted himself to the spot.

'God, the irony. You're not even my husband.' Now she looked at him, laser focused, wound up and ready to explode. 'They're not even my kids, and yet here I am, playing happy families.'

'Dani . . . what is all this?' Ben perched on the arm of the love seat opposite.

'Your search history is very telling, love.' Dani folded her arms. 'It's like a digital fingerprint . . . I can see where you've been.'

'What are you doing?' Ben was genuinely baffled. He looked closely at the computer screen. The article about Karine Mickelsen was open, alongside all the other tabs where he'd googled her, researching her online. Based on his search history, one might think Ben was obsessed.

'I'm just worried about what she's doing here. Something is off. Lily and Nate are missing school, gallivanting around at all hours of the night, bruised black and blue. I'm seriously worried and you don't seem to be.'

'Oh, don't try to turn this around on me.' Dani held up her phone. 'There's more.'

On her phone, Dani showed her Instagram feed. It was the shot the schoolgirl had taken of him inside his car earlier that night. Dani read out the caption while her eyes filled with tears. 'Pervert kerb crawler . . . heading down to Doggers Dive.'

'What?' Ben sat on the arm of the sofa, his hands over his face.

'Do you know how embarrassing this is?' Her voice was sad, resigned to her fate.

'Dani, stop . . . listen to me.' Ben leant forward and took her shoulders, gripping her hard. 'This is all my fault. I was looking for the kids. I swear to you. I saw PC Davis down there. Ask him yourself.'

'Oh yeah, so what did you and your old friend Chris Davis talk about?' Dani was shaking with rage.

'Karine's been asking him questions, sniffing around. I'm telling you, she's up to something.'

'Up to what, Ben? This doesn't make any sense.'

'She's here all the time, in our lives, messing with the kids, investigating the past. This film isn't what it seems. I think she's looking into Annie's murder. I think she's going to try and rake up all the details about the case.'

'Wow, now you're really pushing it.' Dani got up from the armchair and made to leave. 'It's just a stupid horror film, Ben. You're losing it.'

He grabbed her by the wrist. 'I'm serious – listen to me! She's going to try and pin it on me.' His whole body was shaking.

Dani was quiet, finally listening. 'Pin what on you? Annie's death? But Patel . . .'

Ben convulsed as the tightness in his chest sent a wave of nausea through him. 'Oh . . . love.' He had to tell her. That's what this pain was, something leaching on his heart. He needed to get this unbearable weight off his chest.

'I've never told anyone this before.' He rubbed at his sternum. Dani tightened her mouth with quivering breaths. 'Chris Davis doctored the DNA test for me . . . I took a swab from my dad.'

'What are you talking about?' Dani looked confused as she sat back down.

'Before the Patel trial. He switched the sample.'

'What?' She retracted, folding her arms and tightening herself into a ball.

'She was my girlfriend; my DNA would have been everywhere. I was panicking and Chris had access to the forensic team at the police station, or at least his dad did. He helped me. I didn't know what else to do.' Ben was white, his hands were shaking.

Dani stared at him. 'But he went to prison, Ben.'

'Because he was guilty.' Ben was calm. 'Yes . . . and the sentence for that crime has been served.' The pain in his chest had lifted and his hands were still.

'What are you trying to tell me?' Dani stood up calmly, but her knees were trembling.

'I'm telling you that Karine is investigating the case, and if she finds that detail out from somewhere, I'm in serious trouble. She'll burn us to the ground.'

Dani felt light-headed. There was an awful silence.

'I loved her. We were teenagers.' Ben's voice was distant and broken.

'Ben, I think you need some time to yourself.' Dani turned, her eyes searching for her car keys on the kitchen counter. She had to get out of this house. 'I don't know what's happening here, but I'm . . . I'm going to go to my sister's for the night. Lily is having a sleepover at Gaynor's and Nate is upstairs talking to God knows who on the internet.'

She leant in for a kiss and pecked him on the cheek. Her hand touched his face and then she backed away and left the room.

Ben stood at the front door and listened to Dani's car engine disappearing down the street. He turned to the door of the basement, flicked the light switch on and descended the stairs.

The service cupboard door was open and a bundle of heavy-gauge cables trailed along the floor. Ben followed them with his eyes, past the shelving covered with junk, and his wine collection, to the door at the end. The entrance to the garage was cracked open so the cables could pass through.

He opened the door and moved into the empty concrete bunker that was supposed to have been home to a collection of classic cars. The cables trailed across the pristine floor towards the up-and-over double door. Set up in a square, like a hide, were a number of heavy metal trunks, stacked high. Trolleys with piles of cabling and electronics, and two LED large-screen monitors. Ben sat in the fold-up camping chair that was set in front of them and pressed the switch on the side of the monitor.

A flicker of electronic activity burst into life as the monitor turned white, then a time code and date flashed in the corner of the screen. He leant forward to the small electronic box below that looked like a hard drive. He pressed play and it whirred into action. On the screen, various thumbnails appeared with dates and times. Shots of his children, frozen in small postage-stamp-sized icons, and other faces and names he recognised.

Ben sat with his head in his hands for a moment, then moved the cursor to 'Davis'.

'Could have been another Ripper if my dad hadn't finally got a conviction. We all knew who it was anyway.'

Ben stopped the tape. The floor felt soft under his feet and the sensation of sinking into the concrete overwhelmed him. He clicked on the next one: 'Patel'.

'*They othered him, so he buried himself in separate pursuits, solitary interests . . . Pity they didn't find all the tapes.*'

'*You think there were more?*'

'*Well, let's just say some houses were never searched . . . not like ours. Like I said . . . shouldn't have let them in.*'

Ben's heart thumped inside his ribcage and his palms began to sweat as he frantically moved the cursor to fast-forward to the next thumbnail: 'Lynette'.

'*Stringing them all along she was. She weren't a virgin neither. She were on the pill. Din't tell her parents.*'

He stopped the tape and pressed his fists into his temples, then smashed his knuckles hard against his skull, over and over. Like a frenzied madman. He tore at his hair and sank to his knees, pushing his face into the rough concrete floor. But he couldn't cry, for help or for sorrow. Nothing came out; he had no tears. He wanted the flesh to burn off his body right there, but he felt nothing except an excruciating pain in his chest. His head lifted to the monitor.

Ben sat in stunned silence, with his head in his hands. John Maddock had been right. This film wasn't fiction, it was an investigation.

A steely coldness started from the crown of Ben's head and descended through his body. His heart slowed. He looked up from his hands and into the monitor.

He knew what he had to do. He needed to put a stop to this, whatever it took.

He began to erase the hard drive.

44

JUNE 2024

Catherine Maddock looked Max directly in the eye. Her face filled the entire wall of The Volume; the image was distorted because of the format. There was music playing in the background. Mendelssohn.

'The investigation dragged on for almost a year, isn't that right?'

'Yes, the police were under enormous pressure to solve the case.' Catherine held the camera in her gaze, staring directly into Max's eyes.

'And do you think they did?'

'It was never clear what happened at the mill, but we all had to just trust the evidence.'

'All the evidence except for the murder weapon?'

'Yes, that was never recovered.' Catherine swallowed down tears as the past suddenly came rushing back like a flood.

'And there was more than one person's DNA found on your sister's body?'

'Yes.' She exhaled and gathered herself. 'But it was the night of the leaving party. She could have danced with anyone, she could have kissed . . . anyone. She was a teenager. But the fact that they found her blood on Dave's trainers was enough. Witnesses saw him at the scene. All the video tapes he made of her hidden in his bedroom, and the other personal items he stole from her, of course.'

Max closed his eyes; it was unbearable. He knew all too well what Catherine meant by other personal items. The trail that had been left in the wake of his design, and he had done nothing to stop it.

'You were friends with Mark Cherry.' A flicker of something passed over her face.

Max closed in on the screen; he felt tiny in front of her towering image.

'Marcello . . . yes.' She smiled to herself and her eyes found the light at the window. 'Best friends.'

'And yet he didn't testify at the trial, despite being at the scene of the crime.' The interviewer paused.

'Mark . . . wasn't well in the days and weeks following . . .' Catherine stared into the lens again.

'Go on.'

'His mind wasn't clear . . . he . . . he had a breakdown. As an eyewitness, he could have changed everything . . . but he was . . . he was in hospital and then after that, he just vanished. We lost contact.'

Max slowly began to step away from Catherine's face. The music was still playing the undulating chords like waves crashing against jagged rocks, mirroring the violent turbulence surging inside him.

'I just want closure, Dad too. Mum has forgotten; in a way it's a blessing that she has. Everyone got so caught up in the trial because it was all about Dave. But somewhere in the middle of it all, Annie got lost. My sister became just a body that had washed up downstream. I left her that night to go and watch the fireworks. If only I'd stayed.'

Max's mouth tightened as the tears began to fill his eyes and the lump in his throat threatened to choke him.

'They said all kinds of things about her – that she led him on, that she wasn't a virgin. They said that he groomed her. I don't think any of it was true. They were fixated on Dave. A fight had broken out between Ben and Dave over her at the party; they said Ben was defending her. It got violent, but it became all about the boys. My sister was somehow sidelined as a statistic, like she was just a piece of meat.'

Catherine dabbed her face with a handkerchief and recovered her composure, staring directly at Max. The digitised face of his childhood friend penetrating his soul.

'I just wish I knew exactly what happened to my sister that night, what she went through, so that we can all finally rest.'

Max was bent double; he crouched to his knees and clasped his hand over his mouth. He knew there was a way to give Catherine the closure she needed. He had always known there was a video tape that hadn't been seen by anyone else. He had to find it.

Had he started on this journey for her or for himself? To release the grip that guilt had taken on his heart. Perhaps that's how it had all started but now he knew he had to finish the story, not only for Cat but for Annie too.

45

JULY 1994

St Swithin's Day, if it does rain
Full forty days, it will remain.

The month-long heat wave finally breaks with some of the most violent thunderstorms in the region for years. Static electricity crackles in the air as the black storm clouds gather over the open quarry at Mallet Hill. The sweltering heat of the previous month has baked the ground rock hard and scorched the grass. A hose-pipe ban stifles all the usual summer fun of leaping through sprinklers and slipping on soggy turf in back-garden paddling pools. The brook at Cheney End feels like an oasis. There is a stifling tension in the air: something is about to break. It's more than just a weather pattern; everyone feels it. Exams are over, the school term is nearing its end. A feeling of restlessness hangs over the village of Barton Mallet. Hot and sticky nights with the windows open have left everyone tired and irritable. So, when the rain comes, it is a release.

The heavens open at 2 a.m. on St Swithin's Day and the sky crackles with forked lightning. An overwhelming volume of water drenches the clay-baked earth, unable to penetrate. Flash flooding in the region hit the lowlands hard. The brook at Cheney End is swollen and breaks its banks at around 8 a.m. The Water Splash at Water Ford Gate is overflowing into the surrounding fields, but the most worrying breach is man-made.

The small hole in the sluice wall, the handiwork of Davis and

Patel, has opened up a steady flow of water. The mill pond is high, the head race at full capacity and the deep reservoir for the water wheel filling fast. The covered tunnel to the tail race, blocked with shopping trolleys and detritus, won't hold for long. Another night of rain and the dam will break.

'Let's play it again from the beginning.' Catherine places the score on her music stand and picks up the needle from the spinning vinyl LP on the radiogram in her bedroom. She adjusts the RPM, slowing down their 'backing track', and wets the reed of her clarinet. Mark flips his score back a few pages and grips his cello between his legs. He tightens the small nut on the end of his bow and applies more rosin.

The first few bars of 'The Hebrides' overture by Mendelssohn always cause Mark's hairs to stand on end, the undulating chords of the rising arpeggios like the ebb and flow of the sea, and the naming of Fingal's Cave conjured up images of shipwrecks and wild stormy seas.

The rain lashes against the window and the lights in the bedroom flicker. The Maddock Farm has become a swamp of muddy, waterlogged fields after the heavy rain overnight, but the cattle have been locked in the sheds and the sheep herded into the pen, safe and sound for the evening. Mark's socks and sweater are drying out on the radiator and Mrs M made sure they both finished a bowl of beef stew with dumplings before they were allowed upstairs to practise.

Annie Maddock is out this evening and Mark is glad of that. He doesn't want to see her after the shock of her betrayal. He's avoiding her, and anyway, he needs her to be out of the way for what he has planned. He had it all figured out, all under control, but then Annie had blown his cover and now everyone knew. How could she do that to him? She was as bad as the rest of them, worse even because she'd pretended to care. The more he thought about it, the more he hated her. He wanted her to disappear. He wanted to make her sorry. And that's exactly what he intended to do.

'Penny for 'em?' Cat hovers over the radiogram, ready to drop the needle. 'You look like you're about to kill someone, you psycho.' She laughs and kicks his leg with her foot.

'Just thinking.' Mark fingers one of the pegs of his cello. 'Getting into character.' He tunes the G string a little sharper. Cat lowers the needle and the record crackles into the intro.

Mark runs his bow over the strings of Mendelssohn's opening arpeggios. He smiles at Cat as she places the clarinet into her mouth and harmonises to the low turbulent crescendo of the first few bars. Outside, the thunder rises in sympathy, adding an ominous bass to the music winding out of the window of the Maddock Farm.

A few miles away, the stifling tension in the dark sky releases a lash of forked lightning, like a whipped tongue, spitting venom from the sky. The Hanging Tree along the old road into the village is suddenly illuminated. The damp leaves fizzle as drops of water vaporise into a sudden explosion of fire. The old oak ignites, smoking and burning as branches fall and the trunk is severed in two.

'What was that?' Mark stops playing for a second as Mendelssohn's orchestra crescendoes on the vinyl. Cat moves to the window and peels back the heavy curtains.

'It's a fire.' The glowing light in the distance blazes for a moment then dies down. 'Over towards Mallet Hill.' The sheet lightning takes over, accompanied by curtains of wind-driven rain.

Cat's shoulder touches his and she presses into him gently. He smiles at her in the reflection, condensation framing their faces.

'Break time? I'm dying for a cuppa.' Cat smiles and hurries off downstairs to fetch tea and biscuits.

The rumble of thunder recedes outside and Mark rises, ready to do what he came here for. He lays down his cello and tiptoes out on to the landing. He listens from the top of the stairs; the TV is on in the sitting room and the kettle is already whistling on the stove. Not much time. He has to be quick. He creeps along the landing and silently pushes open the door to Annie's bedroom. Without flicking on the light, he crosses to her chest of drawers.

'Custard cream or bourbon?' Cat yells up the stairs.

Heart beating fast, Mark reaches into a pile of dirty clothes ready for the wash and takes something out, stuffing it into his pocket. He can already hear Cat's footsteps on the stairs. Shit. He daren't breathe. He's trapped. He stands in the darkness of Annie's room, heart beating, peering out of the dark as he sees her turn the corner at the top, two cups of tea in her hands and a plate of biscuits balanced on her arm.

'I got both . . . and Jaffa Cakes.' She nudges open the door to the bedroom. 'Oh . . . where are you?'

Just as she is about to turn back, Mark flits over to the bathroom door, reaches in and flushes the toilet. He grabs the towel from the rack and pops his head out, pretending to wipe his hands.

'Yum. Two secs.' He flings the towel back over the bath and pads back into the bedroom, pushing something deep into his pocket, before grabbing two Jaffa Cakes and stuffing them into his mouth whole.

'You OK? You look white as a sheet.' Cat blows the surface of her tea.

'Mmmph ummph and ffft.' Mark splutters with his mouth full.

'You felt fat?'

Mark spits Jaffa crumbs from his mouth, unable to speak.

'Well . . . taking a dump in the middle of a storm isn't going to help much.' Cat giggles, spilling tea on the carpet. They both explode with laughter.

A few miles away, the water in the pond at Blackstone Mill begins to rise. The ancient wheel on its rusty spindle strains under the weight of the water filling the deep reservoir. The rotten blades buckle under the pressure as the metal housing of the central pin creaks and grinds into motion. Buried deep in black mud, the bottom of the wheel begins to shift. Billows of murky silt rise as the tail race releases its blockage and the huge volume of water begins to push. Unable to resist the force and true to its purpose, the rusting ancient wheel untethers itself from the inertia of its metal prison and the mill awakens.

46

JUNE 2024

'DAD!' Nate shouted down the stairs. 'The power's gone out!'

Ben had flung open the basement door, nearly wrenching it off its hinges. He'd picked up the heavy cables trailing along the floor and, with an almighty tug, he'd ripped them out of their sockets, causing the circuit board to short. He had spent the last few hours loading the monitors and the rest of Karine's camera equipment on to the trolleys. He stormed back into the basement and manually opened the up-and-over door. Putting all his weight behind it, he shoved their crap out on to the lower drive. The wheels hit the kerb and toppled over. The monitors smashed on to the flagstones, shattering the glass, and the lids of the trunks burst open, spewing their contents all over the ground. It was raining hard; the electronics would be ruined. He slammed the garage door and stormed back into the basement.

'DAD?' Nate shouted again from upstairs.

He'd decided to keep the hard drive; it was his property now and he had spent all night wiping it clean. He searched along the storage shelving for a place to hide it, his eyes adjusting to the dark. The pile of boxes from his parents' attic, the remnants of their life before, had been moved on to the floor. The blue highchair was tipped over, the old oil paintings lay flat and the suitcases were lined up on their sides. Someone had been down here, rifling through his things.

Ben felt his way back along the line of the shelves to the service cupboard, flipped the trip switch and the lights flickered into life. The security alarm beeped as it rearmed and pin-dot lights in the cameras around the house flashed as the system recalibrated. He headed up the stairs and poked his head around the door to Nate's room.

'All good?'

Nate was standing in the centre of three enormous box lights. A table was set up in front of him, loaded with his special effects make-up. A white towel was on the floor, spotted with blood. Nate was standing with his shirt off, patting a sponge on to his ribs, nursing a livid bruise.

'What on earth are you doing?' Ben stepped into the room. His face was red and beaded with sweat. 'Who are you talking to?'

'Uh . . . don't we knock in this house anymore?' Nate crossed one arm over his chest, covering his body, while pulling at his dressing gown, which he'd draped over the chair. Ben sat on the side of the bed. 'Apparently not,' Nate mumbled to himself uncomfortably.

'Is all this for the film?' Ben scanned the room, looking at the clothing strewn around. 'Tell me the truth, Nate.' His eyes fell on a pair of swimming trunks and then a grey blazer and a blue and red school tie, stuffed into a red leather Nottingham Forest sports bag. 'Oh my God, is that . . . ?' Ben stood and went to the pile of props in the corner. 'Where did you find this?'

'Why do you care?' Nate's eyes met his.

Hyperventilating, Ben's head was light. He felt dizzy as he slowly pulled the old tie out of the bag and turned it over. Stitched into the back seam was an embroidered name badge. B. Knot. A lump came into his throat.

'Your grandma sewed this.'

Ben studied the school tie. There was a cigarette burn on the narrow-pointed end. Lynette Davis's handiwork.

Nate stared at his father, who suddenly looked as vulnerable as a child, turning the faded tie in his hands and picking up the threadbare blazer. 'We couldn't afford the proper one, but she found this at C&A.' Nate had never seen his dad like this.

Ben pushed the clothing back into his old school bag and looked at his son. 'What else did you find?'

'School books, report cards: "disruptive in class, needs to control his temper".' Nate's mouth curved at the corners. '"Thinks he's Gary Barlow."'

Ben cracked a smile. 'Yeah well, I had more hair then.'

'Is that why Mum left . . . and Dani?' It came out of nowhere.

'What do you mean?' Ben stared at his son, confused. 'Because I lost my hair?'

'No, because you lost your temper.' Nate chewed his lip.

'Everyone has a temper, mate.' Ben swallowed. 'I'm just . . . stressed with work.'

'You always say that.' Nate turned back to the table.

'Listen, Nathan . . . Dani . . . Dani has just gone to her sister's to . . . exhale for a bit.'

'Because you're in trouble.' Nate eyeballed his dad. 'Lily told me.'

Ben's head snapped around to his son. 'Told you what?'

'That you've lost all your money . . . she read it online.' Nate retracted from his dad's glare. 'Dad, are we going to have to move? I like it here.'

Ben sighed wearily. 'I can't do this now, mate.' He stood up to leave.

'You drove Mum away and now Dani . . .'

'Whoa . . . wind your neck in, buster.' Ben's voice rose. He turned and took a pace towards Nate, physically threatening. 'Don't speak to me like that, or I'll—'

'Or you'll what?' Nathan was standing eye to eye with his father.

Ben was lost in the moment, truly lost. What was he doing? Was he going to fight his own son? His son, who quite rightly wanted answers. He'd lost everyone he'd ever loved and now he was risking losing the trust of his son. He broke, just about holding back the tears.

The sight was something Nathan never expected. 'Dad?' He was shocked. 'Sorry, Dad.'

Ben gathered himself. 'No, I'm the one who's sorry. Truly, Nate. I'm going to sort this whole mess out, OK?' Nathan nodded at his dad, but inside he was more worried than ever.

As Ben turned to leave the room, a surge of emotion punched into his chest like an electric shock. On Nate's desk, behind the door, was his father's old 1950s tan leather suitcase from the basement. It was open. That case hadn't been unlocked for thirty years, not since his father had died. Most of the contents had been emptied out but there in the bottom was a bundle wrapped in a black bin liner. Ben couldn't breathe, his mouth was dry, he tried to swallow.

His fingers traced the edges of the hard plastic inside. It was a camera. Ben turned to face his son. He stared at the equipment mounted on the tripod. His expression was shrouded in a veil of calm.

'Is that a new camera?'

'Not new but . . . a vintage Hi8. Karine lent it to me.'

'Any good?' The colour was draining from Ben's face. He rooted around in the case, looking for something else.

'Not really, they don't make the tapes anymore.'

Ben's eyes flicked from the Panasonic on the tripod to the tightly wrapped bundle in his hand.

'Dad? What is it?' Nate looked at all of Ben's school things strewn out on the bed. 'I'm sorry, I'll tidy up.'

'It's OK, mate.' The smile was tight and didn't connect with his eyes. 'No harm done, but I need to take these things back downstairs.' His eyes flicked back to the open case. 'If that's all right?'

Nate nodded. Ben turned and carefully placed everything back in the case, registering every item, before locking it and heading out of the room without saying a word.

Nate sat still for a moment, then opened the cassette door on the camera that Karine had lent him.

Inside was the single video tape he'd found in the bottom of the suitcase.

47

JULY 1994

'And now . . . Mark Cherry is moving up into third place behind Chris Davis of Marconi house and Ben Knot of Pasteur.' Through the lens of Dave's camera, a line of students pelt around the running track as he gives his best Des Lynam impression.

Mark's reputation for ducking out of the cross-country run and sneaking off to the chippy with his 'girlfriend' means that his prowess on the sports field is sketchy, but he has really pulled something out of the bag this term. Whispers around school suggest that after so much practice running away from the bullies, he's become some kind of camp Sebastian Coe. Either way, he is kicking ass at the Barton Mallet Secondary School sports day so far, and it hasn't gone unnoticed.

The house teams are largely even this year. 'Pasteur' Red is led by Ben Knot and 'Marconi' Yellow by Chris Davis, but it is Lynette Davis's demotion from house captain that has shocked everyone. Thanks to Mr Branchflower's intervention, Annie Maddock is taking her place as team captain of 'Einstein'. Admittedly, the irony of Lynette Davis heading up team Einstein hadn't gone unnoticed in the staff room, so the decision was unanimous. Lynette is devastated. This is her legacy: demoted in favour of Annie Maddock. She isn't just gutted, she is livid. She has lain awake at night for weeks, trying to figure out a way to nobble Annabel Maddock. Rat poison in her school flask, a trip wire or some other booby trap, Lynette's devious mind has been working overtime. The rivalry has been festering for a long time now, at least from Lynette's perspective. For months, she has watched Annie like a hawk. On the school bus, on the hockey field, in their drama class, at Pen y Fan on the camping trip. She's been biding her time, but now she's ready to strike.

Someone else whose mind has been scheming is Davis; he saw Cherry in the 1,500m trials and he's nervous.

'COME ON, MARK!' Catherine shouts from the sidelines, nearly deafening Patel, who is trying to focus in on Chris.

Patel lenses up, darting between Davis and Cherry. He pans to Knot, who is about 100 yards ahead, turning on to the final stretch to the finish line. As he returns to the two boys fighting for second place, he adjusts the focus. Mark is doing something unexpected, something that a runner with far more experience would do.

Mark's heart is thumping hard as his feet pound the grass. He's been holding back. He's studied Steve Ovett running like this, hanging off the shoulder on the inside lane, tailing his opponent, using him as a pacemaker of sorts. It means a shorter run by the smallest of margins but every foot counts. As they turn the last bend, Mark can hear the crowd roar, and through the cacophony of noise:

'Come on, Bro! DON'T LET THE FAGGOT WIN!' Lynette pours kerosene on an already burning fire.

Mark's heart punches harder, pumping blood into his legs, propelling him faster than he's ever run before. He'll show them. He'll leave them all behind, not just today here on this running track but for every day, from this point, going onwards, for the rest of his life. He makes his move, darting out on Davis's right shoulder and passing him with ease. Davis attempts to stop him by reaching out and shoulder-barging, but Mark is too fast; he thrusts down the home straight and across the line, just seconds after Ben Knot. The crowd explodes. Mark's won silver and is delighted.

In that moment, just as Chris Davis leaps across the line, Patel jogs over and Lynette throws her arms around Ben. As she passes Patel, she whispers something in his ear. She turns to congratulate her brother and starts to cross the field towards Mark Cherry. He is bent over, hands on his knees, gasping for breath. Just as he is about to stand for a victory lap, Lynette takes the waistband of his shorts and yanks them to the floor. Mark's bare buttocks, and everything else for that matter, are on show for all to see. Patel zooms in, laughing his head off as the crowd erupts into more laughter and jeers.

'Oh my God, he's got a BUSH!' Lynette laughs and points.

Mark covers his modesty and pulls his shorts back up, utterly humiliated. Patel runs over, screaming with laughter, trying to get a shot of his bare arse.

'LEAVE ME ALONE!' Mark's voice tremors with fury. Dizzy from the race, his head is swimming; a circle of contorted faces surround him. All of them: Patel, Davis, even Annie and Catherine seem to be laughing and pointing.

'Aw, Cherry, don't be shy.' It's Ben Knot's turn to add insult to injury. 'You should be proud of that thing.' Ben is smirking and sliding his arm around Annie's waist, but she shrugs him off and glares at Dave Patel to stop filming. Mark staggers off to the changing room.

His triumph is marred with ridicule. They always spoil everything. He came in second, but it counts for nothing. Patel has it all on film, Annie was laughing at him, they all were. Is this always how it's going to be? Is there nothing he can ever do to make them stop? He heads to his locker. The plan has been fermenting in his mind like mould. Now it's time to get his revenge. He takes something out of his backpack, sees Dave Patel's sports bag shoved under the benches, opens the zip and places it inside.

He's already showered and dry by the time the others get into the changing room, combing his wet hair in the mirror, calmly watching them pile in.

'All right, donkey boy.' Chris undresses, releasing a ripe stench that clears the area around him by a few feet.

'Did you get it on film?' Ben nudges Patel.

'All of it!' Patel snorts at his own joke and picks his bag up from under the bench. The zip is half open; he is about to stuff the camera inside when Ben sidles up behind him.

'Woah, Casanova . . . what's all this?' Ben yanks at a pair of white lace-trimmed knickers peeking out through the gap in the zip.

'Sod off, losers.' Patel sits on the bench and removes his socks. 'Whose bright idea was this?'

Ben Knot pulls on the zip. 'Duh duh duh . . . de duh duh der . . .' The stripper song accompanies the tease of underwear emerging from the bag. 'Dirty little dark horse, aren't you, Patel.' He helicopters the underwear above his head.

'No idea who they belong to.' Patel is red in the face.

Mark looks at the reflection in the steamed-up mirror, enjoying watching someone else having to endure that sinking feeling in their stomach.

'Unless they're yours?' Chris chips in.

Patel grabs his towel and opens his locker door, but Ben has frozen. He is standing holding the lacy knickers. Inspecting the name tag: A Maddock, in green stitching, sewn into the back.

'Where did you get these?' His voice is trembling with rage. Patel turns to him but before he has a chance to answer, Ben punches him in the face. Dave's head whiplashes back and he hits the deck.

Ben holds the underwear aloft. He scans the room, dizzy with adrenaline.

'You all know about this? Huh?' No one speaks. 'Is my girl-friend screwing him? Someone better pipe up or he's dead.' Everyone is in shock. Dave Patel is on the floor holding his nose as the blood begins to flow.

Dave is on his feet and face to face with Ben. 'Say that again?' The rage between them is terrifying. Patel grabs Ben by the neck, hauling him up like an animal, ready to spit in his face. Then he drops him like a rag and boots the locker door with such force that it buckles like tin foil. He picks up his bag and crashes out of the changing room.

Everyone is in shock. Silence falls over the boys. For the first time ever, Ben Knot is no longer Top Dog, it's all about Dave Patel now. Ben visibly shrinks before everyone's eyes, but he focuses on the door, then his gaze falls on the item of underwear balled up in his clenched fist. No one does this to Ben Knot. No one.

Mark watches with glee, enjoying every single sordid moment. He smiles to himself, imagining the shit Annie is going to be in now. Serves her right for telling everyone his secret, serves Ben right for all the punches.

Serves Patel right for being an onlooker and doing nothing.

It serves them all right.

48

JULY 2024

Lily squirmed uncomfortably in the passenger seat of Dani's Jaguar, chewing her fingernails.

'I'm not sure about this now.' She folded her arms over her chest; the acid-green Poison Ivy catsuit that Dani had ordered on Amazon left little to the imagination.

'What? You look amazing.' Dani indicated and pulled into the school car park. 'If you've got it . . . flaunt it.'

Lily's confidence was waning by the second. 'Nate's supposed to be going as Red Skull.' She opened the door and jumped down. 'I'd better not be the only one in costume. Maybe I should change into my trainers . . . NATE!' She beamed at her brother stepping out of Ben's car, parked across the way. Nate, dressed as Johann Schmidt, with the livid red intricate make-up of Red Skull, was carrying a clumsy-looking old video camera. He turned the camera towards Lily, who was now sitting in the footwell tugging on a pair of Stan Smiths. At the sight of Nate filming her, she leapt up and draped herself over the bonnet of Dani's SUV, giving it a pouty face and a two fingers peace sign, performing for the camera.

A line of Steve Rogers of various shapes and sizes crossed the car park. An Agent Carter dashed in through the double doors, holding them open as a queue of Captain Marvels, Lokis, Rocky Raccoons and Spider-Men streamed into the hall. A stray Harley Quinn with a baseball bat and a sheepish-looking Wonder Woman, with a dog lead instead of a whip, slunk in through a side door, hoping to disappear into the thumping disco darkness of the annual Barton Mallet Pearls Before Swine end-of-term party.

Ben watched as Lily and Nate threw their arms around each other and headed into the melee, towards their circle of friends. Everything was about to change for his two kids. They were at that moment in life when everything that felt sure and certain, everything that defined them, was suddenly about to be taken away. For some kids it was a fresh start, for others it was like staring into the void. Ben remembered how, at their age, he had felt cut adrift and alone. Severing the reins of childhood was a cruel and painful act. School didn't want him anymore; his parents couldn't be there for him; he was on his own.

Lily linked her brother's arm as they entered the school hall.

'What does Pearls Before Swine mean anyway?' She stopped for a second and gazed up at the ceiling festooned with red and gold streamers, bunting made of hundreds of glittering Captain America shields and a DJ desk set up on the stage, pimped to look like the bridge of Star-Lord's *Bowie*.

'Gems of wisdom for a bunch of ungrateful pigs?' Nate scanned the room with his camera, landing on Lily.

'Sweet.' She smiled then pushed the camera away and slunk off towards a couple of her mates standing by a table buckling under a ton of sausage rolls and bowls of cheesy puffs. Lily crossed the empty dance floor. By the end of the night, the parquet would be sticky with spilled drinks and the stifling air heavy with the pungent smell of disco bodies writhing in the dark. Right now, no one wanted to be the first to embarrass themselves.

Outside in the car park, Ben switched off his headlights and sat alone in the dark, watching a rather weedy Doctor Strange and towering Scarlet Witch holding hands as they filed into the school hall. Dani, sitting in her car opposite, flicked on her full beam, deliberately blinding him. He shaded his eyes and dropped the visor.

On nights like this, he wanted to take a snapshot for his memory. His children were growing up too fast; he could feel the wheel of time turning and for a moment he wished it would stop. Or perhaps rewind so he could watch it all over again. It was as if she was sitting in the passenger seat, right there next to him. It wasn't his ex-wife, Ellie, he was thinking about, it wasn't Dani. It was Annabel Maddock.

A prickle of nerve endings that started in his feet, rose through his stomach and ended in the follicles of his scalp jolted him back through time into that same night, all those years ago. Images flashing vividly across his mind. Every frame of every second compressed into a single moment. It was more a feeling than a thought, a sudden rush of pain, mixed with that flutter of teenage thrill. The rules were the rules. If you didn't get off with someone at Pearls Before Swine then you were a sad loser, and tonight was the night.

As that thought passed through his mind, Dani killed her beam. They sat in the orange hue of the school car park, eyeballing each other through steamed-up windscreens. They were like two strangers now. He was about to start the car and head home when Fruity Vape crawled into the car park in the beat-up transit. Karine was riding shotgun; the sound guy and focus puller were nowhere to be seen. Her camera was already on her shoulder as the vehicle slowly tracked around the perimeter of the school hall. Without cutting, she stepped down from the passenger seat and moved stealthily into the shadows like some kind of wildlife photographer. There was a passageway around the side of the building that led to the service area. Karine headed confidently into the shadows, camera poised to capture everything.

Ben kept his eyes fixed on Karine, the fury building inside him. Dani stared at him through her dark windscreen. Fruity Vape was lighting up a spliff; the plume of smoke wafting through the cracked window had a distinctive smell and was far too thick and bilious to be from a cigarette. Ben quietly opened the door of the car and stepped out into the warm summer air. The rain and heat had caused a swarm of midges to descend on the village like a plague, and the landfill on which the school was built was water-logged and smelt like rotting eggs. Ben followed Karine down the side entrance by the kitchens. He counted to five, guessing no more than ten seconds would pass before Dani followed close behind. Sure enough, he soon heard her car door close and her heels clicking on the tarmac. She was following them. Well, let her see what Karine Mickelsen was really like.

Ben hovered in the shadows, observing Karine balanced with one foot on a crate, the other perched on a sill. She was straining to film through a high fanlight window. He watched her watching his kids, studying them through her lens, and he hated her for it, from the very base of his soul.

'Getting everything you need?'

Karine's foot slipped on the crate as she jumped out of her skin. She clattered to the ground, grabbing on to his jacket as she fell.

'Caught red-handed.' She laughed and checked the camera was OK. 'I'm a fly on the wall.' She flipped the camera, turning it on him.

'Be careful, Karine, or I might just swat that bug.' Ben's lip wrinkled. 'It's becoming an annoyance.'

Dani was just about to turn the corner when she heard voices and froze.

Ben remained in the darkness next to the recycling bins. 'I want you and your sordid little film gone.' He took a step forward, his face pale and his voice dead calm. 'I want you out of my life.'

Karine stared at him, then turned the camera on to his face. The rage in his bloodshot eyes was terrifying. She zoomed in tight. 'Oh . . . but I'm not quite done yet.'

'You're done when I say you're done.' Ben's fingers felt for his buckle. He undid it, then slowly removed his leather belt. 'You need to leave my kids alone.' He slowly wrapped the belt around his wrist, clenching the buckle in his fist like a knuckle duster.

Karine took a tiny step back away from him; her voice was shaking. 'Is it . . . making you feel something, watching your children suffer too?'

Ben dug his nails into the belt strap. 'If this is about money, if you're planning on blackmailing me, I don't have any and you can tell whoever put you up to this they won't get a penny out of me.'

Karine frowned. 'I think you may have the wrong end of the stick, Ben. You're letting your paranoia show.'

Ben could feel the blood suddenly rushing to his head. He was fizzing with a white-hot rage. He wanted to rip her head off. 'Be careful, Karine. Be very careful.'

'You do realise I'm filming all this, Ben? And film is forever. Is there something you want to get off your chest?' She panned the camera down to the belt in his hand ready to strike her.

'We had a little accident . . . at the house.' Ben took a step closer. 'Bit of a flood. I'm afraid some of your equipment got damaged.' He pulled the hard drive from his jacket pocket. It had been smashed with a hammer.

Karine stared at him. Ben smiled and threw the broken box at her. She caught it and turned it over in her hands.

'No matter.' Her eyes met his; she was smirking. 'I upload dailies to my editor digitally . . . This is just a backup.'

Before he could answer, a scream pierced the air.

'LILY!' Nate was shouting to his sister around at the front entrance. 'LILY, STOP, COME BACK!'

Ben's head spun to the sound of their voices. Karine's eyes left the viewfinder and found his, shining in the dark. She was already on the move with the camera.

'Leave them THE FUCK ALONE,' Ben snapped, slamming her into the wall with his shoulder.

Karine's face scraped against the bricks, her knees buckling underneath her as the camera slipped from her shoulder. Ben lashed out but Karine ducked and his knuckles grazed the wall as she darted out past him. Ben's hand shot out, grabbing for her, catching a fistful of hair in his hand, but Karine wrenched herself away, escaping down the side entrance. Ben sprinted out after her, but she had a considerable head start now. Nate and Lily were nowhere to be seen. Karine hit the middle of the land-fill site and turned back, still filming, the camera slung low.

Panting and out of breath, she called to him. 'You want to know what all of this is about?' She staggered backwards, taunting him. 'Come on, Ben . . . come and find out.'

Ben lurched after her as she turned and sprinted towards the mill, but she was too fast and Ben slipped and stumbled in the mud. He fell on to his hands and knees. Once he'd scrambled up, Karine was long gone; he would never catch her now. He made a decision. He turned back and strode towards his car.

Dani stepped out of the shadows and pulled out her phone to make a call; it went to voicemail. Hiding behind the recycling bins, she saw Ben stagger back into the car park, covered in mud. She spoke in a whisper: 'Lily, it's me, let me know where you are . . . I'm worried.' She watched Ben open his car door. 'Just text me your location and I'll come and find you.'

Ben started the engine and his wheels spun as he accelerated out of the car park, skidding on the wet tarmac. He slammed a left-hand turn out on to Forest Hill, determined to head Karine off at the bridge. An oncoming car, turning into the estate, swerved, just about missing him, lights blinding and a horn blaring. Ben stamped on the brakes, yanking on the wheel and mounting the kerb. He regained control of himself and the car before flooring the accelerator and speeding off towards the crossroads opposite the Maddock Farm. The shortest route would take him down Water Ford Lane . . . through the Water Splash. He knew exactly where Karine and his children were heading.

Dani's head popped out from her hiding place; the coast was clear. She walked nervously to the front of the school and stared out across the playing fields. Where were Lily and Nate? Where had they run off to? In the distance, towards Cheney End and the mill, a faint light was glowing, illuminating the surrounding fields. Something was going down. Her eyes focused on a figure moving silently towards her out of the darkness. Trying not to panic, she slowly backed away, turned and walked confidently towards her car. Her heart in her mouth, she tried to stay calm as she clicked the locks. The headlamps flashed and the shadow of the man appeared, reflected in the rear window.

Dani opened the door and turned. 'Get away from me!'

Her car key was positioned in her fist like a spike, ready to defend herself.

'Nate? Oh God, you scared the life out of me!' Dani dropped her fist. 'You're soaking wet . . . Where's Lily?' His Red Skull make-up had run down his face and on to the collar of his white shirt, as if his throat had been slit. If he wasn't a terrifying sight before, he certainly was now.

'Karine said we were supposed to meet her.' Nate turned his head towards the mill. 'Down there.'

49

JULY 1994

Dave drops the brown hood of his Obi-Wan Kenobi bathrobe, spits out his chewing gum and puts the viewfinder back to his eye. The cubicles are all lined up along the exterior wall and from where Patel is perched, down the side alley, peeping in through the glass fanlight, he has a good view of the girls' changing room. In one of the toilets, Lynette Davis, dressed as Sarah Connor, is pinning a helpless Terminator up against the door with her tongue down his throat. Patel pans across as Princess Leia enters the bathroom. She dumps a sports bag down on the side and adjusts her earmuff plaits in the mirror before entering the cubicle to pee.

'Come on,' Patel mutters to himself. 'Let me see you.' He tilts the camera, trying to get a better angle on Annabel Maddock.

Sarah Connor freezes for a second and places her ear against the cubicle as Annie relieves herself. Lynette slowly opens the door and spots Annie's bag on the sink. She shoos away her date and, making sure the coast is clear, creeps out from the cubicle, grabs an empty glass Coke bottle from the floor and moves over to the bag. She looks back at Annie's locked door, then plunges the glass bottle into the bag, feeling around for something inside. Shooting another glance to the door, she breaks the bottle with her foot, stamping down on the leather with a muffled smash. She replaces the bag before darting out of the toilets. Obi-Wan's camera whip-pans back to film Princess Leia, who is flushing.

'David Patel! What the hell do you think you're doing?' A side door from the kitchen suddenly flies open.

Patel jumps out of his skin and wobbles on the crate he is standing on. He clatters to the ground, only just saving his camera from hitting the concrete. He is face to face with Mr Branchflower, who steps in close enough that Patel can smell the alcohol on his breath.

'I don't know about perverts where you come from, but we don't like Peeping Toms in this country.'

Dave pulls the rope of his dressing gown tighter and straightens up. 'I'm from here . . . sir.'

'Whatever you say . . . Patel. I'm going to report this either way.'

Dave steps in a little closer and sniffs. 'You driving home . . . sir?'

'Sorry?' Branchflower's spine stiffens.

'Hey, Chris! Your dad on call tonight?'

Chris rounds the corner in a Freddy Krueger trilby, steak knives gaffer-taped to his goalie gloves, clattering along the brick. 'He's sat up at the gates waiting for takers, mate . . .'

'I guess these are not the droids you're looking for . . . sir.' Patel waves a hand in Branchflower's face as Chris Davis spits out a mouthful of Coke.

'Get inside, both of you, I'm locking this door.'

Pearls Before Swine 1994 is in full swing and the entertainment is lighting up the stage. Mark, dressed as Marty McFly in skinny jeans, bomber jacket and sunglasses, is on cello, accompanied by Catherine on clarinet, dressed as Doc Brown in a cotton wool wig, swimming goggles and hairdressing robe. She is perched on a cardboard box DeLorean. Their rendition of 'Smooth Criminal' by Michael Jackson is the highlight of the night so far. By the last thumping chorus, Marty McFly is up on his feet as jumping kids punch the air. Chanting and shouting in anticipation that 'Annie would be OK. Is she OK? Is she OK, Annie?'

Annie Maddock waits in the wings. She seems fine, if a little sweaty under all of Princess Leia's layers, but she is nervous for her solo.

Lynette, or rather Sarah Connor, in her mum's stretch wig, has opted for a lip sync of 'Bat Out of Hell' by Meat Loaf for her performance. She's waving a red silk scarf around while her brother, Chris, circles on his mountain bike, fanning her with a piece of cardboard as a makeshift wind machine. It's somewhat underwhelming. To add insult to injury Chris attempts to steal her thunder by thrashing his Freddy Krueger glove around, which catches on Lynette's wig, yanking it off. She kicks his back wheel and his bike crashes into the boom box, but he saves face by pretending it was all planned. The whole mess of a routine is more comedic than rock'n'roll. The twins leave the stage, on the verge of a punch-up. But then Lynette's attention is drawn back to the spotlight. This is the moment she's been waiting for.

Princess Leia in ballet shoes stands serenely with her arms crossed over her heart, her eyes cast demurely downwards. Patel moves slowly around the perimeter of the room as the love theme from *Return of the Jedi* oozes out of the speakers. The spotlight illuminates the pristine white tablecloth toga as Annie raises her arms like an angel. Patel zooms in closer.

Across the room, a figure in a long black gown that drapes from neck to floor is standing dead still. The grey mask completely covering the face is startling: it's peppered with vicious-looking six-inch nails. The chest plate over the black velvet jacket is shaped like a ribcage. As if on wheels, the dark shape glides across the floor towards Patel. Hellraiser closes in on Obi-Wan: the stand-off of movie heroes and villains is about to come to a head.

As Patel follows the ethereal Leia in a series of flourishing turns around the room, a face suddenly looms into the lens. Close up, the homemade costume reveals its crudeness. The nails sticking out of the grey rubber mask have been fixed with gaffer tape and the velvet ball gown is more Alexis Carrington from *Dynasty* than Pinhead. Ben has strung together a ribcage made from half-chewed dog bones dipped in ketchup. The result is both terrifying and a bit stinky.

'Outside, Patel . . . NOW.' The inside of Ben Knot's mouth is black. He's chewed on an ink cartridge for maximum effect.

Patel pulls up Obi-Wan's hood and covers his face. 'Later. I'm busy.' He turns his back on Ben and lifts the camera to carry on filming Annie's performance. Ben Knot grabs him by the shoulder and yanks him back around. Patel snaps and shoves Knot away. As Ben loses his balance, his foot catches on the gown and he tumbles backwards. A sickening crunch is heard as he hits the ground hard.

'Ah . . . my wrist!'

Patel piles on top of Knot, layers of brown terry towelling and black velvet flying and tearing as a full-on scrap breaks out. Patel's camera skids across the floor into a pair of Converse trainers belonging to Marty McFly.

Cherry picks up the camera and trains it on Patel and Knot. This is all his doing. This is exactly what he had orchestrated. He couldn't have hoped for a more satisfying revenge. He intended to film it and watch it over and over again, revelling in his victory. They had always underestimated him, but he had caused all of this. Let them beat the crap out of each other and ruin Annie Maddock's star turn on the dance floor. Let them suffer.

'Aaarrggh!' A high-pitched scream pierces through the chants and jeers of the Jedi Masters' fight. Annie is sitting on the floor, clutching her foot. The hem of Princess Leia's white gown is spotted with red, and as Annie removes her ballet shoe, it becomes clear why. The shoe is soaked in blood, and the toes that emerge are almost black.

'Oh my God, what happened?' Catherine rushes up and kneels down to help her sister. Cat picks up one of her shoes. 'There's broken glass in your pointe shoe, Annie.' Her head whips around the circle. 'Who did this?'

Lynette grins to herself from the dark corner of the room. Patel and Knot have stopped fighting and Knot is sliding around trying to get up as Dave Patel frantically searches for his camera. Ben charges up on to the stage and tries to pick Annie up from the floor.

'GET OFF ME!' Annie, in floods of tears, tries to stand but the pain in her foot is excruciating. 'Why can't you just leave me alone? What is your problem?'

Catherine puts a hand on Annie's shoulder to calm her down. Ben reels, his fists ball, and for a second it seems as if he's going to retaliate, but instead he turns and smashes out through the double doors of the school hall. The humiliation is unbearable. Patel watches him go.

The strip lights in the hall flicker on and the music is cut. Branchflower totters on to the stage, half-cut, as the sound of fireworks diverts everyone's attention.

'All right, everyone, outside!' He looks in horror at the blood on the floor, more concerned about the mess than making sure Annie is OK.

As the kids stream out of the school hall, Patel lingers. He is torn. Half of him wants to step in and be Annie's hero: this might just be his one and only chance. The other half of him is desperate to pursue Ben Knot and finally show him who's boss. As he turns to leave, he comes face to face with Lynette Davis. She's leaning on the wall, chewing gum as a nasty smile spreads across her face. Catherine clocks it.

She stares at Lynette. 'You did this?' She stands and moves towards her. 'What is wrong with you?'

'Little slag deserved it.' Lynette's head turns to Patel. 'Right?'

Before she has chance to blink, a hand swipes hard across her face in a vicious slap. Lynette strikes back at Catherine, but she ducks and lurches towards the door and Lynette sprints out after her.

There's a sudden explosion outside and the last screaming gaggle of kids swarms out into the night.

Dave and Annie are left alone as the fireworks begin.

50

JULY 2024

Dark, ominous clouds shifted across the moon; the rain was holding off for now, but a storm was brewing. The streetlamps reflected off the wet tarmac as Ben swerved into the centre of the road. At the corner of Barton Rise, he headed down the hill, past the ancient Hanging Rock and out towards Blackstone Mill. He stepped on the accelerator. Why was she doing this to him? He needed to hurry; Karine had Lily and Nate bound to some macabre performance. God knows what she had in store for them tonight, but his worst fears were coming to the surface. She was out of control. If she even laid a finger on either of his children . . . he flinched at the thought of what he would do to her.

At the top of the hill, he could see that the road was flooded at the bottom.

'You're a bad influence on me, Ben Knot.' For a second, Annie was sitting right there in the seat next to him. Had he been the bad influence, or had she?

'I dare you.'

His foot found the accelerator and he plunged the car forward into the deep water of the ford. The vehicle juddered and the emergency brakes locked. The car aquaplaned for a second like a boat, then stopped as the edge of the tarmac road, under the water, slammed against the chassis. The car span in the flow and then water began to seep in through the door.

'Shit . . . shit.' Ben slammed his hands against the steering wheel.

He opened the car door and stepped out into the cold, waist-deep water. Slowly, he waded across to the other side. Soaked to the skin, he staggered out on to the road and began to run, his clothes clinging to his body, weighing him down. It was about half a mile from here. Moving uphill, he was drawn towards the stone chimney of the mill in the distance. There were bright lights glowing from behind the building, silhouetting the mill in the foreground. She was waiting for him.

With each step, he could feel something sinking inside him; the incline was steep, but he imagined himself descending into the darkness again. His legs felt heavy, as if they were filled with lead. He knew this path; he'd walked this road so many times before. As a child, at school on that terrible night, yes, but also on many other night-time pilgrimages to the place where it had happened. Tonight was different. He could sense her waiting. He could already feel his fingers around her throat. He wanted so badly to silence her. He wanted to punish her for what she was doing.

The kissing gate at the start of Cheney End was barely visible and the water from the breached brook lapped over the top. By the time Ben reached it, the flood was up to his knees. He stepped up on to the wooden stile and swung a leg over, splashing back down on to the concrete pavement that led to Doggers Dive. If there were cars there tonight, they would surely be underwater. As the path wound gently upwards towards the car park, the water receded.

Ben stood looking across the field towards the willow tree with the rope swing, where Annabel Maddock had made daisy chain crowns. The chimney stack of the mill thrust ominously into the sky. Ben squinted into the distance towards the very top of the Crow's Nest. High in the tower, a bead of light, no brighter than a candle, guttered in the shadows. Someone was up there. He plunged forward across the soggy marsh of the waterlogged meadow towards Blackstone Mill.

51

JULY 1994

'Let me help you.' Dave kneels down in front of Annie. His gentle voice makes her tears flow more freely.

'It's OK, Dave, I can call my dad. Have you got any change for the phone?'

Patel fishes out a 10p piece from his pocket. 'Here.' He offers her the coin. 'Take my hand.'

Dave puts his arm around her waist and they limp across the empty school hall floor, littered with streamers and sticky with spilled fizzy pop. As she dials the number, Dave pushes the coin into the slot and gently lifts Annie on to a table full of football trophies. He carefully draws her foot up on to his knee and pulls back the torn ballet tights.

'Hi, Mum, it's me. Can you ask Dad to come and pick me up? Yeah, from the party at school. Oh, OK, well, I can wait . . . no, no, I'm fine.' Annie hangs up the receiver and turns to Dave. 'Mum says he'll be about twenty minutes.'

'It's actually not that bad.' He gently pulls out a piece of glass, lodged in her big toe. She flinches at his touch. 'Sorry. Small cut and a bucket of blood . . . You look like Carrie.' He smiles at her and wipes his hands on his Obi-Wan dressing gown.

'Who's Carrie?' Annie sniffs and dabs her eyes with her sleeve.

'Stephen King . . . she gets a bucket of pigs' blood tipped over her at the high school prom.' Dave takes a Swiss Army knife from his pocket, strips a length of cloth from Annie's gown and gently bandages her injured foot. 'I think it's stopped bleeding.'

'What happens to Carrie?' Annie smiles at him.

'Oh, nothing much. She just sets fire to the school and inciner-ates everyone with her laser eyes.'

They both burst out laughing. 'Thanks for helping me.'

'Well, my dad is a doctor, so . . .' Patel flushes.

'Is that what you want to be?' Annie draws up her knees and looks at her toe. 'When you leave school?'

'Yeah, I want to try and get a place at Bamford for sixth form and then hopefully go to med school, specialise in cardiology.'

'You're going to be a heart surgeon?' Her fingers brush his as he withdraws his hand.

'That's the dream.'

'I think I want to study fashion at Saint Martins.' Annie's face glows as Dave smiles back at her.

'You'll be famous.'

'Oh, I don't want to be famous. I just want to do something . . . creative with my life.'

Dave smiles. 'Don't want to be a farmer then, or a shepherd-ess?' He chuckles.

Annie kicks him in the tummy with her injured foot. 'Very funny.'

After a few minutes of Dave's emergency first aid, Annie's wound is bandaged. She hops on one foot with her arm over Dave's shoulder as she pulls on her trainers, wincing in pain.

'Gonna be my knight in shining armour and drive me home then?' Annie turns back with a smile.

'I came on the bike . . . only one helmet . . . sorry.' Then Patel suddenly remembers. 'Shit . . . my camera.'

Annie puts her head against his shoulder. 'Oh, I saw Mark pick it up. He's probably outside filming the fireworks.'

Annie and Dave head outside, sheltering under the canopy of the school as the summer storm blows stronger. The plumes of the glittering gold fireworks fizzle out in the sky.

'Bit of a waste in this downpour.' Patel squints out over the village. The school playing field, backing on to the landfill peppered with gas pipes, appears to glisten with water. A dense thicket of trees shields a row of Tudor cottages forming a small hamlet that runs towards Cheney End and Blackstone Mill.

'Some bright spark is setting them off from over at the mill,' Annie says. 'I wonder who . . .' A deafening bang cracks across the night sky, and a cloud of smoke is followed by a series of Roman candles, whizz bombs and a huge golden fountain, all carelessly expended in one giant explosion.

'DAVIS!' The two of them burst into laughter. These pyrotechnics have Chris Davis's fingerprints all over them.

Another flurry of glittering red and green spinning fire jacks explodes from behind the tall chimney stack, illuminating the treetops and night sky in the distance ahead of them.

'You should go on without me,' Annie smiles. 'Don't want you missing all the fun.'

'It's OK, I'd rather wait here with you.' Patel links his arms through hers, but Annie retracts.

'I'll be fine. Go and get your camera back.'

Dave puts his arm around Annie and pecks her cheek. She laughs awkwardly. 'Get out of here.'

'If you're sure?'

'Go on, my dad won't be long, I'll be fine.'

Patel stands and sighs. It's the end of school. Who knows when he'll have this chance again? 'I really like you, Annie.'

Annie frowns slightly. 'I know you do, Dave, but . . .'

'I know, you don't have to tell me.' Dave winces slightly. 'Is it because I'm . . .'

'No, of course not.' Annie pre-empts the question, placing her hand gently on his.

Dave turns his face away. 'I understand . . . you belong to Ben . . . I get it.'

'I don't belong to anyone.'

Dave's heart sinks at the rejection; his dad was right. He covers his hurt feelings with that dazzling smile. He pulls his Obi-Wan hood over his head and dashes out into the rain towards his chained-up motorbike. He pulls on a helmet and throws a leg over, straddling it like a Hell's Angel.

'All right, Mad Max!' Annie shouts over to him, and he kick-starts the engine and speeds away, heroic robes flowing in the wind.

The rain pattering on the overhang of the school begins to slow as the storm passes over. In the distance, the booming rumble of thunder makes Annie start. She's dressed in little more than a tablecloth and her underwear, and she suddenly remembers her sports bag inside.

She hobbles back into the school hall and heads across the dance floor towards the changing room. In the centre of the room, she pauses for a second as a pang of sadness catches her breath. This is it; their Pearls Before Swine is over. It feels as if she has spent her entire life in this school hall. In a way she has, from the very first assembly when she was four years old, learning the Lord's Prayer, trying to sit still, cross-legged, putting her hand up to go to the toilet. The school dinners she hated, unless there was strawberry milkshake on Fridays. Making Christmas-tree decor-ations out of blown eggs and sequins to take home to her parents. Bringing tins of unwanted mushy peas to the Harvest Festival collection box. Her whole childhood seems to have happened within the walls of this school. But now it's time to leave. Like Alice, she suddenly feels too big for the room; the world she knows is shrinking before her eyes, already fading into memory.

The honk of a car horn outside startles her.

'Dad? That was quick,' she mutters to herself.

She hops into the changing room, grabs her sports bag and limps back to the front entrance. The rain is coming down heavier now and a pair of headlights flash across the glass doors of reception, dazzling her momentarily. The high beam dims as the car pulls forward and the door swings opens. But it's not her father. The familiar battered old blue Ford Fiesta sits waiting with the engine turning over, as Ben leans out over the passenger seat. It's hard to see his face under the silver-grey tape and long nails protruding from his head; the bone-rib waistcoat has been thrown into the back seat.

'Come on, get in.' Ben shouts over the rain, the rubber Pinhead mask puckering around his mouth. 'I'll whizz you home.'

Annie glances back into the hall, that well of sadness still lingering inside her. This is the last time she'll be here and maybe the last time she'll see Ben, for a while at least.

'I shouldn't . . . my dad said he was on his way.'

'Come on.' Ben holds out his hand.

Annie takes a deep breath and steps into the passenger seat and closes the door. 'Goodbye, Barton Mallet.'

'Your buns are all soggy.' Ben puts the car into gear and speeds up the driveway of the school.

Annie cracks a smile, pulling off her Princess Leia earmuffs and leaning her head back into the seat. 'Sorry I shouted.'

The car smells of damp dog and strong alcohol. Ben has been drinking.

'Flash my dad if we pass him on the road. He'll be worried.' Annie wipes the condensation from the windscreen and fiddles with the demister. Ben remains silent, focusing hard on steering in a straight line as they exit the car park and head off through the driving rain.

'That was the turn for Forest Hill.' The little blue Ford Fiesta whizzes past the green gates of the cemetery and suddenly swerves left at the dog rescue. 'Ben, where are we going?'

'Back to where we began.' Ben grips the wheel and turns to her. 'A nostalgia tour.' The sign for Water Ford Gate flashes red as they approach.

'It's under water, Ben, you won't make it through.' Annie grips the dashboard as Ben starts to accelerate down the hill towards the ford and the weir.

Ben steps on the pedal and screams out at the top of his voice, 'Whhhoooohoooo!'

Annie screams and covers her eyes as the car ploughs into the deep ford, waves hitting the air vent and pouring over the bonnet, windscreen and roof, spurting plumes of water like fins behind them. For a second the car wheels leave the ground and float free, aquaplaning across the river. The tyres find the road surface again as the battered old car miraculously makes it across to the other side and speeds away.

'Oh my God . . . you are an absolute psycho, Ben Knot!' Annie's hands leave her eyes. She is flushed and shaking.

Ben, still whooping, continues towards the turn for Cheney End. As they round the corner, the car begins to buck violently, the carburettor coughing and chugging. Warning lights across the dashboard flash red as the engine peters out. Ben steers into the lane leading down to Doggers Dive and depresses the clutch. The car freewheels down the hill and slowly judders to a halt in the car park. Ben brakes, the car stalls, lights flicker off and the engine dies.

'Alone at last.' Ben swallows nervously. 'So now what are we going to do?'

52

JULY 2024

Nathan wrapped his dressing gown tight around him and towel-dried his hair. He stood at the top of the stairs and listened to the silence in the house. Dani had dropped him off at home, bundling him into a hot shower and getting a cup of hot soup inside him before she headed back out to find Lily.

There was something gnawing away in the pit of Nate's stomach. Since the beginning of this last school year, around about the time he'd started making the film, he'd felt as if he was under water. Everything had become blurred and his senses dampened. He hadn't really been listening or paying attention; he had been somewhere else. He'd been someone else, but the person he was pretending to be wasn't real, he couldn't be real. He'd allowed himself to be drawn into Karine's vision. He'd let himself get carried away on a wave of imagination, but time seemed to have slipped through his fingers; he'd lost himself. His mum was absent; she didn't even really know what he was up to anymore. Dani was halfway out the door and his dad was somewhere else entirely. He could run away right now and no one would even notice. He could burn the house down and no one was here to stop him. It had all gone horribly wrong.

His phone buzzed, a text from his sister:

Where are you . . . thought you were doing this too?

Dani said no . . . she's coming to get you. Where are you?

*Waiting in a car for instructions from Karine . . . did you film our
Nicki Minaj dance number?*

Yeah, watching it now. LOL

Nate began to hook up the camera to his TV monitor to watch
the video of Lily, Sam Rathbone and Gaynor Carson twerking to
'Red Ruby Da Sleeze'.

His plan was to cut the most embarrassing bits together as a
special montage to torment his sister at her birthday bash in
September. Happy birthday, Sis!

Nate opened his laptop. Freckles the Bitmoji was frozen on his
RetroFX message board.

The last message had been sent two days ago. 'See ya very soon.'
A cute little wink emoji and an aeroplane.

'Hey, Freckles,' Nate tapped on the keyboard. 'You there?' He
watched the screen, hoping for three repeating dots, but there was
no response. Texting his sister and messaging with a cartoon
graphic deepened the hollow feeling in his tummy. He'd never felt
more alone.

He opened his iMovie program and began to load the ana-
logue footage from the Sony Hi8 camera on to the TV screen,
converting it to digital fingernails in three-minute segments. The
old video tape he'd found in the basement was poor quality and
grainy, and he wondered if the film had degraded after all this
time. Filming on video felt like he was making some kind of cult
film from the seventies. He'd struggled to keep focus and his
handheld technique was a bit shaky. His iPhone used auto focus
on a self-steadying gimbal, but the video camera required a different kind of skill. Nate sat back and watched the embarrassing
'Minaj à trois' come to a bump and grinding end. The audience
went wild.

As Nate leant forward to switch off the tape, a high-angle shot of the girls' changing room suddenly spliced on to the screen.

'That's odd,' he muttered to himself. He watched as a girl dressed as one of the characters from *Star Wars* entered through the door. 'Very retro . . . don't remember filming this bit.'

Nate pressed fast forward and the girl from the bathroom was suddenly centre stage in a white spotlight.

'Definitely don't remember this . . .' Nate hit upload and let the tape play.

The camera panned slowly around the room; the movement was steady and in focus. The girl in white began to dance. There was no sound, but her movements were mesmerising. The translucent white gown draped and floated around her like fluid. Nate leant forward with his hands on his chin, totally absorbed by the apparition on screen, turning on the tips of her toes. Nate yawned and looked at his watch: 11.55 p.m. His eyes drooped as the girl continued to dance; his head lolled forward as sleep overwhelmed him.

'Oh shit!' Nate was jolted awake with a start and his heart raced.

He looked at the screen as a nightmare face, grey with rusty nails hammered into the skin and scalp, lurched into the frame. He paused the tape.

'What the hell is that?' The face on the screen was covered in a grey rubber mask, mouth open wide, black with some kind of sticky slime. Nate rubbed his eyes and tried to focus; he advanced the tape forward frame by frame. As the camera moved, the girl in white appeared again, but now there was blood on her dress. Nate moved to his laptop and uploaded the next three-minute segment from tape to digital. As it rendered, the image on the screen scrambled into a mess of blurred movement and then cut to black. On the laptop, Nate zoomed into the girl on the floor. Above her head was a banner of red, white and blue painted letters covered in sequins: Pearls Before Swine 1994.

'Oh my God.' Nate zoomed in on the face of Annabel Maddock. 'That's her.' He dragged and dropped the thumbnail into a new file. A shriek like a wounded animal made Nate's head snap back to the TV screen. The old tape from the Sony camera he'd found in the suitcase from the basement had been playing on; he'd forgotten to turn it off.

Nate rubbed his eyes and tried to focus; he advanced the film forward. Fireworks fizzled across the shot, lights exploding in the dark. Then the camera jerked violently around, as if someone was running or struggling against the wind. Eventually, there was a series of blurred shots from high above, looking down on to a clump of trees. He paused the tape. Then very slowly began to rewind. The focus moved in closer; the subject was obscured with rain on the lens. He paused the tape again. There in the woodland was a blue car parked up in Doggers Dive. Nate painstakingly advanced the film frame by frame. Like an old kineograph, in staccato movements, a girl in white appeared to fall backwards out of the open car door, lying out onto the ground as a figure in black clambered on top of her. The shot disintegrated again, obscured by rain, but Nate persisted, stepping each frame forward at a snail's pace. Out of the black, a sudden pan to the right and the camera was high up in the tower. It picked up the girl in white again; she was being chased. It slowly began to dawn on Nate that this was Annabel Maddock on the night she was killed. It was a recording of the leavers' party from 1994 and this may have been the last time she was seen alive.

The fight that was happening before his eyes was brutal. The cavernous door to the ruined Blackstone Mill was open and a few kids in costumes streamed out and ran across the grass towards the cover of the dense wooded area behind the car park. The camera panned down and zoomed into the tall lanky silhouette in a Pinhead mask. He was reaching his hand towards her face; the diaphanous chiffon of her costume billowed in the wind. She slapped him away and turned to leave. He caught the fabric of her white scarf and yanked her towards him, grabbing her by the throat. In that second, her foot appeared to slip, and she fell out of sight. The screen went black.

A shaft of light cut across the frame. A fork of lightning lit up the night and a demonic grey face punctured with rusty nails suddenly lurched into the shot. Nate paused the film and with trembling hands began to upload the images to digital thumbnails. There was one frame he desperately wanted to look at more closely. The upload disc spun painfully slowly.

'Come on . . . come . . . on.' The files loaded and Nate froze the image and zoomed in closer. 'No. Please no. It can't be.'

The torn mask hung from the chin, flapping like dead skin, revealing half of his face. The eyes were unmistakable, as was the tiny mole just above his father's eyebrow. There was blood everywhere.

'Dad?'

53

JULY 1994

'It's dead.' Ben's hands grip tightly on to the steering wheel. 'The engine.' He turns the key in the ignition; the dull click makes Annie's stomach sink. Ploughing through the ford at Water Ford Gate at top speed may have given Ben a crazy thrill but he has completely flooded the engine.

He's intoxicated by a skinful of Bacardi. 'Sorry . . . but you have to admit, that was bloody fun.' Ben begins to chuckle.

'All right, Harrison Ford, so now we've wrecked the car, what are we going to do?' Wiping the condensation from the window, Annie leans her shoulder against the door. 'It's still chucking it down out there.'

Ben's head turns to her, his red-rimmed eyes blinking through his grey mask. Something in his body language makes Annie nervous. He's trembling.

'We can't even listen to the radio.' She twiddles the volume button.

A startling crackle of golden rain illuminates the sky from the far bank of the river. The glittering explosion of the fireworks reflects on the windscreen, accompanied by distant howls and screams of delight.

Ben leans back and reaches a hand over her shoulder.

'We'll be OK. I've got a blanket in the boot; we can keep each other warm.' He's quivering with anticipation. 'It's romantic.'

Annie folds her arms. 'Maybe we could just head over to the mill.' She tries not to flinch as Ben's hand reaches her other shoulder. 'Enjoy the fireworks with everyone else . . .'

'I wanted this to happen, you know. I've dreamt about it.' Ben rolls his head towards her, his glassy eyes trying to focus. She can smell alcohol, and cheese and onion crisps, on his breath.

She steadies her nerves. 'You're drunk, Ben.' She smiles kindly at him. 'Come on, let's find the others.'

'That night at my house, when we were looking after my dad . . .' He's slurring his words. 'You said we made a good team.'

'We did . . . we do.' Annie keeps her arms folded tightly across her chest. She can feel the pull of his hand on her shoulder. 'I like you, Ben, but I've told you . . . I'm not ready.'

'It's because you like Patel, isn't it?'

Annie turns to him, wide-eyed. 'Dave? No, where did you get that fro—'

'I thought we had something. I drove through the water deliberately because I wanted you all to myself.' Ben pulls her into his chest; his hand travels from her shoulder to the back of her head.

Annie leans in to placate him, but Ben begins to press her face down towards his crotch. Everything begins to move in slow motion. The heat and humidity in the car, the pain in her lacerated foot and Ben's rank breath meld into an overwhelming feeling of nausea. Now her face is buried in his lap, she can feel his erection through the layers of his costume. Ben fumbles for the fly of his jeans, under layer after layer of heavy velvet.

'Come on . . . help me out here.' He's too drunk to find the zip.

Annie's hand shoots up to push him away and she fumbles for the door handle, but Ben's arm reaches across her and slams it closed.

'You're not going anywhere.'

'Don't be ridiculous, Ben.'

From high in the Crow's Nest at the top of the chimney, Mark has been filming the fireworks on Dave's camera. Roman candles splutter fountains of fire across the water in the meadow. Chris darts out into the open from the shelter of the willow. He lights another fuse, but the crack of thunder followed by a blinding flash of sheet lightning tears open the sky, sending Chris scuttling back out of sight. Mark presses his eye back to the viewfinder and steadies the camera.

Across the other side of the river, in the driver's seat of the car, Ben remains motionless. His hands clutch his thighs and he breathes in deeply, trying to steady himself. Annie daren't move, she focuses intently on the opposite bank. She can hear her friends in the distance, squealing and whooping as they flee from the mill in the downpour. In one swift movement, she lurches for the door handle again. Ben flinches, grabbing a fistful of hair and banging her head into the glass.

'Aggh.' Annie snaps. 'GET OFF ME!'

She pushes him off, slamming her fist into the horn on the steering wheel, then, bringing her knees to her chest, she leans back against the door and kicks out at Ben, again and again, into his shoulder and ribs. Ben grabs her ankle and wrenches her leg, twisting her sideways. He clambers over the seat towards her. The passenger door swings open as Annie's weight throws her backwards. He's on top of her now, reaching for her underwear, fingers finding the waistband and pulling hard to tear them off.

'NO . . . NO!' Annie jerks away violently, but Ben's fingers keep their grip on her neck.

'Sssh.'

'Please.' Annie's voice is muffled as she gasps for air, her face smothered under the black velvet of his cloak. 'Please don't . . . please . . . don't do this.'

She slams her feet against the steering wheel and forces him off, tumbling backwards out of the passenger door into the mud. The torrential rain drenches her as she stumbles and turns, freeing herself from the car. On her knees now, her injured foot buckles underneath her as she tries to get up, slipping in the mud.

The shriek of the car alarm is masked by another distant explosion of fireworks from the tower and a gaggle of Year 11s burst from the doors of the mill, screaming as they hurl themselves out into the thunderstorm. Mark looks into the viewfinder again and zooms in. He can see something happening in the car park but he's too far away to get a clear shot.

The long white Princess Leia costume Annie is wearing drags her down into the muddy water as she staggers on to her hands and knees. The terrifying figure clad in black with the grey Pinhead mask crawls out of the car like a spider, tumbling on to the ground. Slowly, he raises himself out of the mire, the wet robes dragging behind him as he stands to his full height. He watches her crawling away, and slowly stalks behind her. As he gains ground, he lifts a foot out of the mud and stamps on her gown. Towering above her, watching her lash out, slipping and scrambling to get away.

'GET OFF ME!' The fabric tears and she launches herself forward. Sprinting towards the little stone footbridge that crosses the brook, heading towards the mill.

A gust of wind catches Ben's costume like a sail as he spreads his arms and propels himself towards the concrete ledge of the weir. He crosses the water, hitting the riverbank ahead of her, and rounds the corner, cutting Annie off at the footbridge as she trips and stumbles into his arms.

Mark looks up from the viewfinder again as Annie struggles to release herself from his grip. Mark flinches as he looks on. This is awful; he needs to get down to the bottom of the tower and help her.

The growl of an engine sounding in the woods startles him. Mark turns the lens towards the glare of a headlamp cast across the field, illuminating the whole scene. A dirt bike crashes out of the undergrowth, chicaning through the trees and breaking out into the open meadow. From the top of the tower, Mark follows the bike hurtling towards the mill race. Annie clambers up on to the wall of the mill race, but the roar of the motorbike engine catches her. She turns back in shock, staring into the glare of the headlamp, then suddenly falls, dropping behind the wall and disappearing out of sight.

54

JULY 2024

The grass in the meadow was overgrown and the old willow on the bank of the brook was bent double with age, its own majestic size weighing it down into the water. Ben stood in the centre of the clearing, unsure of what he was supposed to do next. His phone buzzed in his jacket pocket.

Keep going, you know where this road ends . . .

Ben trudged across the waterlogged meadow towards the bank where they'd played as kids. A frayed foot of rotting rope was still knotted to one of the high branches of the willow, the remains of a tyre swing. He stared out over the river to the dark silhouette of trees that ran along Doggers Dive. As his eyes adjusted to the dark, he could see that a car was parked up in one of the bays.

'It can't be . . .' As Ben moved closer, the sound of water cascading down the weir grew louder. There, in the car park, was an old blue Ford Fiesta, hazard lights flashing, signalling to him. Ben's head reeled. 'What the hell?'

In that moment, there was a flash of light overhead and the rain seemed to increase suddenly, but the downpour was freezing cold. Ben shivered and pulled his jacket tight around him and scanned the river. He daren't move. A faint light flicked on from inside the car, the passenger door opened and then was violently slammed shut. The horn of the car shrieked out in a constant siren, sending a shock wave through his spine. A figure in a flowing white gown tumbled out of the passenger door, crawled a few feet on their hands and knees, then stood and tried to sprint over the bridge, slowed down by an injured foot. Ben couldn't breathe. This was like one of his nightmares, except he was wide awake. As he dropped to his knees, he tried to cry out, but his throat was constricted in shock and no sound came. He wasn't prepared for this. He'd come here for a fight, full of rage, but now he felt afraid.

At that moment, the driver's door flew open, and another figure spilled out, black robes billowing out in the wind, chasing his limping prey across the car park.

'Oh my God . . . no.' Ben knew what was going to happen next.

He tried to focus on the girl stumbling over the bridge. As he gained ground, she glanced over her right shoulder and Ben recognised her immediately.

'Lily?' Ben was on his feet. 'NO . . . LILY . . . STOP.' He hurtled after his daughter. 'COME BACK!' The man chasing her over the bridge was nearly on top of her now. 'Lily, what are you doing?' Lily hauled herself up on to the wall of the mill race and then suddenly dropped down over the side, disappearing from sight.

An overwhelming rush of rage coursed through Ben. He bolted like an animal in the wake of the man pursuing his daughter. His feet pounded into the wet earth, heavy with mud, screaming like a savage as he gained on her attacker. His arms reached forward, fingertips touching the black velvet cloak fanning out behind the attacker in the wind. 'GET AWAY FROM HER!' He tore at the fabric and wrenched the man backwards. 'LEAVE HER ALONE.'

Ben surged forward and rugby-tackled the man to the ground. They both slammed into the concrete a few feet from the door of the mill and skidded at speed into the stone wall. Ben's arms wrapped around his opponent's neck as he tried to pin him in a chokehold, but he was strong and couldn't be contained. His neck snapped back, head-butting Ben in the nose. Ben's hands shot up to his face as a searing pain sliced through his skull and the blood started to flow. Flipping over on to his back, Ben found himself pinned to the ground, a knee crushing down on one arm, fingers grasping his throat.

Then the rain came to an abrupt stop as if a tap had been turned off. The doors to the mill swung open and a stark blinding floodlight snapped on. Ben lay on his back in shock, his nose pumping blood, as he tried to focus on his attacker. Through his blurred vision, dotted with stars, a face drifted in and out of focus. Everything stopped.

'Hello, old friend.'

Ben opened his eyes and tried to catch his breath. 'Who . . . who are you?' He stared at the man looming over him. 'Why are you doing this to me? Where's my daughter? Who are you?'

'Oh, come on.' The face slowly moved closer to his. 'Surely you remember?' It was a familiar face, older now, hair grey at the temples, but the pale almond eyes, drooping with sadness, were the same.

'Mark?' The fingers gripping his throat relaxed. 'Mark . . . Cherry?'

'I guess.' The accent had changed. 'I was Mark back then . . . but you can call me Max.'

Ben lay on the ground, panting heavily, as the man he had once known as Mark Cherry slowly climbed off him and sank back against the wall. His eyes scanned his surroundings as he tried to orientate himself. A scaffold-like structure was propped up on both sides of the meadow, fire hoses trailing across the ground towards a small clearing on the north side of the mill. Ben flinched in confusion.

'Rain machine.' Max studied him.

Ben's eyes widened as his head turned to the open doors of the mill behind him. Two massive floodlights with thick cables trailed around the corner in the same direction as the fire hoses, towards the dull hum of a generator. Ben's eyes met Max's; his expression was one of bewilderment and pain.

'It's a set.' Max leant forward with his hands on his knees. 'This is what I do.'

The confusion continued as Ben's voice trembled. 'A set-up?'

'One way of looking at it.' Max's eyes flicked to someone standing motionless in the shadow of the mill and he raised his hand as if to stop them from moving in closer.

Ben swallowed. 'Where's Lily? Where's my daughter?'

Max sighed heavily but didn't answer.

'WHERE IS LILY?' Ben rose to his knees, ready to strike out again.

Max inched back slowly. In all the years that had passed, he had imagined this moment, prepared all his lines, replayed and rehearsed this script in his recurring nightmares. A million 'what if's. He'd considered the Maddock family and all of their 'what if's.

Where is she . . . where is our daughter?

Max wanted to throw that back into Ben's face and make him suffer like they had. But he stayed silent, looking at the man who he had known as a boy.

Ben continued, 'What do you want from me, Mark?'

'I want you to tell me what happened that night.' Max moved close enough to feel Ben's heaving breath on his face. 'What really happened.'

Ben's pupils shrank in the floodlight. 'Everyone knows . . . what happened. It's all . . . in the past.' Ben's eyes shot to the mill as a clatter of falling masonry echoed from inside.

'Who is that?' Ben's eyes strained against the burning lamps.

'Look at me . . . tell me what happened. You need to say it, Ben.'

The well-prepared words tumbled out of Ben's mouth. 'Patel confessed, he served his time, he tried to attack me after his parole, the case is closed.' He snatched a breath.

'But we both know that's not quite true. You know that I was filming you that night, on Patel's camera. I saw everything. And you know that . . . because you stole the camera from me.'

Max turned to the figure lurking behind him and nodded. The vast stone wall of the mill was suddenly illuminated in a bright glare. A projector from inside the transit van parked up by the gate beamed a shaft of light on to the stonework, in a perfect rectangle the size of a large cinema screen.

A football match sprawled out over the mill wall: his daughter, Lily, moving at speed across a field, trips and falls. Heavy boots kicking her in the ribs. Nate cradling her bleeding head in his arms. Next, that same boy walking down The Cut, violently struck down by a gang of boys with baseball bats, blood everywhere.

Ben covered his mouth to stem the sob building in his throat.

A sea of blood had flooded the image now, reflecting a universe of glittering stars that turned into the green of an iris edged with thick lashes. The eye blinked, and a single tear of blood fell on to clear white skin as the frightened girl ran through a forest. A monster rising from the earth, soaked in mud, gave chase. As she turned to look back in terror, the face of his daughter Lily burst on to the screen.

Ben stood slowly and moved closer to the projection.

The film became faster now, and more violent: a fairground and the Mouth of Hell, hands and arms reaching out, the face of his son as he choked, gasping for air.

Ben covered his ears to the sounds of his children screaming in pain. He moved closer still as the fire started to rage and the flames from the projection licked up his spine. The furnace dissolved into fireworks and then to a vision in white.

There she was, on the screen, fifty feet high, immortalised forever. The film eased to fifty frames per second as she turned and turned, her long white neck and perfect skin like poetry in slow motion. Her arms swept up high above her as sunshine through the windows flared across the lens, bathing her head in a halo, like the angel she was. It was a masterpiece.

Ben stood still, barely breathing. Nobody moved as the face of Annabel Maddock turned to the camera and smiled.

Ben spun back to Max. He couldn't bear to look at her. Tears were streaming down his cheeks as her face was projected on to his.

'What have you done to them? Where are my children?'

A motorbike engine roared from across the meadow, and a dazzling headlamp lit up his face. He watched the rider in the black helmet plough across the flooded plane, water spraying up on both sides. The camera was strung on her back, one hand balancing the lens, one hand steering. The bike charged directly towards Ben at speed as he cowered back towards the wall, his hand over his eyes. As it came to a stop, the bike fell from between her legs and, without breaking the shot, Karine Mickelsen strode forward towards Ben, the lens close on his face.

'Hey.' Max matched her speed and pincered around to the riverside. 'Hey, over here. Look at me, Ben.' Ben's eyes flicked to Karine, then to Max. Panting heavily, she instinctively moved alongside him, using Max as her 'grip', keeping Ben's eye line directly into the lens.

Max tried to keep his voice steady. 'How does the story end, Ben?'

'Is that what this is?' Ben was shaking now, drenched from the rain and trembling with rage.

'You're the only one who knows. So, what's it gonna be?' Max stopped and grabbed Karine by the sleeve, pulling her tighter into Ben's POV. He whispered in her ear, 'Get in close.'

Ben closed his eyes, as if willing the ground to swallow him up. Then he turned to Karine, glaring into the lens, and violently lashed out towards her, fingers grabbing for the camera. 'Give it to me.'

'Yeah, Ben, just like that, remember?' Max stepped in front of him. 'Remember that night when you chased me down to steal Patel's camera?' Max began to walk backwards, not taking his eyes off Ben. 'Because you knew what was on it, didn't you?' He was baiting him. 'You knew I had the evidence on that tape.'

Ben lurched forward again, like a cobra striking out at its prey. Karine stumbled backwards but held her nerve.

'That's right . . . Come on, Ben.' Max goaded him, drawing him out towards the bank of the river. 'Come after me like you did after Annie.'

In a sudden burst of fury, Ben lurched again towards the lens. Max stumbled back and guided Karine by the arm as they turned and sprinted away, luring him out towards the weir.

55

Annie daren't look back as she clambers on to the low wall of the mill race, her clothes heavy with water. She stumbles, dropping herself down over the ledge to hide from him. The water is inches from her feet as she balances on the edge of the deep reservoir, straddling the cleft in the stone where Davis and Patel had hacked away at the brick. Chunks of mortar crumble under her feet as the flood widens the gap. She braces herself against the wall then edges further out towards the wheel. She waits intently, listening for footsteps, trying to conceal herself from him. She steals a glance over her shoulder to see if Ben has discovered her hiding place. Cutting through the noise of the wind and rain, the growl of a motorbike engine fills her with hope: Dave's here. The beam of a headlamp pans across the darkness like a search light, blinding her. She turns her head away and presses it into the stonework.

Crouched low by the side wall of the reservoir, she waits. The wind is starting to gust harder now, her face is stung and whipped by the driving rain. She can't go back. She looks up to the water wheel, straining with the building pressure of the flood on its rusty axis. Maybe there is a way over? If she can just get to the other side, she can reach the road bridge and make her escape. Her hands reach to grip the ledge and she hoists herself up.

* * *

Max stumbled on to the wall of the mill race, crouched down, just as she had, then stretched his arms over his head and hoisted himself up. Ben darted after him, while Karine struggled to keep pace, falling behind, trying to catch the action. The exact map of that night seemed to replay in the bodies of the two of them. Max had seen her climb, he'd witnessed her desperate attempt to escape, and he began reconstructing Annie's last movements. Just before the water wheel, Max stopped and glanced up to the high tower of the chimney stack. Was this the right place? Was this where it happened? He tried to remember how he had looked down on them both from the Crow's Nest.

'Yes. It was right here . . . wasn't it?' He turned back, breathing heavily. 'Wasn't it, Ben?' Karine had caught up and was now climbing the wall. Max gestured with his head for her to come to his side. He tried to read the expression on Ben Knot's face.

'This was where you trapped her, this is where it happened.' Max pinned himself against the wall and edged slowly towards the wheel, trying to draw Ben closer. Ben was fighting for breath, his eyes looking up to an old broken window in the mill wall.

'What?' Max followed his gaze.

'She was trying to reach the window to pull herself to safety.'

* * *

The headlamp from the motorbike dances across the wall again as Annie rises from her crouched position. There is a broken casement window directly above. She can pull herself up through that window and get to the road, out of his reach. It's her only escape route.

'Annie, come down. It's too dangerous.'

Annie's head snaps round to see a figure standing in the glare of the motorbike.

'Let me help you.' Ben's silhouette cuts a terrifying figure in heavy robes hanging like dripping tar. He drops on to all fours and begins to crawl across the broken wall towards her. The blinding light shudders and bounces off the stonework as the sound of the motorbike engine growls a warning.

Annie strains to see through the glare. 'Leave me alone, please. Go home, Ben, you're drunk.'

'I AM NOT DRUNK!' Ben's voice is aggressive now.

Annie presses her head back into the wooden structure of the wheel, helpless, as the robed figure taunts her, creeping closer on all fours.

'FOR GOD'S SAKE . . . Please . . . STOP IT.'

Crawling across the wall, Ben quickens into a scamper and Annie screams. Her hands fly up to push him away but he's on top of her now. She is buried under swathes of damp cloth, struggling to throw him off, almost suffocating under his weight. A hand presses into her shoulder, pushing her head back into the rotting wood, as the wheel creaks and buckles.

'I . . . said . . . no. NO MEANS NO!'

Annie grabs the hand and grips it before biting down hard into flesh.

'Aagh . . .' He strikes her hard across the face. Then his hands press down on to her shoulders, keeping her in place. 'You think you're so much better than me.'

Annie shakes her head, tears rolling down her face. 'Please, Ben, please stop.'

* * *

Ben hesitated, crouching down on his haunches, holding his head in his hands.

'We can't stop now, Ben, we've come so far.' Max edged closer to the water wheel. 'Just a little bit further. Here? Is this where you killed her?' Karine slowly circled around, pushing the camera into Ben's face.

'LOOK AT ME, NOT HER.' Max was hovering next to the side of the camera now, drawing Ben's eyes into the lens. 'SAY IT . . . SAY THE WORDS . . . TELL ME WHAT YOU DID TO HER.'

Ben stood his ground. 'What the fuck is wrong with you?' He rose up now to his full height. 'You're sadistic.' He staggered, swaying precariously close to the edge of the water. 'Oh my God, is this what the film was for? To torment me? Is this why you've been in my house . . . in my fucking life? You're psychotic . . . both of you.' Ben staggered backwards, closer to the swollen reservoir.

Max moved out from Karine's side and stepped in closer. 'You attacked her . . . didn't you? You attacked her and then left her to die.'

Ben suddenly lurched in close to the lens. 'It was Patel, not me. He attacked her. HE CONFESSED.'

* * *

'BEN, LEAVE HER ALONE!' Patel revs his engine again. He pulls up the front wheel on to the edge of the wall, easing on the throttle as the back wheel mounts. Both bike and rider wobble on to the ledge, balancing precariously as the engine growls harder. Dave suddenly ploughs forward, catapulting himself at top speed towards Annie's attacker. Tight-roping along the broken stone edge, the bike accelerates and the cloaked figure, dressed as

Obi-Wan, stands in the saddle. Then, as the machine hits top speed, he launches himself into the air, landing on Ben's back, and the bike plunges into the water.

Annie seizes her chance. Her feet find the bottom rung of the water wheel and she slowly edges herself backwards, blade by blade. When she is about halfway up, she turns on to her hands and knees and scrambles, frantically climbing the enormous structure of the wheel, towards the casement window.

Dave is on top of Ben now, pummelling him hard in the ribs. Weighed down in layers of heavy wet cloth, the fight is vicious and brutal. Ben bucks him off and they square up, fists raised. Patel tries to land punches to Ben's face but the nails sticking out of the mask catch his knuckles; he can't get close enough to take him out. A heavy boot slams into Ben's stomach and he doubles over in pain. As Patel moves in for a knee to the face, Ben reaches out, fumbling for something on the ground. In a sudden flurry of movement, his hand arcs up from the floor and a brick smashes into the side of Patel's skull. Ben rises from the ground as Patel staggers backwards and collapses, blood pouring from his head.

'Annie, it's OK, you're safe, I'm not going to hurt you.' Ben turns but Annie is already halfway up the wheel, climbing for her life.

* * *

'I saw you.' Max had begun to climb backwards up the rotten slats to the top of the wheel, just as she had done. 'I saw what happened, I watched you do it.'

Karine pressed herself against the stone wall, trying to keep both of them in the shot. She needed Ben's face in focus. It wouldn't work if she filmed the back of his head; they would think it had been faked. She started to clamber backwards alongside Max, up the wheel, keeping one foot on the stone wall for balance. Their combined weight caused the ancient structure to groan and rasp. As if in a trance, Ben began to follow on his hands and knees.

'That's right, Ben, imagine I'm her.' Somewhere in Max's sub-conscious, he had been her, he had felt Annie's pain, he'd been on the receiving end of Benjamin Knot's brutality, every single day of his childhood.

The wheel creaked under their weight, the scaffolding buckled and very slowly began to detach itself from the wall.

'Max, I can't keep him in frame.' Karine hoisted herself up with one hand and sat on the high stone window ledge, her feet scrap-ing the wall, trying to anchor herself. Max held out his hand to her, keeping his eyes on Ben. She passed the lens to him, cables trailing to the main body of the Rialto strapped to her back.

Max pointed it in his face. 'COME ON, BEN . . . I'm the one calling the shots now, I'm the one in control.'

Max stared at him as he moved towards him. The rage in his face was psychotic. Max fumbled behind him and grabbed a steel bar from the scaffold wedged into the wall. He wrenched it out of the crumbling mortar and wielded it like a baseball bat, trying to keep the lens steady.

'Come on, you piece of shit. Show me what you did to her.'

Ben pounced, grabbing at Max, clawing his way up his body and locking his hands tight around his throat.

56

He's on top of her now. Her body pinned down to the wheel.

'Please stop. Let me go.' Annie desperately grips hold of the wooden slats as the rain pelts harder and heavier. He can't let her go, she's the only thing he has left. She's everything to him, his solace, his first love, the only person who cares. No . . . he'll never let her go. Ben leans in close to her face, then suddenly buries his head into her neck, clinging on to her. He is sobbing hard now. Squeezing her so tight, pressing his body into hers so hard, as if he wants to climb inside her. Annie tries to cry out, but he is wringing the life out of her.

'I'll never let you go.' Ben's voice is muffled as his lips brush her shoulder. He squeezes her even tighter.

'Ben?' Patel is lying on the ground, holding his head as blood pours down his face.

Ben tries to lift his head, but the rubber mask rips away from his cheek. He's stuck fast to Annie's neck. He tries to separate himself, but they seem to be glued together. As Ben tears himself away, that's when the blood begins to flow. One of the rusty nails from his Pinhead mask is sticking out of her neck, buried deep. Her mouth is open, and her eyes fixed in the distance. Her breath is short; a gurgle sounds in her throat. Ben pulls the nail slowly out of her neck. Annie's body flinches with pain. 'I'm sorry . . . I'm so sorry.'

As the blood begins to spurt from her neck, Ben's hands shoot out, grabbing at the puncture wound to try and stop the flow. He squeezes tighter.

'Ben, you're strangling her.' Patel is on his feet now.

His head snaps around to Patel's pitiful voice, the torn mask flapping in the wind. He can't see what's happening. Then another voice calls out in the distance.

'HEY . . . STOP!'

Ben's frantic eyes scan the wall, but there's nobody there.

'LEAVE HER ALONE!' Ben's head shoots up to the voice directly above him at the top of the tower and he stares into the lens of the camera that is pointing down in his direction, filming every second of this moment.

'Help me.' Ben's hands are wet with blood. It's everywhere now, pumping hard from her neck through his fingers. He stares down into her face. 'Help. Please.' Ben tears at the chiffon of her train, wrapping a strip around her neck, and pulls it tight, trying to stop the bleeding. The wheel creaks, slowly turning. Trying to keep the pressure on her neck, he shifts his weight to counter hers. On the edge of the moving wheel, they balance precariously over the drop, about ten feet from the surface of the water.

Ben returns his focus up towards the boy with the camera in the Crow's Nest, but he's gone. Then everything happens at once. Ben takes his hands from her throat and makes a break for it, leaping from the wheel back on to the stone ledge. With a rasp of metal, the scaffold slowly dislodges itself from the wall. The sheer volume of water surging out through the tail race drives the wheel faster in a cascade of turbulence. Patel's dirt bike, still hissing and steaming on the surface of the water, is sucked under. The water wheel suddenly jerks, and Annie's limp, swaddled form teeters on the edge, then slowly tips over the side. Already soaked to the skin, she plummets down towards the deep water below, but the cape of her gown catches on the fulcrum of the wheel. Her body is flung sideways and she is wrenched to a sudden stop, hung from the neck. The wheel judders to a halt as Patel's bike becomes lodged underneath and the spindle holding Annie by the throat snaps. She plunges feet first into the deep reservoir and Patel launches himself into the water after her.

* * *

Ben's fingers dug into the veins of Max's neck, and he squeezed hard.

'It was an accident.'

Max's eyes bulged but his hand on the camera lens maintained the shot. He needed this moment, whatever the price.

The cables connected to the body of the camera strained as the wheel began to move. 'Max, you're gonna break the connection.' Karine tried to give him some slack.

Max moved fast, Ben's hand clawing at the fabric of his coat, fingers gripping metal. The scaffold bar sliced through the air and slammed into the side of Ben Knot's skull. Ben released his grip as he fell sideways.

Max was on his feet now, steadying himself on the wooden frame, towering over Ben.

'I always knew how violent you were. You inflicted your cruelty on me, day after day for all those years.' The scaffold bar came down again with force, hitting the wheel, missing Ben's face by an inch. 'But I could take it, all the punches and the bruises and the nose bleeds. But Annie didn't deserve it . . . she loved you.' Max wielded the iron bar, ready to strike for the third time. 'TELL ME THE TRUTH.' With one hand, he raised the iron bar again, and with the other he thrust the camera in Ben's face.

Ben flinched. 'I was trying to stop the bleeding . . . she wasn't breathing . . . she fell over the side.' Ben staggered to his feet, unsteady, his hand held out to stop Max from striking him again.

Blood poured from his temple as he swayed dizzily towards the water. Max stepped very carefully towards him, framing him against the water. The cables tensed. He could go no further. Ben stared over the edge into the water. It was as if he could see her billowing white dress sinking into the dark, her hands reaching out.

'She fell in . . .' Ben took a step forward. 'There was so much blood.' His fingers stretched out towards the vision just below the surface. It was as if he was trying to claw her back. Reaching thirty years into the past. 'She was already dead.'

Max turned to Karine. They had it. They had him, he was unravelling before their very eyes.

Max grabbed him. 'You let Dave Patel go to prison. You held on to the one piece of evidence that could have cleared him . . . didn't you?'

Ben faced the camera, his fingers clutching and clawing at his chest in agony.

'You could have got help, but instead you ran off and left her for dead and let Patel take the blame. Didn't you?'

'She bled to death because I wanted her so badly. I couldn't stop it.'

Very slowly, as if in a trance, Ben turned back to face her watery grave, the place where she fell. Karine tried to find a footing on the rotten wheel as the creak of wood and metal suddenly jolted, causing them all to cling on. Then, almost in slow motion, Ben's body fell forward as he tipped himself head-first into the water.

'NO!' As Max leapt forward to grab him, a huge section of scaffold dislodged from the wall, ripping bolts from the stone-work as the entire structure of the Blackstone Mill water wheel collapsed sideways, hitting the surface with an almighty crash. Max went down with it.

The camera lens was yanked from his hands and dangled precariously, swinging against the wall. Karine reached forward to try and stop it from smashing against the stone.

Ben was now face down in the water as the weight of the structure bore down upon him. Karine scrambled back on to the ledge of the window, reassembling the camera and hanging on to save herself from being pulled over. The structure of the wheel began to sink. Max hit the surface of the water hard, winding himself on impact. He fought to catch his breath as the suction dragged him down. The turbulence of the fast-flowing torrent pulled them both under the wheel, fighting and flailing.

On the other side of the tail race, Ben broke the surface first, exploding out of the reservoir, his body slamming into the sluice wall, gasping for air, hands clutching his chest. The force of the current dragged him under, again and again. His head surfaced as he fought for air, but as he struggled hard against the pressure, he began to lose strength.

* * *

As Annie's limp body sinks into the deep water, her eyes suddenly open, and her arms strike out, breaking for the surface. She's weak and losing strength as the foaming water, red with her blood, sucks her under. Again and again she surfaces, gasping for air, but fluid fills her lungs as she's dragged deeper into the murky blackness. Her feet hit metal on the bottom of the reservoir. Something is wrapped around her leg; the shredded gown has entwined itself around Patel's motorbike. Annie struggles to free herself, but she is held fast. She looks down and tugs at the cloth of her dress. Her hands reach out, lungs about to burst. Then her fingertips soften, and her arms go limp, her grip loosens, and she begins to sink.

* * *

Max broke the surface, his body arching backwards like a dolphin. His eyes black from the silt and his lungs burning as he panted for breath.

His hands clawed at the sluice wall. 'Help me.' As his arms reached upwards, a hand clamped tightly around his wrist and began to haul him out. He was dragged towards the wall of the sluice, fingers gripping the side, against the fast-moving current.

'I didn't mean to hurt her.' Ben stared down at Mark Cherry. 'It was an accident.'

'She was stabbed in the neck . . . you fucking animal.' Max's voice rasped as he gulped for air.

There was never going to be a way to convince him. One of the nails from the mask had opened an artery, and the cut was too deep. But the truth was that he had fled the scene, he had left her there to die.

'YOU'RE A COWARD!' Max exploded at him as he struggled to cling on to the wall, the current tugging at his body.

Very slowly, a darkness descended over Ben's eyes. Max had all the answers now, all the evidence he needed. He would never let this go, there was too much resentment there. Something inside him snapped. They stared at each other, a whole lifetime of damage passing between them; then Max held out his hand to be pulled out, but instead Ben gently placed his palm on Max's fore-head, like a priest giving a blessing and the last rites. Then, slowly and deliberately, he forced Max's head under the water. Holding him there, drowning the evidence.

* * *

Annie can feel another body in the water next to her as a pair of arms slide under hers, trying to pull her out, but she doesn't want to go. It's calmer down here, peaceful and serene. Maybe she can just stay where she is. Her hands reach up to wrap around the neck of her saviour. She turns and opens her eyes. Through the darkness of the water, she sees a face straining in agony, but she is still trapped, tied down by her dress, unable to free herself. Then he floats upwards, fading away. The water begins to feel warmer now. The darkness lifts and all around her is light. The bottom of the weir seems to go on forever, deep and crystal clear. Her dress, like angel wings, spreads wide, fanning out in the water. Annie Maddock lies back, looking towards the surface as the face of Dave Patel stares back at her.

***

A sudden surge of strength coursed through Max's body and his hand thrust upwards, breaking the surface. He seized Ben's wrist and pulled hard, toppling him forward, plunging him in headfirst. Without a second to snatch a breath, his lungs filled with water, thick mud choking him, clogging his airway. Blood from the wound on his head turned the water deep red around him. He was losing consciousness. Ben opened his eyes and stared down into the murky grime. There was something white down there, floating at the bottom; a shred of torn cloth, trapped in the rusty wheel of a motorbike. Ben's eyes suddenly bulged out of their sockets as a stab of pain in his chest paralysed him. Under the water, his body thrashed and writhed in agony as the cardiac arrest finally came. A pair of arms grabbed Ben around the chest and hauled him upwards. Crawling on his hands and knees in the reeds of the riverbank, dragging himself on to the towpath towards the daylight, Mark hauled Ben out of the flood through the black silt. He tipped Ben's head back, forced his fingers down his throat to clear his airway and began chest compressions.

Karine had found her way in through the window of the mill and down the ladder that led to the main hall. She had sprinted around the building towards the road and the footbridge. As she arrived, she scanned the water for signs of life and, pulling her phone from her pocket, she called for an ambulance. Then she slowly picked her way down through the slippery rocks and weeds, keeping her camera high on her shoulder out of the water, until she was knee-deep on the opposite side of the river. She squatted on the side of the bank and did what she knew best . . . continued filming.

Mark pressed his mouth to Ben's, filled his lungs with air, and continued to pump on his sternum. You see, somewhere very deep inside, his fear of Ben Knot was born of a kind of obsession, a twisted love story, a battle with a bully who'd had a grip on his heart since his very first day at school. After all the abuse he suffered, Mark could easily have turned to violence himself, but when all was said and done . . . he was the one with the instinct to save a man's life.

The Cut was going to be the swansong of Max's career. Then he would put it all behind him, all the trauma and the pain and the nightmares. He'd lock it in a box and throw away the key.

Ben was lifted from the ground on to a gurney as the two paramedics took over. Dani's car pulled up by the bridge with Nate and Lily in the back seat, and Max watched as Ben's two children, their faces white and tear-stained, followed their father as he was taken on the stretcher into the ambulance. The shock of what had happened would take a while to settle in. There was never going to be a happy ending.

Max collapsed back into the grass, the water buffeting his body, rocking him gently as he listened to the siren disappearing into the distance.

EPILOGUE

OCTOBER 2024

'I am truly sorry . . .' The man was standing behind him, just a few feet away. '. . . For what we did to you at school.'

Max was removing the faded plastic posy on his parents' graves, replacing it with a small spray of wildflowers. He stood and turned.

Dave Patel's face was thinner now, drawn cheeks and sunken eyes. His skin was sallow. He looked like a faded copy of a man. 'I've seen a few of your films.' The German shepherd snuffled through the flower beds. 'You've done so well for yourself . . . local boy made good.'

It had turned into an Indian summer, a very late burst of warm days and cool evenings, well into the end of September. Max had stayed on in Barton Mallet for a while. He had unfinished business. He swallowed, barely able to speak.

Dave filled the awkward silence. 'I wanted to see her grave.' His voice was soft and light, just as he remembered. 'To finally pay my respects.'

Max gathered himself; it was time to finally face up to his guilt, time to lay all these ghosts to rest.

'I . . .' The breath came out, but no words followed; he didn't know how to form them. 'I ran away. I wasn't very well. I knew the truth. I could have testified but I wasn't capable . . . mentally. They wouldn't have believed me . . . It's me that should be sorry.'

Patel just stared blankly at him, waiting.

'I was too frightened of him. I was paralysed.'

Patel's head dropped and he chewed his lip. 'What's done is done.'

'But your whole life was stolen from you.' Max was struggling to contain himself.

'No, I'm still here. It's Annie's life that was stolen. And I couldn't save her . . .'

The German shepherd padded over, wagging its tail. 'He likes you.' Patel took a deep breath, gathering himself.

Max focused on Patel's eyes. There was a glaze of something there, the institution perhaps, a kind of blurring of the world.

'I'm glad it was you who got to tell the story.' Dave inclined his head.

Max smiled awkwardly. 'We couldn't have done it without your parents' connections.'

'There was no other way. The case against me was watertight. Davis saw to that.' Dave's eyes scanned the cemetery.

'But now the truth will be out there.' Max wiped the soil from his hands.

'What will you do with the finished film?' Patel was smiling now, a light blazing in his eyes as a gust of wind blew a confetti of leaves across the gravestones.

'Karine Mickelsen has big ideas . . . *The Cut* will probably go to Cannes or Venice . . . I dunno . . .' Max smiled sadly. 'She's spending some time with Dani, Lily and Nathan. It's been . . . a bit of a shock.' Max's voice petered out as the scale of this whole thing finally began to hit home.

'What will happen to Ben?' It was extraordinary, but after all that had happened, there was a flicker of pity in Patel's eyes.

'The vultures are circling. I imagine the fraud case will take him down first, and after the banks and the creditors have picked at the carcass, it will be your turn.' Max exhaled and drove his hands deep into his pockets. 'If you want to reopen the case, that is . . . you and the Maddocks?'

'Oh, it's a long road to justice and I'm too old and tired.' Patel's eyes scanned the cemetery. 'And in the end, maybe your film will be enough.'

Max glanced towards the gate. A Vauxhall Astra was kangarooing down the road to a halt by the entrance. The door of the car opened, and a man stepped out.

Max's eyes returned to Dave. 'You know, I once thought this was about revenge, but it was something else. I did it for Annie, and I wanted to right the wrong I had done to you by not coming forward.' In his peripheral vision, Max caught another little person, and his heart skipped a beat. 'This was the only way I knew how.'

Max reached into his pocket. 'Here . . . this is yours.' A small plastic Hi8 video cassette tape with words scribbled in felt-tip pen.

Patel shook his head. 'You keep it.'

A sad excuse for a horn sounded from the stalled Vauxhall at the roadside. Max looked over. Brandon was standing in a full-length winter coat with Charlie in his arms, dressed as if they were going skiing. Americans! Max looked back to Patel, but he was already gone. He turned and walked towards the gates of the cemetery.

'Nice motor . . . you cheapskate.'

'Yeah, Charlie was helping with the stick shift.' Charlie reached out his arms for a cuddle. Max picked him up and squeezed him hard.

'What are you doing here?' Max unzipped the sweltering puffer jacket and smiled at his son.

'We missed you.' Charlie pressed his hot cheek on to his father's and Max inhaled his skin.

Brandon stepped in close and put his hand on Max's shoulder. 'So, wanna show me where you grew up then?'

Max swallowed and composed himself. He stood up and faced his ex-husband and took a deep breath.

'Pfft! . . . Where on earth do I begin?'

Max glanced towards the Maddock Farm and the sound of dogs barking in the distance at the rescue shelter on Forest Hill. Back across the cemetery, through the trees, he could see the chain-link fence around the perimeter of Barton Mallet Secondary School and the sprawling sports complex where the leavers threw their Pearls Before Swine. The Cut with the bugle vine, and the Conker Lady's house, the playground with the rusty witch's hat and the broken swings, where they'd played at the Easter Wakes. The tall tower of Blackstone Mill. No. Too many ghosts.

'Well . . . have you guys eaten? . . . I do know a really good chippy.'

ACKNOWLEDGEMENTS

Thank you to the amazing team at Faber, Lochlann Binney, Louisa Joiner, Mary Cannam, Hannah Turner, Hannah Marshall, Phoebe Williams, Kate Baron and Sam Brown for your trust, enthusiasm and brilliant innovation. (Hannah we'll always have 'getting chased by autograph hunters on scooters in Newcastle'!)

Thank you also to Robin Morgan Bentley, Aurelie de Troyer, Nicola Wall and the team at Audible for opening the door for my adventures as an author.

And my brilliant and patient editor Josephine Lane who kept me on track as I jumped around between decades and continents.

Finally thank you to my agent Jim Gill, you're a friend and an ally, and you are always the best person to be next to at those overwhelming literary events.

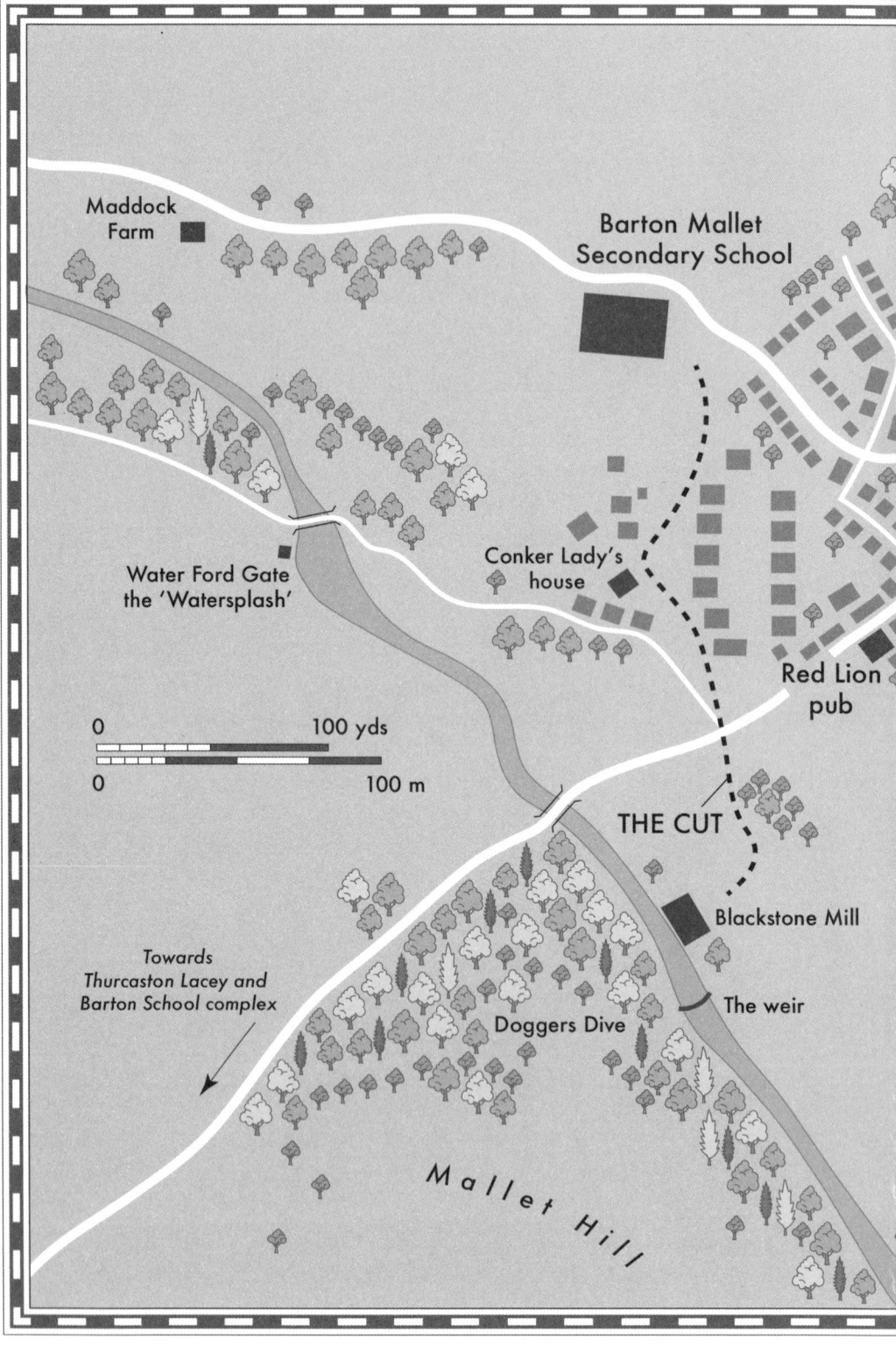

Maddock Farm

Barton Mallet Secondary School

Water Ford Gate the 'Watersplash'

Conker Lady's house

Red Lion pub

0   100 yds

0   100 m

THE CUT

Blackstone Mill

Towards Thurcaston Lacey and Barton School complex

Doggers Dive

The weir

Mallet Hill